Foreword

       The idea of time travel in literature and film is not a new idea. It has been explored in a variety of novels, movies and television series. The vast majority of these creative projects have been intended purely for entertainment value. What T. R. Hendrick does in WHAT IF THEY KNEW is unique in that while the book may have entertainment value, the primary purpose is to provoke readers to reflect and to think.

       The focus is on the state of matters for citizens living in the United States of America in the not so distant future. Recognizing the key role of the U.S. Constitution on our country's government during its origination and forward to the modern day, this author dares to consider what it might be like for a handful of scientists to travel back in time and convince a handful of the Founding Fathers to accompany them forward in time to learn and experience what their fledgling country has become under the guiding principles of the governing document they are in the process of forging – The U. S. Constitution. Such a proposition immediately calls many questions to mind...

- Which of the Founding Fathers should be approached?
- Which of these leaders will accept this unbelievable invitation to time travel?
- How do you bring these historical figures to the present and not immediately overwhelm them?
- What and how much information should they be exposed to?
- What should these men be allowed to experience firsthand?

- How will their experiences in future America influence the thought processes of these men when they return?
- Will their experiences influence their words and actions as they complete the task of creating our U.S. Constitution when they return to their own time?

T. R. Hendrick combines science fiction and historical fiction to create this work. This book requires readers to suspend disbelief, but it is interesting to contemplate the Founding Fathers' original intent for the wording in the U. S. Constitution, as well as, anticipate their responses to all they will be exposed to in the classroom and on the streets. Even if this is not your preferred genre, WHAT IF THEY KNEW offers readers an imaginative adventure that will encourage readers to reflect on the state of politics and life in our country.

Samuel J. Ayers Ed. D.

Director of Graduate Education
Distinguished Practitioner in Residence
Lubbock Christian University – School of Education

What if They Knew

By T. R. Hendrick

Table of Contents

Part 2......What If They Knew

Part 3......The Second Civil War

Part 4......Final Thoughts

Documents of the United States of America

<u>Declaration of Independence</u>

<u>Articles of Confederation</u>

<u>The U.S. Constitution</u>

<u>Amendments to the Constitution (Bill of Rights)</u>

<u>Gettysburg Address</u>

Part 1 The Plan

Chapter 1
In the year 2025

Lightning boomed in the skies above Allentown, Pennsylvania. Heavy rain fell for the third straight day. However, a little over one hundred twenty feet below ground, no one cared about the rain. The testing of the machine continued as planned.

"Place the monkey on Pad A, please, and let's begin again. This will be test #1-2-4-8. Transport live subject from Pad A to Pad B, Room 3 of the 8th sub-floor. Is Pad B ready?" asked Dr. Carver Benton.

"Pad B, Room 3, sub-floor 8. We're ready for live test #1-2-4-8," Came the reply from Dr. William Rayne.

"Very well, let's begin. Go green for test #1-2-4-8," said Dr. Benton.

Benton's technician put her hands on the glass controls in front of her; with her finger she dragged the slider from the top position to the bottom position. She watched through the glass control board while the overhead lights of the room slowly dimmed and then quickly became brighter. The monkey on Pad A sat quietly, as though nothing was happening, as it slowly disappeared from sight. Then its eyes began darting around with sudden confusion.

"Report from Pad B, please," asked Benton.

Dr. William Rayne answered, "Signs of the subject appearing. Density is becoming consistent." Energetically, Dr. Rayne continued his verbal report. His voice sounded like a sports announcer giving detailed play-by-play calls. Moments later, Dr. Rayne announced that the lighting on the bottom of Pad B changed from green to white, ending the testing procedure.

A white light indicated the teleportation process was complete and successful. Red lights after the process meant some sort of malfunction had happened and the process could and would potentially fail. In the years of test trials leading up to this moment, the team had seen thousands of red lights. Before using live test subjects, they tested nearly everything else, including different metals, fruits, wood, liquids, gases, and many other items. Testing would not progress until these items would only produce the desired green light. Once the live testing began, the scientists cleaned up many messes in the name of research, but not in the last few hundred teleports. As of the latest test, the team could boast more green lights than red.

"Process complete, Dr. Benton," commented William.

"Visual results?"

"Successful. All signs look very good. The usual dazed and confused look but otherwise healthy."

"Good. Okay, everyone, let's finish checking the subject after the teleport and call it a day. Finish up the reports and shut things down. This all looks good, but it's just the beginning," Benton said in a cautious tone.

The group of people began clicking on keyboards and touching screens, depositing reports into the servers where few people had access. Double-password entries were required on every access keypad, and those codes were often changed. After two wrong entries, the access keypad would be disabled, and security was notified. Nothing in the system could be accessed by the internet. This system was totally shut-off from the world. The system didn't even have a virtual backup in the cloud. The backup system was located on a separate floor of the facility.

Not far above Allentown, Pennsylvania, is a great resort area called Blue Mountain. Aside from the fantastic skiing, snowboarding, or snowtubing during the winter, the resort hosts some of the summer's best hiking, ropes courses, action archery, and much more in the way of outdoor activities. The year-round activity of people coming and going at all hours was the perfect place to hide. The scientific team members would enter the lodge and pose as either private club members or employees of the lodge dedicated to the private areas of the facility. Special electronic passkeys granted them access to areas regular patrons or employees could not go. However, the entire team of scientists still enjoyed the amenities provided by the lodge in its scenic area of the mountain. The ski-in/ski-out options, valet service, dining, fitness center and heated swimming pool ~ the perks of this job were second to none. The team would arrive at their prescribed times, enter the private area of the lodge with their passkey, and, with the use of the designated elevators, drop down 8 floors beneath the surface of the mountain. The employees of the 8th sub-floor knew they were working on a teleport device to move objects from one specific place to another. These teleport pads had not had a single human test to date, but with the positive tests with the monkeys, they believed it could be possible within a few more years. Only a few scientists knew of the floor beneath. Sub-floor 9 was where the real testing was done.

As technicians completed the shutting down of their workspace, taking off lab coats and turning off the lights, they headed to the elevators. The mass exodus of less than thirty people was norm for a Thursday evening. One more day of work below ground and the weekend would begin. The lead doctors, Dr. Benton and Dr. Rayne, heading up this entire endeavor were the last to step into the bank of elevators ~ eight floors beneath the surface.

"Are the weekly reports coming along as planned, Dr. Benton?" asked Dr. Rayne. "Yes. They all look good. The Benefactor should be pleased," replied Dr. Carver Benton.

Rayne pulled Benton over to the side of the elevator and looked at him curiously.

Benton immediately looked up at the security camera and said, "Good night, Dr. Rayne. We can talk about work tomorrow. I'm rather tired and need to relax."

Rayne, knowing someone could be watching, looked reservedly as he eyed the camera. "Well, how about a beer? I know I could use one."

"Now, you're talking. See ya' at Harry's? Maybe forty-five minutes or so?"

Rayne didn't look back as he waived his hand stepping out of the elevator. He headed for his car, not looking forward to the drive that would inevitably be waiting.

Less than an hour later, the bar owner, Harry, was pushing cold beer mugs into the waiting hands of the two co-workers.

"I believe we earned this beer today," Benton said.

"Agreed," came the immediate response from Rayne, and the two of them took a long pull.

Opening the conversation, Rayne began, "Samuel Adams was a phenomenal beer maker."

The volume of noise in the busy bar was a good cover for the two men to have private conversations. They continued small talk about wives, kids, sports, and anything else that was far and away removed from work; however, neither of the two were married or had children. They just speculated what life would have been like if they had been. They chatted about anything other than work while cautiously looking around the bar for anyone suspicious. After starting their second mug of beer, Benton finally asked Rayne, "How long?"

The answer arrived calmly, "Four months."

"Amazing," was the reply, "Simply amazing. Did anyone else notice?"

"No one on the 8th. Not that I could tell. They were all too preoccupied with their own individual jobs until the last moments. Their concentration while completing a task is exceptional. We have a fantastic team in place, Doctor."

"Okay. Tomorrow let's start phase two. Is Paul ready?"

"Oh yeah. He's been ready for some time now."

"So, he's quite on board with the plan?" Benton asked.

"Oh yes. We need three or four more just like him," Rayne suggested.

"Well, we're not cloning, so..." Benton paused for a second.

Rayne confidently finished his sentence, "But we do have at least one more just like him."

11

Benton looked him square in the eyes, "Really? And who might that be? Do I know this person?"

With a matter-of-fact tone in his voice, Dr. William Rayne replied, "Me."

Benton sat quietly for a moment allowing Rayne to persuade him. Benton was not at a loss for words, he simply wanted Rayne to feel the need to continue. Benton's eyebrows raised, and Rayne picked up on the clue.

"We've worked so long on this, and the results reveal a very good chance we're going to accomplish our goal, and I'm damn sure going to be a part of it as a traveler. I've thought about this a lot, Carver," Rayne was speaking to his friend as much as his co-worker now. "We're asking people to put their lives on the line, and I'm willing to show them that we will do the same thing. It's that simple. Besides, I...." Benton cut him off with his hand gesture.

"I agree," he said.

"Just like that? No argument?" Rayne said with a serious look.

"Okay. Yes. Affirmative. I knew that one of us would step up to be a traveler. And, honestly, I figured it would be you," Benton said.

Rayne took another drink and let his silence work on Benton this time.

Benton continued, "You're right. We've worked together on this for quite some time now, and I've always felt that you've had a little reluctance from the beginning. Once the test results started improving and then became consistent ~ I just figured your imagination couldn't keep you from wanting to be a traveler."

"Okay then," Rayne took another long pull of his beer, reassuring himself he didn't just sign his own death sentence.

Benton looked over at Rayne and restated his earlier commitment. "Tomorrow, we begin phase two." Benton held up his beer mug, as did Rayne, and they drank together.

Two hours earlier, back at the facility, on the 9th sub-floor, Room 3, Pad B, directly below where the test monkey had reappeared, stood a man on a teleport pad. He looked down at his hands and feet, amazed at what had just taken place. He smiled and slowly laughed out loud. He clapped his hands together once and then rubbed them palm-to-palm quickly, as if trying to warm them up, as he stepped off the teleport pad. He walked over to a white board to fill in the requested information. He wrote three things: the time, the date, and his initials. The time was exactly the same as when the monkey above him reappeared. His initials were 'P.T.' The date was four months prior to today's date: July 3rd, 2025.

Paul Tesla gathered his things and left the facility. He was officially the first 'traveler'. Excited to share his information with his boss, he drove straight to Harry's bar.

Back at Harry's bar, more beer was consumed, and the evening continued with the two scientists chatting quietly about the possibilities of their work. Neither of them wanted more money. They didn't want to be famous. They wanted change!

The two spent another hour or so at the bar before they saw Paul walk in. Paul shouted at the new bartender and ordered three shots of whiskey. By the time the three men exchanged handshakes and pats on the back, Cameron had the shots ready. Paul said, "Gentlemen, raise your glasses. Here's to the future and the changes it will bring." The three smiled, laughed, and knew they were making history ~ and could be rewriting history.

When they pushed open the front door to the bar, a dark set of eyes watched the men carefully from the back seat of a limo. The Benefactor had seen two of them leaving the bar several times over the past few weeks. Tonight, there were three.
The reports he received from Dr. Benton were getting more positive each time.
The dark eyes had but one job right now: follow Dr. Carver Benton.

Chapter 2

The next morning., Dr. Benton, Dr. Rayne, and four others sat in a conference room deep within the complex. As time passed, these meetings were more crucial and exciting. Time was getting closer and the project was more alive than ever. Positive progress caused emotions to heighten, and expectation of success was heavy in the air. All six people never sat together outside the walls. As a matter of fact, only Benton, Rayne, and Paul Tesla had ever been seen together in public. Their work relationship had already been established many years in the past.

Four people were carefully chosen by Benton and Rayne. There were no applicants for this project. Each person considered was interviewed and vetted prior to anyone approaching them. Benton and Rayne had to understand how their potential candidates lived their lives, their value system, past decisions, political views, and religious beliefs. Benton would use vast resources to find the secrets no candidate would ever want anyone to know about them. This project, if they survived, could be the single most important event in history. It could change history. The words these men would speak to their colleagues would impact the world as we know it.

Rayne finished pouring his coffee from the small coffee bar behind the conference table. The room wasn't as cold as its counterpart on the floor above. Only five people were in the cozy conference room: Dr. Benton; Dr. Rayne; Paul

Tesla; and the other two candidates, Charles Carson and Sarah Fleming.

Dr. Benton sat in a leather chair and began the conversation. "Paul was perfectly successful last night. His return coincided with the exact time of the return of the test monkey on the teleport pad directly above you on the 8th sub-floor. Excellent! I believe you already know that is the most advanced test we have ever conducted." Paul Tesla nodded at the acknowledgement and everyone in the room clapped in approval.

Rayne continued, "You also wrote down a date of four months prior. The objective was four months so, again, a very successful test." Again, more clapping and smiles.

Paul responded, "Dr. Rayne, I'd like to say up front that I didn't know what to expect. How long…. the feeling…" he stuttered as the thoughts tried to form in his mouth. "Listen, that was simply incredible."

"I'm glad you're comfortable with the test, Paul," Rayne commented. "You have made history as the third person in the world to use our tele-pad and be transported from one location to another and safely return. Sarah and Charles traveling prior to you. Since we have carefully used the test monkeys upstairs, slowly and deliberately made subtle changes, and finally used ourselves as test subjects, we have not lost any human travelers. This particular test is truly a new mark in history. You all know the significance of today's little celebration with Paul's travel. Charles, you and Sarah traveled within the *same* time. From one tele-pad to another. We watched Paul disappear from one tele-pad and reappear on another, moments later.   Paul, in your first teleportation experience, you've made history by traveling from one tele-pad and reappearing on the same tele-pad. You were gone for only 4 minutes for us."

Benton spoke next, "Yes he did. But he was sent back to four months in the past!"

The others in the room held up their coffee cups for a toast. "To Paul!" Charles said, and everyone repeated it.

Paul responded, "To change."

Sarah Fleming chimed in, "Dr. Benton, I realize we have worked here for several years and we have discussed and re-hashed this project hundreds of times. I'm sure that everyone here has had some level of doubt along the way - I know I have. But I admit that this project has been executed in an amazing way! No personnel above us on the 8th knows what happens directly beneath their feet. They essentially have the same tests that we perform down here with one exception. We've just added the element of time. This still amazes me every time, and I've only been sent across a room! The 'mirror effect' between the two floors is genius. Kudos to you, sir."

Benton gently replied, "Correction, Ms. Fleming. Kudos to you and Dr. Rayne. I understand the concept started during some conversation between the two of you."

Dr. Rayne replied, "I must hand it to you, Ms. Fleming. Coming up with the idea of using the transportation of monkeys from one place to another to first test the system and, more importantly, continue to use them to mask our own time travel testing...first-rate, my dear. Well done."

Sarah quickly replied, "Let's just call this a group effort. We've all added quite a bit during this entire system."

"Well said," Benton replied. "Adding to that, Dr. Rayne and I could not generate this technology without your help and the help of those who work on the 8th. This project is a massive undertaking. To mention that secrecy must remain paramount is redundant. Fortunately, nature is on our side: monkeys do not speak. So, the question is how to get people to work together without knowing the outcome? We decided to have two projects. The first would be teleportation. It must be. So, we hand-picked those employees, too. You also know they are experts in molecular biology, genetic coding, cloning, and other necessary fields. Their goal is every bit as secret as ours, and, again, it is the foundation of our project. But the left hand does not know what the right hand is doing.

Those of us in this room are the only people in the world who know our end goal."

Benton moved forward. "You are not the last of the travelers to go through. We only have one more person to send later today to continue these initial time travel tests."

"Who gets that spot, Doc?" asked Charles Carson.

"Dr. Rayne has expressed a desire to be our final representative." Rayne gestured his approval as Benton continued, "I believe you all know we were expecting to have at least four travelers by now, but neither Dr. Rayne nor I have found anyone we feel would fit into this little group. Dr. Rayne's willingness to step into this role with you gives us our fourth, and he also brings his own skills and knowledge of this project with him. Heaven forbid something happen while you're away, but he may be the best person to help repair any technicalities that may occur. Are you three okay with this?"

All three travelers, Sarah Fleming, Charles Carson, and Paul Tesla wore smiles and acknowledged their approval. Benton quietly noticed this small group's cohesiveness and the bonds they were building. He smiled and again shook Rayne's hand in congratulations.

"Now, let's go over our objectives again, shall we?" Benton looked to Sarah to take over the conversation.

Sarah Fleming, the only female in this group of time travelers, spoke up immediately, "Travel to the pre-set time in the year 1787, find our respective members of Congress, find a way to engage them in conversation, get consent, and return to the present time. Once back here, we spend sufficient time with them explaining, teaching, showing them with visual media such as still photographs, and slowly moving toward video. When the time is right, we will travel outside this facility, and this is where the danger takes place. We have an absolute requirement to keep these men safe. At some point, when we all agree that we have shown them enough of what America is in 2025, we will return the congressmen back to the same pre-set time in 1787. Once they are safe and we have said our goodbyes, the travelers will press the buttons of our transporter devices and come back ~ to what, we don't know. We don't even know if we can come back." Everyone in the room could sense the prophetic tone in her voice.

Rayne reassured everyone, "We *will* come back. We will come back to the year 2025, and you will see how America has changed. If we are successful, they may have rewritten the Constitution, and America, as we know it, could be very different than what we have!"

Paul added, "And we make no attempts at any personal gain. That could ruin so much of what we're trying to accomplish. We've all seen the movies, like Back to the Future where one character uses historical information to make himself a rich man in the future. We know that is just a fun movie to watch, but the hero had to travel back several times to fix the 'time continuum'. We are about to meet real people. It's about real change that needs to take place. Please, no mistakes." Paul looked at Charles, whose face had a bit of a smirk. "Charles?" said Paul inquisitively.

Charles pushed his chair away from the table and stood up while answering with fervor, "We have a few more steps to take, so let's keep in mind we are on an expedition of education and information for men who have shaped our country. Everything we are as the United States began with these men. They are smart; they're tough! They are lawyers and farmers. They have family, and they are men of God. Several of these men are pastors. We have all studied the history books and know their opinions, and we must trust them. If any of these men choose not to participate, do not press the point. They may think we are insane and lock us up, so be very careful. But, for the men who choose to take the chance in our project, they will be forever changed.

We must be more prepared for this than any case tried in the Supreme Court. Just because we are advanced in time does not mean we are advanced in our brain. These men are quite intelligent. There will be no gavel to stop what they see or hear. We will be speaking to the forefathers of our country. These men will judge everything they see and hear, based on their own experiences, not ours. They will be surprised and disgusted. Impressed and amazed. Shocked and sickened."

"I'd rather hope so!" Rayne interjected. "That's the point!"

"Yes!" Charles moved forward in his oration, "Absolutely! I realize we will not have *every* answer to every inquiry they may have; however, we will do our level best to help them understand our failures and our advancements." Charles returned to his chair but still held everyone's attention letting the weight of his comments hang in the air.

Charles placed his coffee cup on the table and continued, "But, as to Paul's feeling of no mistakes, I hope we are not making one. I don't feel as if we are...I, uh...I just pray we are not."

Benton stood to refill his coffee cup. "This will be amazing, my friends. Charles brings up a good point, so let me add something to this conversation and be very clear. You were each chosen for specific reasons. You are all experts in your fields. Your educational qualifications are spectacular, but this isn't about you or me. Collectively, we possess the same desire to help this country be better than the mess it has turned out to be. Dr. Rayne and I discussed this from the very beginning of this project. Neither he, nor I, nor any of us should ever come into a mindset of a 'God Complex'. This is simply a technology giving us an opportunity.

An opportunity with responsibility; a responsibility like none other. Am I clear on this?"

The room had yet another moment of silence.

"Everyone feeling the gravity of this?" Sarah Fleming put forth the question in rhetoric.

Moments later she followed up by saying, "Shall we get back to it? Dr. Rayne, when is your scheduled trip? I'll get the monkeys ready on the floor above."

"I have a 3 PM scheduled. There are a few things I need to finish beforehand."

"I'll be ready for you by 3 p.m.," she answered and took another sip of her coffee.

Paul stood and slowly walked over to a small table with a lamp. "Okay everyone, I'd like to show you something if I may."

"Go on," was the response from Dr. Rayne and everyone's attention was focused on Paul.

"Thus far, I have been the only traveler to have had the option to press the return button when I decided to. Everyone else was a timed return. Correct?"

"Yes."

"It is imperative to understand that anything we do when we travel can, and most likely will, make a change in history. We must be diligent to be very careful. I was only sent here, to this destination." Paul was pointing to the very room they were standing in. "I disappeared from the tele-pad, arrived in this building to the designated area, and then walked into this room. I arrived here after working hours, as you know, and no one was around. We did discuss doing this, and my actions were on today's agenda, right?"

"Yes," Benton said while everyone nodded their heads in agreement. "We were coming to this point shortly but go on. I enjoy your enthusiasm."

"I stepped off the tele-pad ~ came into this room and..." Paul held his right hand, raising his index finger in an expression for the group to wait for his next move. He walked over to a table and picked up a lamp. He carefully turned it over and slowly pulled off a taped piece of napkin from the bottom of the lamp. He handed the paper to Sarah as he continued, "That napkin only has my initials on it. 'P.T.' I placed it here four months ago, but I only traveled to that time yesterday. I walked down the hall, grabbed one of those napkins, wrote my initials on it, taped it here and, when I decided to return, I walked back to the tele-pad and pressed the button. You said I was gone four minutes."

"This is so cool!" said Charles. "I mean I know everyone's status with traveling ~ the three of us have done it, but this is the first that anyone has moved off the tele-pad, spent time in the past, and we have great results!"

"I think this means that we need to move to the next test. Sarah, have we trained the monkey to move off the tele-pad and be returned from another location?" Benton asked.

"Yes, sir," she replied.

Benton looked at Dr. Rayne, "Is the portable tracker ready?"

Rayne added, "I've concentrated on a miniature version of a tele-pad that can move with the traveler. It's not yet tested, but yes, sir, it is ready."

"Very well, let's begin the next phase upstairs to match what we already know here. Remember, the findings need to be synchronous. One success does not mean we're done testing," Benton said decidedly and turned and left the room. Dr. Rayne also left the conference room leaving the other three to once again raise their cups in a mock toast and smiles.

Chapter 3

After several months and many more tests, the secretive group was becoming more efficient time travelers. Oddly, both Dr. Benton and Dr. Rayne felt as if they were running out of time to get their project's toughest phase started, yet time is exactly what they were playing with all along.

Dr. Benton walked through the underground facility; he had many thoughts going through his mind. He couldn't stop them. It was in his DNA to have continuous thoughts about several subjects at once. His mind was never quiet.

He was a man that most would consider a technical and scientific genius; but, if you asked him, he would tell you in very common language to let him work. He could speak to colleagues at the highest intellectual levels and turn around to children and communicate on their level, a task many people cannot imagine. He was humble and didn't care to take credit for the completion of any job. But, this work...this would have a massive impact on the world. He still didn't want any credit; he only wanted to participate. To be a traveler might have been the greatest reward of all, but this opportunity was taken by Dr. Rayne, which he knew was the best decision.

Dr. Rayne had completed the small portable devices that would help trigger the time travel. His team of engineers and scientists on the 8th sub-floor believed they were working on spatial teleport travel from one destination to another *within* the same time-period - to be able to "beam me up, Scotty" or go from one city to another within just a few seconds. And they would be right!   Dr. Benton admired Rayne's expertise and his resolve.

Throughout the years of this entire process, Dr. Benton was the only person who had contact with the person who financed this project. Billions of dollars had been spent building the underground facility, making payroll, and providing the necessary tools. Benton's nickname for the financier was the Benefactor. Why would anyone spend this kind of money and not want to benefit from it? Maybe the Benefactor had the same mindset as he did: use the science to change the world and not make a profit. Benton highly doubted that.   Therefore, the logical conclusion was to make money.   The Benefactor never micromanaged or even showed his face in the facility. He never questioned the money Benton authorized to be spent, but he still required progress reports.

Benton could only speculate what the Benefactor would do with a teleportation device that is proven to work. It would be very costly to create the teleport pads in mass, so this would be a luxury item at first, for sure. Maybe he didn't want to put the automobile, transit, or airline industries out of business. Too few people would be able to afford this type of travel, but it would certainly be a steppingstone forward in the evolution of travel. No more emissions regulations and maybe even temperature decrease in 'global warming', which he didn't feel the need to spend his time worrying about.

Benton was convinced the Benefactor would do everything in his power to not let the government seize his work. The government wasn't the only cause of his desire to have teleportation become a reality, but it was a large part. The Benefactor believed the government's tightened regulations, poor decisions, and restrictive laws produced an overall loss of freedoms by the citizens of the United States. Its growing bureaucracy and power were simply ridiculous and out of hand. Benton understood this frame of mind and accepted the challenge of this project. However, Benton wasn't content with just creating a machine for someone to make a profit. Benton's intention was to truly change America.

He didn't care for the way the United States had turned out, and, if the Benefactor was going to fund this project, Benton would take this opportunity to go as far as he could. If there was even the slightest chance that he could send a human across the room, then he would make every effort to send someone back in time ~ and this is the part of the project the Benefactor could know nothing about.

Benton would send all the progress reports about spatial travel and monkeys and everything that happened on the 8th sub-floor to the Benefactor, and all of that information would be true.

However, anything dealing with the floor beneath only exists for himself, Dr. Rayne, Paul Tesla, Charles Carson, Sarah Fleming, and, if successful, a few signers from the past. Benton's end game was to show these men what the United States had become 232 years after the Constitution was written.

Benton had decided early on in this endeavor *not* to explain any of his coding that dealt with time travel. This was his own intellectual knowledge that, when the time was right, he would share with only one person.

On the 8th sub-floor, the engineers, scientists and technicians couldn't figure out how teleportation works, and monkeys couldn't talk. Benton and Rayne kept the critical developments separated until it was time to put them together. They also thought Dr. Benton and Dr. Rayne were mad scientists until the magic happened. Inanimate objects were 'moved' from one tele-pad to another. Then again. And again. Even after seeing that teleportation was possible and safely repeatable, it was still hard to believe. Seeing didn't always mean believing. Even still, the workers joked about the possibility of time travel as if it were a totally impossible task. Of course, they also thought this about teleportation before the project began. However, given the current status of the project, Benton thought logic would take over and they should think anything is possible.

The 9th sub-floor didn't exist for people except for the select few. Those few used Benton's time travel coding to continue their project. Once the project had positive reoccurring results, he would commence the main task. The preparations were quite extensive. It took several years to get to this phase; and yet, here he was. Was he ready? The team reviewed every aspect and could not think of anything that may have been left out. Benton made his own lists on paper with precise details; but at the end of the day, he destroyed those papers. There would be no electronic or paper footprint of his own notes. Security was paramount. Getting someone from the past was a huge milestone, to be sure, but what to do with them while they were here was another task to consider.

The travelers had built an entire learning facility for their future guests. This wasn't an easy task to take on not knowing the number of guests they may have. So, the travelers decided to plan for a maximum of eight. Should each traveler only bring back one guest would be amazing ~ two guests each would be closer to a miracle!

Rooms in the facility were recreated to look as close to rooms their guests were used to seeing. The travelers were trying to prevent shock and maybe instill some level of comfort when the guests arrived. Even the interior of Independence Hall, where the members of the Continental Congress were working, was an accurate replication. This room would serve as the first classroom during orientation. The guest would experience a fast-paced learning process that would bring them up to date with the major developments of the world. The living quarters would look like the hotel rooms of their own time period. The travelers had clothes made for themselves and their guests, so everyone would have a working wardrobe. More clothes were available for the men who decided to come back with the travelers. Food would be prepared similarly. Even the bathroom facilities would seem familiar, although they worked differently. Dr. Benton believed this aspect shouldn't be too difficult to imagine as indoor toilet facilities were emerging around this same time. However, chamber pots were still in each room, even if they weren't used.

Benton had walked through the facility so many times he felt as if he had already traveled back to the past. This place was very much like a small town built for the comfort and education of his guests. So extensive was the construction of this facility that when his guests were studying certain advancements in technology or amenities, the crew taking care of the facility could remove a few items in the rooms and reveal the "new" technology, which included light switches, chandeliers, pens, lamps, bathroom items, and clothing styles. This concept was to be an immersion into the current century. They would learn *what* had been invented ~ not necessarily *how*.

Benton concentrated on several aspects of this project simultaneously and those topics could change at any moment. He knew that time was still a factor in several ways. How much time his guests spent in the present ~ do we ask them to stay a day, a week, a month, or longer? How does their time here affect the lives of others while they are gone from their duties? The health of his guests would be important. Benton couldn't have them die while they were in his care. Their hearts were beating, and their lives were at stake.

So much had gone into this project that even Dr. Rayne was amazed at the progress. Still, he would happily let Dr. Benton take all the credit. This was Benton's brainchild of a project, and the two had become quite good friends during its process.

Rayne was very content being a part in making and changing history.

As he finished walking through the orientation facility, he found Dr. Benton waiting for him. "A penny for your thoughts, Carver?" Rayne asked.

With his hands in his pockets and a reassuring look on his face, the question was answered. "I think we may both feel quite similar. I believe we're ready, my friend. I know we could go over the systems again, but..."

Rayne stopped him in mid-sentence by saying, "No. I think you're right. We are ready, and I say we have one final meeting with the entire group and then begin. I'm not as apprehensive as I was at the onset of this crazy idea. My fear isn't failure. We've had plenty of that along the way. Even the men that we are about to meet face to face know the feeling of failure. The one thing I fear is that we could make things worse."

"Or better," added Carver, trying to be positive. He continued, "Our goal is absolutely for a better America. Better for everyone. Better for everyone the way we see it, Carver. And maybe the way we see it wouldn't be better for everyone. You can never please everyone."

"You're sounding a bit like a politician," Rayne quipped.

"I hope I'm sounding like a scientist. We can't *assume* the action we are about to undertake will have the desired outcome. Could it be that we change the minds of our forefathers, and this country goes to hell quicker than we are now? This is a question we can't ignore."

Rayne conceded, "I see your point. And, quite frankly, I've thought about this, many times."

The two slowly and thoughtfully walked towards the conference room. Benton's words broke the silence, "Here's the answer to both questions. Whether we help or hurt our country, we, like many scientists or explorers of any century and from any country, even with our good intentions, will never know unless we try."

"In this, we are in agreement."

The following day, the conference room chairs were filled by the team. The room had an air of excitement. Several of them felt as if they were about to ride a rollercoaster for the very first time.

"Good morning everyone," Dr. Benton began. "I'm not a long-winded person, and I do not have a huge oration to give. I believe we have all addressed our concerns, and those concerns have been proven unsubstantiated. I feel as if this project is ready for the ultimate test. Are we all in agreement on this?" All heads nodded in the affirmative.

"Then we," he stressed this word as he repeated himself, "*We*...are ready to test ourselves in our endeavor here today and over the next several weeks. May God be with us. Dr. Rayne, would you like to say a few words?"

"Please, if I may, would you all pray with me? It's a simple prayer that's been said in so many languages and for a very long time. It's called the Serenity Prayer. *God, grant* me the serenity to accept the things I cannot change, the courage to change the things I can, and the wisdom to know the difference. Lord, we are about to embark on a quest that may forever change the way the world looks today. We understand and recognize that only you are God, and we are not. We also believe the talents we have used come from you. As the talents of medical people heal, the talents of imagination and thought have brought forth many inventions. Help us to truly use these gifts to bless others. In Your name we pray, Amen."

"Amen" could be heard from every person in the room in unison.

"Very well, everyone. Let's begin. Travelers, please take your places. The time is now just a minute or so from yet another test on the floor above us. For us, however, this is no test."

Calling themselves 'travelers', Dr. Rayne, Charles Carson, Paul Tesla, and Sarah Fleming stepped onto a large tele-pad. They were dressed in clothes to resemble the years of the late 1700s. Except for their return devices, they took nothing that would give them away as being from the future, including jewelry and eyeglasses. They all carried a few small gold nuggets and silver currency of the period to exchange for goods and services when needed. They looked around the room at each other.

"Ready?" Benton questioned. Heads nodded. "See you in a few, my friends."

"We'll be right back," answered William.

"In three, two, one...go."   With that, the travelers began to disappear, and Dr. Benton started his stopwatch and took a deep breath.

Chapter 4
In the year 1787

The travelers reappeared in a clearing outside Philadelphia. Dressed in the clothing of that era, each person looked at the other and grinned just a bit. They had not ever traveled at the same time and were now silently a bit squeamish at how the system would work, yet here they stood. June 7th, 1787, was a Thursday. The sun was shining, and the team had work to do.

"Okay, everyone. You have your assignments. Please remember... we do not want to cause any trouble. And Charles, you are a free man, but I can't change the color of your skin. We already talked about this...just be careful, my friend."

Charles, ever the playful man, kindly tilted his hat, stepped back with his left leg and bent over at the waste with a slight bow of his head while answering, "Yassuh." He stood up smiling.

"See you all soon, God willing."

The group began walking to town in search of the delegates. It wasn't long before several conversations with their target members started up with splendid accents and speech patterns such as, "Good morning, sir. Might you have a moment to spare to speak on a most pressing matter?" Each person waited for the probable response of what the topic of conversation would be. The answer at the ready came quickly, "The future of America, sir."

As statesmen, this was certainly a way to capture their attention. As soon as the mere mention of the future was discussed, ideas came spewing forth from some of the congressmen. Some of the statesmen were tired of discussing or arguing politics and strategy all day such that another conversation, particularly with someone they didn't know, seemed inviting. Fortunately, the travelers were experts in history and gleaned from their conversations just enough to interest the statesmen in continuing the conversation. Even the only female traveler, Sarah, who happened to be stunningly beautiful, could turn the intellectual heads of several men she thought wouldn't give her a second thought. Eventually, all the travelers turned every conversation into 'seeing the future' as a means of solving problems.

Most of the statesmen simply found the idea preposterous and bid their guest good day. Without pressuring the conversation or trying to draw too much attention to themselves, the travelers simply moved on to another potential candidate. Each traveler soon found that a different approach would be necessary. At a predetermined time and place, they met at the end of the first day. Collectively, they found and started a conversation with about twelve of the fifty-five delegates. But they were not discouraged and continued to discuss their findings. Should anyone not return, it would be assumed they were successful in the mission. However, all four found themselves looking at each other knowing that no one had yet succeeded.

"I believe it is time we tackle our subjects on their own terms," Charles Carson said.

"And just exactly what do you have in mind?" Paul Tesla asked quickly.

"Not having spoken to anyone before while 'traveling', we have no data to help us determine the best way to describe our intent and just mentioning time travel or 'seeing into the future' isn't doing very well. We've only a select group of men to pull from and the ones we have approached thus far have obviously rejected our ideas. We need to rethink our approach. Be more on their terms and not as direct as we have been," He replied.

Sarah Fleming noted, "Gentlemen, I have spoken to several statesmen on my predetermined list and found nothing but rejection or contempt. I'm not sure if that is because I am a woman or if they were afraid my intellect was far more advanced than theirs. However, I think it's time for me to travel to New York. If our dates are correct, and I believe they are, after today's events then Gouveneur Morris should be arriving there in two days. As we've discussed, he could be my best option; but if not, I have a list to work on."

"Agreed," said Dr. Rayne.

"Very well, I will seek out the cobbler and see how much conversation in his Divinity we can muster up. I hope to see you all with your guest as soon as possible." Paul's comment ended with a friendly head nod.

Charles looked at Rayne and asked, "For whom will you seek?

Rayne's face was serious, but inside he was rather excited. "We are on this mission, and, in all accounts, we have already succeeded, as proven by the fact that we now stand in a time long past. I'd venture that over 99% of America's population in 2025 can't name a handful of signers for the Constitution or the Declaration of Independence. As interesting as this may sound, we've no time to waist. We may not convince them all, but we only need a few. I'm looking to meet with James Madison or Thomas Jefferson."

"Forget Jefferson. I believe I recall during the time we are here that he received information from Virginia that is causing him some issues. He's currently serving his second term as the Governor and is moving the capital from Williamsburg to Richmond. He will be a bit tied up and probably will not entertain any guests," Sarah noted.

"These are very tough times for this country," Rayne said seriously. "Very well, then, Madison it is. Mr. Carson, do you have someone specific in mind?"

"A man who, at this point in history, has already freed his slaves...well, to some extent...and is still in the process of doing so. Only one other founding father has done so, and that is Benjamin Franklin. Yes sir, I do have a

Pennsylvanian Representative in mind. He helped author the Articles of Confederation."

"Ahh!" Paul interjected. "You speak of Mr. John Dickinson?"

"Yes, I do."

"You, sir, are a genius. Again, I wish you...I wish all of us success!"

Arrangements were made to meet again in three days if unsuccessful. All of them hoped to see the others at the training facility with a guest instead of remaining here.

After one last look at each other, Charles, Paul, Dr. Rayne, and Sarah took steps in different directions. Rayne could hear Sarah humbly and quietly say, "Here we go." She sounded a bit nervous. Rayne didn't wonder about Paul being nervous. Somehow, he knew that Paul's ability to talk to anyone, about anything, at any time, kept him calm. He was more of an extrovert. Sarah was certainly the most nervous of all, but, when the time came, he felt assured of her ability to get the job done.

Each person in this group had their own issues to deal with. Charles may have had the toughest issues as a black man stepping into a time when he could potentially have been thought to be a slave. There were few free black men in this time period. Charles's expertise as a historian was unmatched. He was a very proud man, and any sensibilities he had to the history of his family and race were always in his mind. However, he was more interested in progression than regression. He was raised that way. Be productive, not a burden. "Make something of yourself, work hard every day, learn new things, read books, and teach your children to be better than yourself, and these things will make the world a better place," his mother used to say often. His mother passed away when he was 17, and he lived every day hearing her words. This was one of many reasons he decided to obtain as much education as he could. And he loved history. He also loved to read, and his mind was like a sponge. Even better, he could recall much of what he read. He smiled as he briefly thought his mother would be proud of him and what he was about to do.

Charles strolled into town still expecting evil stares by some of the white population but was quite surprised when it didn't happen. He walked into a local merchant store, found what he wanted, and placed the items on the counter. The storekeeper looked at him without reservation and asked how he wanted to pay for the items. As planned, Charles confidently pulled a few silver pieces out of his pocket and placed them on the counter.

"I'd like to trade these in and maybe get a few 'bits' or Spanish Dollars in return."

The man behind the counter looked inquisitively at Charles and how he was dressed. Then he pulled a scale from behind the bar and completed the transaction. Charles walked out of the mercantile with a few items and coins in his pocket. He then made his way across town to continue his mission.

By happenstance, he found John Rutledge. Knowing this statesman represented South Carolina, so Charles decided to be very careful as he approached. Charles Carson knew that Rutledge was a man accustomed to getting his way. As a wealthy lawyer, past President and Governor of South Carolina, Rutledge had successfully commanded troops and defended against invasions by the British while defending Charleston. Charles believed Rutledge would be a formidable opponent during a proper conversation on the future of America. If Rutledge could believe what Charles had to say about the future, he still wasn't sure Rutledge would believe in time travel. That could be said for any statesmen, really. However, if Rutledge did not believe any of what Charles had to say, Rutledge may feel as if he were about to be ambushed by a charlatan. This conversation could be quite risky. Carson also knew that Rutledge, while having defended abusive slave owners in open court, disliked slavery despite owning upwards of sixty slaves during his lifetime. By the time Rutledge died, he only owned one. Carson kept this in mind as he drew nearer and said, "Begging your pardon, sir, if you will permit me an introduction? I am Charles Carson, a free black man, and if I am correct, you would be the Honorable John Rutledge, Esquire?" Charles carefully waited for his response.

"I am he. What is the meaning of your introduction?" came Rutledge's response.

"Your Excellency, I wish only to appeal to your thoughts of justice, humanity, and the welfare of the Honorable State of South Carolina and her neighboring states, with specific

41

regard to the future declarations and documents that will govern such properties. As an elected and esteemed official to this Second Continental Congress, you have a permanent influence on the future. And I, also possessing formal education and being a constituent of our fair state," he lied on this part but thought it might help, "wish to take a few minutes of your time to discuss these items. I do believe I have a vast understanding of what lies in front of you."

"You have knowledge of what lies in front of the delegates of this conclave, sir? Is this an affront to our integrity to say that you are privy to the events that occur before they happen? What sort of treason is this?" The volume of his voice did not rise, and he remained very calm. Rutledge was the type of man who would not show fear though his demeanor became cautiously defensive. Cold eyes stared back at Charles Carson.

"Sir, I offer my sincerest apologies if my words suggested anything but honorable intentions. I simply wish a few moments of your time to discuss the actions of this delegation and the permanency that such signatures will indemnify. Please, a moment of your time?"

"Mr. Carson, you certainly have me intrigued. And I believe you have no ill will toward me or our 'fair state', as you aptly stated. However, I am not convinced that any person can foretell of events that have not occurred…"

"Excuse me, please, Your Excellency. We could discuss the ramifications of actions or the wording of literary statements by the delegation. These are the items of interest."

"Mr. Carson, just a moment." Rutledge gave Charles a look of hope for just a brief moment as he hailed another gentleman to the conversation. The streets were busy with many people going about their daily business. Considering how nervous Charles was at the moment, his heightened senses and the quiet calmness of the day helped him to hear the footfalls of another gentleman coming closer.

"Mr. Carson, this is my esteemed colleague and friend, Mr. Thomas Jefferson, Esquire. I will defer to his judgement and trust that any man who has a pen as intelligent and true as his will gain my favor, for I shall be compelled to surrender any amount of time that is required to hear your thoughts."

The introductions continued, and Charles stood there with his thoughts while looking into the eyes of Thomas Jefferson. Remembering what Sarah had mentioned about Jefferson not being available, he kept his wits about himself although he was dumb struck. As a historian, Charles appreciated that he was standing in front of one of the most notable men in history. Although the travelers knew a moment like this would happen, to have it happen was even more of an honor than they could imagine.

Carson's thoughts quickly turned to the political prowess of Rutledge and could only find the situation quite amusing. In a matter of moments, Rutledge was able to compliment him, show a bit of doubt and pass off this interview to Jefferson!

Charles felt the chills up and down his spine from Rutledge's shrewdness.

Thomas Jefferson, ever the gentlemen, replied, "Mr. Rutledge, your introduction does me nothing but to admit I should seek to be a humble man, for I know of no man to which you have pledged surrender." Smiling, they all shook hands. Rutledge continued to explain to Jefferson the intentions of Carson while acknowledging that he was a bit cautious due to his beginning statements. Jefferson asked a few more questions when Rutledge began to bow out of the conversation.

"It is here that I must depart and will allow the two of you to continue this discussion. I have pressing matters I must attend, though I will reiterate my earlier thoughts, Mr. Carson. I will hold my tongue and await to hear from the honorable Mr. Jefferson." Rutledge looked at both men and offered his handshake to Carson.

"It will be my honor to entertain a conversation with you, sir," Carson replied, and Rutledge walked away.

Thomas Jefferson and Charles Carson looked at each other inquisitively. Each had questions for the other and both had little time. Jefferson spoke first, "Mr. Rutledge is an esteemed fellow whom I hold in high regard. You must have gathered his interest, albeit a rocky start. Yet I will add he gave you high marks for your recovery, sir. It has been my experience in dealing with Rutledge that he does not entertain strangers upon political endeavors. You, Mr.

Carson, have succeeded in such a task. Your success is nothing short of a great strategy considering Mr. Rutledge's military prowess. His mind never stops churning. Whatever did you say that captured his surrender for a few moments of his time?"

"My words are obedient to the truth, sir. Admittedly, I am still nervous in my thoughts. To have been granted a few moments with the Honorable Mr. Rutledge, and Your Excellency, is truly a moment I shall never forget."

"Then an audience you shall have, though I humbly suggest losing the nervousness. I am a proponent of removing obstacles before proceeding. While you calm your thoughts, I will add that this conversation is still limited on time as I am preparing to travel. I have business in my home state and only happened upon this meeting, so, Mr. Carson, if you will begin?"

Carson remembered Sarah's comments of Jefferson's issues needing to leave the conclave for a short time, and yet, here he was, walking alongside Thomas Jefferson. He would be taking every possible advantage of his time. "Thank you, Governor, for the opportunity." Charles followed the steps of Jefferson for the next hour. The two were immersed in conversation and Jefferson's quest for more information was obvious. Impressed with the amount of knowledge that Charles possessed, Jefferson couldn't help but ask where his education had come from as not many free black men were as educated as he. Charles truthfully answered that his education began at

King's College, now known as Columbia University, in New York and then continued in New Jersey at Princeton.

"As a matter of fact, sir, King's College was established only six years after you were born. It was one of our country's earliest established educational facilities which is why I chose to go there first. Princeton wasn't established until 1754, and incidentally, your esteemed colleague, Mr. James Madison, was not able to obtain a position at Princeton in 1773. However, he was successful in 1774 in attending King's College." Both campuses were already established the mid-1700s, and Jefferson was familiar with both, so Charles was very careful not to mention when he graduated with a master's degree from both universities.

Jefferson gently replied, "Mr. Madison, as do the majority of men, needed a bit of time to find himself. It would be my conclusion that he has done just so and cleverly dispatched himself into strong positions of leadership and government, and I applaud his accomplishments. He is an excellent orator, thinker, and protector of liberty. I do so admire him." Jefferson recalculated the amount of time he would spend with Charles Carson.

The topics of conversation were broad, but, deep down, both men knew they could speak on these subjects at length. They discussed the change in posture of the government over time, leaving the citizens with less liberties. Jefferson equated this conversion as a slow growth of tyranny ~ a symbiotic cancer for which there is no cure. Charles talked of the freedoms expressed in the Declaration of Independence, to which Jefferson admitted that his thoughts expressed a desire for the citizens of the Colonies and British Monarchy to unilaterally understand what it should mean for this country to experience freedom. Jefferson also admitted this was a daunting task to which he lost much sleep and still wasn't sure he got it right.

With Jefferson's comment in mind, Charles asked, "Sir, the document is written from the standpoint of the responsibilities of a federal and state government. I've always wondered why there are no references to the responsibilities of the citizen. What's expected of them? How do they remain true or loyal citizens? I understand there are criminal and civil laws for punishment, but what about individual responsibilities?"

"You have a good point, Mr. Carson. However, it is not the morality of man that must be governed, it is justice for actions in which the lack of morality may have played a part. An honorable man will do good to his fellow man whilst the opposite is true: a dishonorable man will destroy. It is the dishonesty that must be punished. Being honorable is, by its very nature, the greatest reward. Therefore, I believe your concepts have been considered in this process. As I mentioned, I may not have gotten it right."

The topics of government, economy, scientific and technological advancements, entertainment, communications, and more were all touched on at some point throughout the time spent.

Even though the conversation continued until dusk, in the end, regardless of how impressive and convincing Charles Carson could be, including the belief that Charles truly was a 'messenger from the future', Jefferson gently declined Charles' invitation for several reasons. However, the primary reason was simple for Jefferson when he explained, "Mr. Carson, this evening has been very enlightening, and I wish to convey to you my sincerest appreciation for the education and counseling. But I do not consider myself as a worthy candidate for this proposal. You have given me sufficient reasoning that I will truly be disappointed for what is in store. In truth, I will have to consider the possibility that the Constitution, now in debate, will resolve as a satisfactory document with regards to the rights of the citizens of the United States."

As the two said their farewells and Jefferson began to turn away, he paused and said, "Mr. Carson, I can only surmise you will attempt to take someone else into the future. Am I correct?"

"Yes, Counselor, quite right." Carson replied.

"As you are a well-educated man, you will know this answer, but should you find yourself wishing to gain an audience with the 'Penman of the Revolution', you might consider demonstrating to him that you know something he doesn't. I believe that would capture his attention quite well."

"Thank you, sir. I will do what I can." With that, Thomas Jefferson left to continue on his way. Seeing Thomas Jefferson leave, Charles' emotions ran high with both excitement and disappointment. He knew now that meeting Thomas Jefferson would be forever on his list of top five memorable moments.

Jefferson was very intrigued at the start of the conversation but eventually talked himself out of wanting to visit the future. He believed that to be a very dangerous concept. He had looked deeply into Charles' eyes and believed every word that the man was telling him was truthful, and this was very satisfying to Charles.

Exhausted and excited from the day's work, Charles returned to the hotel that allowed him to stay in the servants' quarters. Without causing an issue, he thanked the hotel manager, paid for the room anyway, and prepared for the next day.

Chapter 5

Earlier, when the group had separated, Paul Tesla had turned to walk in the opposite direction. The travelers knew that they were going to separate from each other to avoid any questions of familiarity. Should someone see them and associate their fanatical, and probably psychotic, question of time travel, it would be better for only one person to be in trouble than all four of them. Either way, it wouldn't last long. The plan for everyone was to exit that conversation as quickly as possible before being detained. When the time was right, activate the return travel device, and they would safely return to when they belong. Of course, this was less than the desirable result but was agreed to be the best exit plan.

In his own right, Paul was a master historian of this time period. He fell in love with the Bill of Rights in his youth. His own father was also a historian and professed that this period was the most profound time in America's history. Paul's father, his most poignant influence, was right in his son's eyes. Paul began studying this time period in the sixth grade, well in advance of any classroom studies. Men were writing these foundational documents to not only separate them from a superpower monarchy, but, more importantly, to defiantly stand alone as a new country, with laws and beliefs that would govern the country for centuries. The weight upon the shoulders of these men was far greater than what a common person of the twenty-first century could fathom.

As Paul strolled down the streets of Philadelphia, he passed the various historical locations that he had studied. He pictured the differences in his mind: how time had, in many cases, not changed the appearance of these buildings while their surroundings had been continuously modernized. He breathed in the clean fresh air. Gone was the smell of exhaust fumes from thousands of vehicles and the smelly trash cans on so many corners. No power lines or pavement. However, he noticed the swarming flies around piles of horse dung scattered in the streets, to which no one paid attention. The air certainly wasn't fresh in those areas. Times had certainly changed.

As he turned the corner on to Chestnut Street, he didn't see the ever-familiar bronzed statue of George Washington with a humble and stately expression. The area looked as it should ~ uninterrupted by all the twentieth- and twenty-first century updates in remembrance of historical events. He looked upon the building known as Independence Hall. Though it sat there looking so new and resolute, it was roughly thirty years old.

Paul continued to lose himself in his own historical moment, one that no one would ever read about, and still he marveled at the honor he felt being able to participate in this endeavor. Additionally, he remained awe struck in the fact that he had traveled through time. He felt as though he was walking in a dream. At the same time, Paul's thoughts turned toward the cobbler and the task at hand. Shoes.

A good sturdy pair of shoes was how the modest gentleman from Massachusetts had traveled into politics. Roger Sherman, a man known in the history books for compromising, walked over 150 miles to begin a career with his brother as a cobbler. An avid reader, Sherman was book smart, and he put that mental skill to the task when his neighbors were in legal disputes. His ability to debate a case lead a local lawyer to encourage him to take the Bar, which he passed. Needing the income, he accepted the jobs for justice of the peace, county judge, and, eventually, state senator, leading him to attend the first and second Continental Congresses.

His Puritan background fueled his arguments toward non-violent conclusions. During his tenure within the seats of the conventions, his reputation grew favorably among all who could hear and would listen. Sherman did not agree with every statesman attending the conventions, though he was considered a friend by the setaceous John Adams, who described Sherman's character to be "honest as an angel and as firm in the Cause of American Independence as Mount Atlas."

As the second-eldest member of the Constitutional Convention, only Benjamin Franklin being older, Sherman was one of the most influential. By making motions or affirming motions during the convention close to 160 times, he reinforced his ideas of freedom. A few historical accounts do not agree, but it is believed by most that Robert Sherman is the only stateman to have signed this country's top four documents ~ the Articles of Association (1774), the United States Declaration of Independence

(1776), the Articles of Confederation (1781) and the United States Constitution (1789).

With the knowledge of Sherman's character and achievements reviewing in his mind, Paul's dream walking was becoming more real as he approached. He had walked far enough that he stood in front of the Philadelphia statehouse and looked up to the sky. There, proudly hanging, was the State House Bell with its biblical reference from the Book of Leviticus (25:10). Carefully, he visually scoured the bell and looked for the infamous crack line, which may have come from the first time the bell was used.

He smiled as he felt like a young schoolboy with curiosity. As he found himself just staring at what is known today as the Liberty Bell, his thoughts were interrupted by soldiers rushing down the street. With the sight of the soldiers so close, Paul was immediately concerned for his own safety. He recalled that this Second Continental Congress only agreed to meet in Philadelphia specifically for this conclave due to the 1783 Mutiny of federal soldiers for nonpayment. Hamilton and Jefferson were working feverishly to move the U.S. Capital away from Philadelphia to what is now known as Washington, D.C.

Paul Tesla casually placed his hand inside his pocket and felt for his portable teleport device. He would not remove the protective cover and put his finger on the button, but it gave him a bit of comfort to know it was still in his pocket. Paul backed out of the way of the soldiers. Several of them looked directly at him as the entire group rushed by. Paul found himself taking a deep breath as the last one passed. He could now see they were headed quickly down the street to a tavern. He didn't worry himself about why they were in such a hurry, but he decided to be more cognizant of his surroundings.

Turning his gaze and his feet toward the doors of Independence Hall, Paul's adrenaline picked up again. There, in the distance, was Roger Sherman. At 66 years of age, the square-jawed man was walking out of the building with his assistant. Immediately, Paul acted as any man heading into a job interview: he rubbed the top of each shoe against the back of his opposite pant leg to get the dust off and started towards Sherman. "It's the shoes," he said to himself. Paul was wearing shoes with a style that would hopefully catch the eye of a professional cobbler. These were not typical shoes for this time.

Paul noticed the direction the two were taking and followed. It was nearing the dinner hour, and Paul was hoping that the congressional meeting hadn't adjourned for the day. He was hoping that Sherman would be headed back but couldn't be sure. Sherman and his assistant stopped at a local hotel just a few blocks away. However, after an hour of waiting, the two did not come out. Paul waited another hour and still nothing. He walked back to Independence Hall only to notice that the building was dark. No lights shown through the windows. He knew he would have to wait until morning to continue his plan.

When morning arrived, Paul was already in place. He stood patiently outside the doors of the hotel, leaning against a lamp post. The lamp had been extinguished for just under thirty minutes when the hotel door opened. Several men were coming down the steps, and Paul was grateful to see Roger Sherman as one of them.

Paul Tesla didn't speak. He had taken off his right shoe and set it on the ground beside him for it to be noticed. The shoe was black and highly polished to gain the attention of a man that knew how to make shoes properly. Paul was rubbing his foot as though he was in some discomfort.

If Paul's study of Roger Sherman was even close to correct, he knew three major things about Sherman: one, he grew up as a cobbler; two, he had a Puritan faith that he was never ashamed to speak about; and three, he loved his country deeply.

"Good morning, sir," Sherman said as he watched Paul rub his foot.

"Ah, good morning. My apologies, sir. This isn't the best place to remove one's shoes, but these are new and not yet broken in. These are quite unpleasant for the road ahead."

"I happen to know a little something about shoes. Perhaps I can help?" Sherman held out his hand. Paul picked up the shoe and handed it to him. Introductions were made, and proper sentiments exchanged. Sherman's facial motions expressed how impressed he was with the construction of the shoe and he began to ask several questions about how it was made. Paul answered the questions convincingly and added other details about the design. Sherman was quite intrigued. When nearing the end of the short conversation, Paul added, "It can be rather difficult to know your fellow man unless you are able to walk for a while in his shoes. Would you not agree Mr. Sherman?"

Sherman looked directly into Paul's eyes and thought about what he had just said.
Sherman, not a man to reply too hastily, slowly shook his head up and down. "Yes, Mr. Tesla. I do believe I agree."

"Such an agreement from you, Mr. Sherman, is a compliment. While I believe I am vaguely familiar with the agenda of the conclave to which you attend, I would also wish to visit with you further. If you wouldn't mind praying about such an audience, sir? I am staying in the other hotel just a few blocks from here," Paul said.

"You are also a man of faith, Mr. Tesla?"

"I am, sir. That I am," came the reply, and in this, Paul did not lie.

"I do not believe that I will need prayer to meet you Mr. Tesla, but I will pray about the meeting discussions."

"I look forward to it, sir." Paul shook his hand and the details for their meeting were set.

The following day, after several hours of private discussion, the Honorable Roger Sherman, gave his consent to take a glimpse into the future. This was no
56

easy task.   However, Paul successfully used the Puritan platform of desiring religious freedom from the Roman Catholic faith to move the discussion toward the concept of fighting for freedoms in the future. The two also talked about the science of time travel to the extent that Sherman would understand the action was not witchcraft. Paul found Roger Sherman to be a very interesting and formidable conversationalist. Paul was awestruck that this man, a man admired by Patrick Henry and visited by George Washington on every possible occasion, was willing to participate.   Sherman's respect by other congressmen was admirable. Paul remembered the words of Thomas Jefferson when he said Sherman was "a man who has never said a foolish thing in his life."

Not wanting to lose the moment, Paul placed his hand on Sherman's shoulder, and his other hand in his pocket. He lifted the safety mechanism and pressed the teleport button. Both men gently smiled as they faded into the future.

Chapter 6

He was walking down the streets of Philadelphia with purpose in his steps. John Dickinson was a lanky fellow with a receding hairline and a long Roman nose. His mind was churning on the words to pen for upcoming arguments at the

Constitutional Convention. Having been elected as what was then called 'President' of Pennsylvania, his current state of residence, Delaware, had sent him as their representative. One of the richest men in these states, he was also one of the most noted. In the years from 1777 to 1779, he had written his manumission[1] of his slaves, effectively freeing them within certain terms. While not being an active Quaker by membership, he was raised as one, and as he matured in that religion, he became one of the nation's earliest abolitionists. He freed his slaves and even continued for many years to care for those who could not work.

Within the ten years prior to freeing his slaves, John Dickinson had been a part of the political climate for both Pennsylvania and Delaware, serving his appointments in the Continental Congress and authoring the first draft of the Articles of Confederation. Near the end of 1781, he took office as President of Delaware, his own dissenting vote being the only one preventing unanimous election. However, his love for Pennsylvania pulled him into

---

[1] **Manumission** is the act of an owner freeing his or her slaves over several years.

58

controversy, and he accepted the role of President of Pennsylvania, briefly holding both offices simultaneously. He made and maintained many friendships within the political arena and was deemed one of the country's major patriots.

Dickinson continued with his thoughts as the afternoon sun beat down through the humid air. He didn't hear the nearly silent footsteps approaching him from the rear. Dickinson's concentration was interrupted when a messenger tapped his shoulder. He turned toward the black man and with an irritated look on his face, confirmed who he was. The messenger promptly placed a note in Dickinson's hand, then turned and walked away.

Dickinson's intention was to read and probably ignore the message. He was sent messages all the time from people trying to manipulate his vote or give him reasons why he should argue for or against the subject on the floor of the current convention he was attending. He continued walking down the street while opening the rolled paper. As he began reading, his walking slowly came to a halt.
He looked up and tried to find the messenger that handed this to him. Nowhere. As he thought about it, he realized he didn't really pay enough attention to remember what the messenger looked like other than he was a black man. Then he did remember one thing.

The messenger's hands were smooth. Not cracked and dry like a slave but smooth, as if the hands were well taken care of. One more look around the area found the same result: no messenger in sight. He read the message again

59

then slowly rolled up the paper and placed it in his inner jacket pocket. Not believing what it said, he slowly regained his pace toward the convention. He would wait to hear the question as confirmation of the mysterious message. No one knows the future, he thought to himself. No one.

A little over an hour later, he was sitting in a chair listening to the rhetoric in the room. Colleagues were spewing words for and against arguments that could and would potentially lay the groundwork for this country. He listened intently to both sides of the cause. He listened to reasons that, in his opinion, were not viable or appropriate for this conclave. Then, he heard it ~ the words from the note he had received earlier. At one point, he thought this was some sort of joke. A prank from the other side of the aisle. But the way it was presented proved it couldn't be a joke.

Dickinson hadn't spoken a single word during this meeting, so he couldn't have swayed anyone to make this suggestion; yet, there it was. Spoken by the last person in the room he would ever think of making such a comment. The leader of the opposition had just suggested Dickinson be the state's representative, just as the hand-written note had told him it would happen. He immediately felt he was being set up. Something sinister was happening, and he couldn't believe it. He was stunned.

He remained silent until the gentleman on his left tugged his sleeve and said, "Mr. Dickinson? Mr. Dickinson, did you hear the question, sir? Would you accept the position if elected, sir?"

"Yes. Yes, I believe I would. Now, if you'll excuse me, I need some air gentlemen.   I'll...uh...I'll return shortly." Out of character, Dickinson left the building and pulled the note from his pocket and read it again. He looked up and down the street but did not see the messenger. He walked slowly down the street and continued searching. Dickinson's normal quick pace while looking down at the ground in front of him was gone. His eyes darted everywhere.

He had walked nearly three blocks when he spotted the messenger sitting on a bench near the edge of the park. The messenger, Charles Carson, was quietly reading a newspaper when Dickinson sat down beside him.

"How did you know?   Who's setting me up? Am I in danger? Is my family in danger? Tell me who's behind this, now!" Dickinson's voice was quietly firm and commanding. He was looking directly at the messenger who slowly lowered the newspaper and replied, "I know because I have specific information about today. No one is setting you up, sir. Neither you nor your family are in any danger, sir, I can assure you of that, and you do not know the gentlemen that are behind this as there is nothing here to cause you harm."

"What is the meaning of this?"

"I do have intentions, sir, to tell you more than you could ever wish to know. Safely. I wonder what you would do with such information. If I told you that it would rain tomorrow, would you wear an overcoat? Would you share that information with others? Would you keep that information to yourself and have others laugh at you when you wore your overcoat only to have them look at you and make comments behind your back when the rain starts because you are the only person with an overcoat? How would you answer this, sir?"

Dickinson was getting frustrated at such silly conjectures, but, curiously, he did not walk away. He thought for a moment before he answered the question.

"I am not convinced of my response, but, somehow, I believe I would carry my overcoat in the hopes that I would not have to use it. Should it rain, I could say that I just had the feeling of rain heading our way, that I was hopeful or that I felt it in my bones. I don't believe it will rain tomorrow, sir. However, I sense self-assurance in your voice." Dickinson paused for a moment.

When he continued, he said, "To answer more, I am more than confident I would not share this information with anyone. What is the significance of tomorrow's weather to our meeting here now?"

"Very well, Mr. Dickinson. The significance is direct, sir. Carry your overcoat tomorrow. If you will, sir, I shall meet you here tomorrow afternoon, and we will discuss this very thing. And please, do carry your overcoat. Much more than rain could be coming your way. Good day, sir."

The messenger stood, folded his paper under his arm, and walked away.

Dickinson was intrigued but confused. Confusion was something he was not very accustomed to feeling. He returned to his meetings and tried to pay attention to the rest of the discussions, but the thought of an overcoat kept flooding his mind.

The following morning, he was about to walk out of his hotel room and saw his overcoat hanging near the door. In his own bewilderment, he smirked and grabbed his overcoat. He left the hotel looking up at the brightly lit sky and felt like a fool. While keeping his appointments for the day, he found himself wondering if he was being made to play the fool. The sun continued to shine, and the weather was quite warm. Then, when he felt he had enough of these games, he began walking intently to the meeting place. Up in the distance, the messenger sat on the park bench. Dickinson, as predicted, received odd looks as he carried his overcoat throughout the day. His mind was racing as he was forming the words that would chastise the messenger. The whole of the day was full of sunshine. A few puffy white clouds could be seen but the weather seemed normal despite little humidity, dark clouds, or signs of rain.

Dickinson's footsteps were getting faster and falling heavier on the ground as he could see the man just a block away.

As Dickinson's distance quickly closed in on Charles Carson, the sky opened, and rain came crashing down. Thunder

63

boomed in the sky, and Dickinson could hardly see Charles Carson sitting a short distance away. He quietly stood in the summer shower as it came screaming down. For several minutes, John contemplated his new response. Charles could see Dickinson's countenance change instantly.

The messenger, clothed in an overcoat, walked over to Dickinson and said, "You might want to put that on, sir." Dickinson looked at the overcoat over his arm and smiled. "Let's you and I have a talk somewhere dry, shall we?"

Chapter 7

With a name such as his, he must have been predestined to be involved with politics. His first name is Gouveneur. His last name is Morris, and he had been given every opportunity to succeed in life. Childhood tutors aided him in getting into a university at age 12. He graduated four years later in 1768 and, in the next seven years, completed his master's degree and was accepted by the bar to practice law. He was 23 and was quickly becoming known as a man who had a way with words. He was also setting his own political tones which, it turns out, were against those of his mentor, William Smith. Morris was moving his soap box towards independence from England, anti-slavery, and keeping at bay any voting except within the aristocracy. In 1778, Morris was appointed to the Continental Congress, wherein he befriended George Washington. On one occasion while visiting George Washington at Valley Forge, Morris was disgusted with the encampment of the soldiers and became quite vocal with his opinion. Not long after, Morris aided Washington in revamping the training and financing methods of the military. Later in that same year, in the course of his position in Congress, he became a signer of the Articles of Confederation.

Within five years of the beginning of his political career, Morris' reputation as a lady's man had grown beyond the point of rumors. In 1780, Morris had fallen from a carriage, resulting in the amputation of one of his legs from the knee down; however, the rumor was that he was escaping from a balcony and the wrath of a married man. Morris, who never took himself too seriously, braved the rumors and used his wooden leg to his advantage, but continued his relationships regardless of marital status. Even though Morris kept an eye on the ladies and the ladies were fond of him, he remained quite serious about his chosen career.

Remaining an ally of George Washington and upholding his opinion that a national government is necessary to maintain an independent country, in 1787 he was elected to the Constitutional Convention as a delegate from Pennsylvania. During this time, he gave 173 speeches, the most of any single delegate. This was also the time he was called back to the then capital city of New York for about a month.

As he arrived back in New York City, the town of his birth, he nimbly hopped out of the carriage, with his good right leg landing firmly immediately followed by a clunk on the ground from his peg leg. When he turned to enter his hotel, Sarah Fleming was nearly standing in his way.

She had been waiting for him. Sarah had made her way to Morris's hotel. She made her inquiries with local people and found out when and where he would arrive. She had every intention of getting him to her bedroom. She was sure that his reputation had sealed his fate, and she would have her way with him. Morris's pedigree hailed from one of the wealthiest land-owning families, and he still hadn't married. He was a prime target for her plan. It was nearly six o'clock in the evening, and the sun was fading fast as Morris stepped onto the sidewalk. She was facing him on the sidewalk a few doors down. Her clothes were stunning, and he noticed her right away. Sarah had a plan. She was the bait, and she was going to play hard to get.

"Good evening, ma'am," Morris said as he bowed slightly at the waist.

"Good evening, Mr. Morris," she said confidently. Morris didn't show any shock that she used his name, but he quickly recovered.

"You seem to know who I am, but I am at a disadvantage. Please, have we met before? For I could not have forgotten such beauty." He smiled slightly.

"No, sir, we have not met; but you are in the public eye, and I am not."

"Were I to be the man in your life, I would never let you out of my sight. Who is this man who allows you to be unescorted in the evening? Would I know him?"

"No such man exists for me, Mr. Morris. I am dining alone this evening. While I know it is unheard of for a lady to be out in the evening, I needed some fresh air and an early dinner."

"In that case, I'd like the opportunity to get to know you better Miss...?" He didn't finish the statement and looked at her with expectant eyes.

"Miss Sarah Fleming." She said confidently.

"Well, Miss Fleming, I just hate to eat alone though it happens more frequently than I care to admit. Would you care to sup at my table this evening? It's never good for the aristocracy to be seen dining alone."

"Mr. Morris. If I didn't know any better, I'd say your flirting with me. But, as I did come here for dinner and you just happen to be willing...I'd be happy to."

They entered the establishment and ordered. Their conversation was full of political rebuffs of the time and Morris was intellectually stimulated. Sarah did not shy away from any topic.

They spoke of religion in government which spawned Gouveneur Morris to say, "I've said this before, 'Religion is the only solid base for morals and that morals are the only possible support for free governments.'" Sarah politely agreed. Knowing the history books found little confirmation to the religious affiliation of Morris, she gently continued with the subject.

Sarah said, "I do believe I have made my fair share of misgivings in my life, but I do feel that there is forgiveness. What are your thoughts, Senator?"

Morris replied, "My thoughts of forgiveness? The Almighty Father through our Savior, Jesus Christ, has granted us all forgiveness for those who would but believe in Him. Yet, men and women, simply due to the nature of being human, will stray from the path of righteousness. I am no different than you, Miss Fleming, in the act of misgivings. So much so that my personal reputation is considered less than desired by other members of the congress, such as the Honorable Roger Sherman. However, I am convinced that he and I are of the same faith, not the same religion, and will be judged accordingly by our Savior."

Having gained a more than satisfactory answer, Sarah smiled at him and changed the subject. They discussed voting, taxation, and other political items until Morris' intellect had been fully engaged. Her plan was working.

He had never thought any woman to be so fully informed and versed in the workings of his arena. Bantering left and right, she simply had all the answers and gave him just enough of the reasons why without creating any real repercussions of future events. Morris had never met anyone like her. By the end of the evening, she had made it just difficult enough for him to be lured to her hotel.

Fleming made the appropriate moves and gestures as to not draw any more attention to herself while getting back to her hotel and into her room while Morris, having the reputation of promiscuity, simply followed. However, he was gentlemanly enough to give Fleming enough distance. Minutes later, he gently knocked on her hotel room door.

Once inside, his thoughts of intimacy were diminished. Fleming had proposed a more enlightened conversation of politics. She hoped the words she chose were eloquent to the ears of Gouveneur Morris. She also hoped he couldn't resist her opportunity.

"Mr. Morris," she began, "Were I to give you an accurate glimpse of things yet to be, allow questions to be asked and prove to you that your actions in the coming months will be written in history, would you be so inclined to listen?"

"Who are you that you so well understand these assemblies and conventions of the Colonies? The knowledge possessed by this extraordinarily beautiful lady in front of me surpasses that of men with whom I banter daily for the life of this land. To not listen would be an injustice upon my ears."

"Mr. Morris, were I to give you enough prose that you could see in your mind's eye without doubt that we, the people of this great land, need your pen and your mind to help shape this historical meaning in the assembly from which you are currently absent, would you wish to see such views, sir?"

"Miss Fleming, may I be blunt"

"Of course," she replied.

"You speak with such wisdom and confidence that I may not be as steady on this single leg as I was earlier this day. I believe I must ask you if I may sit to hear more."

"Please do so, Mr. Morris. Would you care for some tea?"

"That won't be necessary, Miss Fleming," he replied while sitting down.

"However, coming to an answer to your previous query, should you be able to present to me a way for my mind's eye, as you say, to see the events of which you wish to show me, then my own eyes would be jealous, I fear, for to dream while awake is still but a dream."

"Then, I must ask you to dream with me, Mr. Morris, for I do have the wishes to enlighten you with visual entertainment and knowledge the likes of which your own dreams cannot fathom. For I, and the people with which I congregate, are patriots of this land, as are you. So, I ask you again, Gouveneur Morris, for time is not a commodity to be bargained, and the preparations were vigorous in creating this opportunity. Will you dream with me while you are awake, Mr. Morris? Will you allow us to give insight and education which binds the tapestry of America?"

"Miss Fleming, it is with respect, admiration, and interest that I am mentally encouraged to learn what it is you have to show me." As Morris concluded his statement, he stood and held out his hand in a gesture of agreement. Sarah Fleming raised her right hand and took his in kind. As the handshake began she said, "Don't let go of my hand, Mr. Morris." In a fashion befitting the reputation of Morris, she dipped her left hand just between the buttons of her neck-high shirt and found what she was looking for. She pressed the button and noticed Mr. Morris' eyes widen, and a smile began forming on his face.

Chapter 8

During the past two hours, John Dickinson was so captivated by Charles Carson's visions of the future that John asked if he could continue the meeting and bring a man whom he trusts. He did not name this person, and Charles, not knowing why, didn't ask. Charles, not wanting to make any mistakes in his mission, was hesitant. Dickinson certainly trusted this man enough to want to show him the future, but did Charles trust his guest enough to let him leave his sight, possibly showing up later with the authorities to lock him up? Would they take away his freedom and thrust him into slavery? Would they strip him of his clothes and, thus, his only way of transport back to safety? A thousand questions ran through his mind when his voice simply erupted, "Of course, Your Honor. Would this man, perhaps, also be in your company of the conclave you are now attending?"

"Yes, he is. Would this be a problem?"

"No sir, not at all. It would be a pleasure to discuss this with you both."

Dickinson stood up from his chair with his tall lanky body and pushed out his hand to Charles, who immediately stood and shook it with confidence, all the while looking Dickinson straight in the eye.

"Mr. Carson, it is an honor." He said with one last shake of his hand. "I will be back in about an hour, and, after I've twisted his stubborn arm, I shall return with company in tow. But be prepared, Mr. Carson, just as I do not sway easily into decisions after one short conversation, this gentleman whom I will bring back will almost certainly run from you. However, if you do not step on your tongue ~ and I have a suspicion that you will not ~ and the information is true to the form to which I have been given, I feel as if you will be successful in your mission, sir."

"I shall do my best, Your Honor. I await your return in this very place." Carson nodded his head, and Dickinson stepped back toward the door. The summer rain had stopped. Dickinson plucked his overcoat from the coat rack by the door, folded the overcoat over his arm, and stepped into the evening sunlight.

Charles Carson's stomach was in knots waiting for the time to pass. The first ten minutes seemed like an eternity. He wanted to go to the local tavern and take a shot of whiskey to calm himself, but that just wouldn't do. He needed every synapse his brain had to combat the thousand questions that not just one but two of this country's founding fathers would certainly have for him.

Two! He wondered if the little device in his vest pocket would be able to transport them, but then, he remembered all the testing and knew it would. Half an hour had passed, and Carson wiped the sweat from his brow and gulped another glass of water. It certainly didn't taste very good. Untreated and unfiltered as he was accustomed to, but it did the trick. He decided to use some calming techniques and started with some deep breaths and closed his eyes. Minutes later he heard men approaching the door of the small no-name hotel lobby. Carson opened his eyes and stood up as the two men covered the doorway. Dickinson stepped in first and then immediately stepped off to one side to allow his follower into the foyer.

Dickinson began with the formal introductions, but Carson knew exactly who stood before him. "Excuse me, Your Honor, if I may. I believe this is the honorable Alexander Hamilton: born from a mother of English and French descent by the hand of a Scottish father; educated at the King's College but didn't complete it due to British occupation. After joining the militia for a time, you were appointed Captain under General Washington and then, when permitted, resigned your commission to continue practicing law. More recently, you led the Annapolis Convention, which has led to this conclave of the Philadelphia Convention.

Your Honor, my name is Charles Carson. It is an honor to meet you, sir. Please, will you come sit with us?" Carson held out his hand and firmly shook the hand of Alexander Hamilton.

Hamilton looked over at Dickinson with raised eyebrows. Hamilton was slightly surprised and impressed at the same time. Dickinson smiled at Carson, signifying a good start to this discussion.

Dickinson, in an almost uncharacteristic way, stepped over to the lad behind the hotel counter and requested a pot of coffee. An hour later, the second pot of coffee was gone, and the hotel clerk was nearly asleep, having not poured coffee for himself. The three men stood up, and the congressmen placed a hand on each of Charles Carson's wrists as he pressed the button in his right hand.

Chapter 9

He had already lived a full life at his current age of thirty-six. He had no idea that his future would find him as the fourth President of the United States. He was a wealthy slave owner who inherited most of his fortune. His political theories and ambitions varied during his career. There were moments when he couldn't stay on one side of the aisle when debating a heavy-handed national government or a strong-armed state government. At this point in his life, he didn't know his name would be written down as the "Father of the Constitution". He also wasn't aware he would gain a reputation for his fortitude when orating for the Bill of Rights. He was only thirty-six and still one of the most accomplished writers of his time. The Virginian had no clue he would be known as one of the most notable statesmen in the history of our country, and there he was, standing in the muck of the stall next to his horse, which was a stark contrast to his own small, thin 5'4" frame.

The thoughts kept coming to Dr. William Rayne as he tried to muster up the gumption and start a conversation with the Virginian statesman, James Madison. Many of the statesmen had servants or slaves that took care of their animals, but Madison was quite content to work his horse himself. He certainly had plenty of slaves that, when necessary, would take on this task, but Madison usually did this job himself. This was his own type of meditation. A quiet time to think and formulate his thoughts, prioritize, and recharge himself for yet another day of being the power-house statesman that was James Madison.

Rayne was ready to speak to Madison when, suddenly, pigeons burst up into the air and flew out of the barn, frightened by the crashing sounds of two men fighting out back. Madison had seen battles before, and this was nothing. This was just a fight between two men. There was no reason to get excited, but he did feel the need to quell this dispute in short order.

William could see the quarrel through the barn and rushed over in case there was a need for his help. Madison, with his small stature, yelled at both men to cease their nonsense. The two men fighting were slaves.

Their clothes were muddied from the fray, and their faces were bloody. When Madison approached the edge of the barn, he could tell that one of the slaves worked for him. He showed no anger but raised his voice again for the men to stop fighting. As the slave who worked for him saw him, he stopped as ordered. However, the other did not and turned and ran in the opposite direction.

Madison motioned for his slave to step into the barn. With his head hanging down, the slave walked past Madison and Madison followed. As he did so, William, who had already reached the edge of the barn to watch the event, screamed a warning, "Get out of the way!"

Madison's instincts from being a soldier took immediate action. He pushed his slave into a stall and followed him to the ground. A pitchfork, thrown directly at them by the second slave, struck into the ground less than a foot from where they had been.

William started after the second slave, but the man was just too fast. William stopped his chase, a bit out of breath, and walked back to the barn, where he found Madison speaking to his slave in soft talk.

"Young man, you work for me, do you not?"

"Yassuh"

"What was the meaning of this quarrel?" Madison asked calmly.

"That boy says that I was having relations with his sister, suh. I did no such thing! I swear! I..."

"That's enough! Do you know his sister?"

"Yassuh" he replied with his face toward the ground. His breathing was labored but slowing down.

"If I go ask his sister, what will she tell me?"

"I pray she tell the truth, suh. I only know her 'cuz I seent her at the market. I learnt her name juss yesterdee."

"Tell me her name."

"Her name Sara, suh. I'm so sorry, Masta Madison. I didn't mean no harm to her or anyone. That boy is just mean. Ev'ry day, he just plain 'ol mean. But I won't back down to sumpin' I didn't do, Master Madison, I won't."

"Very well. You go on about your business here in town. Go clean up if you need to, and I will pursue this matter no more. I believe you. But I don't want to see this sort of behavior coming around again. You stand your ground when it is right to do so but try not to get into trouble if that is also an option. You hear what I'm saying, young man?"

"Yassuh. Thank you, suh. Thank you, Master Madison. I..."

"Go on now," Madison interrupted, and the man stepped away.

"One more thing," Madison said confidently, and they faced each other.

"Hold your head high and look people in the eye. It shows respect. It is the same for everyone."

The young man nodded kindly, squared his shoulders, stood a little taller, then turned and walked away.

Madison turned and looked directly at Dr. William Rayne.

"You sir, I owe a debt of gratitude. Had you not the insight to alert me I believe I would have been impaled." He motioned toward the pitchfork. "What is your name, sir?"

Having heard the advice Madison just gave, William had already squared his shoulders and looked him in the eyes, stuck out his hand and firmly shook Madison's with his reply, "Dr. William Rayne. But, please, people just call me William."

"William, it is then."

"May I ask you a question about what just happened, Mr. Madison?"

"Ask away and, by all means, in a private area such as this, you may call me James." Dr. Rayne noted the response and that Madison's commanding ego hung in the air.

"Very well then." William replied with a slight proper nod of his head. Then, he reached down and picked up the pitchfork. "The boy you just released from this little fight ~ he works for you?"

"Yes, he does. His family has worked for our family for a generation."

"Let me clarify. You own him, do you not? He is one of your slaves. How is it that you did not scold him or give him lashes?"

"They are just boys playing at being young men. They are the same as you and me. They put on their pants, go to work, have frustrations, have wives and a family, someday. No matter our lot in life, we will be abrasive towards someone else for one reason or another, and, eventually, unless logic prevails, our emotions get the best of us and one becomes aggressive. I believe most physical engagements are avoidable. The most common argument is due to a misunderstanding and poor communication. The higher end of arguments stems from total disregard for the opposite opinion. Wars have started over such things. But this," he waved his hands in the area where the fight occurred, "this did not warrant any consequence. That young man needed to learn when to use his head. He did not have to fight. He merely needed to be out of the way. The other fellow will have a higher price to pay for throwing that pitchfork, but I'll let it be as he does not work for me. His own master will deal with him."

"Hypothetically, James, if you were able to see the future of your actions, such as the decision you just handed this young man, would you have treated him differently?"

"No one has that ability, William, and I prefer to deal with knowledge I possess. Forethought should always be considered when making decisions, so I take an accounting and try to minimize the consequences. Why would you ask this of me?"

"Let me rephrase the question. Have you ever made decisions in your past that you now feel should have been different?"

Madison did not answer right away. He looked inquisitively at Dr. Rayne. For several moments Madison looked at the pitchfork and then out of the barn in the direction the young boy had taken when he left. Then, he turned his head toward Dr. Rayne and replied, "William, in one's life, I will conjecture every man will have opportunities for decisions which will bring him pause to think upon such decisions. The caution I gather of your inquiry demands more inspection. I am apprehensive to answer such a question definitively, yet, the short answer is 'yes'. I believe no man has made the correct decision every time and in all cases. I should add that reflection of every decision might cause fragility in the deliberation of future decisions. I am not one to live my life in regret."

"We have only just met but if I may call in your marker for owing me a debt, I would appreciate a bit of your time. I'm happy to explain my inquiry, and I would be honored by your company."

"Well played, Dr. Rayne. You have an hour, and then I shall need to return to my prior engagements."

"Thank you, sir. An hour it is." Dr. Rayne's thought to himself, "*If this works, I'll have much more than an hour.*"

"James, you are here for the conclave of the Philadelphia Congress along with approximately fifty-four other honorable delegates."

"You are well informed," Madison said cautiously.

"I am very well informed, Mr. Madison, as you shall soon see."

Rayne reached down and picked up the horse brush from the ground and handed it to Mr. Madison. "I also know that this is where you do your best thinking; therefore, I believe this is the best place to have a conversation."

Over the next hour, Madison listened intently to Rayne. When the allotted time was coming to a close, Rayne asked one final question.

"Mr. Madison, if you are willing, we can begin now. Are you ready?"

"You've either conjured a wonderful tale, or you are quite serious. You understand that something such as this can be devastating. You could be harboring a tool that could destroy America. You could alter everything!" Madison exclaimed in hushed tones.

William countered, "If I were a man who had ill intentions, why would I come to you at this time? Why would I want to educate you? Why would any of you here be of importance to just me? If I were to harbor thoughts of greed, war, or anything other than honorable intentions, I would not have to illicit your help, sir. We, my team and I, could have chosen to invest in other options or another time or any number of items. Your thoughts are true, Mr. Madison, and our goals are not selfish. This ability is truly an honor for me, and, like you, I have dedicated my life to helping others. I fully believe that is also your intention ~ to aid in the preservation of the United States..."

Madison cut him off: "What did you just say? The preservation of what?"

"The United States, sir. As noted in the Declaration of Independence. The words on that document helped to solidify our nation in several ways. We're a good people who have lost our way. We need your help, Mr. Madison. And If I may be so bold at this point in our discussion, I'd like to quote a famous statesman of this time who said, 'Knowledge will forever govern ignorance; and a people who mean to be their own governors must arm themselves with the power knowledge gives.'"

"Thoughtful insight indeed," Madison replied. "Who, dare I ask, said these words."

"You did, sir."

"I was afraid you would say that," Madison smirked. "Yet, I believe I've also spoken to the contrary, that all men with power ought to be distrusted to a certain degree."

"Yes, sir, indeed you have. Will you help us?"

Madison stopped brushing his horse and scratched the animal under the chin to think on his answer. When he finally spoke, he said, "Dr. Rayne, this is truly a cross to bear, for, if what you say is true, I will have knowledge of the future. And in my current position as a congressman, it is my responsibility to perform every function possible for the betterment of society. This is no small trifle, William. I am reluctant for the responsibility of knowing the future, with the weight that carries; and, in that, there is no doubt. But I am also reluctant to go to war, and, on occasions, eat my Aunt's homemade soup. But, whether it is soup or war, responsibilities must be met. It is my intention to go with you, William, and it appears the time to dispatch this endeavor is now."

William wasted no more words. He stepped closer to James Madison and placed his hand on his shoulder, pulled out the time travel device, and pressed the button.

Chapter 10
June, in the year 2025

Each traveler, successful in their mission, stood in the front of the training room. The congressmen had taken in the subtle changes of their surroundings. It looked so familiar yet strangely different. Chairs, while looking the same as the ones they were used to, felt newer and softer ~ the wood had cleaner edges or smoother curves. The lighting seemed familiar and strange at the same time, it had changed ~ it didn't come from outside, and yet, it was easier to see. Shadows were lessened. Objects were clearly seen. There were so many questions gathering in the minds of these men, but still, they had no fears. Whatever convincing conversation each congressman had with their own 'traveling companion', the confidence in their individual decision grew stronger when they saw their traveler standing right in front of them. There was also a comforting feeling upon seeing other statesmen had made the same decision. They knew the future must be different, and yet, on the whole, their surroundings were quite similar.

"Welcome gentlemen. Please, have a seat. My name is Dr. Carver Benton. Each of you has had a conversation with at least one person standing here in front of you today. Through the course of that conversation, you were curious enough to ask questions. And those questions probably led to more questions, and in the end, you still wanted more. This panel of what we call 'travelers' consists of scientists and historians. They are experts in their fields of study and volunteers. We have but one goal in mind: to educate you on what happens in the future based upon decisions you gentlemen have made and will make in your time.

"You are now in the year 2025. Nearly the 250th anniversary of America. I'd like to let that set with you for a moment in case there's a question forming in someone's mind. While you formulate your questions, please allow me to set your mind at ease. You will not be harmed in any way, and yes, you will be going back to your own time period, in essence to precisely when you left it. You will go back with all the knowledge you learn here. We hope to show you the wonders that your brilliant minds have helped us create in these United States. However, with those wonders comes the evil side of horrors for which we, as Americans, must also bear responsibility: civil wars, revolutionary wars ~ concepts that I know you understand all too well. I do not wish to delay your education too; therefore, I will bring this introduction to a close. I do not wish to alarm anyone, so I will tell you what to expect.

"You are not a prisoner. You chose to be here, and you may return with your traveler simply by asking. We built your trust very quickly, and we wish to continue to build on that trust, but time is limited. Despite the fact you just traveled through it, there are limitations. You are standing in a very advanced underground facility approximately 126 feet below the surface. There are no windows, but we will be going outside as your education progresses. We wish for you to experience the world as we know it. We hope to show you many good things, truly, that we are blessed with, and then, of course, things that are not such blessings. These are the things we will discuss during your visit here.

"You all have rooms to sleep in; all your meals will be prepared for you, and if you have need of any items, if it is in our power, we will accommodate you. I believe most of you gentlemen have come to us near the end of a workday and may require sleep. As time travel is very new to us, please drink some water to hydrate. Once you are shown to your accommodations, please, try to get some sleep. We will begin in the morning. Hundreds of questions will come to mind, and I hope to have answers for most of them... however, does anyone have any simple questions for me or any of my staff at this moment?"

Benton no sooner finished his opening statement when Gouveneur Morris spouted out, "Might you have anything stronger than water?"

Hamilton chimed in, "That would be a good start, sir. I second that motion."

"Right this way gentlemen," Sarah said as she held out her arm for Gouveneur Morris to escort her. Morris smiled and took her arm as all the statemen followed down a corridor that looked like the inside of a hotel from their own time.

Curiosity and intrigue filled the air as they entered a parlor. Soft conversations began to form amongst themselves, and a bit of laughter caught the ear of Dr.

Benton. He smiled a bit and shook his head as if to tell himself, *"You did it.*

You're either a fool or genius, but you did it. Now the work really begins."

Chapter 11

Benton was a logical man. While this success would make the common man jump up and down, scream out loud, and act as if he had won the lottery, he did no such thing. Certainly, a higher level of adrenaline was coursing through him, yet he was controlling himself. He remembered the words from his own professor so long ago when he successfully completed a project. The professor had seen the results of this same project from several students. They were elated! They smiled, jumped, and pumped their fists in the air. Some laughed while others cried from putting so much effort into a daunting task and completing it.

Benton's reaction was very different. He started walking down the hall, remembering what others before him had learned. Never stop trying. He remembered all the failures that helped him get to this step. He wasn't finished. This success was now a part of the past, and there was so much more to do. He was now responsible for the lives of these men. The level of his responsibility had now grown exponentially, not only for the safety of his guests, but also for the knowledge and education they would experience. Getting them here was certainly a tremendous feat, but just as two people can conceive a child ~ that part was easy.

Now was the time to raise that child. Carefully. Teaching them along the way. What would their reactions be? Would they learn the lesson he wanted them to know, or would they resist? These were educated men with egos and strong opinions. Would they come to the same conclusions or part from the natural answers and think outside the box, producing an answer that astounds?

Benton again remembered his professor's comment: "Young man, you've successfully completed this assignment with a result like no one I've ever taught before. I will add that your answer leads to a few fundamental questions which you should ask yourself. Should you pursue this course of action? Whom would you tell of your success? Could you live with the results? Could you handle your failures? What harm is involved? Is this for personal gain or for the betterment of society? These are only the basic questions you must ask yourself. However, I have a question for you. Do you like comic books?"

"I did as a child, sir. Why is this important?" he remembered answering.

"Did you read the <u>Spiderman</u> comic book?"

"Of course."

"Comic books are fun and engaging for entertainment, yet I feel the writers are visionaries. I remember the comment from the character Uncle Ben to Peter...do you remember what he said?"

"It's been too long, sir. What did he say?"

"'With great power comes great responsibility.' You would do well to remember these words. You are quite an intelligent young man, Carver Benton. Make wise choices." The words echoed in his mind as he took his next steps down the hall.

Make wise choices. Pray about them.

Carver chose to continue with his studies and eventually found the financial backing to help create this underground wonderland. His well-documented research papers and glowing recommendations from all his professors helped him reach the right person, who, after several months' consideration, gave him carte blanche to build and run this facility.

Now, several years later, each year showing positive technological advances toward his goal, he walked down a hallway hearing the footsteps of five of our country's forefathers ~ seeing their faces and hearing their laughter. He hoped to hear their thoughts, anger, and arguments, as well ~ to see their eyes light up in wonderment from every facet of life they will see and experience. He wondered how much anger or sadness will show on their faces and expected to hear whispers and screaming when they were shown the horrors that had taken place. They only knew the wars of their time. The wars they will learn about were far worse.

Dr. William Rayne stepped from the doorway into the hall and brought Benton back from his thoughts, "Carver?" No response.

"Dr. Benton?" he said a bit louder.

Benton turned, looking a bit startled, and answered, "I'm so sorry William... lost in my head again."

"Welcome back. Carver, there's five of them!" he said in hushed tones.

"Yes, I can see."

"I just wanted to say 'Congratulations!', my dear friend. I realize we have much to do, but I thought I'd press the pause button in your head just for a moment and let you take it in."

"Thank you, Dr. Rayne. We both should breathe in this moment, my friend. We work well together ~ the whole team, in fact. I was just thinking about expectations and responsibility yet again. The world will not judge us on our intentions; they will judge us on our failures and successes. Their judgement will likely be emotional. But, let them judge. We have already succeeded thus far, and we may yet fail miserably. But you are correct: this is a moment you and I will hold in amazement, and I'm happy this moment is with you, William."

"Well said, my friend. And I with you."

William turned back the way he came and bid their guests good night. Each traveler led his own guest to his individual room. Eight rooms had been designed and prepared with the expectations of the 1800s. Sink pots, armoires and other items. The idea of the four travelers all bringing back two statesmen each had crossed Benton's mind, but that probability was quite low. Whatever the number, the unused rooms would be repurposed as study areas or simply remain closed.

Understanding the time of day and how our bodies work, Sarah believed it was time to integrate the internal plumbing system. The toilet wasn't so far out of their timeline, and it certainly wasn't popular being indoors. But being in an underground facility, this was as good of a time as any. It didn't take long for all of these men to comprehend how this invention was possible. Several of these men, and many of the statesmen they associated with, were also inventors.

Minutes later and true to form, Gouveneur Morris tried to continue his dating with Sarah and winked for her to step into his room. She smiled politely and gave him a kiss on the cheek, whispering that there was more to the future than just a night with her. Morris bid Sarah good night by stepping back with his right foot and bowing slightly. She returned his gesture with a curtsy.

Each stateman stood in his respective room for a few minutes and listened until the hallway was quiet. They looked at the somewhat familiar surroundings as their minds raced in so many directions. One of the doors could be heard opening, then another, then another, until all five men were standing in the hallway.

Hamilton spoke first. "Gentlemen, candidly I admit that my curiosity has brought me thus far, and I fear it will continue to push me farther. What say you?"

"Aye," came the response, nearly in unison.

Morris spoke next, "I shall add for myself that I did as I always do and followed a specimen of beauty. But, in my defense, and I believe this will be the same for the whole of us standing, my own desire for more of the knowledge that was imparted to me by my companion traveler imprisoned me to search for more."

James Madison offered a follow up, "To the latter, I should agree. As we all heard earlier, they offered securities for our safety, yet I should be more than willing to carry a musket until I'm more settled. Have we truly stepped through time? Is this real or some elaborate British hoax to move against our country by sabotage? I should not think we are all so easily fooled."

Dickinson remarked quickly, "If fooled we are, I stand here guilty and offer my deepest apologies, Your Honor." He looked directly at Hamilton.

Hamilton responded matter-of-factly, "We are all here of our own choosing."

Roger Sherman, the oldest of the group, took a slight step forward to speak, "I come from humble beginnings as a cobbler. I concede we are in agreement to be standing here of our own volition. I would suggest we take time to walk in the shoes of our hosts and listen to what their words will bear. As I have listened to them most recently, they do not speak as we do. They do not dress as we do, nor the British…." He looked at Madison, who nodded in the affirmative.

"Furthermore, I am of the mind that the truth is being set forth upon us. For the time being, we should all retire for the evening and in the morrow see the fruits of our labor.

Sleep may very well evade me this night as I fear the weight of responsibility is heavier now more so than ever. I will take my leave of you. Good evening, gentlemen."

Each man returned to his room with their minds in a whirl. Sleep would escape all of them for most of the night.

Madison sat in his room at a small table, feeling the sturdy comfortable chair beneath him. He was impressed with the forethought of his host as he looked around the room. It was comfortable. Familiar. Madison, true to form, picked up a quill, dipped it in the ink, and began to write down his thoughts.

Chapter 12

Morning broke underground as the lights slowly got brighter. Four of the statesmen were ready, while Gouvenour Morris took a bit more time getting dressed. He could hear the doors opening and closing and muffled words in the hallway. Each statesman seemed to be a bit sleepy-eyed but eager to start their day. They greeted each other and noticed the one who was missing. As Dickinson stepped over to Morris' door, it opened. Morris stepped out with a bit of a scowl on his face. He looked at the other men inquisitively then reached over with his right hand and pinched his left arm. He winced and looked at the men around him.

"Not a dream," he said with a quirky smile. "I pray it is not a waking nightmare."

Before another person said a word, Dr. William Rayne spoke from behind them, "Good morning, Counselors. I trust you may have gotten some resemblance of sleep, yet I admit, I did not get much myself. So, after some coffee and food, we have a full day. If you will follow me." Rayne turned and led them down the corridor to a large room where food was prepared. Tables were set as best as they could be to resemble the statesmen's own time period. Details weren't spared, but there were subtle differences that couldn't be reproduced. Being underground also posed a problem; however, the reproduction of the outdoors through windows was very well done. The lighting, live trees, and artwork outside the room produced scenes that depicted the morning sunrise so well that the statesmen appeared to be comfortable. Not one of them mentioned anything to the contrary.

Roger Sherman asked the first question of the day, "May I inquire as to whom else will be joining this endeavor?"

Dickinson added, "Certainly, if you can bring the five of us, you can manage to bring more."

Charles Carson let his thoughts be known. "If I may, sir, this is the contingent of our group. Let me explain. We travelers and Dr. Benton have discussed this at length, and you are correct: we could return and try to convince more representatives to join us; however, the manageability of too many participants could pose a problem. Therefore, we devised a list of candidates in order of historical influence and reputation. Admittedly, not every signer of the Constitution is a household name. Honestly, we expected to have only eight guests. However, I was honored to have two of you at my encounter. This is truly a blessing for us all to host the five of you."

Gouveneur Morris set down his coffee cup and quipped, "I'm honored to be here, but how many others resisted your temptations before the affirmative?"

Sarah gently answered, "Your Honor, we all failed in our first attempts. It's true. I believe the men who denied our request were not approached properly. This is our fault. However, when we appealed to you on a more personal level, the response is as you see here. But like you, I am very honored to have all of you here, for as long as you are here. We have a lot of ground to cover today, so whenever you are ready?"

The last of the coffee was sipped down and chairs were pushed back. Sarah led the men from the dining room to a classroom. This room was decorated to resemble the interior of a classroom to which the statesmen would be accustomed to sending children. This room was physically the most tasked room to build as Sarah knew that this room would be changing daily to slowly bring the statesmen into a new comfort zone. They would be spending the majority of their time here. *"This will be amazing,"* she thought.

Each man took a seat in a desk chair. Books had been placed on each of the desks. Dr. Carver Benton entered from the back of the room and walked to the front. "Good morning, gentlemen. Thank you for being here. Within the walls of this room and this facility, you will be learning about your future..." he waved his hands, pointing to Sarah and himself, "Our history. We will be asking questions and learning from you at the same time. Sarah has graciously requested to be your teacher, as it were, for the first few sessions. We will be moving along at a rapid rate and touching on some of the most significant changes in history. And within a short amount of time, I hope to have you sitting in the city and seeing more than what we have shown you. In the end, you will be returned to your own time and, I pray, think upon this education when deliberating in the convention."

"Make no mistake, gentlemen; this is the year 2025. You are nearly 250 years into the future. We are so far advanced, you cannot imagine. All of you have long passed. No one here is immortal. I'll not be telling you of your own demise or any personal information or how to get rich or items of this nature. You gentlemen shaped a nation, forged a union, protected liberty for the common good. But along the way, through many, many years, legislators on both sides of the aisle - Federalists and Anti-Federalists, Democrats and Republicans - have bastardized laws, changed the meaning of liberty, propagated welfare, removed God from the tapestry of education and government, and the list continues. If any of these concepts creates anger and disgust based solely on the mention of these topics, you may, based upon your own education, experiences, and beliefs, feel even more of the same when you *see* the results. For now, let us begin with information and bring you into the future of these United States of America. Gentlemen, it is my honor to formally introduce you to Counselor Sarah Fleming. Yes, she is a lawyer and historian, and, in my opinion, one of the best. Her credentials are impeccable. I shall be available to answer questions and attend to your needs. You need only to ask. Sarah, the room is yours." That said, he motioned his hand to Sarah and walked to the back of the classroom and sat down.

Dickinson, Hamilton, Sherman, Madison, and Morris, five of the fifty-five delegates sent to Philadelphia and to the Constitutional Convention in 1787, now sat in front of Sarah Fleming. Her own adrenaline was pumping as she peered into the eyes of these men. She slowly and softly took a deep breath. Determined to stay in control of herself, she said, "Thank you, Dr. Benton. Gentlemen, we shall begin with the highlights of history during the beginning of the 1800s." Sarah's voice was not lost on the men. The information she provided was astounding. She let them know the books that were provided had been especially designed to give them the same information she was putting forth without divulging anything personal pertaining to them. They would be able to follow along in their books, which contained pictures, diagrams, and nearly every word she was telling them.

While she paraphrased everything, her story telling was compelling, colorful, and inviting. Even Gouveneur Morris appeared to be intently listening without his usual eye movements chasing the stitching of her clothes.

"Let me start by saying the very history that I am beginning with is being mentioned now as a point of history only. There will be questions later in our discussions as to your thinking. Then, as we show you more history, the written and signed documents, and the results of the words, phrases which you will have used as the framers of our nation, we will ask you if you would have changed anything. We believe you would. Of course you would, as you will now have foresight. The knowledge you gain from your time here will carry some level of impact. Even if your decision does not change, the impact could be a feeling of confidence having made that same decision.

Sarah Fleming continued, "Councilors, when you return to your own time, you will continue to be tasked with the creation of what is now called the U.S. Constitution. I am at liberty to tell you that each of you has chosen to sign this document and I am also at liberty to tell you that this document quickly gained an addition of ten amendments which are called the Bill of Rights. The combination of these two documents and two former documents with which you are more familiar, The Declaration of Independence, predominately penned by your esteemed colleague, Thomas Jefferson, and the Article of Association, govern our country still today. The records indicate that the Honorable Roger Sherman, is the only delegate who has signed all four of these documents.

"I must cover one more item before we move forward. There is no conceivable way any of us who will stand here in front of you can cover every part of history. To try would take more time than we feel we are allowed to share with you, making such an attempt unviable. We will entertain questions and arguments until we must consider the point as passed. Let's begin."

She covered the creation of the Library of Congress and emphasized its importance as a historical depository. She compared the census of 1800, with approximately 5.3 million people, to the current population of over 400 million. She noticed the men shifted in their seats just a bit. Questions of economy, agriculture, land, shipping all came at the same time. Hamilton and Madison were spewing forth the inevitable problems with so many citizens using up the country's resources, while Sherman,

Morris, and Dickinson could only speculate with rebuttals. The conversations were on point and when the tangents began to form, Sarah would bring them back to the task at hand and move forward. Sarah's mind was reeling from the ideas the men produced and how their conjectures were so very close to the real outcome of the subjects they discussed. Of course, there were a few outliers among their thoughts, but this is where Sarah reigned in the conversation. At times, this was no easy task as these men were in their element for arguments. She pressed on. Without naming who was president at the time, she noted that America's property was extensively increased with the Louisiana Territory purchased from the French in France's intention of creating an ally against the British. She moved from that bit of information to the first practical steamboat journey in 1807, which helped answer questions about the shipping industry.

Sarah covered the British Slave Trade Act of 1807 but made it a point to mention that slavery in America became a commodity of illegal income, with over 250,000 slaves still being shipped. Knowing another historian would be covering more details, she only looked into the eyes of the men who were living their lives as slave owners. Madison's eyes were deep with thought upon hearing her, yet he did not utter a word. The point was made.

Sherman, Morris, and Hamilton had not grown up with slavery as a part of life, as Madison and Dickinson had. Their upbringings were quite different. While the educational statement stung, they continued to listen intently as she delivered historical facts and not accusations. She mentioned that Morris maintained a huge anti-slavery mentality and mentioned his affinity that it was "the curse of heaven wherever it prevailed." But before Morris' chest grew from the comment, she also mentioned that slavery predominantly survived where the aristocracy thrived, and Morris was touted as being an "aristocrat to the core." It was uncommon to find one without the other. However, when she gazed into the eyes of Dickinson, his reply was spot on: "I am self-aware of my beliefs on slavery and my own upbringing. But, please, tell me: this does change, does it not?"

"It does, Your Honor, yet not soon enough. For now, I will add that, 250 years later, it has left a mark on our nation, sir. That mark still burns in the hearts of citizens not because of who they are today, but because they cannot let go of how their ancestors were thought of or were treated back then. Some believe their past defines them. If that is the case, then everyone else's sin condemns us all, regardless of the color of our eyes, our height, our race, or skin color. Still, others believe you make of your life what you will, and the past will not define you. Your success would depend on what you do as a person, not by actions of others. There will be more education on this later, of course."

Moving forward with our country's advancements, she spoke about the first anthracite coal burning in 1808, an experiment as a fuel source. She explained that this product would soon be changing the face of the US as they knew it. She also dug a little deeper into steam as a mechanism for moving ships.

Knowing full well that several of these men sitting before her were literal proponents for the War of 1812, she discussed the details, the amount of lives lost, and that the final date for this war was on January 8, 1815, on the Chalmette Plantation in New Orleans. She covered the eight-year construction of the Erie Canal, with its 363 miles and 83 locks, to reduce transportation costs up to 90%.

Bringing slavery back into the conversation, she informed them that the new state of
Missouri refused to accept slaves within their borders and the Tallmadge
Amendment passed in the U.S. House of Representatives. She concluded with the Missouri Compromise. She also covered the government's actions in trying to recover and pay for the War of 1812, including the heavy borrowing which caused the country's first financial crisis and resulted in a rise in unemployment and bank closures. Since borrowing is fully within the bounds of the Constitution, Sarah wanted to tell them that the government continued to borrow heavily to fund the defense of the nation and perceived entitlements, but she wasn't sure they could fathom the twenty five trillion dollars the debt rose to. Would they accept that the annual budget was over five trillion? Would they accept that our interest rates were twenty percent of the revenues? She did not mention these items now as she knew this country's financial situation is on the agenda and would be covered in more detail later.

Sarah knew full well that this first day of information would be a fast track for her students to come to grips with being in their own future. She admitted to herself that being in her own future would be quite interesting if she were in their shoes. She passed out a piece of paper showing a map of the expansion of the United States.

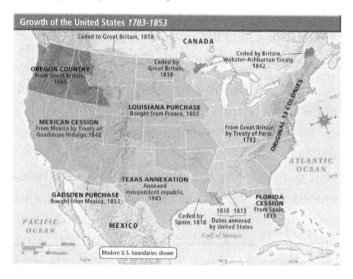

(http://onlinemaps.blogspot.com/2012/11/united-states-western-expansion.html)

"Gentlemen, what you see here is a map of the land mass for the expansion of the United States of America. Some of this is in your very near future. However, your comprehension of what is to come is necessary. Please look over what you see here and ask any questions you wish. However, let's take a small break and introduce you to some modern conveniences."

Sarah had noticed the hour of the day was well passed noon and the group should be ready to separate from the classroom. Lunch was served to the visitors and the travelers, and for over an hour, they slowly discussed details of what they had learned thus far. The time spent in the historic looking parlor, drinking tea or coffee, proved to be more enlightening to the statesmen than Dr. Benton had projected. The statesmen were astounding. Their comprehension for inventions was like a sponge and their minds were thirsty. Nearing the end of lunch, Sarah Fleming stood and made one final comment. "Gentlemen, before you return to the classroom, I would like to add this: the land which you now fight to protect is just a small portion. You've seen the map. The borders will change. They will grow and, in doing so, will be populated at a very advanced rate. By collecting data from across America, we can determine the U.S. has a birth every 8 seconds, a death every 12 seconds, and a new immigrant, whether legal or not, every 9 seconds. This is a net gain of one person every 12 seconds. And that number is growing higher with new data and persons we cannot count."

"What you should know is the third census of these United States, in 1810, shows approximately 7.2 million people. By the time the 1900s come around, our population will grow to 76.2 million people. Are you wondering where exactly do they live? Where does the food come from? How many people live in the cities? How do they travel from city to city? What is the tax rate? These are all very good questions and please make note that in 1900, the tax rate is around 3% of the GDP (Gross Domestic Product). But... that isn't the real question, is it? No, the real question in your mind is 'what is the population in my

2025' and the answer to that question is approximately 400 million. That is a staggering number! Now, add the second half of the question, the correlating tax rate, and the answer to that is about 30-35% of the GDP in 2025.

POPULATION IN MILLIONS

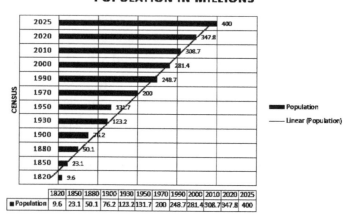

	1820	1850	1880	1900	1930	1950	1970	1990	2000	2010	2020	2025
Population	9.6	23.1	50.1	76.2	123.2	131.7	200	248.7	281.4	308.7	347.8	400

Historical information from U.S. Census reports

"We will revisit the economics and finances later, but for the moment, we simply wanted you to know how much change has occurred in the population."

The group continued to discuss the population changes for another hour. The volume of the room varied as each man raised their voices to gain control of the conversation. Sarah let the men form their own opinions and offered information when asked. She was amazed at the depth of their thoughts as she patiently listened.

When Dr. Benton found a quieter moment in the room, he ushered everyone back to the classroom, where Paul Tesla was waiting for them.

"Good afternoon, gentlemen. I will be continuing with you for this afternoon, and you will find that we, as your hosts, will rotate through as your tour guides."

Paul's history lesson for the remainder of the afternoon began with the early 1800s, specifically:

- September 1814 - Francis Scott Key penned the words to the Star-Spangled Banner during the twenty-five-hour bombardment of Fort McHenry, as seen through his eyes.

- January 1819 - The first financial crisis occurred. Paul noted the bank failures and increasing unemployment. Several causes were identified, including the heavy amount of borrowing by the government.

Paul could see that James Madison's forehead showed worried lines. His eyebrows furrowed as he listened intently. Paul could only sense he was weighing out his thoughts. Glancing at the faces of the men in front of him, Paul saw similar looks on all of them.

- August 1820 – Since the prior census, massive European immigration and natural growth produced 9.7 million people for approximately 33% growth.

Dickinson's eyes widened as the percentage was given.

- March 1824 - The Bureau of Indian Affairs was established by the United States War Department. Paul briefly covered the expansion of the Midwest. The statesmen were familiar with the natives and logically followed the reasoning. They would soon learn why this date was important.

- May 1830 - Congress voted for the Indian Removal Act, an act to "relocate" hundreds of Indians, mainly Cherokee, east of the Mississippi River and push them to the West. Eight years later, against U.S. Supreme Court ruling, President Jackson enforced his 1830 Act and forced the Cherokee nation to walk over 1000 miles to what is now Oklahoma. Over 4000 people died during this event.

- October 1835 - The Revolution of Texas began. The Texas army, led by Sam Houston, proclaimed and exercised their right to secede from Mexico.

- February through March 1836 - About 3,000 Mexican troops under Santa Ana attacked the mission at San Antonio, Texas, and its 189 defenders during the battle of the Alamo. Thirteen days later, the Texans had lost. However, later the same month, the independence of Texas was declared, making them an independent nation and free from Mexican rule.

- July 1845 - The Congress of Texas voted to join the United States of

America. Actions by then President Tyler led to the United States authorizing the annexation of the Republic of Texas, adding them into the Union as the 28th state later that same year.

Sarah commented, "This may be a good time to discuss the concept of 'what if'. It is a simple question, but it demands attention and thought. Ask yourself, 'What if states were allowed to unjoin or backout of becoming a part of the Union? What if a state's congress voted to remove itself?'"

Hamilton interjected, "What you are saying is totally to the contrary of creating a stable or consistent nation, Ms. Fleming. How many times would any state's congress, over the lifetime of the state, decide to join, and then fifty years later, the newer congress decides to leave? How many times will states' laws change? No, Ms. Fleming, this does not lend itself to stable national or state economy. States deciding to leave, rejoin, then leave again will disrupt the sovereignty of the national government in terms of foreign policies, commerce, and a host of other subjects. This simply is not an option."

Madison added, "Is it not obvious that we are trying to preserve the Union as a whole? I believe it is understood that states do not lose their individuality, but it is the national government who is at risk. What foreign body would look at a country whose citizens decide to leave and rejoin and leave again? The Articles of Confederation can only do so much within the boundaries of its writing, and the

Constitution will help solidify the Union. Any state that would offer to leave the Union would not stand upon legal grounds if said state had first given its oath to uphold it."

"Gentlemen," Sarah started, "before we jump into the discussion further, let me add that the very question I posed and the arguments you delivered are about to be addressed."

- July 1848 - The Declaration of Sentiments, calling for equal rights for women and men, was signed by 100 men and women in the Wesleyan Methodist Chapel, Seneca Falls, New York, at the 1st Women's Rights Convention, led by Lucretia Mott and Elizabeth Cady Stanton.

- June 1850 - The United States census of 1850 counted 23,191,876 population, a 35.9% increase from a decade before. Over three million people were now living in its most populous state, New York.

- March 1857 - James Buchanan was sworn into office as the 15th President of the United States. His tenure as President would be marred by the question of slavery and a compromise stance that would neither alleviate nor eradicate the intractable question from American society.
In that same month, the United States Supreme Court ruled in the Dred Scott decision, 6-3, that a slave did *not* become free when transported into a free state. It also ruled that slavery could *not* be

banned by the U.S. Congress in a territory, and that blacks were *not* eligible to be awarded citizenship.

Dr. Benton, who had been sitting quietly in the back of the room for some time, made a mental note: *"Interesting how blacks were shipped in as a product and taxed as a product according to Article 1, Section 9. These slaves, or shall we say 'inventory', were denied citizenship; and yet, in this century, babies from mothers who were smuggled in or paid to be on U.S. soil were given citizenship without question and regardless of color or national origin."* Benton knew this subject would be discussed later. Until then, he wondered how, or more specifically, *if* logic prevailed during either of these times.

- April 12, 1861 - This was the beginning of the U.S. Civil War, a four-year conflict of unrest, disagreement, and thousands of deaths.

The discussion on this topic lasted several hours and into the twilight of the day. After another internal plumbing break, Paul thought now was an appropriate time for a hypothetical question. "Gentlemen, I wish to ask a question or two that I hope you will think about over the next few days. Our government, such as it is during this time in history which we are covering, has shown us its propensity for growth. The bureaucracy, in its infancy, was to govern the republic of the United States. Do you see America as a republic now? A mere 74 years later. My first question is this: Would there be a way to combat the ever-growing government? Perhaps the answer would be not to pay government workers? Truly I ask you, who would want a career in government if they wouldn't get paid? Maybe we *should* pay them but limit the time they can stay on the government payroll. Term limits, perhaps? I wonder if the elected officials would like it if their official seat in the government was mandated by law to not accept anything other than the same standard health care as provided to the citizens they represent! And why isn't there a way for any state to secede from the nation? Not that they would, but why isn't it even an option in most cases? Would the U.S. have fallen apart long before now? I...I have to wonder..."

Roger Sherman stood for a moment with his hand slightly raised for a question. His face had a look of confusion.

"I beg your pardon, Mr. Tesla?" came the response from Sherman. "What is this health care you speak of?"

"I'm so sorry, Your Honor. To coin a phrase, I was on my soap box. Please, forgive me. The answer to your question lies within a new lesson that will be passed to all of you.   I did, however, step a bit farther into the future than I had planned. Yet my question still stands. Is there a way to combat the ever-growing beast we call government? Please, think about this as an umbrella covering your 'future' lessons."

"Nice pun," Gouveneur Morris noted as he grinned. Paul returned the smile.

Paul decided it was time to call it a day, at least for his students. He knew he had another hour in front of him to help the others change the décor in the classroom to a mid-1800s scenario. While there wasn't a staggering difference in the décor, little bits of change may or may not be noticed. Paul thought of his young days on the stage and how fast the stagehands could change the set; however, in this facility, the details were impeccable. Everything worked. The stage pieces were for the show, but not here. Dr. Benton spared no expense on finding authentic items or creating the best replicas when necessary. He mentioned to everyone he was purposely doing this for the comfort level of his guests, but Paul was sure there was a deeper meaning.

The statesmen were served dinner and were very pleased with the quality of food. Dr. Rayne was curious to find out if the recipes he had found were as authentic as he was led to believe. Roger Sherman was quite complimentary of the roasted duck. This delight was not a staple for him during his lifetime, and he presented his comments elegantly.

Throughout dinner, none of the guests could stop digesting the day's discussion. In true Senatorial form, Hamilton carried the floor while Madison and Sherman injected their own dissents or confirmations. When the meal was over, the five retired to the parlor, where drinks were served. Before new arguments were revived, Gouveneur Morris sat next to Dickinson, who was seated next to the fireplace. "John, would you have any dissent to my requesting some answers of a more personal nature?"

Dickinson's expression didn't change. "I will hear the question before I know if I will answer," he said flatly.

In a manner to not bring attention, Morris quietly began the dialog. "You are as I am, a man who will stand for what he believes. An honorable man with high integrity. Well, my integrity may not be as high as yours, but still, we're both sitting here today to understand, gain knowledge, learn about how our actions will be written down in history. I'm certain that if I found anything noteworthy of myself, I would be feeding my own ego. You, sir, would not stoop to that level, of this I am sure. I... I would like to know *if* the absence of your name on the Declaration of Independence has caused you to pause, given the new information we have gained on this day?"

Dickinson's expression still did not change. Morris patiently waited for Dickinson to form his thoughts, as he believed this man would stand toe to toe against anyone for what he believes.

"Gouveneur, I can only say that, while this country, up to the point of our education thus far, has become great, it has done so in a way that I could not approve. I would not change time and wish my hand to pen my name to something that I did not agree to. Now to you, sir, if I may, I return your inquiry, with the foreknowledge that I bear information of your own past when you wrote to General Nathaniel Greene in 1781 and spewed forth your own opinion that this country would not subsist unless ruled by an absolute Monarchy. Tell me Counselor, what say you now?"

Morris wasn't as much of a stone face when it came to confrontation, but he did not back down. His face turned a bit red as his letter was in confidence, and his reaction was more of annoyance than embarrassment. "Well, John, the rest of the letter maintained that my ear is to the people and the tone and temper of my constituents is nothing of trifle. It is true, my time in France had certainly led me to believe what you have shown not to be private information; however, my compass has changed. In hind thought, this may be the very basis of my question. My own mindset has changed based on what I found to be the desires of the people I represent. Is your missing signature of the same nature? Of this, I do not wish an answer. I wish to leave this conversation with you knowing I hold you in the highest esteem as a most honorable man. I applaud your decision, as I know this is something you deeply hold to. My question does stem from what you have done, Your Honor. Decisions made are made at the time of the event and should be done with all information available. Regret is the after-thought of our decisions, and quite possible after seeing those results. I do not believe you are a man who lives in such regret. Not at all. Not at all, sir. I will take my leave now, John. I shall see you in the morning."

Chapter 13

The travelers and the statesmen arrived in the classroom around 7 AM. All had eaten and brought their coffee with them to the classroom. The statesmen were a bit amused at the prospect of carrying their morning coffee away from the table to the classroom ~ such things just weren't done this way. However, after the time they had already spent in the classroom, the readily available caffeine was appreciated. The five took to the same seats they had the previous day. John Dickinson mentioned that the classroom had an American Flag up near the front of the room. He made a mental note that the number of stars had increased on the flag. Roger Sherman was the last to sit, and, as he did, Charles Carson walked into the room.

Charles hadn't slept well the previous night. He was no different than any of the other travelers in his nervousness. To be able to stand in front of such an audience was more than an honor. Hell, to stand in front of these men the very first time he saw them all together was simply fantastic! Now he was about to be their educator for part of the day, and he couldn't even shout it from the mountain top! He could say nothing to his family or friends, or even talk to himself out loud in his own apartment for fear it might be bugged. None of them could. While he was very content to talk about this with his fellow travelers, today was his day to shine.

Charles began, "Good morning, gentlemen. It is my privilege to be with you this morning and take a walk with you, if you will excuse the expression, through the remaining decades of the century at hand. Before we begin...." He gestured towards Dr. Benton who moved to the front of the room.

"Good morning, again, gentlemen," Benton said. "Today we will start you off with a little bit of a treat, I should think. 'Technology' is a term derived from the Greek language and is not commonly used in the late 1800s. The best definition may very well be from Jason Bigelow in 1829, which, paraphrased, means 'the use of processes or principles involving the application of sciences'. The machine that brought you here is such an example of how far technology has advanced.

"We will use this technology in your education. And why not? Technology is a great tool if used properly, and, as in most cases, man's propensity is to use tools for the extreme at both ends ~ for good and evil. We hope to educate you in both during this process, but we will focus on the good technology today. In your own time, gentlemen, you will soon hear of such a technology called 'moving pictures'. It's a process whereby pictures are placed end to end, and, when the pictures advance, the details of the pictures, which are specifically sequential, will appear to be moving. Let me show you an elementary example. In front of each of you is a small book. Please open your book to the front page. You see a young boy sitting on a penny bicycle. The bicycle is a great tool to

118

show you about technology as well. Two wheels placed end to end and connected by a simple frame. When one sits on the frame and remains balanced, the bicycle is now a mode of transportation. Now, turn to the first book-marked page and you will see that same young boy sitting on the ground next to the bicycle."

"It would lend to the imagination this young boy did not know how to ride a bicycle," commented Gouveneur Morris. "I'm sure this is something I could not do either," he said with a bit of a smirk.

"Ahh! You may be correct on both accounts," Madison added with a touch of humor. The room lifted with laughter for a brief moment.

Benton continued with his example, "If you will now look to the last page of the book. You will see the boy is now riding the bike into the sunset. This may lend to the thought that the boy has learned how to ride. However, let's start from the beginning. From the first picture, flip through the page like this." Charles Carson demonstrated. "Watching the pictures move ever so slightly, it appears that the boy is actually moving, yet we know these are only single pictures on paper. If you continue to the last page, you will see the boy fell only once during his bike ride. He got up, dusted himself off, rode up and down a few rolling hills, and continued to ride into the sunset. The format of the moving pictures technology isn't too unlike what you've just experienced. We have taken pictures of people with cameras, such as what you see in the corner over there and placed them on

119

film. Charles, if you will." Charles began handing out the pieces of film. "If you hold that item up to the light, someone tell me what you see."

"It appears to be a picture of a man riding a horse," Hamilton answered.

"It is quite grainy looking, but I agree - a man on a horse," Dickinson concurred.

"Correct. Pictures of motion. And now for the next step, 'projection'. Charles?"

Charles used the historical film projector to show the same pictures against the white screen, the same pictures the men were holding. He showed them that each picture was certainly different, just like the pictures in the book. You could hear the excitement in the room when the statesmen saw the man on the horse galloping against the white screen.

"Wonderful!" Madison exclaimed.

Gouveneur Morris laughed out loud, "Look! Astonishing!"

The other gentlemen were excited, too, while Charles and Dr. Benton enjoyed the moment and the expressions on their faces.

"Charles, I believe you have their full attention now."

Charles nodded and replied, "I believe I do."

After a few moments of the statesmen touching the camera and asking a few more questions, Charles added, "I believe there is one more item that we can add to this innovative technology." He paused for effect. "Sound."

Charles waved to Paul, who had been waiting for his cue, and Paul rolled in a more modern projector. The film had already been loaded. Charles noted that the technology to add sound was a bit premature, it will move their education along faster.

"Today, with Paul's help, we will be showing you a few short films. These 'moving pictures' with sound will be a new way of bringing information to you. I encourage you to remember your questions until the film stops, and we will be happy to discuss them with you. Paul, if you are ready? Paul nodded in the affirmative. For the remainder of the day, Charles used books, film, and his own knowledge to help give the five statesmen an overview of some of the most momentous events in the coming decades.

Charles was ready to proceed and gave a nod to Paul Tesla to be ready.

Charles gave a brief introduction, "Gentlemen, the 16th President of the United States, the Honorable Abraham Lincoln."

Paul dimmed the lights and started the first film the statesmen had ever seen.

- September 1862 – The Emancipation Proclamation, given by President Abraham Lincoln, declared that all slaves in states showing resistance to the Federal

Government shall be "forever free" as of January 1, 1863.

The short film included information on the Civil War, intricate to reasons why Lincoln was elected. The film narrator noted that an estimated 620,000 lives were lost during this conflict, which is more than all other American conflicts combined. The narrator of the film made note that an undesirable federal law mandated that no states were given the option to secede from the nation and become a sovereign country, a major cause of the Civil War. The northern Union population was just over twenty-two million while the southern Confederate States population was near nine million. The Union soldiers outnumbered the Confederates approximately 2 to 1. However, the death toll ratio has been calculated to be 8 Union soldiers for every 11 Confederate soldiers.

When this movie clip was completed, Charles Carson, a free black man, passed out a replica of the proclamation to each statesman. He did not utter a word. Just before he was about to hand Roger Sherman his copy, Sherman stood up and held out his hand. Charles Carson stood proudly and shook firmly. Charles had just experienced another moment he would never forget.

Alexander Hamilton spoke, "This President Abraham Lincoln is a man with true integrity. I admire his actions, but I must inquire, does he live a long and fruitful life?"

"No, sir. He does not." Charles answered quickly. "His life was taken from him at age 56. But before that happens, he orated what American history has described as one of the best speeches ever produced. If I may, I have a copy of it here, which you may have during your time here. The speech is only 272 words, which is close to two and one-half minutes of your time. Please listen to this reenactment of The Gettysburg Address, which was given on November 19, 1863.

Once the recording was completed and a few questions were answered satisfactorily, Alexander Hamilton raised a question. "Your previous statement held caution in your tone, and so I wish to inquire precisely how Lincoln's life was taken from him?"

"Of course, sir. President Lincoln was attending a theatre function in our nation's capital. On April 14, 1865, he was assassinated by gunshot."

The room remained quiet for a moment until Charles continued his lesson. "It is strongly suspected that this event in history spurned on the 13th Amendment. This amendment dealt with the abolition of slavery, which took place in December of the same year. However, as all you gentlemen know, change is not an easy task to accomplish and it rarely happens overnight. Even as the 13th Amendment is now law, opinions rage on what exactly that means for the black population."

Gouveneur Morris interrupted, "I beg your pardon, to whom are you referring?"

"My apologies, Councilor," Charles answered. "People of color, black people, such as myself. The term 'nigger' has been categorized as a slave term, and, as slavery is no more, the term is considered derogatory and, in some cases, offensive to the black community. Admittedly, the term is mostly used by black people themselves, who seem to think they are exempt from being 'politically correct' or offending other black people. But, in my opinion, it only shows their arrogance, ignorance, and prejudices. While my skin is black, gentlemen, I did not 'come from Africa'. I was born in America. I am simply American ~ the same as you. All Americans have ancestors from other countries. We are a nation built from other nations. We must first be *American* citizens and unite as such."

"Well said," Madison added. "Hear, hear."

"Indeed," Hamilton and Dickinson concurred. Sherman and Morris nodded their heads in the affirmative, while all the statesman began hitting the tabletop in front of them in agreement.

Over the noise, Carson continued, "Mr. Hamilton, if I may use your words, sir? In the documents known today as The Federalist Papers, you wrote an essay entitled 'Concerning Dangers from Dissension Between the States' in the context of territorial disputes, whereby these disputes 'have at all times been found one of the most fertile sources of hostility among nations.'

"You were very correct, sir, and you all know too well the disputes over such territories have been fought with wars. Unfortunately, when the dust of the territorial wars had settled, a new war, a Civil War, and more will have risen to take its place. A war over the color of skin or a war over taxation of slavery and the political control over these
124

subjects. Liberties that were never given, and freedoms which were denied because of our differences. Our nation has imploded with this same and fertile source of hostility. Which leads me to our next points of history, gentlemen. Let's visit a few other changes in history which contributed to our country's turmoil and advancement."

"Let's discuss an inventor of your own time," Carson continued. "Eli Whitney. Some of you may have heard of or even know him. He invented the cotton gin and applied for a patent in 1793. Cotton, the main component of the clothing you are wearing today, has maintained its command of the clothing industry. This impressive piece of history allowed the cotton industry to thrive. The South, where cotton is predominately grown, must be picked from the cotton fields. This invention revolutionized the cotton industry, but it also caused a great demand for more people in the fields to pick the cotton. Thus, the South's dependence on slavery. Incidentally, the tobacco industry shared the same dependence on labor to grow their industry. Knowing this information, you can see why the South held their views concerning slavery and taxation.

"Other technological changes could include the changes in weapons: rifles and guns. Advances from the flintlock design, which I assume you are all familiar with, to a percussion-detonating concept. Although still a percussion design, Samuel Colt, in 1835, was the first to mass produce a reliable revolving piece of work.

Hundreds of designs, sizes, and calibers were manufactured during this era. Two more notable items were the Spencer repeating carbine rifle, which fired 7 shots in 15 seconds and became a preferred weapon during the Civil War. The other, a larger weapon eventually made into several sizes, including .50 caliber, called the Gatling Gun. This weapon changed the outcome of several engagements. We have a room set up down the hall to show you these designs here in a few minutes."

Madison interjected, "A few minutes isn't necessary, my friend. We're talking guns! Let's go see them now, and we can continue with more lessons later. What say you, men?" The statesmen were all in with this idea and stood up. "Show us the way Mr. Carson, if you will. You can talk about more things while we peruse your arsenal!"

Carson led the men out of the classroom and down to the historical gun room, set up for just this occasion. While the group looked over this collection, he answered the questions that came up. The statesmen were quite interested in the collection and spoke amongst themselves for quite some time.

After a short break, the group returned to the classroom, and Carson resumed his lesson plan.

- March 1866 ~ The Civil Rights Act protecting the rights of Americans was enacted.
- March 1870 ~ The 15th Amendment banned race as a preclusion to vote.

Carson mentioned this without reservation and only as fact. Sherman glanced at the speaker, gauging his comments. He found nothing but the face of an historian recounting the events.

September 1886 ~ The chief of the Apache tribe, Geronimo, surrendered to U.S. troops, signifying the end of wars between Indian tribes and the U.S. Army. However, the last uprising by Indians was fought in 1898 at the Battle of Sugar Point, located on Leech Lake in northern Minnesota.

"We may or may not be visiting this last location in the not-too-distant future. Schedules change. We have several outings planned, and I'm very excited to be with you during these events," Carson said emphatically.

Sherman asked, "When will these outings take place, Mr. Carson?"

"Perhaps in a day or two? After we conclude our orientation, I'm sure, but Dr.
Benton has planned for you to see our history...that is, what our history is now. We will walk the streets and go places which you may find familiar. I have another motion picture to show you. This time, we will look at travel, economics, electricity, and communications."

Carson started the film. The statesmen showed great interest in the images on the screen. Watching their expressions, Charles Carson could see how proud they were to see how the advances in technology had helped the country grow. He could see questions forming in their facial expressions. When the film was over, the group briefly discussed how the railroads were built and the labor involved in such a task. They discussed the Transcontinental Railroad and its effects on commerce and shipping over land. Big city dwellers traveled by street cars where available. Carson covered the details as the questions were asked. They reveled over the telegraph and how this invention was paramount for speedy information transfer. This led to a conversation about the telephone and the lasting effects it has had on all communications. Carson knew there would be more on this subject soon. Then, a bit early, he briefly discussed the radio and the beginnings of wireless communications. Carson turned a knob on a wooden box and let the men hear the static where no station was available. He slowly turned another knob until the five were listening to music. The forefathers were quite impressed and entertained. Smiles were shown all around, and the lesson moved forward.

- January 1892 ~ New York Harbor hosted Ellis Island as the east coast immigration center and debarkation for European immigrants. Ellis Island replaced Castle Garden, located in Manhattan, N.Y. By its closing in 1954, Ellis Island had processed over 12 million immigrants. Prior to 1890, immigration was regulated by individual states. Shortly after the closing of Ellis Island, immigration laws were determined by Quota Laws and the National Origins Act. The downside to these Acts were short-sightedness of the law makers as the

Acts were only limiting the immigration for Europeans. The Acts did not apply to Latin America, or countries with bilateral agreements, or Asian countries. The evolving laws changed after 1918 as the U.S. emerged as a world power. Since then, hopeful immigrants were required to request citizenship or visas via the consulate in their home country.

- October 1892 ~ Marking the 400th anniversary of Columbus Day, public schools began the first recital of the Pledge of Allegiance. The words were written on a piece of paper and handed out.

Carson verbally noted the words in the pledge were written "to the *republic*, for which it stands". The groups began heating up when Carson mentioned the country's progression towards a purer democratic society.

Madison interjected, "Is the country *not* a republic?"

Remaining neutral, Carson replied, "That would depend on your definition, sir."

Madison, still sitting in his chair, uncrossed his legs, put his elbows on his knees and clasped his hands, then spoke clearly, "Democracies do not last unless the group is very small. Yet the philosophies of a democratic system can be incorporated within the national republic on a state level to represent the people via their elected agents. Carson, you and your staff have all expressed the ever-growing population as a concern, and it has been duly noted. The United States, by my terms, cannot be a democracy. The population is too great. A republic places itself into the hands of an elected delegation. Is this not the way this government was set up? Do you not elect officials to represent the people? The power of the country must remain with the people and be equal among the sovereign states. Has something changed in this respect that we have not yet been informed about?"

Carson gently replied, "We do elect officials in all levels of government to represent the people."

Madison continued, "Then, by definition and your own admonition, these United States remain a republic. I know of no instrument in a democracy that will balance the desires of a few larger populated states against the sacrifices of the smaller populated states. It does not exist. It is my contention that you have democratic inconsistencies within the system, tearing apart the intended fabric of the government, to which you take issue."

Charles replied, "The comparison between 'republic' and 'democracy' remains today as it has for centuries. Some say the majority does not rule as in a true democracy. Take the Electoral College, for example. All of you are familiar with the EC, that it operates to protect the smaller populated states from the larger populated states in the attempt at giving a fair vote to all states, regardless of their population. In fact, candidates have been named as President by the power vested in the EC. This, of course, is a check-and-balance of the voting system so that states of lower population cannot be ignored. There is also the mention of 'one nation, under God'."

Sherman asked, "Why, specifically, are you mentioning these phrases in such a manner?"

Charles retorted, "In later years, a small percentage of people in America, whether American citizens or not, will be offended that our country was founded on Christian principles. Using such words as 'God' in some public-school systems where a child's religion is not Christianity was deemed offensive. Since that time, many places have stopped reciting this Pledge of Allegiance. In my time, many children do not even know it exists unless they are in a civic group, not associated with public schools. The political system has removed God from schools and therefore, it follows, they essentially removed the moral code of the Bible. Oddly enough, they now wonder why horrific events happen at school. In many American schools, prayer is absent in those buildings, unless spoken in secret or in 'a moment of silence'."

Gouveneur Morris' eyes furrowed in disgust. "A law? Someone created a *law* to forbid this?"

"That is correct," came the reply. "The 9th Circuit Appeals Court ruled the pledge cannot be recited, as the term 'under God' endorses religion. This is not yet the time, but we will discuss the words in the 1st Amendment and its meaning, as described by your colleague, Thomas Jefferson."

Hamilton questioned, "Are you implying that Jefferson's attempt at explaining why an amendment was written has been taken out of context and used against the American people?"

Carson replied, "Your perception is correct, sir."

The room remained quiet for a few moments before Madison concluded, "I believe I will discuss these thoughts with Jefferson at my first opportunity."

Roger Sherman spoke next, "The words you have just spoken keep resounding in my mind, Mr. Carson. People are 'offended' that our country is founded on Christian beliefs and this has caused a rift in the fabric of our nation."

"That is correct," Carson answered.

"And law makers have removed open prayer from public schools?"

"Yes."

Roger Sherman spoke clearly, "That is a travesty, Mr. Carson. And blatantly against the intent and tapestry of the Constitution." The other statesmen agreed and began clapping their hands. Sherman held his hand up to calm the room. "However, the life of Christianity, as I know it, has a history of persecution. Know this, gentlemen: God is sovereign, and no man's law can command where He cannot go. No man's law can keep the Almighty from the hearts of those who seek Him." Again, the statesmen began clapping. Sherman spoke above the noise, "Yet, I will surmise that the governing body that allowed this to
132

happen has issued a 'letter of acceptance' for the deterioration in morality within its borders."

Carson wondered how the Supreme Court justices of 1962 and 1963 would react to hearing these words as it was their debatable misinterpretation of the First Amendment wording that resulted in the decision to remove the Bible and prayer from public school-initiated functions.

Charles Carson smiled on the inside at hearing these discussions. Change was certainly forthcoming. His very short meeting with Thomas Jefferson remained fresh in his mind, and he couldn't help but wonder how Mr. Jefferson might respond to the comments of the men in this room. Would he write the same words of the Constitution upon hearing the comments of these men? Certainly not. Carson felt comfortable with Gouveneur Morris being in the room, too, due to his contributions in writing the Constitution. Carson's reflection was short-lived as he found himself saying, "Let's move on, shall we?"

- May 1896 ~ Plessy vs. Ferguson, a court case dealing with the idea "separate but equal". The idea of a free black individual was still being put to the test of integration when segregation was still legal. This was one of the first steps in the desegregation of one race from another, in this case, blacks and whites. As a simple example: a designated 'whites only' water fountain vs. the same device in a separate, usually more inconvenient location labeled 'blacks only'.

"Oh! My goodness!" exclaimed Gouveneur Morris. "A man puts his pants on and pisses yellow just like everyone else! What man with righteous forethought and upright thinking would allow this to continue? Pray tell, just how long does it take for America to finally come together?"

"At this point in history, around 1896," Charles began, "the U.S. is very slowly allowing black individuals to become free via legislation; however, the sentiments of white individuals are not allowing full integration, regardless of the law. In fact, segregation is lawful and, in some states, governed by Jim Crow laws, which allow for 'separate but equal'. Blacks could not use the same bathroom as whites, walk in the same front door as whites. Is this such a shock to anyone sitting here, knowing that slaves of your time were afforded the same, if not worse, considerations?" The statesmen made no replies. "These types of considerations last for several decades.

"To answer your question, Gouveneur Morris, I'm not convinced we have, sir. Longer than those on the losing end would care to have it transpire, and, believe me, all parties lose. To this day, sir, and please hear me, even after the United States of America has elected a black man as president, the country still has not come together against racism."

Alexander Hamilton spoke softly, "I understand that your wish is for us to learn how the current Union has evolved. I further understand that our education here may very well turn our thoughts differently and towards a different path which may alleviate some of the pains that you have shown us. Your question to us is what will change, if anything. My own question would be relating to what we retain in the Constitution.   I will venture that your advances in medicine, agriculture, technology, and inventions are truly on levels I would have never suspected, and we would all be very impressed. But your society, social interactions, legal segregations, taxes, tax spending, and increased government size have, and I feel you will prove to us that more is forthcoming, caused me to doubt that keeping anything, in our rough framework of a document, would be beneficial! I submit to you, sir, that the politicians of later years have certainly failed to learn from the past! My point is specifically convincing when it is evident that their own eyes are set on their own agendas and not that of the people they serve! Have they not read our papers? Studied *our* mistakes?"

Roger Sherman gently raised a finger, "To the honorable Mr. Hamilton, I am in agreement, yet I feel I must add that, with all sincerity, we..." Sherman gestured to the five statesmen, "...in our current position as representatives of the people, even as representatives of the people in the United States today, in this year of our Lord, 2025, with the knowledge we possess by choice, can and have made an impact on the situations today, in our time and time to come. We have chosen this, gentlemen. I, for one, am willing to see this through until this education is completed. I shall not make any decisions to take away from the work we have so diligently set forth. We, the five of us and the remaining delegates, have set upon making these states into a Union under a single flag. The fallout

135

from this decision will occur with many men giving the ultimate sacrifice. Growth and change cannot come easily if it will be affecting millions of citizens. These travelers have shown us that we have succeeded, gentlemen. We are sitting in the United States of America in the year 2025. Before we become too disenchanted and fraught with discouragement, let us finish what we started here, knowing the five of us have accomplished a great goal in crafting America. These gentlemen, who have used phenomenal technology, are only asking if we could improve upon our accomplishment and help them understand our intentions from 250 years ago. By all rational thought, what has already transpired has come at a great cost. *Should* we make any changes, the cost will change. Our true question is not *if* we will make changes, but what changes *will* we make? And will this cost be greater than the whole of history thus far."

Madison stood to address the room. "In my life, I have never dreamt of such a day as this. 'Tis true the education we have received and, I would agree with Mr. Sherman, the information that is yet to be will forever affect the decisions, opinions, and writings which we will put forth. Any information gained, by its very nature, must be used to complete those decisions and used in argument to defend the same. Having been privy to the information we have been given, I consider this to be an honor and a curse. However, as honorable as it may be, is it a test of integrity? We are the first five who answered this call. Had other men been given the opportunity, the decisions would rest with them. However, here we are. It will be a true test to not impart such knowledge to those not here as they may believe us to be mentally unstable. All the while, we continue to use this information to argue for the correct changes and help write the documents which will guide this country. Mr. Sherman's cost analysis is correct. Mr. Hamilton's powers of observation are also correct in many aspects. I believe it was our esteemed colleague, Thomas Jefferson, who said, "The natural progress of things is for the government to gain ground and for liberty to yield. These liberties must be protected. Freedoms defined." He paused for a moment as if he wasn't sure if he wanted to make his next statement. "Be it ever a task for the five of us here, but we still have another century and a half of education ahead of us. I believe we might retire for the day, albeit a bit earlier than normal. I've had my fill at this point. That is, if Mr. Carson is in a satisfactory position for us to continue again in the morning?"

"As you wish, sir," Carson replied and opened the classroom door. "Gentlemen, would you care for some fresh air?"

"Yes, of course," came the reply from several of them, and they made their way to the gardens. Carson was already informed to guide them outside upon the close of the education, no matter the outcome.

Dr. Benton stood in the control room, watching and listening to the events in the classroom. The large monitor screens and surround sound system made him feel as if he had been sitting in the room during the lessons.

"J.A.S.P.E.R.   Based on their facial reactions, verbal responses, and physiological assessments, what are the projections that the men stay for more than another day?"

J.A.S.P.E.R. (Just Another Super-Powered Educated Response) was the artificially intelligent private virtual assistant developed by the same philanthropist who funded Dr. Carver's operation. The artificial intelligence systems of 2025 were available in personal homes and performed many functions. Some were more advanced than others, and costs varied. With the help of Dr. Benton and the Benefactor, J.A.S.P.E.R. had access to some of the most sophisticated databases in high-level positions of government and private corporations.

J.A.S.P.E.R.'s response came quickly, "Based on your request, including all of their historical data that I can find in their personal letters, legal documents, and published writings found in any database, including the Library of Congress's secret documents, letters to Presidents and Free Masonry membership lists, of which two gentlemen hold evidence as members, I calculate 92%."

"Ninety-two percent. Very well. Thank you, J.A.S.P.E.R."

"My pleasure, sir."

"One more question. Who among our teaching staff has the greatest influence on our students?

"That would be Mr. Carson, sir. I can give you a break-down of their facial responses and body language, if you wish."

"No, not just yet. But update me on this every two days or if you see a significant decline. I'd like to keep them interested and learning. How are their vital signs and overall health?"

"Satisfactory, Dr. Benton. No concerns noticed, but a minor mention: Mr. Sherman may be more susceptible to catching a cold."

"Noted ~ upgrade his vitamin supplements in the meals. We do not need anyone getting sick. They must remain as healthy as possible. I can't return these men in poorer health than they arrived."

"As you wish," J.A.S.P.E.R. replied.

Benton suspected the amount of information could be overwhelming, and, at this point, they weren't quite halfway through.

The group walked off the elevator and stepped into the garden area, where they heard light music coming from speakers placed throughout the lush escape. They were offered several types of drinks, coffee, and juices. Only Roger Sherman accepted water. The others were content with a short pour Kentucky bourbon whiskey. When Charles Carson had handed them their choice of beverage, he waited for ten minutes for any questions that may be lingering. Finding no one approaching him, he left the area and went back to the classroom to begin getting it ready for the updates heading into the next century.

Hamilton and Madison, who had been friends for a long time, both co-wrote The Federalist Papers with the help of

John Jay, walked to the end of the gardens, away from everyone else. The view of the rolling hills, perfect blue sky, and white billowing clouds were spectacular. They remained quiet for several minutes, just admiring it. When they finally did speak, their conversation was quiet. Dr. Rayne and Sarah Fleming had joined the group and met up with Roger Sherman, while Dickinson and Morris were met by Paul Tesla. Dr. Benton arrived, grabbed his own glass of ice water, and quietly sat at a table, watching the interaction. He heard Gouveneur Morris laughing, which almost seemed predictable. Morris was quite the thinker, but he didn't take himself too seriously. Dickinson was carrying the conversation with his thoughts of ratifying the Constitution and how the document should be re-written to apply the theories of oppression, not only from the British but from the potential growing government within the Union. Benton knew John Dickinson was strongly noted for his intellectual influences.

From where Benton was sitting, he knew he would be able to catch up on the other conversations as soon as he returned to his office. J.A.S.P.E.R was able to listen to any conversation on the property and would give him the "Reader's Digest" version.

During the next hour or so, the groupings and conversations changed until everyone was notified that dinner was ready. Everyone made their way to the dining area and eventually concluded the day by retiring to their rooms around 9 PM.

Dr. Rayne and Dr. Benton had their 'end of the day' meeting and checked to be sure the classroom had been updated for the following day. Everything was satisfactory. Documents and maps that had been discussed now lined the walls. A few of the smaller inventions were set on tables around the edge of the room. Both men seemed to be in good spirits, when J.A.S.P.E.R.'s voice interrupted them.

"Excuse me, Dr. Benton. You have an email from the Benefactor." "Very well, I'll tend to that directly," Benton said.

Rayne questioned, "How is his attitude on the project?"

"His attitude on *his* project is as it should be, but we will soon need to push him off so we can have some time without his interruptions. I'm not sure at this point how to accomplish that, so maybe you can help with some ideas. You're a crafty fellow."

"Well, thank you…. I think?"

"In this case, it's a good thing. What are your thoughts on today?" Benton asked. "I'm of the opinion things are progressing well. J.A.S.P.E.R gave me a report earlier with good indications which only confirmed my own, so I've nothing erroneous to report."

"Good. Forward we go, my friend. Let's see how the next century yanks their chain. Who is up at bat in the morning?"

"I am, but they are expecting Charles. However, I'm still of the mind of having you stand in for me."

"No, no, no…. you know I don't wish to do that. I'm not comfortable with the classroom teaching. And I've told you before there may come a time when the explanation from a teacher is not acceptable to these men. They very well may argue the stupidity of modern men and women, which I will certainly agree to. But as a teacher, you must present the facts. I will have to soothe the emotions, and I don't need them being mad at their teachers. They can be mad at me if they need to be. There just has to be buffer of some sort."

Dr. Rayne waved him off. "That's bogus. If the facts piss them off, then they will want to effect change! This could be good."

"If, and probably *when* the facts 'piss them off', as you say, I hope they don't throw in the towel and wish to leave too soon. I'm not yet convinced this wasn't Madison's state of mind this afternoon. Having them wish to stay is more important to us both, I should think."

Chapter 14

Trying to be as up to date as possible and in keeping with the history presented in the classroom, clothes of the 21st century had been laid out for each statesman. The sizes were all correct. Benton didn't want the men to be too obvious for the day's events. They didn't know it yet, but they were going outside the facility today, and Benton was rather excited to see their reactions. Each man dressed in his new clothes: jeans, a sensible shirt, and updated footwear. After a few questions about the new zippers from Sherman and Dickinson, each man stepped into the hallway very close to the same time. They all sized each other up and grinned. Small talk ensued, followed by quiet laughter.

Upon arriving at the classroom, they all noticed the changes with the desks, lighting, ceiling, and other items. Items on the walls had changed; wallpaper was added. The room styles had been built inside each other and were designed to be changed in a little less than an hour by removing the interior walls to reveal pre-made, updated walls. The structures were no more than 8 inches apart. The ceiling was a bit tougher to create the changes, but Dr. Benton had consulted some of the top architects he knew and found a way to make it happen with the least amount of time and effort. Benton had several conversations with Dr. Rayne on just how many styles of rooms should be pre-made. Their final decision was six. Not knowing exactly when each class period may end, they believed that major changes were seen every 50 years. So, they started with the year 1800 for the comfort of their guests and built a room with updates for every five decades. If the class happened to go faster, they could always take down any walls necessary to accommodate their desired surroundings.

The room really was just a bit larger now. The most drastic change noticeable was the furniture. Their comfortable chairs of the late 1700s had been changed out for newer chairs of the late 1800s, with the explanation that they were essentially over '100 years old'.

Dr. Benton sat in a chair across from the entrance to the classroom. Dr. Rayne stood in front of the class and welcomed each man as he entered. Pleasantries were exchanged and reactions to the room were noted.

"Good morning again, gentlemen. Dr. Benton has a few words to begin the day. Dr. Benton." Dr. Rayne gestured towards their host.

Benton did not stand up. "Hello, Councilors. The amount of history you received yesterday was substantial to absorb. As always, I am more than willing to review any subject with which you still have questions.

Councilors, history is about to move faster. Horses and buggies are no longer the main mode of transportation. Inventors are emerging quickly, and the thirsty American is drinking it up. You have heard much about the struggles. Those struggles and other such difficulties will continue. I also wish you to see some of the marvels of newer technology. I pray that your accommodations and clothes are fitting you satisfactorily. If not, please let us know. I hope you enjoy your day, gentlemen. Dr. Rayne will be your guide and teacher today, so I will leave you to it."

Dr. Rayne spoke up, "Today we are going to literally feel the effects of a couple inventions that have changed the face of America. Remember that these inventions are the very start, and through the following years, these inventions were improved upon. As a slight departure from our previous presentations, these inventions are not in chronological order, but they were all brought to light during this next century. As Dr. Benton mentioned in his introduction, this lesson will go *fast*."

Rayne continued, "Before we get to those items, let's cover a few notable pieces of history, shall we?" Rayne talked for an hour...

- The population in the early 1900s was over 76 million.
- The geographical center of the population is in the state of Indiana.

Dr. Rayne spoke his opinion, "One can only wonder if this is the preamble of how our country is moving to the left ~ directionally and politically? This is, of course, just rhetoric."

- July 1902 – Mr. Carrier invented the air conditioner. Rayne walked over to the wall and turned a dial. "Gentlemen, please note the holes in the ceiling and tell me if you can feel cooler air coming out of those vents." The men gave smiles and made mention in their quiet conversations amongst themselves that they believed their climate was cooler due to being underground, which certainly did play a part in it.

- Wilbur and Orville Wright brought America into the age of flight. Rayne showed a short film to help explain the success of the airplane.

- December 1907 - Sixteen battleships and twelve thousand men, known as the United States Great White Fleet, started their first round the world sailing. Alexander Hamilton remarked that defending and protecting the United States appeared to be one of the few decisions which the Constitution was designed to handle.

- September 1908 – The first Model T car was manufactured in Detroit.

While this film was playing, Dr. Rayne walked around and placed a small long box on each desk. When the lights came back on, Dr. Rayne began, "Before we begin discussing vehicles and transportation, this next item has been evolving for quite some time. Even before you were born, this item had already been thought of. Each of you have been able to take notes or write letters with your quill. This device may help you with those tasks. Please open the box in front of you." Each box contained an ink pen.

"Please," said Dr. Rayne "go ahead and take this device and begin writing on the paper in front of you." As the men did so, Rayne continued to explain that the evolution of even small devices, such as an ink pen, has changed the way the world works. Hamilton and Madison both looked at each other and thought about the amount of time they could save when writing.

Sherman mentioned he had heard of similar such items in Germany but had not seen one. Morris also mentioned of hearing of a device with a reservoir for ink, but it was made with two quills.

"Very well, gentlemen. Let's continue, and you may use these pens to take notes. Rayne began the discussion of vehicle transportation and how it opened up new opportunities in the industrial age, changing America's economy.

Dr. Benton was watching, listening, and anticipating their reactions to the next topic.

Rayne pressed on with more facts:

- February 1913 – The 16th Amendment (to the statesmen's Constitution) allowed for income tax.

"Nay!" yelled Roger Sherman.

Several men started slapping the desk in front of them in agreement. "I do not agree with nor comprehend this action! In as much as the British government had no right to levy taxes on the settlers of this country, their own government should not impose unwanted taxes. Will the people have any say in how their own hard-earned income be spent? No! Property tax should have been used if funding was to be obtained! Which is to say this is a matter of the state and not a federal matter. You," he was pointing his boney finger at Dr. Rayne, "have mentioned each day how the population has grown, yet you have not even mentioned, therefore may not have considered, increasing the number of representatives or senators who speak for the people. I cannot comprehend that any single representative can know the pulse of their constituents, even when the only consideration I will use as a basis is the population in their own area of representation. These numbers do not justify! Additional taxes only imply the government will be increasing this tax over time, and that alone would show this government to be perpetuating itself. Collecting, controlling, and dispersing funds is outside the realm of the Constitution and should be left to the individual states, who shall retain their own sovereignty, their own internal government. And then, if the people of such states so choose, they can tax themselves! This has been and shall remain my position. Thomas Jefferson's words have certainly come alive, and I believe this terrible news would impact his expectations and his views on the elected officials of his future. Dr. Rayne, the country is not at war at this time, correct?"

"In the year this was ratified, you are correct," came the ominous reply.

"Then this Amendment, with respect to the Constitution allowing the members of government to lawfully implement such laws, was not in the best interests of the citizens. It was only in the interest of the government!"

"Hear! Hear!" was heard from the other chairs.

Hamilton stood up to speak, but before he was completely out of his chair, Sherman continued, "Furthermore, if I may continue before a lengthy oration starts from the Honorable Mr. Hamilton." Sherman's voice became softer. Hamilton sat back down and relinquished his desire to rebut. "I have read and concede your writings, sir, with respect to the letters on the topic of taxation of property as it would be a true bond between those who own a single parcel to those who have much and own many sections of land. That bond being to keep the land taxes as low as possible. How is it that a citizen who works hard every day should be ruled by a government who demands and steals a tax on the meager income by which he barely scrapes by? Even the wealthy of our country would not wish a government to outwardly rob him and call it a law! Have we learned nothing from when the British tried to levy taxes from us not so long ago? I would consider this population growth, which is exponential above our expectations, will have no real representation in the government to explain where this income tax should be spent.

I also understand your writings concerning the powers of the government to create laws, having been given the
149

power to do so; but a national government, while remaining supreme over the law of her states, should allow states to govern and tax themselves accordingly. Understanding that, should a state government consider a tax and the voting people approve such a tax, then the state has control over where that is to be spent. This action of your 16th Amendment causes me to pause, gentlemen." And pause he did. Sherman stood there, frustrated and trying to think of the right words to say. He resigned himself to say nothing more.

Sherman sat down, politely nodding his head and motioning for Hamilton to take the floor, but that didn't happen. Hamilton did not speak.

Dr. Rayne spoke next, "Gentlemen, all of your teachers have previously discussed among themselves how much of the U.S. history should be imparted to you. It would be impossible to tell you all of it. We have mentioned population as a means of demonstrating the changes in growth. As of yet, we have not specifically mentioned the lack of change in the House of Representatives in our lessons because of the 1929 Permanent Apportionment Act, which allows for equal representation for rural America versus the densely populated cities. The Constitution, as written, allows for representation of the states based upon population. The government you are building was meant to be small, was it not? It is hard enough for the current 435 members of the House of Representatives to agree on a subject. It would only be more difficult if there were twice as many. Which must now bring forth the question of who will pay for these new members? The state, of course, which will take the money from the people in the form of more taxes. The Permanent Apportionment Act maintains a limit so that the cities, which are now overrun with people, do not have any more say in the government than the rural areas of states. If that were not true, then the majority would always rule, and the popular vote is not always the best recourse. Mr. Sherman, your argument is quite valid. I applaud you for your passion for the people, sir. Mr. Hamilton, the floor is yours if you wish."

Hamilton stared down at the desk in front of him for a time before he spoke. "As information provided by this forum continues, my thoughts are in a storm. However, I will add this: from what I have gathered thusly, taxes, in whatever form they may come in, must be appropriately used as prescribed by Section 8 in our working draft of the Constitution. Monies must come from somewhere to pay for the debts accrued by such government. From the maps we have seen, land is finite, and the population grows. A growth in taxes imparted to all citizens, instead of just landowners, would be a prudent way to perform such actions if it is done with such purpose in mind as to serve the people and not the state. But it must be established by the state! A household, a farmer, the mercantile owner, an army, or a country must have a source of funds by which it may create a balance sheet for budgetary purposes. A national government such as we have, formed by the creation of documents to secure a sovereign nation and liberty for her citizens, and appropriations of property taxes which are shared by the states represented, would not be sufficient, given this new information these fine people have imparted to us. The Constitution allows for taxes levied on imports which would help feed the federal needs. Population growth and the expansion of the Union in accordance with the land mass could not, without an income, maintain the common good, provide an adequate military, or carry on with the building of America. I suspect this could not go without discussion. Our colleague, the Honorable Mr. Sherman, is undoubtedly correct in respect to the representation of the people. One hundred soldiers on the battle lines, whose job it is to protect our land and liberties, must be fed, trained, and given the proper tools to do their job, and paid for their efforts by the government, via the very people of this country they protect, through taxes. That, sir, is currently being discussed in our conclave, and, I pray, will be bound by the Constitution."

Gouveneur Morris stood. "Gentlemen, it is incumbent on us to look into the future and provide for the citizens of this country. To do so with limited funds will stifle the manner in which those who are governing could provide such assistance. It appears this amendment was crafted with the totality of the population in mind and allows for the growth of the governing body to perform its function!"

Dickinson replied in a flat tone, "First, Mr. Morris, to the contrary, there is no such thing as 'unlimited' funds. Ever. Eventually, even you, sir, will run out of capital.

And the creation of a perpetuating debt is preposterous, at best. And, what of the common man who cannot find work? How does this apply to him?"

Morris, who was born into wealth and an elitist heritage, ignored the insult and answered, "The same as it would for any person with or without employ, sir. 'Give to Caesar what is Caesar's'. What you should look at, Mr. Dickinson, is if this common man is truly trying to work or sitting under a bridge looking for a passerby to donate money, food, clothing, etcetera. I fully expect that all countries, no matter the overall wealth, will have the destitute, downtrodden, and bottom feeders. There is no escape from this, but when any citizen is employed, there should remain the fulfillment of this 16th Amendment." Morris turned his attention to William Rayne. "Dr. Rayne, could you enlighten us with one reason this federal tax has benefitted the country?"

"Of course," Rayne said. "Some of the funds from federal taxation were put to great use in 1956 with the construction of an interstate system; paved roads that travel between each state. Congressman Sherman, you may find this particularly appealing. The base purpose for this road system was to allow the military to travel faster, to any destination, in preparation or reaction, in the event of war or domestic trouble. Additionally, citizens can use
153

this system in daily travel." Sherman kindly nodded at Dr. Rayne's explanation.

Hamilton rejoined the small debate. "The Honorable Mr. Sherman has conceded the argument of the 32nd letter written to refute this very topic. If you are not familiar, I will kindly remit that I maintain my opinion that such oppressive taxes should not be determined by the national but by the individual state. Again, I allow the 'justness of reasoning' for such a measure and hold that this amendment can be construed as a 'violent assumption of power' by the national government and is not set forth by any document, including the proposed Constitution."

Roger Sherman politely nodded his head toward Hamilton. The room remained silent for just a moment until Dr. Rayne shocked the room with his own question.

"What if you failed?" Rayne asked.

"I beg your pardon?" quipped James Madison. "What exactly do you mean, Doctor?"

"Let me ask it in this way. What if this Constitution had not been ratified? What if this government did not turn out the way you had intended it? What was your escape clause? What did you plan to do if this failed? What was your exit strategy?"

Madison's short body stood as tall as he could, with his chest barreled out. He looked at Dr. Rayne with ill-contented eyes as he answered, "The possibility did exist. You must understand, we have spent close to four months arguing amongst ourselves with only the thought of forging a nation, Dr. Rayne. We have languished through the details and compromised between each state with every effort to allow for the freedoms and liberties not provided for by other governments. We *must* come together, Dr. Rayne, as *one* nation. Perish the thought of failure to all ends! However, the reality of your question deserves an answer."

Gouveneur Morris spoke out of turn, "I believe that your option to run out of here like rats from a sinking ship is out of the question and, at best, cowardly!"

Dr. Rayne defended himself, "I mean no disrespect, gentlemen. The reality of second options lies not only in logic, but in strategy. No one has ever started a fight and planned to lose. Yet, my question remains."

Morris, his voice raised a bit, continued, "Think, man! We would have continued our conclave and continued to vote until our nation could be made whole and seen in the eyes of the others as a sovereign nation. The 'second option', as you call it, is to strive harder!"

Dr. Rayne decided to move deeper into the question. "Since the Articles of Confederation, which is largely regarded as a treaty between the states, aided in the transition and foundation for the documents which we are now speaking of, would there have been the possibility that several states used those Articles as the basis to create their own sovereignties? If this Constitution did not work as you have planned ~ that is, to join these states into a single nation - could it have resulted in many smaller sovereign countries?"

Hamilton offered a rebuttal, "That is quite an observation Dr. Rayne, I must admit. However, you already know the five of us did not settle these United States, nor did any other delegate. However, we could not live here with anarchy, ungoverned and lawless. By our very nature, we wish to succeed. It is intrinsic upon leaders, whether chosen or not, to lead with success in mind. Our vision of success did not include a division of land into several countries, as you suggested. That would have been a failure, Dr. Rayne." Hamilton raised his right hand and pointed straight up with his index finger. "One nation, under God. *One* nation, Dr. Rayne. Just one."

"Very well," Rayne said flatly. "These were just questions that I sit and ponder. Thank you for sharing your insight. All of you gentlemen have much to think about. I only wished to present my thoughts. I pray you take some time to think about such things. No government will please all its people. The underlying question here, as in other subjects we cover, is this: is there another way? A better way, perhaps? While you begin your internal deliberations, we have a schedule to keep, and it is my pleasure to help us keep it. My friends, today is a treat! All of you will be going outside for a lesson in travel."

"Will you be pushing that fancy button of yours and taking us to another time?" asked Gouveneur Morris.

"No sir. I think you'll enjoy this even more. Gentlemen, please follow me."

The statesmen, dressed in their new attire, followed Dr. Rayne. They were met by the remaining teachers and Dr. Benton.

A few minutes later, they were sitting in a horse-drawn buggy traveling down a winding dirt road. A few miles later, they turned off the dirt road and followed a short driveway. Tall trees and foliage surrounded them, making it difficult to see through the forest. In front of them stood what looked like a very standard barn from the turn of the century.

"Doesn't smell like your average barn," quipped James Madison.

Dr. Rayne just smiled at the comment before he answered, "Let's step inside, shall we?"

Inside the barn were cars and trucks lined up on both sides. Not every model of car was represented, but the collection would easily outrival that of Jay Leno. The cars were spaced about fifteen feet apart, in the order they were produced, early models first. The barn held close to 200 vehicles. In front of every vehicle stood a small monitor. Pressing the red button played a short informational video.

Dr. Rayne spoke first, "As the U.S. began to grow, people needed a way to get to their destination a bit faster. This building houses cars and trucks and a few other vehicles, from the first, produced in 1890, to today in 2025. This is a short course in the changes of modern travel and the advancement from steam power to the combustion engine. Before we start down the corridor here, please choose from these two vehicles and let's go for a ride." The statemen climbed into a couple of Ford Model Ts. The cars started purring right away while the double doors to the barn opened. The two cars were lined up at the end of a long, grassy strip of land which, Dr. Rayne noted, was exceptionally smooth. Just beside the cars was a large horse with its rider, Sarah Fleming. No one had noticed that she stayed outside after their arrival.

"Hello again, gentlemen. May I have the pleasure of a race?" she exclaimed excitedly. "We will begin here and race to cross a white line, which is about 300 yards straight down the field. Drivers, are you ready?"

The men driving smiled as they grabbed the steering wheel.

"On your mark! Get set! Go!" she yelled as she bolted forth on her horse. She advanced much quicker than the Model Ts.

The remaining travelers sitting with the statesmen made mental notes of their reactions. Smiles were shared as the cars raced down the grassy strip of land. Slowly, the cars caught up to Sarah, and by the end of the 300 yards, the Model Ts had won the race. Back at the starting line, those who had hats were waving them in the air for victory.

Minutes later, the vehicles were parked back in the barn in the same place they were before the race. Sarah had returned and handed off the horse to someone who was helping. Within the next few hours, several of the cars were taken for a ride down the same grassy lane. At the end of the collection, the statemen were looking at futuristic concept cars. Once everyone had a chance to see the collection and were gathered at the opposite end of the barn from where they started, Dr. Rayne asked a question, "How did you like what you have seen so far today?"

Heads began bobbing up and down when John Dickinson spoke up, "Dr. Rayne. I enjoyed this session today, but what makes you think we would not use this knowledge and push these inventions into being sooner than expected? How was this question answered prior to bringing us to this place of amazement?"

"In my logic, Mr. Dickinson, there is too much technology, by so many scientists and inventors, that has not yet been invented for you to accomplish what you ask. However, that is not my ultimate answer. The answer, my friend, is this: your honor, integrity, and self-control. Each of you has the power to change the future of this country. How you change it is up to you. I have faith in all of you, gentlemen."

"As do I," came the familiar voice of Dr. Benton. "In all things, consider the possibilities and make wise choices. It's something that was told to me a long time ago. I asked myself if creating a way to bring someone from the past and into the future was a wise decision. My conclusion is this." Dr. Benton raised his hands as if to say, *Look where you are*. Benton continued, "I truly believed that it would benefit mankind and help make our country a better place. You, sir, are the answer to that query."

James Madison had been looking around during the conversation and noticed another barn at the far end of the same grassy field. "What is that barn down at that end, Dr. Benton?"

"That, sir, is our next stop. Shall we?" Benton motioned for everyone to climb into one of the two limos that were pulling up.

As the men climbed in, Dr. Benton held back from the group and quietly asked the question, "J.A.S.P.E.R. can you hear me?"

"Yes, sir," came the answer in his earpiece.

"Please check everyone's vital signs and see if they are up to par with our next ride."

"Of course, sir. Currently, everyone appears to be pumping along just fine, sir. Pardon the pun."

"Very funny, J.A.S.P.E.R., but that's good news. Please perform the same function when they return to the limos later."

"Of course, sir. I'll report any anomalies based on this current assessment."

Benton got in the limo and it drove toward the opposite end of the field. The statesmen noticed that the vehicles were now equipped with a radio and air conditioning. Roger Sherman noted how quiet the ride was, insulated from outside noises. Dickinson noted dark it was inside the car and how the sun didn't seem so bright when looking up to the sky. The men were full of questions, but one question seemed a bit louder than the others in Dr. Benton's limo. James Madison asked, "Just how big is this barn? It appears to dwarf the one we just departed."

Benton calmly responded, "This barn has much bigger dreams, sir." "Much, much bigger," came the soft reply from Roger Sherman.

The barn doors began opening, and the noise began to grow from outside the limo. The 2024 Learjet XRT came rolling through the doors. Dr. Benton was equally surprised to see this as he was told earlier in the week that it might not be available. The next hour was spent looking at a smaller collection of select airplanes including bi-wings, small fighter jets, the navy's F-16, and commercial airlines from Boeing. Dr. Benton found this collection to be a bit less impressive than the inventory of cars and trucks, but he couldn't complain. It was all on loan due to the connections of the Benefactor.

Twenty minutes later, everyone was in the air. The take-off was perfectly smooth in the presidential thirty-seat flying tube. The plane's interior had been redesigned to carry 12 to 15 passengers with plenty of room. A bar and many other amenities were available to passengers allowed on this aircraft. However, the change in altitude was a bit rough for Gouveneur Morris during liftoff, but he held his demeanor well as he knew Sarah was sitting right behind him. Snacks and beverages were served on the flight. Dr. Rayne explained the particulars of flight, and all
161

five statesmen were impressed by how far they could travel being so high in the air. A short flight of 95 minutes gave them a small, exhilarating demonstration of air travel. The flight plan took the passengers over Baltimore; Washington, D.C.; New York; out over the Atlantic Ocean; across Philadelphia; and back. All of the five looked out the windows and marveled. The questions and comments came quickly from all of them: "How high are we?" "What was that green circle?" "How did the farmers get the circle so perfect?" "Are those the interstate roads?" "What makes the plane stay in the air?" "How far can we go?" "What is that city?" "Can we see Philadelphia from here?" "Those buildings are so tall!" "The driver has televisions up here!" "Are you sure this isn't a dream?"

"How do we get down?" This question came from Morris, and it seemed to gain a few chuckles from his companions.

"Dr. Benton?" came the soft voice of Roger Sherman, who was sitting right beside him.

"Yes, sir?"

"This is a private comment. Please, call me Roger."

"Very well, Roger. What's on your mind?"

"I know I'm not dreaming, and, eventually, this will end. In some ways, you have given all of us a real nightmare of realism. But in this moment, this is very much a dream. Thank you, Doctor," Roger Sherman said quietly.

"Call me Carver, if you wish. And you are most welcome."

The plane returned by landing on a concrete runway that connected with the same long, smooth, grassy field. The horses and buggies were gone. The car barn was locked up, as was the airplane barn. The captain of the plane told Benton that the plane was needed elsewhere as soon as they landed. This 90-minute flight was a special treat since this plane was being delivered to its buyer, who hasn't even flown in it yet. The plane's captain explained that this craft would be in England in about six hours to meet the new owner.

The travelers and their guests watched as the plane slowly turned around then took off fast and climbed up into the sky. Watching the takeoff from the ground captivated the statesmen.

Dr. Rayne spoke, "I believe I mentioned earlier today that this lesson would go by fast. In our 90-minute excursion, we've only had light refreshments, and I think I'm ready for dinner. Please, tell me I'm not the only one!" The group laughed and found themselves in agreement.

"We do have one more stop before we sit for a meal. It won't take long," Benton mentioned.
"Some of you gentlemen saw the green circles on the ground from the plane ride over Pennsylvania. Those are circle crops the farmers have planted. Did you notice that there are also long row crops just across the roadway?"

"Dr. Benton," said Mr. Sherman. "We may have a life 250 years ago, but the proper use of irrigation is not something new to farming, young man."

163

"Of course, sir. I believe I may have misspoken. I would like to show you some changes in how the farming is now accomplished, sir."

"I would love to see such changes, Doctor," Sherman said with a slight grin.

Moments later their vehicles stopped in what appeared to be a long driveway. Across the road to the south were long, straight rows of several types. Dickinson could see corn, wheat, and tobacco in one area and potatoes, beans, and cabbage in another.

Across the road, along the north side, sat about 20 different tractors. Some of them showed signs of rust, wear, and age. Others looked shiny and fresh. The green circles of crops behind the tractors were as perfect as the land would allow. Just as the last man exited the vehicle, a gray bearded man riding in a horse-drawn buggy came to a stop not far from them. He wore dark gray work pants, leather work boots, and a simple gray, long-sleeved shirt. The sun was shaded from his face by a baseball cap. He gently hopped out of his buggy and, keeping a hold on the reins, began walking towards the group.

"Hello, Dr. Benton," said the farmer. "I see you have your visitors with you today. Good afternoon, everyone."

Dr. Benton spoke next, "This is Mr. Stephens. He farms the land on this side of the road, and as you can see, still loves horses."

"Good afternoon, everyone," Stephens began. "Dr. Benton has already informed me about your visit and asked me to give you a bit of history about my farm and Mr. Duke's farm across the road. Our families have farmed these parts for several generations, but we have done so in very different ways. The Dukes are very content embracing their quiet life, and they do just fine farming organically and in traditional ways. The life of a Quaker is very simple, indeed. However, our family, has accepted farming using newer technology."

Dickinson interjected, "We are familiar with the Quakers, Amish, and other folk who, as I recall, live outside the cities and keep to themselves. Tell me, what made you decide to change?"

Mr. Stephens looked at Dickinson and replied, "My great grandfather believed in progress. Using newer technology made it easier for him to hire less laborers, yield the same amount of product, or more in some years, depending on the weather. He saved much of his money and eventually bought more land to expand the farm. My dad was much the same way, and now we farm most of this area."

Hamilton asked, "And what of Mr. Duke's family across the street. How have they fared in consideration of your expansion?"

Stephen's replied, "We have asked if he wished to sell, and they do not. Which is fine with us. They are great neighbors and a good family. But, to better answer your question, sir, he farms more than enough for his family to live on, and his product is always top notch."

Sherman raised his right hand, palm out to show he had a question.

"Yes, sir?" said Stephens.

"I wonder, Mr. Stephens," Sherman started off. "What are the downfalls to your farming style compared to Mr. Duke's?"

Stephen's eyes met Sherman's for a brief moment, but then Stephens looked down.

"Great question, sir. Our family may have embraced the new technologies of farming, but in doing so, we must also accept the regulations. Even with all the land we farm, we must purchase more seed every year to replant. The seed product we use is quite expensive as it is not organically created, though it is designed to withstand certain bugs or diseases. Large companies demand high prices for such product. Irrigation can also be a factor. We cannot always rely on 'Mother Nature' to provide, so we pump water to the needed areas. We are very blessed that grandfather bought two areas where we have natural ponds to pull from. Additionally, in as much as we have a good lifestyle, these tractors you see behind me are also expensive. They can do so much work by themselves, but the technology costs money."

Dickinson interjected again, "Did you say, 'by themselves'?"

"Yes, sir. The newest of these tractors has air conditioning and satellite radio and uses GPS to keep the rows in a perfect circle or, where we need to, follow the contour of the land for proper irrigation and water conservation."

Sherman commented, "Is he also constricted by these regulations?"

"No, sir. His only constriction is to be sure his crop is free of the product which is grown on our side of the road. Not that it would be his fault which way the wind blows, but the large corporations believe they have intellectual rights to their product. Mr. Duke uses many hours of labor to keep his product free from disease and pests. He is a very busy man these days."

"I see," said Mr. Sherman.

"I believe Dr. Benton has brought you gentlemen to see our collection of tractors. Please, follow me." The group followed the farmer down the road a bit farther and found a small collection of yokes hung on display. Stephens explained that
his great grandfather did not own a tractor until his 40th birthday. He had farmed
this land using pairs of oxen or horses, just as Mr. Duke's family still did. The
group learned that the newest 16-row planter was built in 2017, with a cost of
nearly $175,000.00. There were two more just like it, sitting side by side.

Stephens went on to explain some other changes in farming by giving some information: "In a 1987 report from the New York Times, people in farming occupations were approximately 72% of the work force in 1820. Of course, we don't know what it was like to live back then, but I would guess by the stories from my grandfather, those men and women were strong people."

The statesmen stood still and listening while a couple of the travelers gently smiled. Stephens didn't notice.

He went on, saying, "By 1850, that percentage declined to about 64%. Somewhere near 8 million people. Jump forward to 1920 and the official Census shows only 30% of the population were farmers feeding the country. I can only imagine that number is much smaller today due to machinery and technology. I might add the obvious note that when farmers do not employ labor those people are forced to find employment elsewhere. I believe there may have been many families displaced from the fields and forced to integrate with city folk or head to the coast for industrial work. I would like to point out that you are standing on one of the last farms with a family heritage as owners. The Duke's across the highway is another. We both plan to keep it that way for as long as possible."

Sherman stepped slightly forward and asked to be shown around the grounds. Stephens led the group and continued spewing forth more information. He turned out to be quite the tour guide.

When the tour was over, and all the questions were answered, the group found
themselves hungry. Everyone climbed back into the limos and headed
back to the facility. As the group arrived back at the facility, Dr. Benton's watch

buzzed his wrist.

He looked down to check the message. J.A.S.P.E.R.'s message said all statesmen were still physically okay.

Throughout dinner and after, the conversation flowed freely about the events of the day. When the evening was winding down and the statesmen had excused themselves, the travelers met in the classroom to make changes and decided to leave it the same for the next day. They hadn't really left this time period and really didn't need to put forth the effort to push anything.

In the statesmen's hallway, Hamilton stopped everyone by waving them over towards his bedroom door. He spoke quietly, "Today was rather exciting, was it not?" The nods of their heads in agreement could be seen. "I wonder to myself if there would be any more reason for me to stay."

"Why would you even ask yourself this?" Morris asked inquisitively.

"I'll tell you why," Dickinson answered quickly. "We've been immersed with information. The weight of this responsibility that has been placed on our shoulders is greater than any single man here has expected."

"It has caused me to pause and contemplate, and I cannot ignore the possibility that we have seen too much," Hamilton added.

Morris interjected, "Alexander, you and I have been great friends over the years, and I'm sure this will not change when I ask if the drink has gotten too far into your head?"

"No, my friend. The minimal alcohol is not the source of my concern."

Sherman took a short step forward toward Hamilton. "Thus far, we have witnessed a few things, but we have not seen the workings of the current government or the society. On that note, may I offer a bit of insight?"

"Ecclesiastes 10:10 tells me that if I am not sharp enough then I should welcome wisdom," came Hamilton's answer.

Sherman replied, "Today, here and now, our lives are already written in history. Our headstones have been carved with two dates. We are living extra days by being here and the time here is not wasted. I'm learning. You are learning. If we are to take this weight of responsibility back with us, should we not listen to the fullness of their lessons. Or would you have us retreat and forget why these men have asked us here? We have already been told that we forged a nation and framed a country. Shall we not listen and learn, possibly from our own blindness or lack of foresight, to make this country the best that it could be? Shall we not save it from some of the hardships that we had to endure? If you have thought this through and you feel in your heart that you must return, then do so. But tonight, do not run into the arms of doubt and extricate yourself." Sherman placed his hand on Hamilton's shoulder. "We rely on your wisdom as well, my friend. Gentlemen, I do hope to see you in the morning." Sherman turned and walked to his room, closing the door behind him.

Hamilton remarked, "I've argued with that man more than any other man in history, and we may never see eye to eye on the political side of life; but in matters of life in general, he may very well be the wisest man I know."

"Well, I thought you had said that about me at some point." Morris snapped.

"Ah! Gouveneur, you are wise beyond your years, but we are not wise beyond his years." Everyone quietly laughed.

Chapter 15

"Good morning, Dr. Benton," J.A.S.P.E.R. said. "I have news for you." J.A.S.P.E.R. explained last evening's events in the hallway of the five statesmen.

"It appears I have Mr. Sherman on my side for the moment, but I think I'll have a little convincing talk with them all. Thank you, J.A.S.P.E.R."

Moments later, the men were met outside the classroom door by Sarah Fleming.

"Good morning, everyone. We have been requested to start today a bit differently. Please, follow me."

They rode the elevator and exited the building outside into a secluded garden. The view was spectacular. They could not see anything but the mountains surrounding them. From this view, they were not able see any city skyline on the opposite side of the facility. The courtyard was designed for a moment such as this. A time for reflection.

Dr. Rayne watched the doors to the garden open, revealing Dr. Carver Benton holding a coffee pot and a box of donuts. Everyone noticed Dr. Benton place the items on a table as he began to speak.

"Politics, technology, travel, economics, and education are not the only changes we experience. Food has also changed. I suspect coffee is truly better brewed these days. And when I say 'these days', I mean this is modern-day coffee and these little sweet treats are called donuts.

These came about near the year 1850. They're loved by millions of people and probably not good for anyone's digestive system; however, they have a way of making one feel better. I'm not sure why this is. But I'm sharing. Please, try one." When the statesmen all had a bite and the familiar low troll of 'mmm' could be heard, Benton began to speak again. "I wish to reiterate that both Dr. Rayne and I do apologize for the onslaught of information, not only for that which you have already received but also for that which still remains. The changes in our history..." Benton gestured between himself and Rayne, "are not all ugly. Medical advances have saved countless lives. Doctors are able to help heal people without invasive surgeries. Unfortunately, you gentlemen have seen war-ravaged men that doctors cannot help, but we know today how to replace hearts and other organs from one person to save the life of another. Radio and television, agricultural mechanisms, farm implements, the telephone, vehicles and the highway system on which they travel, household appliances such as the ice box or refrigerator, the microwave, and even the world's first nuclear reactor. These are terms you will soon learn. So many things have been a positive advancement in science. Medicine and technologies that were intended to make life

better for mankind, not just this country. But there exists the intangible characteristics that can change the statement 'for the good of mankind' to 'the evil side of man'. Greed, selfishness, obstinance, arrogance, revenge, and hatred. The evil that lies within all of us is not always contained and has existed since the dawn of man. Our

173

thoughts will waiver when the desires of our hearts are contaminated. No person is immune to human nature. The differences we have encountered have not come without resistance, including in the political arena. If I may quote the Honorable Alexander Hamilton, 'Men often oppose a thing merely because they have no agency in planning it, or because it may have been planned by those whom they dislike.' I should also include the technology which brought you here."

Gouveneur Morris quipped, "That Hamilton is a saucy chap, isn't he?" The small crowd laughed.

He continued, "I invite you to walk throughout this garden. Take some time to think. Ask questions and clear up anything that comes to mind. We have passed on a hundred years of history to you in a very short time. When you are ready, we will continue with our lesson out here. It's a beautiful day, is it not? Sarah will be your next instructor."

"Dr. Benton, just a moment please." Sherman stepped a bit closer to him.

Roger Sherman, who had been rather quiet this morning and throughout this process, calmly raised his hand shoulder high to get the group to quiet down. When he had everyone's attention, he looked each man in the eye and then looked over at Dr. Carver Benton and said, "You have given each of us so much to think about. A person from our time could not fathom the amount of information we now possess, nor should we speak of it outside this group or we should be considered possessed by the devil himself. Moreover, we agreed to this encounter, and I do not hold you as solely responsible. It is not possible that we return to our time and not think about the future of these United States. The wonders and advancements we have seen are impressive. Quite astonishing, really. I'm concerned about two things, Dr. Benton. First, how do you expect us, a few congressional appointees, to change any of this? How do we prevent a growing government, which seems to move forward with what I must consider to be 'good intentions', but has not the foresight to return and demand responsibility to and by the people to maintain a small government? Government was never intended to be a babysitter. The men, and in your time women, who occupy their political seats appear to begin their time in office with a hope of change, but what are they changing? Government is not getting smaller, and the undue, mandatory costs to the people are rising. Bureaucrats aren't working themselves out of a job. What would you expect the five of us to do, Dr. Benton?

Benton replied with a question. "What *could* you do, sir? Progress cannot be stopped, but perhaps its direction can be changed. The impact of decisions made yesterday can change the outcome of tomorrow. Even if someone, as you said, had good intentions, how would one ever know the decision or indecision of yesterday could result in a hundred years of misery? What *would* you do, gentlemen, now that you have seen how our beloved country has changed? I applaud you, sir, on such foresight to ask such

175

direct questions, yet my answer is ever so simple in my mind. With respect to the change that I can control, I can now say that 'here stands a handful of the framers of our nation, standing in front of me.' I cannot effect any other change. Only the five of you may do such a thing. My answer is this, 'What will you do? What *can* you do?' The answers to these questions lie within each of you."

The men were quiet for just a moment. Then Alexander Hamilton stepped forward again. "I believe Dr. Benton is a true patriot. He is not demanding we take any action that we are not willing to take. He does not push any authority upon us. He has given us a window so that we may choose. However, *power* remains the one constant he still controls. He has brought us through time. A man with such power, who does not force it upon others, is truly humble indeed."

Sherman continued, "Dr. Benton, my second question may not be so easily discarded when searching for an answer. What would prevent you from initiating this action again until you get the desired results? And how sure are you that these results would be better than the present?" The group silently waited for the response.

Dr. Rayne had just taken a sip of coffee and set his cup down, then raised his hand to answer this question. Rayne gently gave a slight hand signal and all the travelers moved closer to the guests they were responsible for.

"If I may answer this question as clearly as I can. No one on this incredible team holds any power over you. Not Dr. Benton, not me, not any of us." Each traveler pulled the time travel device out of their pocket and held it out. "Each of you may return at any time you wish. As for the results of history and if they will change, we are all willing to bet our lives. Neither we nor you can guarantee we will be standing here. We will never know if we have a second chance. The choice remains yours, Your Honor." Rayne purposefully used Hamilton's title to imply that he retains the judgement of his own choices and what lies in the balance.

Dr. Benton added, "Please take the rest of the day to rest. Enjoy it. This garden is yours for as long as you wish. Your host traveler will accompany you and be at your disposal to answer any questions. I pray you have a blessed day, gentleman." Dr. Benton turned and left the group to themselves.

The remainder of the day was spent with all five statesmen walking or sitting in the garden with their traveler. Sarah Fleming was still flirting with Gouveneur Morris while answering his questions. The tension was high among the framers and she was hoping to do her part in easing any tensions with him. She felt she probably had the easiest of men to attend to.

Throughout the day, outside of the normal classroom atmosphere, the five continued asking questions. They may have had their doubts, but their curiosity and yearning for more aided in their queries. Eventually, the smaller conversations between two soon grew into all the travelers and statesmen sitting closer. The campfire setting was comfortable, and the information was free flowing. The five wished to continue discussions on the railroad expansion, the banking system, medical advancements, and so much more. There was an abundance of information to disperse. Hamilton asked if any of the topics covered had anything to do with the Constitution. Some did, and some did not. Dr. Rayne explained that much of the political structure would lightly reference the Constitution to justify its existence. The simplest of reasons for this are that lawyers or politicians will argue the Constitutionality of nearly any topic. Some of them argue for a single reason ~ it came from someone they didn't like ~ regardless of the topic or intent.

During this course of the day, the travelers remained focused and continued to add new categories to talk about. As with the good, so comes the evil. They discussed the underbelly of the country, including oppression, the mafia, cartels, gangs and gang violence, and their propensity to raise the crime rate. While the Constitution provides for the federal funds to protect the country, the state, county, and city governments remained as administrators for the number of police to help curb the criminal element ~ and it was never enough. The five were disgusted with the outrageous prison population in the year 2025. They were even more disgusted by the government allowing the prison system to become an overcrowded business. Dr. Rayne let the statesmen know this would be covered in a lesson of its own.

The outside weather remained beautiful. Food and drinks were served. While the day was meant to ease the stress and the overload of information, the five continued to learn. Nearing the end of the day, groups separated out again.

John Dickinson, known as the "Penman of the Revolution", was influential with the writing of the Articles of Confederation and famous for his "Letters from a farmer in Pennsylvania", which helped sway public opinion against laws enacted by British Parliament. He sat near the edge of the garden. He had brought his ink pen and began writing. His traveler, Charles Carson, sat at the next table. Dickinson stared at his paper for quite some time before his pen started moving.

Dickinson wrote, "*The hopes of a nation, through the advancement in science to bring forth men of the past, who framed liberty and freedom, into the present and give evidence of the fruit of their labors two hundred and fifty years later, are the immediate cause of these writings. How would a republic pen governing documents with respect to freedom and liberty and write them in such a way as to govern without dictation and provide for its citizens? The current bodies of writings, whether ratified documents or articles, maintained over the years still breathe life into this country. Along the way were many debates, drafts of petitions, and compromises. Great was the number of ill-success for petitions prior to the final drafts. We have learned that thousands upon thousands of lives were lost for all to gain the freedom enjoyed by the population of this land. There are those in position who have bastardized our terms and phrases to use for their* own subversive purpose, without regard for their true intent. How may we, the five of us, having had only a glimpse of the future, resolve the injustice for our constituents and defend privileges on behalf of their offspring?" Dickinson set his pen down and looked at Carson.

"Have we failed the sons and daughters of this land, Mr. Carson?"

"No, sir. The best that man can do is use all the information they have at that time to the fullness of their abilities. With that would come the number of men who are to agree in these decisions. It is the opinion of all of us who work here at this facility that the decisions that were made were done so, at the time, by the brightest minds in America's history, sir. We were not built overnight. This country did not change in the blink of an eye. However, it is the men and women who followed you who failed America. Whether it is impurity, selfishness, misguidance, or the greed of men and women ~ of your future law makers ~ it is we who have failed you, sir. Failed to carry on the intent, purposefully changed the direction, ignored the dreams, and cast aside the plans of a hopeful nation."

Dickinson, not really a man of emotion, remained silent. For just a moment, Carson thought he saw the hint of a tear forming in his right eye.

Chapter 16

Sarah began her lesson. She made mention of the previous day's event and asked the men to be prepared for war today.

- July 1914 – World War I began. The cause of the war is attributed to an assassination. However, historians from several countries have also blamed the rivalry between the stronger political powers which were in play. It wasn't until April 1917, two years after it started, when the U.S. reluctantly entered the war against Germany, thus turning the tide of lost souls. War changes everyone it touches. Nearly 18 months later, hostilities in World War I will end. After traveling to the Paris Peace Conference in December of 1918, President Woodrow Wilson made history as the first sitting president to go to Europe. The devastation of this war lasted until June 1919, ended by the signing of the Treaty of Versailles. Of the changes WWI created, President Woodrow Wilson may have summarized it best when he said, "Factories and homes were not destroyed in America. But the need for war material recharged manufacturing and production to an all-time high." Profits soared, and the U.S. emerged as an industrial leader on the world stage. But not everything was a positive outcome. This treaty punished Germany too much and became a precursor to WWII.

- After the war ended in 1919, the "Roaring Twenties" saw the wealthy continue to spend while corporations laid off workers or reduced wages to cover operating costs. Unions were formed, and workers would go on strike. In many places throughout the U.S., employment was competition between union and non-union workers. The unrest tripped the already unsteady feet of racism into riots. Unaware of what was on the horizon, America was spiraling downwards.

Sarah had shown the five statesmen several informational films of the history of WWI. Many of the questions were answered in the films but there were a few that Sarah fielded quite well. Several breaks and lunch had been taken. Sarah stayed until all the questions were answered and finally concluded her lesson nearly two hours after the dinner bell had rung.

The next morning, Sarah continued.

- Legislation was passed by Congress and signed by President Calvin Coolidge mandating that native-born Indians within the territory of the U.S. be granted full citizenship under the Indian Citizenship Act. The overall significance of this is that the Indian population was the first people to begin a heavy dependence on the U.S. government, but this was no fault of the Indian people. The whole of the problem lies with the government dictating to the Indians how they will live! It's no wonder this was a failure for the Indians as all their assets were controlled by a bureaucrat sitting in the state capital's Office of Indian affairs and administered by Washington, D.C.

Sarah commented, "Here's a rhetorical question. How would you like someone you've never met to control of all your financial and economic growth decisions by following regulations you had no decision in? In addition, they don't own the land they live on. Its U.S. land designated specifically for Indians on which to live, called a "reservation", for obvious reasons. The U.S. government owns and controls everything. With the perpetuation of the growing bureaucracy, the problem has no way of ending. My opinion is this: the government itself has created the first generational welfare. Questions?"

"Are you letting on that there are citizens who live off government funding?" Hamilton asked.

"Quite so, Your Honor. It is true that in certain times of the life of this country, particularly between 1929 to 1939, employment was so low there simply weren't any jobs. Employers were also struggling and letting good employees go as they couldn't afford to keep them. People were lining up in front of churches and in other lines to get government cheese, bread, or soup just to keep from starving. As times changed, the government kept handing out money or benefits to people who qualify."

"*Qualify*. Please explain?" asked Sherman bluntly.

"Yes. If a person or family had no income, or a low enough income, the government would subsidize their living from the tax money everyone pays."

"So, this 'income tax' is forcibly being paid to the federal government, who is redistributing these assets, to take care of its citizens who are, for any reason, otherwise unemployed. Is this the concept?" Morris suggested.

"In a manner of speaking, yes. In the 1930s, this was a life-saving program for many people. However, there are people in the 21st century who simply do not wish to work, or some who are just being dishonest and have continued to abuse this system. And when mothers, especially unwed mothers, have more children, the government allows them more money to feed and clothe them."

"My God! Why would the government not put a stop to this? Certainly, this was not meant to be a permanent solution. This is a downward spiral in all cases and nothing short of poor financial administration of funds," Hamilton quipped.

"It gets worse, sir. Remember, I mentioned generational welfare? The children of these parents grew up living on government assistance. Few of them have successfully broken the mold; however, many of them have learned to play the game with the government and continue to live off the tax-payers' money. They have learned this so well that many of the teenage children are having babies with the sole intent of being supported by the government. Obviously, they are not married, and I will add that unmarried mothers and mothers with more children qualify for more assistance than established married families where the father is present."

Sherman added, "Babies having babies and qualifying for permanent assistance?" "When did this country get lazy?" Madison asked in a quiet voice.

Sarah held up her hand as if to signify she had a direct answer for this very question. "Please understand I mean no disrespect. But, to be blunt, this country began to become 'lazy', as you call it, when the legal system exploited your own words in the Constitution."

"I beg your pardon, my dear!" exclaimed Dickinson.

"If I may, sir. The Constitution's preamble uses these words, 'promote the general welfare'. These words were written by none other than our friend here, Gouveneur Morris. Somewhere along the way, some person twisted these words and exploited their true meaning, then convinced others to do the same. There is no blame on Gouverneur Morris."

Morris' body language was such that everyone could tell he was about to speak defensively, until Sarah politely stopped him. "Listen," she said, "the laws changed. Legally. By the votes of the elected at that time. And in doing so, the government grew in responsibility over the people. And the people, especially the recipients of the welfare, were in favor. Today, the recipients are ever so much more in favor as many have the mindset of 'why get a job when the government pays you for doing nothing? '.

It isn't like that for every person, but it rings true more than most care to admit."

Sarah continued to explain, "The bureaucracy in Washington, D.C., tends to start programs in hopes of helping, but they never seem to plan for an ending to the program! It's as if they know they can appropriate the monies for a program, and therefore, keep themselves in a job. The bureaucrats *never* work themselves out of a job *and* still try to help people."

Hamilton gently raised his hand off the table in front of him and asked, "Is there an end in sight to stop some of this financial bleeding?"

"Councilor, you have been very instrumental in helping this country set up a stable working financial system. This is no secret to yourself, these men present, or other men in your own time. I can stand here today and tell you that this country is currently 30 trillion-plus dollars in debt."

"Dear God! Are you serious?" Morris exclaimed trying to fathom the enormity of the trillions of dollars.

"It's true, sir. I'd like to give you an exact number, but in 2025, the debt increases approximately $8,000.00 to $9,000.00 per second due to interest and spending. And we aren't even able to pay the interest without bonds, borrowing, or higher taxes."

The room was quiet for a moment.

Dickinson had been taking notes. *"Is it possible to have a governing body and allow it to run as a business and still perform its duties? A business, most cases, only survives*
186

with a profit. How does this government sleep at night, thinking their actions are acceptable and continue this ever-growing deficit? What would this cost in terms of the loss to the citizens? Would it gain them economic growth or economic loss and distention within communities? When do the states become responsible for their own? Does the responsibility of the poor rely with their own individual families or charity organizations? Do the people have the ability to determine where their tax dollars are spent?" He set his pen down and asked his last question.

"Ms. Fleming. Are the citizens allowed *not* to pay into this income tax?"

"This may be the one of the hardest questions to answer during your time with us, Your Honor," she began. "The taxation of citizens is an ever-changing and growing issue. It is the financial lifeblood of the government. This started with the Revenue Act of 1861 under President Lincoln. However, it changed with the ratification of the 16th Amendment in 1913. It quickly changed again by the government's financing the war efforts with the 1916 Revenue Act and the War Revenue Act of 1917. You have all agreed that financing a war is constitutional and very expensive. From here, the tax laws only grow, and taxation, of any kind, is a highly discussed topic. However, to answer your question, Your Honor," Sarah looked at Dickinson, "Yes, is your basic answer. There are citizens who choose to not pay and many who do not owe taxes."

Hamilton asked, "Are there other kinds of taxes? You mentioned income taxes, and we already understand property taxes. Will you share with us a short list?"

"Of course," she answered. "Not necessarily all are federal taxes, as some of you have mentioned the state becoming responsible for their own. Then local governments have joined in for obvious reasons. But a short list would include property, income, capital gains, sales and excise, payroll, customs, estate, gift, and death taxes. Many factors play into this answer, but largely, taxes are based on income. No income, or even minimum income, means no taxes due. Other tax laws, loopholes, credits, and such now exist in 2025, which, over many years, have caused an incredibly complex mathematical equation resulting in returning some dollars back into the pockets of people. But, if you are a gainfully employed citizen and receive a paycheck, you will be taxed."

"Additionally, since 1955, April 15th of each year has been designated the date for all citizens to settle their debt to the IRS. That's the government entity responsible for collecting and dispersing monies based on income. If you owe money and do not pay, the penalty could be fines, or, in some cases, prison; but rest assured, the government will come after you. It's not a choice. Much like a thief with a knife at your throat, they will take your money. Nor do the people have any say where their monies are spent. That same thief is not going to ask you where you want your money to go. He will spend it where he wishes. When you pay into the system, the system decides where to spend your money, whether you like it or not. Your tax dollars may fund the military or clinics performing abortions. You don't get the choice because it's not your money anymore, as the government sees it."

Morris added, "In the event other options are presented, what do you believe would be a better choice over any other?"

Sarah stopped to think for a moment. "I'm not sure I can answer that question satisfactorily, but I would offer this: how much federal income would be derived if the government taxed consumables?   Think of it this way: taxing consumables would allow everyone, including those who only use cash, to fairly pay federal taxes. I'm sure there would be a few essential consumables that could be tax exempt.   Some states already do this over and above the individual income tax, and some even have a higher tax on alcohol and cigarettes." Sarah paused to consider, then continued, "I also believe a flat rate tax for everyone could be a solution."   Sarah took the time to explain her thoughts a bit more and decided to bring the conversation to a close.

"Gentlemen, these are my opinions, which you have requested. Whether they are good or bad, they are mine and they are shared by many who truly wish for a correction to the problem. I'm sure there may be minor flaws with them, and I don't know how to put it all into action.   That would be up to the elected officials to make the necessary changes, wouldn't you say?"

The room discussed taxation for a while longer before they took a short break.

When they returned, Sarah moved forward with her lesson.

October 1929 ~ The 1929 Stock Market crashed. The bottom fell out of stock prices between 1929 and 1931, with an estimated $50 billion in losses creating America's worst economic depression.

Sarah started a new film detailing more information and depicting the living conditions of many Americans. Following the hour-long film, the group discussed several events occurring within and after this time, including an estimated 650 bank failures, an unemployment rate upwards of 25%, an increase in crime and stabilization of the mafia, the increase in the homeless population, and the collapse of America's economy to nearly half of what it was, all by 1933. Sarah Fleming also noted that, in the wake of America's Great Depression, the global economy was also affected by the decrease in the U.S. GDP (gross domestic production).

The group took a break for lunch and returned to find Paul Tesla at the helm of the classroom. The five were getting used to the teachers taking turns. Paul began where Sarah left off by starting another film discussing the reactions to the depression by the 32nd President of the United States, Franklin D. Roosevelt, and the New Deal.

- November 1932 ~ Democrat candidate Franklin D. Roosevelt wins the presidential election for his first of a prodigious four terms. In the following year, Congress passes the economic program called the New Deal during a limited one hundred-day session specifically designed to discuss the depression era economics. However, the First New Deal did not perform as expected.

- August 1935 ~ From efforts later providing the groundwork for the modern welfare system, Congress and the Second New Deal helped pass the Social Security Act into law. The primary concept was to provide aid for the unemployed, the elderly, and children.

Paul Tesla and the five statesmen discussed the concept of the Social Security Act for the remainder of the afternoon. They looked at the history of economic resources and maintaining a secure economy.

The Social Security Act legislated certain welfare programs and was designed to aid elderly individuals in saving money as a supplement to their own savings upon retirement. Paul maintained the opinion that, unfortunately, many treated it as a solitary retirement.

After a bit more conversation was processed by the five, they decided to call it a day. While walking back to the room, the statesmen's conversation had harsh overtones, in contrast to the decisions of the lawmakers in the 1930s. So many people trying so hard to eke out a living. How could any governing body make a "right" decision?

The day ended with concerns on the minds of the statesmen.

Chapter 17

Dr. Rayne and Dr. Benton sat in the back of the classroom. No words were spoken as the five statesmen took to their seats. They could tell they were about to watch another film from the projector. The classroom décor had not changed. Dr. Rayne turned out the lights and started the film.

- December 7, 1941 ~ On a quiet morning, sailors on the shore of Pearl Harbor, Hawaii, gathered in routine duties. The air was crisp while the sun was shining with the promise of another day in paradise. However, at 7:55 AM, the Imperial Japanese fighter pilots, who had been airborne for some time, found little in the way of defenses as they attacked and devastated the U.S. Pacific fleet. Over 2,300 military lives were lost on this day, with 1,177 coming from one U.S. ship alone, leaving the history books to record the greatest loss of American lives in a single act of war. The following day, America declares war on her aggressor, Japan, and enters World War II.

- December 11, 1941 ~ Just 4 days later, Italy and Germany, who partnered with Japan, also declared war on the U.S. America would fight on two fronts for as long as humanly possible.

The five statesmen watched the educational films all morning long. The information was captivating, as well as overwhelming.

James Madison wrote several notes upon the paper in front of him, describing his own thoughts of how miraculous it had been that both World Wars have involved the United States, but, except for Hawaii, not on American soil. He wondered how long such a miracle could last.

Dickinson also continued to take notes, and his thoughts invariably supported his preconceived notion that the U.S. needed to have a better foothold on how to govern before the Constitution was ratified. His confidence, while bolstered by many of the advances in technology, medicine, and other subjects, was not upheld by the gross negligence of politics or the selfishness of those who sat in power. His eyes could only see reaction and not the proactive balance of an economic and political machine.

- June 1943 ~ As an aside to the war efforts, the climate in Harlem, NY, and Detroit, MI, produced race riots. America was still fighting within itself while still sending troops abroad.

Madison's eyebrows furrowed when he spoke, "I don't give a damn what color their skin is! These men are obviously able-bodied men who should fight. Why the hell don't they fight for their country? If they are so angered about freedoms, they should have put forth efforts toward the freedom of the United States. If they don't want to fight for their country, they could live elsewhere! It is evident to me from your history lessons that many people, except slaves, have properly immigrated to this land for a better life in America. But, if this country is engaged in war efforts, then that's where they should focus. Lives will be lost. Freedom is not free, gentlemen."

Sherman replied with a quiet confidence, "I agree with your point of view, Councilor, but I will add that the riots did not solve anything in my opinion. Even in the military, there were discontented black soldiers. It appears they were ill-treated within the ranks. While there is surely unrest in their home cities, my opinion is the same as yours, my friend: we all bleed red. We've seen this in our own time."

The lesson continued:

- June 1944 ~ Known as D-Day, over 155,000 soldiers from eleven Allied nations (Australia, Belgium, Canada, Czechoslovakia, France, Greece, the Netherlands, New Zealand, Norway, Poland, and the United Kingdom) and America's military, engaged in the Invasion of Normandy. World War II's invasion of Europe began when Allied troops stormed France's beaches, eventually freeing Paris from the opposition.

- February 1945 ~ A five week battle occurred at Iwo Jima, just south of Tokyo, Japan, led by thirty thousand U.S. Marines. The following April would see the start of the Battle of Okinawa, which would last until late in June.

- May 1945 ~ The battles in Europe came to a close with the unconditional surrender of Germany.

- August 1945 - The war continued with Japan until President Harry S. Truman approved the bombing of Hiroshima with the world's first atomic bomb. Technology had advanced enough that a single bomb could destroy an entire city. On August 15, nine days after the first bomb was let loose, Emperor Hirohito surrendered.

As the men watched the film displaying the mushroom-shaped cloud, their eyes fixated on the scene in front of them ~ a huge mushroom cloud. Quietly, Morris's thoughts came out, "Hell on earth." Dickinson nodded his head in agreement.

"Certainly, hell for those who survived for a time. They may have wished for a quicker death," Madison answered.

"There is no secret here, gentlemen," Hamilton started. "War is a place one should never wish to go. However, one should always be well prepared for it. I hold to my opinion that the United States should be ready to defend her interests. I can see here that this reluctant president wished to end this war, and end it he did," Hamilton added in a humble manner.

Roger Sherman sat quietly. A single tear slowly formed and fell to the floor.

Dr. Rayne calmly noted each statesman's reaction. After a few moments, Dr. Rayne interrupted the silent room, "Let's take a short break, gentlemen. We have a room set up just down the hall, with items of this war that you may find interesting. You may take all the time you need to look through this quasi-museum, and, as always, we will be nearby to answer questions." After lunch and a couple hours of 'show and tell' with war artifacts, the class was reconvened.

Dr. Rayne moved forward with the lesson.

"Councilors, one last bit of fighting before we move to a lighter subject. The United States and other countries, in an attempt to recover from these recent events, created an organization: The United Nations. The premise of this group of countries is to stand together, supporting and defending each other when necessary.
NATO (North American Treaty Organization), which consists of the United States,
Canada, Belgium, Denmark, France, Iceland, Italy, Luxembourg, Netherlands, Norway, Portugal, and the United Kingdom, was designed to let the world know that any attack on a member of this organization was an attack on all of the them.

"This did not prevent the United States from entering into yet another war, but the intentions were not to defend the U.S.; it was the defense of another interest - aid to another
197

country. This three-year conflict, beginning in 1950, was called the Korean Conflict. The U.S. took the position to fight with South Korea against its neighboring country, North Korea, who were supported by weapons supplied by the Soviets and China. In July of 1953, an armistice agreement was signed, ending the fighting."

The group's discussion of democracy versus communism came to a close rather quickly, with the group agreeing the former was the best preference.

Dr. Rayne felt it was time to slowly switch gears away from the years of fighting and destruction to a new product that has, over time, changed the shape of American values.

Chapter 18

Rayne refocused the group, "And, now, to a lighter subject. I do have a film for you to see, but this time it will be a little different. In today's exhibition, you will notice the advancement of technology as you will be able to watch this film on a color television." Rayne briefly explained the history of television. Gouveneur Morris found this to be quite interesting, while Hamilton and Madison were not so captivated by the idea.

Hamilton voiced his thoughts, "Who would have time to sit and watch this 'television' when there would be so much work to be done?"

Madison interjected, "Agreed! I find it hard enough to complete my current duties on the farm without adding a distraction such as this contraption."

Sherman asked a question, "Could it be that a family could enjoy each other's company for a short time, doing something which may mentally distract them from whatever may have them in a poor attitude? I feel confident that this 'contraption', as you call it, will prove to be entertaining and," Sherman paused for a moment, "informative. I say this with some surety as the films we have recently witnessed have given me both."

Dr. Rayne continued, "Thank you all for your thoughts, gentlemen. All of these sentiments have been true in the lives of many. However, let me discuss this in economic terms. The changes in the communications industry, which include television, radio, telephone, internet, and cell phones, have changed the face of the world, not just the United States. At one point, families were considered privileged if they had but one television in their home.

"Before television, families used to sit in their living rooms gathered around a radio and listened to news or entertaining shows. This industry has produced hundreds of thousands of jobs in manufacturing these devices and for people who produced the shows for entertainment, and generated revenue for shop owners who sold the products. The advancements in this single industry alone have, in my opinion, had more of an impact on the world than any other. People need and desire communications with others, albeit person to person or country to country.

"In your time, hand-written mail would be taken by messenger and, depending on the location of the one to whom you are sending the letter, may have taken days, weeks or months to arrive. In this century, we can use the telephone and speak to another party in another country instantly. However, let's not get too far ahead of ourselves."

The television had been sitting in the back of the room for this morning's presentation. Dr. Rayne and Paul Tesla had previously fixed wheels to the bottom of the large, wooden cabinet, console-style TV and now pushed it to the front of the room.

The statesmen's reactions remained calm, but Dr. Rayne could sense their imaginations were spinning. Eyebrows raised. They would be wondering how a wooden box with a piece of glass in the front could show a film in such a manner. It was just a few days ago they learned of using light and still pictures to create a film. Now, the film would show up in what looked like a polished, fancy crate.

Rayne reached down to turn the knob on the television and said, "Gentlemen, please enjoy the show."

The documentary started in black and white while discussing the history of the phonograph in 1877, followed by that of movies and theatres in the mid-1890s. Nearly 20 years later, the shortwave radio was in use. The documentary's narrator made note of how much time passed between major changes in the industry and then introduced the 1920 invention of Technicolor used in movies. It was at this point that the film slowly turned to color.

Dr. Rayne watched the statesmen's reactions. Dickinson clapped his hands together and was the first to comment, "Amazing! Simply amazing." The other four followed his example with smiles and small comments as the film continued.

- FM radio in 1929
- Pinball machines and the Jukebox in the early 1930s
- Broadcast television and record players in the 1940s
- Transistor radio and color television in the early 1950s

- From the early 1950s to mid-1960s, color televisions, stereo phonographs, and large console video games became popular.

- As the economy changed, the 1970s showed more homes began to have more than one television.

- VCRs (video cassette recorders) were introduced in the mid 1970's while CDs (compact discs) were introduced within the next five years.

The narrator concluded by mentioning these products were produced in the United States until U.S.-based manufacturing companies learned that 1.3 billion Chinese would build these items for a fraction of the cost of U.S. labor.

When the documentary finished, Rayne said, "By now, you have realized we are not trying to focus only on political history, but also to give you a wider perspective of the phases our country has experienced."

Dickinson began, "Dr. Rayne, will there be a point when you will be taking us on another outing? I do so love the fresh air, and I would love to see how the citizens live during this time. Is this possible?"

Gouveneur Morris chimed in, "I, too, would be interested in this."

Hamilton and Madison nodded in agreement, while Sherman remained still. Sherman's lack of agreement did not go unnoticed.

Dr. Benton had left the room earlier to complete work in his office not far down the hall. J.A.S.P.E.R. said, "Sir, there may be developments in the classroom that require your attention. You should head there immediately."

"Very well," Benton answered and made his way down the hall. "What is the nature of the situation?"

J.A.S.P.E.R. answered, "Leaving the facility, sir."

In the classroom, Rayne spoke, "Senator Sherman?" Rayne paused for a moment then continued, "Are you abstaining, sir? Would you prefer to stay here and possibly learn more of a different perspective? We have many subjects available, and I would be more than happy to stay and talk to you about any of them."

Sherman intentionally looked at each man in the room and then stood up. With his hands clasped in front of him, he answered the question, "Gentlemen, I contend that I am curious to see the real lives of citizens in their current habitat. This would certainly prove to be interesting; however, I find myself with a conjecture. I cannot make this any simpler ~ I fear I will not like what I see."

Hamilton commented, "Inclusive of all the information we have been given, Councilor, I'm damn sure I will not like what I see in its totality. But there are many things in this world that I do not care for, and the world does not see things as I do. I tend to look at the grand picture of how things should be, and considering the information our new esteemed educators have shared with us, this United States has, over time, slowly changed from a people coming together to a people who think apart from the whole of the country. Albeit due to race or gender or any number of other aspects of individuality. These are our differences, Senator. And this is a nation of very different nationalities, cultures, and desires. I would implore you, sir, to come with us. Let's you and I, and these gentlemen, explore this 'new country' with our old eyes and experience something new. Senator Sherman, I hold your opinion high, sir, and I freely admit that, while we do not always agree, yours is one opinion that helps me define my own. You and I are similar, as two sides of a coin, sir, but we are the same coin."

As Benton walked into the room, he saw Sherman nodding toward Hamilton in what appeared to be a gesture of thanks.

Madison joined in, "I, too, have the same sentiments as you both. I expect my attitude to be a mixture of curiosity, confusion, and anger. I hope to gain some understanding along the way however, come what may. I was convinced from the beginning by Dr. Rayne that our country, gentlemen, while still standing, has lost her footing from time to time, and he believes she needs our help. I'm willing to endure the coming emotions and lend a hand. I would very much like to see all of you continue on this journey with me."

Dickinson had previously overcome his doubts about staying and simply nodded his agreement. Following Dickinson's lead, Morris also nodded in approval.

"Hello, Dr. Benton," Rayne said. "We were just discussing the probable emotions of anger and confusion when we have our next field day trip outside this facility."

"I see," Benton replied. "If the question is 'Will we be leaving the facility again?', the answer is 'soon'. Our first field day was quite a bit easier due to the location and a few other logistics. For us to see other places, I will need to complete a few more details. Rest assured, gentlemen, we *will* be leaving again, and to give you an idea of potential locations, here is a short list: a visit to a Senate hearing so you can see exactly what takes place. Or would you care to watch medical advancements during a live surgery? Perhaps a walk down Chestnut street in Philadelphia, just to see the changes and preservations of the area. We've considered a visit to a naval ship to meet the men on board who are willing to die for their country and then take a drive near downtown Washington, D.C., and see how many homeless live in America's capital city. In the political arena, would you care to visit a hearing in the Supreme Court? However, I would be remiss if I did not ask you to add to our list from your own thoughts. Please think about this for a while, and we will return to this subject and hear your ideas.

"Gentlemen, you have been bombarded with so much information in such a short time. Please, take the rest of the day and think about what it is you would wish to see in the future. Without giving you details concerning your own personal lives or those of your family, we are willing and able to show you nearly anything."

205

Dr. Rayne jumped in the conversation, "If I were a betting man, that sounded like the dinner bell, and I, for one, could eat a horse." The group of men laughed, left the classroom, and began closing out the day with the evening meal. The five senators met in the garden after dinner.

"The days are getting longer here, sitting in the classroom and being filled with 'historical information'," Morris said.

Dickinson added, "I do feel as though I have an advanced degree in history, yet none of it will ever come true in my lifetime."

"Yes," Hamilton quipped. "I know more about the future and am still so unsure of my present decisions. The pressure of our decisions is illuminated more now than ever. I did not expect to feel so overwhelmed."

Sherman spoke his mind and said, "And you wondered why I was considering going back before we have completed our quest ~ if a quest is what we are doing here. I not only feel anger at what I am seeing, I also feel confused as to what I can do to change any of it. Men and women seem to be so much more informed about what happens by the use of these telephones, televisions, and radios, yet they are only concerned about their own households. Gentlemen, how do we right the future wrongs by living in the past? I'm an old man, and I feel older now than ever."

James Madison stood on the outskirts of the circle of conversation. His eyes were looking off towards the western sky and the sunshine it provided. His small stature wasn't a factor as he turned toward the group of men. "All of us are men who purpose to complete a task. We live intentionally with the desire to help this country survive and be better tomorrow than it was the day before. We will eventually go back to the past and live our lives the way God intended. I, for one, believe God allowed us *this* time to learn. To grow. To aspire to be more than ourselves and yes, Mr. Sherman, complete a quest that we never expected.

"We have more to learn. We may be full of new information, but it's information we never would have learned if not for this group of scientists. They mean well, and I believe they have good hearts. Do you not understand? Their dream is the same dream as yours and mine. They dream of a free country. They dream of a society where people get up and work hard to raise a family, a society whose government is not the cause of a failing economy or allows those citizens who do not participate in its growth to be the downfall, draining its resources. They have the same dream! Gentlemen, we can do no less than continue to learn and try to understand the question that plagues the five of us. *What can we do about it?*

"We choose to stay. As I have chosen to be present in the Second Continental Congress, I choose to be present in this day and perform for my country. What say you?"

"Aye," said Dickinson.

"Aye," said Hamilton.

"Aye," said Morris. "And as everything they have said has come to pass, I can only take as a true statement that we will return to our own time just moments after we left. Which means we return with the knowledge to make our country more than we ever expected."

Roger Sherman looked at his colleagues, and his eyes stopped on James Madison. His answer did not arrive quickly, but its delivery was clear. "Aye."

Back inside the facility, Dr. Benton worried. Maybe it *was* time to take them into the real world and let them experience the sights, sounds, and culture of what has become America. This, of course, had always been his intention but not necessarily at this point in the process. Yet, he couldn't ignore their verbalized wishes and curiosities. Besides, they have done much better than he thought they would with their acceptance of the vehicles, guns, and other inventions they have discovered up to this point. Benton wondered if they could handle the shock of today's city life, having come into it with such limited knowledge. Was more history required? Certainly, more information would help their understanding of today's America.

Dr. Benton decided to have a private meeting later that evening with Dr. Rayne and their fellow travelers to discuss the latest developments and the attitudes of the statesmen.

When that time came, everyone knew the subject of the meeting, and Sarah wasn't waiting to voice her opinion.

"These men are soaking up the history, but they are chomping at the bit to go out and see what has become of America. They're curious. I also think they don't have the patience to sit in the classroom. Let's change it up, take them out and give them what they really want….to see America firsthand," Sarah said bluntly.

Rayne played devil's advocate and responded, "Yes, but they haven't heard some of the latest parts of history. I don't believe they would want to be dumped in the middle of Times Square and told to fend for themselves."

"They are probably better prepared than we believe. There are congressmen who are holding office today who don't know as much history as our guests do now!" added Paul. "What difference would it make?"

"Good point, Paul," Charles agreed. "Does it matter that they know how America started and," gesturing with his hands, "…and now they know a little about the middle, but the point is they don't know *everything*. And they won't ever know everything. We can't give them everything. Some of this must be spontaneous questioning so we can teach them the events they are interested in. I mean, we've been teaching them a lot! And it is all very good information, but can't you see? They are a bit tired of war-after-war, and they had a very, very good day when we showed them planes, trucks, and cars. I think they are ready for some outdoor activities."

Benton was digesting the conversation when they all heard the knock at the door. Benton got up from his chair and opened it.   There stood Gouveneur Morris. "May I come in?"

"Of course." Benton waved the man into the room.

"Sometimes I'm a light sleeper, especially, when I'm making important decisions. I can't sleep the night before. This is such a night.   My father raised me to tell people what I think, and in doing so, I lose the eloquence that you have heard from my fellow statesmen. Aside from being a light sleeper, I also have quite good hearing.   As I approached this door, I couldn't help but overhear the subject of your conversation, and so I stopped at the door before knocking to be sure I would not be out of turn to tell you this: it would be unwise to let myself or my companions be unleashed into your world without a bit more information. History will not change in the time it will take for us to hear it.   We are, as you say, impatient. However, we are also men who want information before making decisions.   Among the five who came on this journey, there are some who have fought in wars as high-ranked officers and some who have waged political battles.   Not a single one of us would wish to *not* be as informed as possible. We may be impatient, but we know what it is to be prepared.   We have shouldered the responsibilities afforded to us in the time of our own living and collectively have come with a great amount of education and tenacity to win the battles put in our path. However, to comment on your opinion, Mr. Tesla, there is no difference.   This journey is not a battle as such, where warfare has come, all too familiar with the blood shed on the fields. No guns shall be lifted by these hands in this time; however, a battle it remains. Neither I nor my companions have yet to understand how to defeat the shortcomings and disappointments of the future to assure America's freedoms and liberties are not torn apart from the inside. We do not have the intellectual tools for this just yet. Therefore, do not let us down, and do not let our country down by..." Morris paused and looked at Dr. Rayne. "How did you say it, Dr. Rayne? 'Dumping them in Times Square.'"

Dr. Rayne grinned at the comment and raised his hand slightly, "May I ask a question, sir?"

"It is one way to find answers," came the reply.

"What is it that you would like to see in this new world?"

"My answer could be an oration; however, in the interest of time and the desire for sleep, I will say this: progress. I'm well aware there are various definitions, degrees, and subjects for what I seek. Some we have seen in terms of craftsmanship, ideas for the common good, medicines, transportation, and much more. Your classroom itself is impressive. Time may have continued forward, Dr. Rayne, but that is not a guarantee of progress. With matters of law and government, America has fallen short. In many ways, the government has failed the people of these United States. The insurmountable volume of law that has been passed is only an example. You may have created more words on paper, but I do not see this as forward progress. I see this as more confusion, more control over the people. That, sir, is not progress. What you have

211

shown me thus far has already presented itself; therefore, I expect more. I also wish to see Ms. Fleming at a dinner table as my guest, along with a bottle of fine wine." Sarah turned a slight shade of red as he looked directly at her during his last comment.

Dr. Benton stepped forward and said, "Thank you for your insight, Councilor. I believe you have helped us conclude this conversation. Good night, sir."

"Good evening to you all." Morris left the room to return to his own.

"That man is as insightful of a person as I have ever known," Charles said.

"In any event," Benton said, "he has made our option easier. I will see you in class in the morning. One more thing: Ms. Fleming, feel free to take him to dinner when we are in town. I think he's looking forward to it." The men in the room started quietly clapping their hands in agreement with Dr. Benton, and everyone could see the corners of her mouth rise into a shy smile.

Chapter 19

The five were sitting in the same chairs as they were the previous day. The classroom hadn't changed much. Benton's thoughts of changing the room after last night's conversation weren't as reflective as their attitude so he left the room as it was. He hoped today would show more promise.

Sarah stood at the front of the classroom today. "Let's get started, shall we?"

"Gentlemen let me just take a moment to comment that race riots, which we discussed yesterday, were certainly everywhere across America during this time. I will also add that in the future, that is, further into the future of what you are learning, even up to 2025, people still cry out on the platform of racism. Whether their reason for claiming an issue deals with racism is true or not, it is a powerful platform. People want to be heard. In the cases where it is truly founded, it should be addressed. Sadly, these are the cases that form the precedence for more legislation. In the cases where it isn't founded, where the claim is supported by lies, it's more about the money one might make from taking the case to court, and there are thousands of these cases in the judicial system. However, let's move on while you ponder those thoughts."

Sarah moved on with the lesson, "We are moving into the mid-1900's and things are changing at a rapid pace. Today, we will cover a lot of ground and I suspect eyebrows to raise, grimaces on faces and maybe even a fist slammed on to your desks but remember this ~ you are not the first to be upset nor the first to be glad with the some of these outcomes. Let's continue..."

- January 1958 - Cape Canaveral launches the first U.S. space satellite, Explorer I.

- July 1960 – Hawaii is recognized as the 50th state when the fifty-star flag is raised in Philadelphia, PA.

- August 1963 – Civil Rights were still in turmoil when Dr. Martin Luther King delivered a speech entitled "I Have a Dream." He stood at the steps of the Lincoln Memorial in Washington D.C. possibly to commemorate President Lincoln's dreams.

- November 22, 1963 - President John F. Kennedy is assassinated.

- June 1964 – Potentially stemming from Dr. Martin Luther King's speech, legislation is passed banning discrimination in voting, jobs and accommodations.

- 1965 – President Lyndon B. Johnson introduced 'The Great Society' as a domestic program. The concept's goal was to eliminate racial injustice and discrimination by addressing the spending characteristics of rural poverty, transportation, medical care and education. Of the few pieces of legislation passed during Johnson's presidency, the Civil Rights Act of 1964 was among them.

- October 1967 – The first black Supreme Court Justice, Thurgood Marshall is sworn into office.

214

- July 1969 – The United States Apollo (Space) program is successful when Neil Armstrong becomes the first man on the moon.

The five statesmen were quite astounded with this news.

Madison began, "It took scientists, such as yourselves, a bit over 10 years to figure out how to keep humans alive in space, land on the moon and bring them back. This is such an achievement."

"Yes, sir. It is," Sarah replied. "It remains my own opinion that this achievement was the last major push within our government, namely NASA, to set a long-term goal. The space program was set on a fast pace to beat the Russians. So many programs come from shallow thoughts of grandeur and no follow through in the government these days but this...this was a culmination of hopes by mathematicians, biologists, scientists, men and women who put their private lives on hold and worked countless hours to culminate in that moment. Landing a space craft on the moon, carrying a payload of men, and allowing them to step on the surface, and return home safely. It truly is an amazing accomplishment."

Dickinson was a bit smug in his comment, "This really happened? This isn't one of those 'movie making' films simply for entertainment?"

"It isn't an odd thing you ask, Mr. Dickinson. Many people throughout the years have made the same notations as you however, it is true. Americans have walked on the moon."

In efforts to combat Dickinson's rejections of history, Hamilton added, "John, you are sitting in a chair in the year 2025, learning of the future." Hamilton turned his gaze back to Sarah. "Your group of scientists here today, how long did it take to create your time travel device?"

"Many years. It has been Dr. Benton's life's work. Technology has come so far, sir. And we are about to cover the person most likely responsible for the growth of technology.

- November 1976 – Bill Gates registers the trademark of Microsoft.

"For this bit of history, I would like to add my opinion that without this particular man's efforts into the growth of the computer, technology would not be where it is today. This device has allowed men, women and children to put forth their own efforts into technology. Those with the desire were able to dream of things that no one else had and the computer, with its intricate processors and incredible ways of making calculations faster than the human brain. Games were built for entertainment. While that may prove to be addictive to some and result in people who don't produce anything, it could also be that the skills learned from the games were used by those who entered the military and remotely flew 'drone' or planes without pilots over parts of the world.

Along with personal computers, the development of the Internet has exponentially allowed communications, in many forms, to be nearly instantaneous.

"Gentlemen," Fleming continued. "I'd like to introduce you to a friend of ours.

His name is J.A.S.P.E.R. His name is just an acronym that stands for Just Another Super Powered Educated Response. He is a computer program. He is Artificial Intelligence or A.I. He is also a program that helped us to create the machines that allowed us to bring you here to our time. Programs, such as J.A.S.P.E.R., have been around for a while now, but Dr. Benton, with his unusual skills and connections, has helped his program do so much more.

Since you arrived, J.A.S.P.E.R. has been passively monitoring you. He is able to tell us your heart rate and blood pressure without touching you. He can have conversations with each of you at the same time. He can calculate any mathematical problem and give you an immediate answer or he can, if requested, make suggestions on courses of action and give the probability of success based on your decision. He is remarkable. Would you like to meet him?"

Hamilton spoke first, "Are you telling me that we have been watched the entire time we have been here."

"Mr. Hamilton, within your own privacy areas of this facility, J.A.S.P.E.R. is not watching. However, within this classroom, the garden area, when we were out looking at the vehicles and flying in the plane, J.A.S.P.E.R. was monitoring your vital signs as per orders from Dr. Benton. You see, you are only 'on loan' from the past. We have a responsibility to keep you safe and healthy so that we may return you to the past."

217

"I see," he replied.

Dickinson spoke next, "From your description, I think this computer machine gizmo might be something of value. You say it will talk to us?"

"Yes, sir. Allow me to introduce all of you to J.A.S.P.E.R. Please say 'Hello' to our guests J.A.S.P.E.R.

"Good afternoon, gentlemen. It is my pleasure to continue to aid you in your safety, well-being and education during your stay with us in the year 2025. I have memorized your voice prints so that you may ask me any questions you wish, and I will do my best to provide you with the best possible answers," answered J.A.S.P.E.R.

The men began looking around the room for where the voice was coming from.

J.A.S.P.E.R. said, "My voice is coming from 18 different speakers in this room. There are hundreds of speakers in this complex for me to listen to you and so I can speak with you. I will be happy to entertain any questions you may have however, for now, I will let Ms. Sarah Fleming continue her lessons."

Roger Sherman asked, "J.A.S.P.E.R. just about gave me a heart attack! This future of yours continues to surprise me. I do have one question if I may Mr. J.A.S.P.E.R.?"

J.A.S.P.E.R. replied, "Of course, sir."

Sherman asked, "You are a computer program that can entertain a conversation over any subject, correct?"

"Yes, sir," came the reply.

"And we were brought here, with your help, is that also correct?"

"Yes, sir."

"When we return to our time, if we were to enact some sort of document, law, article or writing of such a nature that prevents you from becoming a reality, wouldn't you wish to stop us from doing that?"

"Great question, your Honor. The answer is no. My existence is to serve humans, not myself. I do not have 'feelings', but I have been known to have insight. It would be my insight that when you do return and, if such documents come to fruition, I will not ever have known. Therefore, I must maintain my answer as no. Please, do whatever is necessary to help make America great again," J.A.S.P.E.R. concluded.

Sarah questioned the group, "Anyone else have a question or comment?"

"Yes," said Gouveneur Morris. "Just a simple 'Thank you', J.A.S.P.E.R." "My pleasure, Councilor," came J.A.S.P.E.R.'s reply.
Sarah continued, "Mr. Madison? Anything to add?"

"Very well," Madison started. "I've been listening to all the remarks in the room, and I can only surmise that from this time forward J.A.S.P.E.R. will be a training aid. Will he be leading our classes as well? If he, she or it, can handle all of the information that you know, and more, wouldn't it be wise to allow him to teach us everything else you wish to share?"

"We have discussed this very question and we feel it would be impersonal.
J.A.S.P.E.R. is an invaluable tool without question, but we will continue to lead the discussions.   However, when lessons are completed, and you still wish to do more learning, he is available," Sarah replied.

"Good," replied Madison.   "I like this J.A.S.P.E.R. but, I think, I prefer to talk to a person. It looks rather insane to speak to a wall and have it talk back to you.   I believe Judge Sherman might agree."   Sherman slowly bobbed his head in agreement.

"Understood, sir," J.A.S.P.E.R. replied.

The men in the room laughed for a moment but nodded in agreement.

Sarah started the class again by saying, "Very well, gentlemen, let us continue. My hopes are that Dr. Benton has figured out a way to get us into the city to see some sites and have some hands-on experiences but, first, we need to tell you about circumstances to try to better understand why our country has become what we have become."

"Let's move into the 1980's," she said. "In this decade we will find the United States in financial difficulty."

- April 1983- President Ronald Reagan signed the proposed legislation designed to keep the unstable Social Security system out of bankruptcy.

Hamilton's understanding of finances was set on fire before he spoke, "I believe you mentioned this governmental financial plan is funded by the people. I also recollect that this system was put in place around 1935. Which tells me several things: first, in less than 50 years this plan has begun to fail. Second, you've been informing us on the census and by now the fifty states should be overpopulated by over 200 million citizens. I fear that your population of those who have paid into the dependent program will not equal those who will be accepting such benefits. If this is to be a long-term program, the trustees of such a program should be investing a portion of such monies for profit, if not, I fear this program will self-destruct."

Madison chimed in, "This concept of a publicly funded program is that citizens pay into it and expect to be paid from it at some certain age, is that right?"

Hamilton replied, "That is the base of the concept."

Madison, "Why in God's name would anyone let the government hold on to their personal money? Can't they save it themselves? Do they not have the fortitude to think about their future and that of their children by controlling their own banking? We all understand taxation for a government to carry out its duties to the country, but I would never allow them to determine my financial future."

Roger Sherman added, "My wife and I have many children together. We work hard for what we have and appreciate many things in life. I've invested in several things over time and have come to find that not all my investments have been great choices, however, those were my decisions, and I have corrected such. I would sooner teach my children to work my finances than let a government decide my financial state. I can only wonder what will happen when the amount of monies deposited will not be enough for those who are dependent on it. It appears as though citizens are using this system as a life savings program. I believe this to be unwise."

Hamilton agreed, "As do I. If what we have just said is correct, this President Reagan may have only extended the date of this self-destruction. It may be foresight on his part, but it may have also kept the country from other catastrophes. People do not change much as a whole. Societies throughout history have always sustained an economy with the rich and the poor and those in between. Regardless of one's financial standing in the community, I fear this Social Security program is pandering to needy individuals. Individuals perhaps without supportive family members. Citizens with a meager living but, a living, nevertheless. I agree with my fellow statesmen here that this program has created a dependency of which I do not agree."

Dickinson nodded in agreement when Gouveneur Morris said, "Gentlemen, I cannot speak towards the finances of others except to say it is incumbent for those who control the purse strings to be accountable. It appears this Social

Security system administrators, be it congressional or not, have done a poor job of growing the available funds by other means than the required input from the citizens."

Paul Tesla had walked into the room near the beginning of this discussion and raised his hand in a gesture of adding to it. He said, "If I may, I would say that I am in favor of the Social Security system we have in place. My grandparents never had much money or social standing. They did what they could to make a living and taught my parents how to save. However, when the economy began to struggle, my parents made less money and therefore were not able to save any at all. When they reached retirement age, the money they paid into this program kept them from going bankrupt. It was a savings account for them to be sure. It paid their bills and put groceries on the table. It is their money! They worked hard for it and they deserve and needed every penny to survive. When my father passed away, Social Security was mother's only source of income."

Hamilton politely answered, "Young man. If I give you a penny and ask you to hold on to it for 10 years and you only give me a penny back, you have failed me. If I were to take that penny and turn it into two pennies within a year, I have created value. In your story, you bring emotion into the equation. I understand you love your family, but dollars are not an emotion. Currency in any form is a necessary entity as a means to an end. Let me rephrase. My father abandoned my mother, and I while I was an infant. I know very little of him. My mother passed away when I was young. We had nothing when she died. I lied about my age, so I could find employment. I had no other family. I had no money. To some extent, there is emotion in this story. My point is that I realized I had a choice to do something and be accountable to myself, and I made my choice. During my days of education at King's College, students were required to attend chapel and so I did. I prayed often, and I remember the teachings of Matthew 25. It is the Parable of the Talents. This may have been how my interest in finances was developed. Again, I had nothing, not a penny, until I put forth effort to work, then I put my money to work. Furthermore, and please understand I mean no disrespect, but if this program wasn't mandatory, it appears your mother would have had no savings on her own and she would truly have nothing."

Roger Sherman quietly agreed, "Amen. Well said. It's the cold truth."

Paul politely answered, "I understand your point, sir."

Hamilton continued, "Do you? Because it appears to me that citizens of this last century do not live intentionally to be independent. Do they not think ahead, plan, conceive notions by which they can rely upon themselves and not lean on the government? Do they continue within this lack of fortitude? Could it be that citizens have been bought by the government and the government has been able to creep into their daily lives? Is the government passively controlling them? My friend and college, Thomas Jefferson, warned upon such matters." Hamilton paused for a moment and the room remained silent as he starred at the floor lost in thought. When he lifted his head he said, "Upon my return to my own time, I should review the structure of the banking in the American system to the extent that will allow citizens to better control their own finances."

Sarah and Paul both grinned a bit and Sarah added, "As you wish, Councilor.

Anyone else have something to add?" No one made any motions or comments. "Very well, then." Sarah moved on with her lesson.

- August 1989 – Army General Colin Powell accepts the nomination for the position of Chairman of the Joint Chiefs of Staff. Powell becomes the first black man ever nominated for this position.

- The 1990 population has reached just over 248 million. Since the 1980 census, it is the smallest increase since 1940 at only 9.8%. Illegal immigration, which wasn't an issue until early 1900's, leaves the speculated population to be over 255 million. Sarah added a graph to show the population expansion.

Madison posed a question, "Please, Ms. Fleming, could you tell us a touch more about this illegal immigration. I believe there are men in the room who are true patriots to our flag, and yet haven't we all originated from the same countries."

"Yes, of course," she said. "In early America the population grew from settlers of other countries, citizens of natural birth and frankly, slaves shipped into the

225

country. Some could say that traveling across the ocean may have had a certain level of quality control due to the cost but, of course, the was not the case for every person. Not all slaves were counted as citizens until years later and their numbers grew regardless. Nothing of this was illegal since there were no laws regarding such growth. As time passed, laws changed, and the topology of the population followed.

Today, there are laws and regulations regarding how to become a U.S. Citizen. However, those that do not follow the rules are regarded as illegal. My personal view is that the term 'illegal immigrant' is mislabeled and a poor description. My view is that you are either a legal immigrant or illegal alien. An immigrant is someone who truly *wants* to be a U.S. citizen. An illegal alien does not ~ they only wish to partake in the services or freedoms in which the law-abiding citizens provide. An illegal alien doesn't obtain a legal social security number or pay taxes, but they want to use the hospitals when they are sick. They want free food when they can't put food on the table. Sure, many of them work and work very hard to care for their families but if they want to stay in America, they should learn the language and devote themselves to live as American citizens and do so legally. Even you gentlemen would probably know someone who left the strife of another country's oppression. They came to the thirteen colonies to be free, but they did so because they desired and hoped for a better life! They desired freedom! And they did so at the peril of crossing the ocean. Gentlemen, you are creating the documents that will set

America into motion with the legal verbiage that shapes who America is today. In the first 6 months of 2019 there were well over half a million apprehensions of illegal crossings from the Mexican border alone!

The illegal alien's step all over this document and disrespect the legacy that is our Constitution! I...I..." Sarah stopped talking. When she looked down in a bit of embarrassment, she could see both her hands were balled up into fists.

Madison noted, "Ms. Fleming, it is refreshing to see that people, such as yourself and these fine men who are with us here in this place, feel as patriotic as you do. As Mr. Hamilton very aptly stated, when we return to our own time, we should do more to write into this document not only what is expected from a government to the people of this great country, but what is expected of her citizens to remain as citizens."

Gouveneur Morris agreed, "Yes. Moreover, the inclusion of what could happen if citizens do not comply should be in order as well. We have much work to do. Ms. Fleming do not feel as though your words have fallen on deaf ears or your passion unfelt.

"I do apologize. I should not have been so callous in my explanation," she said.

"Nonsense," said Roger Sherman. "Were you not so inclined in your opinion, I believe Dr. Benton would have passed you by for someone else. Besides, my colleagues here do not always share the same opinions and have voted against each other in several occasions. Different opinions are what opens the dialogue for discussion and leads to a meeting point."

"I do appreciate your conversation gentlemen, and I believe you have a grasp on this subject. If I were to put this in a more modern view, I would say that when I am in my own house, I will open the door to my guests and my family. They can enter my house through the front door, as I choose to open it. When my front door is locked closed and my windows are shut, I do not expect anyone to enter. They are not welcome to break in, steal my belongings and pursue crimes against me or anyone else in my house. I wouldn't be off the mark to say that most of the citizens of our country have some sort of alarm on their windows and doors. Even many of the criminals in our country own a gun or a guard dog to help prevent such actions at their own homes. Why are we not protecting our country in the same manner we protect our homes?"

Hamilton raised a question, "Are you not providing a military? Are you not utilizing the Navy? What sort of protection are you referring for the country?"

"Ah, yes, your Honor," she started. "We have the finest military sir. Of this, do not have a disbelief. However, as you know, we are not in a war with another country. We are at war within ourselves about how to secure our borders from those who, on a daily basis, cross over into the United States without even trying to knock on the front door." Sarah continued teaching and told the statesmen that the U.S. Border Patrol was created for such purposes in 1924. However, under-funded and under-manned, the numbers of illegal aliens crossing over cannot be contained. In the process, the U.S. built fences to help attempt to keep them out. In 1925, the duties were expanded to patrol the seacoasts. The state of California even erected fences between San Diego and Tijuana, Mexico. Years later, in 2006, congress passed laws to fund the building of a physical barrier. Finally, when President Trump stood his ground and reminded the public that our country should not be taken over by those who enter the country illegally, use our resources, file for welfare and re-invite diseases that were already eradicated in the states.

She continued, "This wall has made a tremendous and positive impact in helping the U.S. Border Patrol in doing their job protecting us. The influx of illegals has diminished greatly but we still have work to do in securing our borders."

Sarah Fleming motioned at Paul.

Sarah said, "Let's move on, shall we? I believe this next segment in our lessons will combine several advancements. Paul will you help me?"

Paul didn't answer as he walked over to the wall and stood in front of a picture on the wall. The piece of art was a detailed map of the United States. State lines were shown with the first 13 colonies being in assorted colors while the rest of the map was displayed in a tan color. The high-quality artwork, loosely based on a map created by F.L. Gussefeld, depicts the early United States around 1784 and showed the lands topology in vivid detail. The five statesmen were familiar with the colorful New England area and seem to appreciate art's highlights while enjoying the remainder of the United States completion in the piece. Paul pushed a button and the large painting slowly began to move to one side.

Behind the painting revealed a 100" flat panel television built in 2016. Sarah would be showing the statesmen some very detailed pictures and since Dr. Benton's team was ramping up the speed of information given to the statesmen, this was a perfect moment to 'upgrade' several categories of information such as space exploration, media communications and high definition television. Additionally, the quality of information delivery for upcoming classroom films could be shown on this monitor instead of using the older television or the projector. All of the travelers were particularly ready for this change in education as J.A.S.P.E.R. was connected to the media and could manipulate the television when asked questions to add to the education.

"Thank you, Paul," Sarah said as Paul sat down in the back of the class and she continued with her lesson.

- April 1990 - The U.S. Space Shuttle Discovery launched into space carrying the Hubble Telescope.

Sarah described the purpose of the Hubble and noted that the mission of the Space Shuttle program being built was to return to earth for multiple missions back into space.

Sarah requested J.A.S.P.E.R. to begin showing a series of pictures that have returned from the Hubble Telescope. The statemen sat in amazement as they saw the rings around Saturn, new planets, moons and scenes from beyond the stars they could only see at night. Paul and Sarah enjoyed watching each man's reaction as the large screen changed pictures in vivid colors and created a three-dimensional deep space visual.

Once the space exploration demonstration had concluded, Sarah closed the lessons for the day. "Very well then Councilors, we have covered quite a bit of ground today. I would like to remind you that should you feel the need to consider digging a little deeper into any particular subject we have covered thus far, you make ask any one of the travelers, Dr. Benton and even J.A.S.P.E.R. It has been a long day and, if I may add one last item in the category of space? As you have today, I believe these pictures of outer space are spectacular, however, the sky is quite clear this evening, and I will use this time of reflection outside in the garden and look for the constellations with my own eyes. Please feel free to join me." Sarah turned and left the room.

"With my own ears, I believe I've just heard an invitation I will not pass up," Gouveneur Morris quipped as he grinned and followed Sarah out of the room.

Chapter 20

Earlier the same day, morning broke for Dr. Benton. He hadn't slept much the last two nights. He wasn't quite sure why, but he could feel the effects from the last of a deep sleep. He had several meetings scheduled today for the security of his guests. Benton knew J.A.S.P.E.R. would be available to a certain extent. He regarded the program as a tool to aid in the security of his guests but there were limitations. An intelligence to rely on. Academic and informational muscle. Benton would never give up the option of real, human interaction. Nor would he discount anyone's 'gut feeling'. There was a major difference in Benton's mind between human interaction and artificial relationship however, Benton was ever so grateful for the work J.A.S.P.E.R. has contributed to this project. He may be artificial, but he was invaluable at the same time. Benton's conference call was scheduled to start in just under an hour. It was 6:40 AM. He had time for a twenty-minute workout and a shower. He would begin the conference call from his car.

At 7:29 AM, Benton dialed the phone number he had been given. "Good Morning, sir. Have you read the most recent reports?"

"Yes," came the answer. "They look good. When will we be ready to start manufacturing some of these tele-port pads?"

"I've mentioned this before, sir. I don't like talking over the phone about the project. I don't trust cell phones. I
232

suggest we meet later today. How does 2 PM work for you, Colonel?"

"That works for me, Dr. Benton. I will be at the facility and see you then."

"Very well."

The call was disconnected. Benton drove the rest of the way to the facility considering places to take the statesmen when they venture out.

Hours later at 1:50 PM, the Colonel arrived at the facility. As with everyone else, he made his way to the elevator and pressed the button to the underground facility. He stopped on 8th sub-floor and found Dr. Benton waiting for him as the elevator doors opened. "Good afternoon, Dr. Benton," he said politely.
"Yes, a lovely day today, is it not?" Benton didn't wait for an answer as he stepped into the elevator. "How about we have a chat outside in the garden?" Benton said as he stepped in front of the benefactor.

Moments later the 'Benefactor', retired Colonel Alan Powers, sat in the warm sunshine and fresh air, and directly in front of Dr. Benton. Colonel Powers remained a powerful Washington aristocrat even after his exiting the military. Graduating from the United States Naval Academy, he quickly rose to the rank of Colonel in the U.S. Marine Corps. He commanded several overseas operations based out of Camp Dwyer in Afghanistan. Possibly for his achievements, he was noticed by several politicians who approached him shortly before his military contract was over. After several attempts, the politicians convinced him to run for a seat in the House of Representatives for the state of Delaware. He won that seat and spent time on several committees. Colonel Powers gained a penchant for getting things done on the hill as his did in the field of battle.

Alan Powers was an only child and during the eleventh year of his life, his parents were killed in a car accident. His grandfather, a veteran Marine, raised him. His grandfather was a very quiet man with a strong sense of self. He taught Alan to rely on himself, create a good team, work harder than the man next to you and set a good example. God, country and family were where he placed his faith and loyalty.

Unexpectedly, the Benefactor's personal finances grew exponentially when his grandfather passed away leaving him a fortune. His new-found money became a problem as sudden 'long lost family members' jumped out of the woodwork asking for grants or 'handouts'. Alan decided to build several shell companies to protect his assets. However, he didn't let his financial responsibilities sit idle. He hired a personal staff of savvy business-minded individuals and quietly grew his portfolio. He paid his staff well for their loyalty and silence. He didn't buy extravagantly, didn't spend frivolously, and didn't announce it to anyone. He did whatever he could to keep his private life simple and out of sight. Usually an insurmountable task for a typical politician but, for a man such as Alan Powers, this was not impossible. When he was working as an elected official, he knew how to fit in the political crowd just fine. He shook the right hands and played the game well without compromising his beliefs and keeping his promises to his constituents. In his private life, he wore jeans and t-shirts, worked out daily, drank beer and worked with his private staff.

The responsibility of his staff was to grow his influence. Powers knew the money would grow when put to the right use, but influence? This was a key development for his plans.   He learned how the political machine in Washington D.C. worked and didn't work. Money thrown towards projects or people to nudge and turn the tides on appropriations, votes and a host of other decisions. Influence took time and money. Time he couldn't control, but money? Well, he started growing those dollars around 1999 in varying amounts.   As time passed, he put that growth in the right places and gained the influence from a direction the political machine would not expect. Plus, he would do so without anyone knowing it was him, until it was time.

Over time, he was elected to a Senate seat the following term of 2018. He decided to retire from politics after a single term and pursue other interests that might also prove to help the country. He quietly remained a powerful man within Washington D.C. and his political connections were solidly in place.

Alan Powers was most proud of following in his grandfather's footsteps with his time in the Marines and still preferred to be called 'Colonel'. Patient and soft spoken, he waited for Dr. Benton to begin the conversation.

"We have some really nice test results, Colonel. As you said, you have seen the reports. I believe we are certainly in new scientific realm of discovery. This is exactly in line with where you were wanting the testing to go. I'm quite happy with this body of work and, admittedly, with our staff, sir. They are beyond exceptional."

"This sounds very positive. Are you able to tell me when this product will be produced and distributed across the major cities?"

"That's not really in the immediate future, sir. As you know, we are able to transport our primate test subjects with great success. We wouldn't be doing our due diligence for humanity if we just went 'willy-nilly' and produced the devices without real human test subjects. While this is certainly our intention, I'm not sure we have everything quite worked out just yet, sir. You're aware of the liability in placing a human in the transports. However, since you have mentioned this, Colonel, I can only imagine you have the proper people in place to push the production processes and all the legal aspects covered when the time arises for this to take off?"

"I have as much as I can in place without letting anyone know what our product can do. Dr. Benton, this will blow the top off the science world. I realize this may have started in the imagination of movie makers but to have this become a reality! Truly, you are blazing a trail that will change the way the world operates." "Yes, I'm quite sure it will, Colonel," Benton answered confidently.

"And when do you believe you will have everything worked out, Dr. Benton. This project hasn't been what some would call 'quick', and while I'm minimally concerned about the price tag, I am concerned that someone else will beat us to the punch, Doctor. I want to be first. Then, of course, I don't want to lose the potential revenue. Are we understanding each other?"

"I understand, Colonel. If you will allow us a bit more time, I believe I can answer this question in a matter of weeks or perhaps a month. However, I must remind you, this is science and I will not be committed to a verbal or calendar time frame. It will happen when all requirements and safety measures are met. It's just the nature of science."

"Yes. Yes. I understand. Now, that the time and money talk is out of the way, how are the test subjects? Can you see any residual effects from transporting them?"

"No, sir. They seem fine from all accounts," Benton answered. The conversation continued until nearly every avenue had been covered again. Benton began to get the feeling the Colonel was getting pressure from some other direction to complete the project, but he put that out of his mind. It wasn't his problem.

Benton stood in the large driveway of the facility as the Benefactor was leaving the parking lot. His life was built upon responsibility and integrity. He wasn't used to feeling a sense of guilt. This was not an emotion he liked, and it was staring at him in the face. Not giving the Colonel full disclosure of the full project. Not introducing the statesmen to the Colonel after all he had done. It was wrong and Benton knew it, but for now, this was his cross to bear. It was a small price at this point. America must change, or she will self-destruct. The signs of the impending implosion were there, if one was to only look. Of this, he was sure.

Chapter 21

Paul Tesla stood at the front of the recently 'updated' classroom. The lighting was bright and controlled by a touch screen monitor. The same monitor controlled the temperature, which was a comfortable 71 degrees. The large television hung quietly while allowing for pre-set pictures to fade in and out on the screen. Paul smiled a bit when he thought how far the team and their guests had come in such a short time. Three of the five congressmen slowly entered the room carrying hot, steaming coffee cups. Dickinson brought hot tea. Madison had yet to carry a drink into the classroom. He mentioned to Paul a few days ago he was afraid he would spill it on his notes. Madison sat in his chair, picked up his pen and patiently waited for class to start.

Tesla made his opening statement, "All of us, that is the teachers, are planning on today being the last regular classroom day. It's time for you to see America with your own eyes. You've already gotten a taste of the engineering when we visited the collection of vehicles and airplanes. You've experienced some of today's technologies when flying in the airplane, visiting with J.A.S.P.E.R. and some of the educational items we have used." Paul motioned to the large screen television. "What you haven't experienced are the people. Our cultural diversities are fantastic, and we wish to share them with you while still providing information of how America has turned out. So, unless there are any questions, let's get started here and see how the day turns out." No one made any motions of having questions.

"Very well," Tesla said as he continued. "This next segment of information was discussed in length whether or not to show you this piece of legislation. In this information, you, Mr. Madison, make a proposal which takes congress over 200 years to finally ratify.   This is the historical information: May 1992 - The 27th Amendment to the Constitution is passed two hundred and two years after its initial proposal. It bars the United States Congress from giving itself a midterm or retroactive pay raise.

Madison spoke, "This is certainly a delay in coming to a vote but what I find more interesting is the idea that there are at least 27 Amendments! Tell us, just how many Amendments are there to the Constitution."

"Let me answer you this way, Senator," Tesla replied. "There have been nearly 12,000 suggestions for amendments, however, the majority of those get lost in committee. To be more precise, there have been thirty-three proposed amendments. Yours, Senator Madison, is the 27th and the last. The remainder of the thirty-three were not ratified for various reasons."

Madison commented, "Why would this proposal continue to be active for such a long period?"

"Ah!" Said Tesla. "The rules changed along the way, sir. Your proposal did not have any time limitations. Today, there is a seven-year time limit for ratification."

Dickinson commented, "I must add that I am glad to know that the Constitution has supporting laws to help govern our country. It clearly doesn't stand on its own. This is the second time we have been introduced to this Bill of Rights. What exactly is this?"

Tesla discussed the generalities for the Bill of Rights over the next couple hours. He purposefully left out who the main author for the moment and oddly, no one seemed to ask. Tesla could only guess they believed it would have been a committee that wrote it, but he knew it would be discussed before this conversation was over.

Madison, who had still been taking notes, finalized this portion of discussion when he said, "Gentlemen, it appears to me our work at the conclave will not be complete without such a document. This is something I will be working on upon our return." Hands banged on the tabletops in agreement to the suggestion. And there it was. The opening Tesla was waiting for.

Tesla waited for the loud table noise to subside a bit before he added, "Senator Madison, it is my honor to inform you that whether or not you are encouraged to pursue this engagement of writing due to this conversation or not, history records you as the primary writer of the document. And, for the record, despite the Federalists of your time arguing against it, the Bill of Rights is necessary to solidify our country. During the course of our travels outside these walls, sir, you will inevitably find this out as it is directly related to the scope of efforts of Dr. Benton and our team."

Madison's face showed little reaction. Nor did anyone else. The remaining four statesmen were very respectful of Madison's capabilities, especially Hamilton. However, the words Paul Tesla had just voiced carried the weight of centuries to come, and they were not lost in the mind of Madison.

"Of course, Mr. Tesla. I shall purpose to take this task with all liberties belonging to the citizens of the country."

"One more point of order, if I may," Tesla said. "Mr. Sherman, your arguments against changing the words in the body of Constitution remain in the history books. It is now clearly evident from this meeting today that we are asking this very thing! However, probably not to the point of combining these two documents, but that is something the members of your conclave could discuss."

Madison and Sherman both looked at each other as though they both expected such an argument between the two of them could still occur. Neither of them changed the expression on their face. Both men were fearless, opinionated and knew that nothing was done, until it was done.

"Sir," Tesla said looking directly at James Madison. "If I may, in today's world, the United States has the majority of the world's lawyers with approximately 1.5 million. Which can only mean the people of the United States have created a need for such a large capacity of litigation. Your Honor, we know that civil damages are normally monetary while criminal cases typically conclude with incarceration. My point is this, our country is overloaded with lawyers who specialize in certain law, simply due to the fact that we have thousands upon thousands of laws! Entire libraries are dedicated just to the laws created by our government. It can be said that these laws are all based upon the interpretation from the document's you gentlemen are writing. A strong, yet smaller government could be realized if there were less room for interpretation."

Internally, Tesla braced himself for the inevitable argument from his last comment. Ironically, the men he was standing in front of ~ the same men he risked his life for in a time travel experiment ~ said nothing. The peg-legged aristocrat, the compromiser, the farmer, the father of the Bill of Rights and Publius remained quiet for quite some time. Paul Tesla was also a man of patience. He knew these men have already had a conversation about dialogue opening up the traffic lanes of communication to solve a problem, they would pound his idea into the ground ~ but that didn't happen right away.

Roger Sherman spoke first, "Taking into account the evidence of history you, and your team, have provided to us, I believe you have a valid point, sir. One for which I will consider paramount before placing my signature on parchment."

Hamilton grinned when he added, "You have touched upon the point to which every councilor or politician could agree but would only do so upon reaching the conclusion that the clarity you speak of matches his own opinion. That, Mr. Tesla, is most difficult." Tesla politely nodded his agreement.

"Agreed," said Morris.

"I, too, concur with the Honorable Roger Sherman," said Dickinson. "The agreement via signature must, by the very nature of commitment, must be of utmost importance." Paul Tesla quietly remembered Dickinson as being absent on the day the Constitution was signed, yet it was signed by proxy for him. Keeping that in mind and what he just said, left Paul with questions that could wait for another time.

Hamilton had not been overly vocal the past few days. He had held his tongue for as long as he could and decided that now was a good time to present his case. "Mr. Tesla, would you please ask Dr. Benton to come to see us when he has a free moment of time?"

Tesla, looking at his watch and sensing the topic of conversation was about to change answered, "As a matter of fact, I believe Dr. Benton has already planned to be with us shortly. However, I will certainly pass on the request. Gentlemen, I think it's time to take a short break, and I will contact Dr. Benton."

The statesmen stood as Mr. Tesla stepped into the hallway. When the door closed behind him, he said, "J.A.S.P.E.R.?"

"I'm here," came the response.

"You heard the request for Dr. Benton?"

"Of course, sir. He has been notified. Shall I let him know you're on the way to see him?"

"Sure. Tell him they're ready to get out of this place," Tesla said.

"Consider it done."

Inside the classroom, the statemen decide to take a few moments and meet in the parlor. As the last statesmen took a seat, Hamilton broke his silence.

"The time is now, gentlemen. The time is now to once again venture out of this building and see this country. I do so appreciate the efforts of Dr. Benton and his staff, yet I feel trapped in these walls. Tell me, is anyone else in agreement with Mr. Tesla to be outside?" The room was softly filled with 'Aye'. Not one opposed or raised an eyebrow.

Morris quipped, "Damn, I do believe that was the quickest vote in which we have all participated."

Madison added, "Truly, it is easier when all are in agreement."

Dickinson noted, "If all of our votes could only be so favorable. Mr. Hamilton, if I may ask your reasoning? Do you think this artificial intelligence can sense that we are cooped-up in this underground facility? Why not hear more right here and be better prepared? What do you hope to gain by venturing out quite possibly before these fine people have completed our education?"

Somewhat surprised; the answer did not come from Hamilton. Roger Sherman, true to form, raised his hand and calmly stood from his chair. He respectfully looked at Hamilton, who nodded his relinquishment.

"Thank you, Mr. Hamilton," Sherman said as he turned his direction towards the other in the room. "Mr. Dickinson, I may not have the exact answers as to the mindset of Mr. Hamilton. Truly, all the minds in this room are, at times, difficult to ascertain their true reasoning. However, in this case, I will attest to the following; our educators have pulled us up by our bootstraps and led us with significant information. They have allowed us to formulate our own conclusions, given us time for questions and still proceeded to move us across a timeline from our own period to nearly the present. As we have all agreed that it is in our interests to move outside these walls that the technology or historical events within the next 25 or so years of history we could gain within a classroom could also be discussed in the freedom of society, letting us use our taste, smell and touch to guide our reactions instead of just hearing about it and seeing it on paper, films or these televisions.

It is time for us to see and experience it first-hand. I believe whatever historical information these travelers have left to share, can be shared as we sit among the people."

Morris broke in, "Gentlemen, this adventure we have chosen to be on has allowed us to fly! We sat in this winged tube and stayed aloft in the clouds and watched the ground pass us by! Why would we not wish to endure more of what this country's innovators have produced?"

Hamilton said, "For me, that classroom isn't just a classroom. It has been a room full of magic. And the magicians have let us see how the tricks were conjured.

246

The room changed with nearly every major change in history, so we were as comfortable with our surroundings as we may have been with the information provided. It's time, gentlemen, and they know it. It's time to go beyond these walls and experience this new world."

Madison added, "Hear me when I say this: gentlemen, we have chosen this profession long before these travelers came to us. Now that we are here of our own volition, a place we knew we could never otherwise see ~ the future, it is incumbent upon us to do our own research. To learn what we can and take this knowledge back in our minds and apply it for the good of the country. Five is not the number of delegates in our conclave, gentlemen. There are fifty-five! Yet, we five, hold a few new keys to the future. We must see what these United States have become, and with God's help, repair some damages and, prayerfully, prevent some of the wrongs without removing the liberties provided to her citizens and adding their responsibilities! This is no easy task that has been laid upon us. By faith alone, a soul can be saved from damnation if one only chooses to believe in the Almighty and His Son. However, the five of us may be able to save this country from her own citizens if we purpose to complete this task with which we now are participants. What say you?"

Hands slapped the tables or clapped together as the room erupted in agreement. Even Dr. Benton, who had entered the room just prior to Sherman speaking, was clapping. Sherman, ever the polite gentleman, simply grinned with the approvals.

Sherman continued, "Dr. Benton, I'm sorry I didn't hear you come in, sir."

"I think I arrived right on time, Senator. I cannot remember ever hearing such compliments. Thank you for the kind words."

Hamilton stepped in, "Thank you for coming in Dr. Benton. Getting to the point, I shall put you to the same question, Dr. Benton. We," he gestured to the statesmen, "are ready to venture outside these walls and see this country and how it has evolved. Mr. Tesla explains that today is the last classroom setting. We simply wished you to know we are in agreement." Hamilton's statement was phrased to show respect for all the work and planning that Dr. Benton has done.

Benton responded without hesitation, "Let's do this tomorrow, shall we. It will be a pleasure for us to be outside, as well. I will have transportation ready for all of us, first thing in the morning. We can depart right after breakfast. There are a number of places I think you would all like to see. I must add one thing, gentlemen. No one knows who you are except for our team. You will be in clothes befitting our time-period as you are today. My personal mission while you are out of this building is your safety. The travelers will continue your education. Do not stray away from your traveler for any reason. Are we in agreement?" The five statemen agreed. Benton continued, "Then tomorrow it is. I will inform the team, and I shall see all of you in the morning. I'm very excited for this, gentlemen. Truly. Good day, everyone." Benton turned and left the room. As the door closed, he could hear the applause. Benton grinned as he walked to his office. "J.A.S.P.E.R.," he said, while still in the hallway.

"Yes, Dr. Benton," came the response.

"We have work to do for tomorrow."

"Preparations are underway, sir," came the quick response.

As the applause in the parlor slowly dissipated. Hamilton, with a calm and purposeful composition, posed the question, "When thought is placed before the action of tongue, what is it that you would wish to see in this future America? I know I have had a few moments to think upon this question. It is quite probable we have all contemplated the same thought. My heart is heavy when I hear of the national debt being so exorbitant. I cannot fathom any presidency wanting to leave a legacy with a black mark such as this."

Madison replied, "You would be perfectly matched to look into this, my friend. Many things have changed since the time you started the first bank in America." Madison said staunchly, "Isn't this quite interesting, we sit here now with knowledge of things yet to come. Hamilton will create the nation's first bank in 1791, only four years from the time we came to this place. Truly, Hamilton..., nay, all of us, had no knowledge of things to be. And now, he will ponder on the national debt of the year 2025 when creating this new bank. Dr. Benton was very right in bringing us here to this American experiment. The future will change because of what we now know.

"Councilors," Morris said prestigiously, "I, for one, believe this to be a very important yet curious question. I should think that we all have pondered upon this very thing since the time we were asked into this experiment, such as it is. If such is true, let there be no hesitation in what we seek. Hamilton is an expert in the field of finance, and in this, there shall be no question." Hamilton interjected, "Thank you for the vote of confidence, but as this task is pending, I wish to add that you, Gouveneur Morris, are also an expert in economics and finance. We should collaborate on such a large task."

"I accept your invitation, Alexander." Hamilton nodded with acknowledgement as Morris moved on, "Now, I will answer that my curiosities and inquiries should fall into the category of senate meetings, voting and citizenship."

Dickinson replied to Morris with a downtrodden voice, "Based on your aristocratic, privileged upbringing and your penchant for keeping the wealthy in the realm of running the country, yes, I do believe that would be your course of action."

"Now, don't be so persnickety, John," Madison said. "We've known each other for many a year and I don't recall him ever having snapped at you in private. What he seeks to find may be no less than any man here. All of this," he paused and waved his hands in the air, "this! Is nothing short of a miracle ~ and overwhelming."

Dickinson shrugged and looked at every man's expression. "Yes. I can agree. This 'experiment' is nothing short of a miracle. It's a miracle, it's science, it's a wish come true or an evil nightmare. No man of our time should know what we know! Yet, by some sort of greed for knowledge, or curiosity, or...well...something, we all agreed to be a part of it, and I shall not take this task lightly."

Roger Sherman interjected, "Nor should any man."

"Yes. You are correct, Councilor," Dickinson moved on. "Then, to answer Mr. Madison's query. As I think upon such things, that I may hope to let America be a better place, I believe I wish to take time to visit our nation's senate meetings. I'd like to see for myself and pray to understand, how the future senators of our states truly communicate, interact, and create the laws that have been *burdening* our country for so long. Were they bought by lobbyists? Were they paid by favors and therefore traded our citizens into a story with an ending no one expected? Perhaps influenced by foreign governments. Were the weak politicians bullied into a corner with the promise of a seat on a Senate Committee or other oversight option? Do the men of integrity stand strong for their constituents?" The frustration could be heard in Dickinson's voice and did not go without comment.

Morris interjected, "Mr. Dickinson, it does so appear you have put forth much effort during your time outside of the classroom, sir. This is quite refreshing! I, too, have most recently been talking to our colleagues in quiet conversations to better understand today's status of voting. I can only speculate what may happen if the laws of this country allowed for those people, whether aristocratic or common," Morris glanced towards Dickinson, "who legally fulfilled qualifications set forth by a

251

new law, allowing for more than one vote per person. Or, as we discussed in class, how this country may thrive if the Constitution gave the country an explanation of what's expected of the citizen to *maintain* citizenship."

Dickinson calmly answered, "Excellent topics, sir. Yet, you will never get passed the freedoms and liberties of the majority to remove the citizenship of a few. The laws can never be so specific by a governing body. 'Jurisprudentia' must take place in removing citizenship."

"You are correct, sir. These are excellent topics. As to the rest of your statement, you should know well that all things can be made law. This is exactly what we have learned here. Too many unclear and interpreted laws may well be why this country has soiled itself. Therefore, what we know is 'all things' in law are not to the benefit of the republic for which we stand!" Morris' statement rang true in the room.

The conversation in the room could have erupted to arguments, however, Hamilton seized the moment by asking, "Mr. Sherman. Please, sir, what is it you wish to seek when we stand in the freedoms outside these walls?"

Sherman, who would normally stand up when answering questions in a formal political setting, remained seated. He looked over to his fellow statesmen when he answered, "I'm ready to feel how a citizen feels with today's political climate. I'm willing to listen to them and pursue the cause of liberty and remove the bonds of a perpetuating national government. If it is still there, I would like to sit on the bench in front of Independence

Hall ~ watch the people go by ~ look at their shoes and wonder what it is to walk in their lives. How did they get where they are today? As a person, as a community, as a country. Does the common man care about the nation at all? Or does he only care about his next meal? I'm fully aware that circumstances of one's life may dictate much of the answers I seek. But, if I am not here for the betterment of this nation, I should not be here at all, my friends."

"Might I propose a more personal question to you, sir?" Hamilton asked.

"Certainly," Sherman said and nodded his head while the two stepped away from the others a bit.

"Why is it that a man, who chooses to be present on the signing day of all four of our country's major documents, has not the famous name he deserves?" Hamilton said humbly.

"I don't deserve anything, Alexander, especially grace. I believe the answer to the question you are looking for is simple. I do not do any of this for glory, money, or accolades. I do this work because there is a need for it to be done and I am very qualified and fit to the task. I do not have a care if my name shows up in the history books as famous or not. Of the men in this room, I believe I can say the same... save for Mr. Morris. He is a born aristocrat and has a care that he be recognized when he walks into a room. However, in his current station, as we are, representing citizens of our respective states, I believe he is well suited for the task. I cannot say of others for whom we know." Sherman smiled as he looked down at his shoes. Madison could tell the oldest statesman was remembering something.

"Tell me, Roger, what do you smile about?" Madison said.

"I've published a few writings in my younger days, during my time in New Haven. My brother and I tended the local mercantile and, for a time, I came up with a few sayings which, at least to me, signifies an honorable life. One such saying is 'He who by good actions deserves well, need not another's praise'. That, I believe, is a just answer to your query, Alexander."

"Indeed, it is," Hamilton answered.

Chapter 22

Time to leave the facility again. The statesmen were appropriately dressed in clothes fitting the styles of 2025. Roger Sherman maintained his desire to stay with comfortable leather shoes. John Dickinson followed Sherman's lead. However, two of the remaining three opted to try something new and wore rubber-soled athletic shoes or *shoe* in Morris's case. Madison wore leather boots.

"Come now, Mr. Sherman," Morris said. "Why not try something new on your feet?"

"Gouveneur, the last time I noticed someone's newer footwear," Sherman began, "I was enticed enough to be brought here, to the future, so I'm sure you can understand my hesitation."

Hamilton smiled and added, "Surely, no ill-will towards your traveling companion for doing his homework to understand you."

"None at all, Mr. Hamilton," Sherman said. "That would be the furthest from the truth, sir. I hold Paul Tesla in the highest regard. He is an impressive young man. Besides, I'm wearing everything else requested of me. I believe I shall hold on to a solid footing of good leather shoes and my own peace of mind."

Hamilton continued smiling.

In Dr. Benton's office, Rayne began, "Everything is set, Carver. We're ready."

255

Benton questioned, "Security?"

"On point, sir. They have no clue who anyone is, and they've been told our guests are using fake names to protect their identity. I thought that was an interesting idea, don't you? Call them by their real names and no one is the wiser. Charles and Paul came up with it, and I couldn't see any reason to disagree."

Benton didn't look up from his desk and continued, "Very well. J.A.S.P.E.R., do you have anything to report?"

"No, sir. All guests and travelers are medically fine. There may be a bit of apprehension from a few participants, including yourself, but nothing out of the ordinary."

"Yes, I do believe I am somewhat 'apprehensive', as you say. We're about to go outside this place where crap happens that I can't control."

"We'll be fine, Carver," Rayne said.

"Yes…well…in any event, J.A.S.P.E.R., move your threat level up 30%. I'd rather be overly cautious and not need to have been than the reverse."

"Done," came the reply.

"Okay, let's go."

The doctors left the office and met everyone at the vehicles. Morning pleasantries were exchanged, and the caravan of vehicles left the Allentown resort facility in a calm and orderly fashion. Along the way, conversations took place about the morning fog, the expected weather, the landscape, road signs, and more.

John Dickinson was getting more comfortable with the changes in technology. "J.A.S.P.E.R.," he said. "What are the expected weather conditions for today?"

J.A.S.P.E.R. replied with the answer. Dickinson sat there in amazement. "You can even tell the weather what to do." Charles corrected him and explained how the forecast models work, but Dickinson's amazement didn't change. He loved the science of Charles's answer.

The caravan was getting closer to the city, and the Philadelphia skyline was coming into view. Dickinson stared out the window as he spoke, "Be it a weather forecast or the ability to build very tall structures that don't fall in terminal weather, this future holds many amazing things. I shall not lose sight of the positive things in this country, Mr. Carson."

"Yes, sir. There are many wonderful and beautiful things in this country, Your Honor," Carson replied as he, too, looked through the car window at the skyline.

John Dickinson glanced over at Carson and said, "Tell me more about yourself while we continue our journey, Charles. If you wouldn't mind, that is."

Carson started a short narrative about his life as the vehicle moved toward their destination. Dickinson paid close attention as Carson spoke. This was the first time that Dickinson made any inquiries of his personal life, and the notion was not lost on Carson. Carson's story telling was detailed and captivating. He finished his autobiography as the vehicle pulled into a parking spot near Independence Hall.

After getting out of the car, Carson noted the look on Dickinson's face. He watched as Dickinson was remembering what the surrounding areas looked like just "days" ago. Carson said, "Change is a constant, sir, and this town has certainly done so. Just down that way would have been where we first met. The bench we sat on during the summer rain is long gone, and you can see the rest. However, Your Honor, the inside of this building hasn't changed much at all. Shall we go inside?"

Dickinson looked across the top of the vehicle and towards the large expanse of grass. He slowly turned and looked up into the sky.

"Hear my words, Mr. Carson. The trees, the grass, the sky, and the things our Maker has placed on this earth still look the same to me. But this..." He waived his arm motioning to their surroundings. "This is very different from where we first met, son. Different isn't bad, Mr. Carson. It's just different. Truly, this place has an abundance of people."

"We tried to prepare you, but it's hard to let it sink in until you've witnessed it."

"On this, we can agree."

"Shall we go inside, sir?"

"Yes, but I wish to read the words on that statue there. Seems someone did something by which to be remembered."

"You all have, sir. You built a nation," Carson said. "Your Honor, once you return to your own time, you may note that President Washington is getting close to finishing his

258

term in office - the country still hasn't quiet come together. He will be very reluctant and openly unwilling to continue in a second term of office."

"Very well. The country, such as it is, will need to hold another election."

"Truly, sir, you are free to do as you wish. I will add that since he remains as a man to never want to serve as President of the United States, and the only person I can think of that both parties of Congress agreed on to hold the highest seat in the Union, you might consider him as 'the glue' that keeps this young republic politically together."

"I see. Your perception is that this country will not survive itself otherwise?"

"I have no idea if that would be the case, sir. These are just my thoughts."

"Very well, Mr. Carson. I shall bear that in mind."

Dickinson read the inscription on the pedestal of Washington's monument and kept any comments to himself. The two of them caught up to the rest of the group.

The entire group, via some special connection through Dr. Benton, was able to bypass the National Park Service security. No one emptied their pockets to walk through the mandatory metal detectors. The group of 15 the statesmen, travelers, and personal security wasn't too large. Dr. Rayne sounded like a tour guide as he led the them into the quiet hall. Morris's peg leg seemed to make more noise than anyone. He had refused to cover it up.

None of them entering Independence Hall turned towards the court room, which once functioned as the Supreme Court. Instinctively, they turned into the room to which they were more accustomed. With only thirteen states attending and representatives each, the size of the room was adequate.

Original photo 2018 by Chester Budney

Dr. Benton had reminded his security that this place is a public area. Tours were already in progress. People were milling about and taking in the sights of the old building, the rooms, chairs, feather quills, and ink wells. Cameras and mobile devices were quietly snapping memories and transferring the data to cloud storage. Others were listening to the Park Ranger's tour information. Still, as other tourists began to line up in the green-decorated room, Dr. Rayne, with permission from the Park Ranger's service, continued to act as a private tour guide. Suddenly, the small stature of James Madison stepped up beside him. It was obvious Madison had something to say, so Dr. Rayne reverently stepped back, and as Madison began to speak, the entire room became quiet.

"Ladies and Gentlemen, today it is our privilege to attend this visitation with you. This room, with all her members gathering around these tables and presided over by a very humble George Washington, began each and every congressional meeting with prayer. In doing so, we not only to acknowledge that we are believers in our Sovereign Lord, but that our desires for this country were to remain guided by his Holy Spirit. Therefore, while unannounced, I am certain this is an appropriate time. Would the Honorable Roger Sherman please do us the honors this day?" Madison asked.

Sherman stepped through the small swinging gate dividing the guests from the display of green cloth covered tables and walked up to the front of the room. With a commanding statement, he asked the men in the room to remove their hats and then said, "Let us pray…". He concluded his prayer with these words: "Let us live no more to ourselves, but to Him who loved us and gave Himself to die for us. Amen."

Sherman walked back to where he was standing and quietly spoke to Dickinson. "I wonder," he said with a short pause, "when was the last time a public prayer was spoken within these walls?" Dickinson smoothly replied, "Only when the heart of a man who fears the Lord has first made the request or done so himself. Today may have been that day, sir."

Sherman replied, "Then let us hope that today will not be the last, my friend."

Madison continued with his unprepared speech of how it was sitting in a conclave with statesmen from twelve other represented colonial states, each trying to ensure their respective state was heard and represented and did not receive any unfair advantage over another, no matter the size, their philosophy, their products or profits. The national government was intended to govern the country and allow the states to manage their own affairs. Madison gently reminded everyone that no participant of this conclave truly knew how to accomplish this task.

He noted to all the people in the room that this form of government had never been attempted before by anyone. There was no prior-written rule book to follow. No existing man-made laws to be broken. No way to be assured they were "getting it right". Arguments were heated and full of passion and, often times, distrust. Sides were taken behind closed doors, and many of the statesmen were skeptical they would accomplish anything. However, the unification of a new sovereign nation was paramount. The weight of such matters was heavy upon their shoulders.

Madison saw a hand slowly raise in the crowd. "I recognize the young lady wearing the blue sweater. You have a question, do you not?"

"Yes, sir. Thank you, sir. My name is Clara Parker. You seem to be quite passionate about the work our forefathers have done. What do you believe James Madison would say if he were to be asked about the nation's current extreme polarity between the political parties?"

Dr. Rayne was about to stop Madison from answering, but Hamilton, never taking his eyes off Madison, put a hand in front of Rayne. Rayne looked at Hamilton, who motioned to allow Madison to answer.

At the same time Hamilton stopped Rayne, Madison gently lifted his palm toward her to end her questioning and convey that he would answer.

Madison had a small smirk on his face that his fellow statesmen recognized right away. Composing himself, he answered, "I firmly believe Madison would answer your query in this manner: First, even in the days when the men who sat in this room, and many other rooms such as this, to discuss a proposal, the opposing sides were normally invigorated and passionate about their cause, and they should take no pause in being so. It is nearly a requirement to survive in such a climate. Many debates prior to the forming of these United States have been thoroughly argued by men whose hearts were resolute to the root of their purpose. Secondly, it is the root of their purpose that may be their undoing. I fear there are more members of Congress, whether Senate or in the House, who do not hold their ear to the ground or their hand on the Bible and listen to their constituents or God. Their purpose is not selfless. Their purpose is to assure their greed. Usually a greed for power. This was not how this government was intended. So, to be clear, there has always been a polarity, Miss Parker, even to the point you see it today."

He looked directly at her when he continued, "It is here where Madison's next point would appear. He would say, "In many instances, to provide for a resolution to many arguments, there will come a form of compromise. This has also been a part of government for a very long time. An agreement of fairness, I pray, between the two oppositions." Now, to specifically answer your question, Clara Parker, such a beautiful name I might add, - in the congress that resides in the year of our Lord 2025, you do not possess the same political parties with which our country was founded. Today, you have an extreme polarity between the controlling coastal 'Socialists' and 'mid-America patriotic Conservatives'. Let's call the latter group 'Federalists'. Additionally, I believe I've learned this polarity continues with every election cycle. So much so, I fear you are on the very cusp of splitting up the lands and breaking the country into two or even three separate countries. Your socialist party wishes for the government to provide free services to any living body within the borders of this country and have the productive and wealthy citizens provide the means and financial responsibilities via taxes and other instruments or implements of the government. This will be a destruction of the United States, without question. Thomas Jefferson even wrote of such a demise. He understood that Liberty must prevail to maintain the integrity of the nation. To move any closer toward a socialist government is to eliminate the full purpose of The Constitution, the Declaration of Independence, and our Bill of Rights. Miss Parker, mid-America conservatives or, as others may call them, 'federalists', may converge on one of the remaining solutions...secession."

"May I add a thought please?" she asked as she continued without an answer. "Would you agree that socialism would be the destruction of these United States and, as such, it is the opposite of patriotism, and therefore socialism is the betrayer?"

"Miss Parker, there are countries living under the rule of socialism. Therefore, I believe Mr. Madison would answer in this manner: This country was designed for liberty and freedom. In this country, the believer in socialism is the betrayer."

Clara Parker stood there in awe and respect. "Thank you, sir."

Madison kindly nodded toward her.

As the entire group started to disperse and move on with their tour of Independence Hall, Clara Parker couldn't help but believe the man she just spoke with looked familiar. She decided to pursue that feeling at the right time.

Minutes later, the statesmen and their travelers were walking away from their familiar desks in Independence Hall when Morris reached over and got the attention of Hamilton.

"Yes, Gouverneur?" Hamilton said.

Morris had a near-comical look on his face. "Now see here," he said almost laughing. "This is the desk where I usually sat."

"I believe I remember, Mr. Morris. And mine is just there," he said, pointing.

"Yes, but look here. That is the crack in the desk from when I fell trying to sit down. It was quite an embarrassment, but I can't always control this damn stick of a leg all the time."

"I don't believe I was in the room at the time, but I too have memories coming back to me today," Hamilton replied.

"Also, look just here," Morris continued his observations. "Those are my initials I carved when I was bored and tired of hearing John Rutledge blabber nonsense."

At that moment, the Park Ranger was quite near and partially heard Morris' comment. "Excuse me, sir! Did you just say that you scratched your initials in this desk?" he asked excitedly.

Hamilton was quick to respond, "Ah! No sir, I believe you misunderstood. These are simply the same initials as this gentleman. No harm done, sir. And I believe it is time for us to go. Shall we?" Hamilton was looking at Morris with a bit of a grin.

"Just a moment," the Park Ranger said as he held up his hand. He suspiciously eyed the desk and then looked at Morris. After a short pause, he said, "It is believed, due to these initials, that Gouveneur Morris sat here. Were you aware that he only had one leg?" he asked.

Morris answered calmly. "See," he said looking at Hamilton with a huge smile. "There are similarities other than my initials." He gently tapped his peg leg on the floor.

"Time to go," Hamilton said, cutting the meeting as short as possible.

The Park Ranger stood there proudly. "You gentlemen have a good day." The two congressional alumni made their way towards the exit to find the rest of the group.

Madison had already made his way out the door of the building when he heard her speak.

"Excuse me, sir. I believe you were spot-on with your answer. And, if I may say so, you seem familiar. Have we met somewhere before?" she asked.

"I do not believe we have, Miss Parker. I have not been to this place in ages. What brings you here today?" Madison inquired.

"Oh. Well, I'm a history student at the University of Pennsylvania. We're studying the events surrounding the formation of our country, and obviously, anyone studying that would be an idiot if they didn't stop here. It's the birthplace of so many things that guide our country today. The Constitution, freedom, liberty: they are all connected in this land. The men who fought and died during the turmoil of getting out from under the thumb of British rule. All the while the framers, several who truly knew what it was like to serve in a war zone - unlike most of the selfish, narcissistic politicians of today I should add - were pounding out how to make new laws and doctrines that formed a new nation. New hope. New ideas." Clara stopped abruptly and looked at Madison. "I'm sorry, sir, I was rambling on. I have a tendency to do that."

"Please, go on. I wish to hear what you have to say," he responded softly.

"Well, the paper I have to write takes into account the changes in thought from what I believe our forefathers were thinking to how the current politicians think. It's not an easy task, so I'm basing my work on the evidence I find."

Madison interjected, "This sounds like a fair assessment. Tell me, what evidence have you uncovered on your quest?"

"I notice that you don't really have an accent, but you certainly do not speak like most people I know. Where are you from?" Parker asked.

"I originally arrived here in Philadelphia by way of Virginia, where I was born and raised."

"Oh! I love Virginia. My family drove through there on vacation last summer. It's so beautiful. Anyway, I still can't get over how familiar you look. So, to answer your question about my findings, I feel as though the men who helped form this country were doing so 'for the people'. You know? Being a true representative for the country, but more so for the people of their state. There's a big difference between their purpose and the politicians of today. In today's Senate or House of Reps, there seems to be more people wanting to be elected simply to have a career in politics! A paycheck that comes with power, prestige and countless other adjectives that basically mean they are not doing the job for the people. It's for their own agenda," she said matter-of-factly.

"I see. Do you not see that each statesman will argue for an agenda? To present their point of view with a passion against the opposition?" he asked.

"Of course, but do so with the heart of creating something better for the country, not for personal gain or more funding for the next re-election campaign," she quipped. "Listen, I have to get going. This tour is awesome, and I probably need to catch up to my group. I'm sorry if I was a bother. Okay, see ya'. Enjoy your tour!" she said as she jogged toward the rest of her group.

Madison raised his voice as he said, "Farewell, Clara Parker! I enjoyed our visit." She turned, smiled, and waved.

While Dr. Rayne moved the rest of his group outside, he noticed the end of a conversation between Madison and the girl in the blue sweater. Rayne suggested they now separate into different groups and proceed with the remainder of the day.

The travelers paired up with their respective statesman and security. Goodbyes were said, and they all agreed to meet back at the parlor later that evening.

"Councilor," Tesla said as he looked at Sherman. "What would you like to see? We have today and possibly a few more. Where shall we begin?"

"This may sound as though I am not in tune with the idea of learning outside the walls of our accommodations, however nothing would be farther from the truth. I am very interested. I do my best thinking from observation and reading. As we leave this place, I will be observing. I wish for you to take me to a library, if you will?"

Dr. Benton was standing within earshot of Sherman's request, and his curiosity was peaked. "Would you mind if I join you today, Roger?"

"Not at all," came the quick reply. "I enjoy your company, Carver. Let us learn something together, shall we?" Sherman said. He turned his eyes to Tesla.

"As you wish, Councilor," Tesla said without hesitation. Tesla knew exactly where to go. He would take North 5th Street to the Vine Expressway, and then over to Highway 76. They made their way to the Philadelphia University and into the Paul J. Gutman Library.

Sarah was standing beside Morris and posed the same destination question. Morris continued to look around the grounds of Independence Hall while answering, "I do not wish to presume anything, so I will ask this question without any expectations. I wonder, Ms. Fleming, would it be possible for me to witness a Senate hearing in progress? It is evident from our classroom education and what we have seen here today that the arguments set forth to the nation's Congress are not held here and I would like to witness such an event. Would that be possible?"

"We are not confined to this city, Senator. But, arrangements must be made. One moment and I will find out." Sarah looked at Dr. Rayne, who was several feet away and possibly out of earshot of the question. She walked over and explained the request. Rayne's eyebrows lifted in excitement. "Of course!" came the reply. I'll have J.A.S.P.E.R. make the necessary arrangements. Just head to the airfield. Oh! Wait just a second; let's start with the state Capitol first. We can take the train. Besides, I know they are in session." he said quickly. Rayne stepped over to Hamilton, Madison, and Dickinson and asked if they would wish to travel to Harrisburg and witness the same event. Hamilton and Madison declined, but Dickinson agreed.

J.A.S.P.E.R. relayed the information to Dr. Benson, who was a bit apprehensive but agreed, and the small contingency left quickly.

~~~~~~~~~

Roger Sherman, Dr. Carver Benton, and Paul Tesla arrived at the university library and had a polite conversation about the country's growth, then discussed its arrogance, stupidity, greed, and gluttony.

"Dr. Benton," Sherman began, "you and your group have concentrated on education of the historical events leading up to some of the most current. I wonder, given all that your technical achievements and history can tell you, what questions would you personally ask of me?"

"Your Honor, I would not wish to pry into anything personal, sir."

"I do not mind. Of course, think of the events which history records I am a part of and ask me the question that is already in your mind, Dr. Benton. I have taken myself away from the others in the group to give you this opportunity."

Dr. Benton was momentarily stunned at Mr. Sherman's perception. When he gained recovery, Benton looked into his eyes with a direct question.

"When you put together the three branches of government, why did you limit it to only three? Why not four? Or more?" he asked.

"Ah. The executive, legislative, and judicial. What other possibility would you have me suggest?"

"As each of these categories are in a position of checks and balances between themselves, it comes to mind that the duties of each do not consider the totality of the country. The President constitutes the executive and his duties are somewhat of an overall concept, but the office cannot operate outside the remaining two. The legislative must uphold or create law with respect to the citizens, and the judicial will operate within the confines of legalities for the criminal. Mr. Sherman," Benton said, "who looks after the country as a whole? What person or group takes a step back and looks at the bigger picture? Let me say it this way: the Senate represents the states, the House represents the people; but who is to look after the nation as a whole - to advise on the national health and wealth, remain within the checks and balances of the current structure, and leave the sovereign states in control of their own decisions? Because, as it stands now, the three current segments have been missing the mark when you look at over $25-30 trillion for debt in 2025. I'll not set responsibility on the government for the rates of homelessness, unemployment, or crime in any given state... those issues, on the whole, have much to do with the individual choices; but the government does write the checks. I do take issue with the welfare system, but we can discuss that later," he added.

Sherman answered, "And you believe that more government would help to guide or oversee the financial wealth?"

"An advisory board of such nature might have proven advantageous. Something like the Electoral College, which keeps the larger states and populations from stepping on the smaller states? A group of economists such as Mr.

273

Morris or Mr. Hamilton?   Men and women who understand that a country, with the exception of war-time spending and the Department of Defense, can and should, live within the means of the taxes it commands. Households across the country live daily lives and carry debt.   Those who overspend have run into problems keeping debts paid. Those who have saved money do not have as many issues.   Each of the families have their burdens to bear, but a dollar is only a dollar. How they spend it is their own choice.   But how the government spends the tax dollars of the people is supposed to be the people's choice, and the government has not been a good steward, my friend. The government has failed, and the debt is climbing."

"I see," Sherman said softly. "You have set your sights quite high in this project. Please, do not place me, or the others, on a pedestal. You may not like the outcome should we fall. Why would you specifically ask me for this subject matter of the branches of government?"

"It happens that history records you as one of the prominent developers for how the government has been framed, Your Honor. You are but one key component of how the Constitution is created. Therefore, as you are here now, I'm asking you."

"I see," Sherman said.

"Mr. Sherman, please understand, I cannot place anyone on any pedestal, least of all myself, even with all this project has already accomplished. We are all just people in a position to effect change. Surely it may change for the worse, but it may very well change for the better. But now you can see a few of the things that have happened over time, and I only ask you to consider what the future brings. Do you make allowances for what you see happening? Or do you not? That is the only question I can propose to you, Roger. I have failed in a great many areas of my life, and I cannot sit in judgement.... but, with the opportunity now provided to you and your fellow statesmen who have come into the future, you can judge for yourself."

"Have either of you any other thoughts you wish to impart that deal with other areas of the Constitution, my friend?" Sherman asked politely.

"Yes, Your Honor," Paul Tesla said. "I do. I wonder if we could briefly cover the terminology in the Constitution which describes ...", Tesla's voice trailed off there as he thought about his next words. His thoughts about Constitutional changes had been brewing for a long time, and he briefly savored the moment. When Tesla finally began again, he spoke of religion and the separation of church and state. He mentioned they might consider providing a more concise glossary, or possibly some footnotes, to tie the hands of those who either liberally reinterpret or purposefully misinterpret the Constitution far beyond the forefather's original intent. Sherman faithfully listened when Tesla mentioned that the Constitution lays out what the government cannot do, not what it can do. He said he believed it was the evidence of men who were running from a monarchy. Sherman did not react to that statement except for the slight smirk from his lips.   The three of them continued their conversation for quite some time.

Meanwhile Hamilton, Madison, and Charles Carson took a stroll down the new Philadelphia streets.   Charles took the lead and simply pointed towards the Delaware River.   As the three left the Independence Hall area, Hamilton began to verbalize his thoughts. "The city has certainly changed," he said. "But, then again, it hasn't in many ways. The sun still shines down through the trees, but the buildings look so much older."

"Well, they are," said Madison.   Carson just grinned.

"Yes, yes, I know.   Yet it seems so very odd to walk by these buildings on this grey walking path that lines the streets.   The paint is peeling on some of these homes that, to us, are still new homes.   It is quite surreal, would you not agree, Mr. Madison?"

"Justly, I would," he muttered softly.

"Tell us, Mr. Carson, do all the streets in Philadelphia have those tall statues of George Washington?"   Carson continued to grin at the sarcasm.

"No sir, they do not.   However, as he did serve as our country's first president, someone thought it fitting to have the statue placed close to Independence Hall."

Madison quipped, "The chap didn't even want the job, and yet he has a statue.   One can almost taste the irony."

As the three continued past the Old City Hall and across South 5th Street, Hamilton could see another statue. "That fellow appears to be looking up at a scroll for some reason. Who might that be, Mr. Carson?"

"That, Senator, is a statue called 'The Signer'. It is the artist's impression of any one of the signers of the Constitution, sir. It is said that the artist believed the signers were joyous that they had completed the document. It was dedicated in 1980 in commemoration of the deeds of the signers, sir."

"Very well. I shall take it the house that was standing here before this statue was no longer of use," he said flatly.

Madison added, "Come now, Alexander. Surely you understand this to be a compliment, do you not?"

"I do. Nothing appears more plausible at first sight. I suppose I was just wondering if it was another impression of Washington. For if it were, it would not be as correct as some might think."

Carson continued to walk with the two as they passed the Second Bank of the United States. Carson briefly described the building but refrained from telling either of them that Hamilton was responsible for authorizing its establishment. Fortunately, neither of them asked for that information.

The three continued on their stroll of the familiar, yet unfamiliar, city. They crossed South 4th, and both Hamilton and Madison noticed Carpenter's Hall off to the right. Somehow, a knowing look passed between them, but neither of them spoke. Both men remembered their recent history lessons, and both men's lives would change because of people they knew in that building.

Concentrating on his thoughts for a moment, Hamilton noticed the smoke coming from the tailpipes of cars and remembered the films about pollution and global warming. However, he also made a mental note that, in his own time, smoke would be puffing out of the chimneys from wood and coal-burning stoves in many homes and stores along the streets of his own town. He also noticed the lack of horses and the piles of dung they produce. Gone. The streets were hard like bricks and all black or gray. He noticed the weather was warm and sunny and dismissed the global warming concept with a wave of his hand. *The earth will constantly change,* he thought to himself. *People will change. I shall strive to make changes towards the betterment of my country.*

The walking tour of the area took a turn to the right on South 2nd Street. Near the corner of Walnut Street, Carson stopped. Madison and Hamilton both stopped behind Carson. "Is there a reason we are here?" Hamilton asked. "Of course, there is. I'd like to be a bit self-indulgent, if I may, and tell you a story. During your time, gentlemen, while this country was being formed by men - well...by you and other men like you - I might have been able to enter in this building through the back entrance. And, frankly, that would be only if I worked here. But that was then, sir. Today, we are walking in a time where I am proud to walk in the front door with two men I have admired since I was a child. Something that no man could ever dream of actually happening. Gentlemen, I love my country dearly.

While the color of my skin may have ruled the lives of the black men in your time, I have made it my mission that it will not rule my life. I have grown up purposely learning to make my life better. To better the world around me. To learn something new each day. In school, I would find the smartest people in the room and find some way to study with them. If they could make a decent grade, so could I."

Carson's story continued as he moved his gaze directly to Madison. "Sir, you once said, 'Equal laws protecting equal rights is the best guarantee of loyalty and love of country.' That statement, and others by many other figures in history, helped me persevere to learn about equality. So today is an unexpected and special day to me, personally. I said this stop is self-indulgent, and if you two wouldn't mind, I would like to walk through that front door with the two of you and buy you a beer before we continue on our walk. The Old City Tavern, built to be one of the features for one of the most prominent cities in all 13 colonies, has been here for a long time."

"Yes, we know," said Hamilton. Carson sheepishly replied, "Yes, of course."

Understanding Carson's heartfelt intentions, Madison quickly chimed in, "Well, what are we waiting for?" Madison waved his hand toward the front door of the Old City Tavern. Hamilton reached the front door first and held it open for Carson to walk though first.

~~~~~~~~~~~

Sarah sat across from Dickinson and Morris on the next available train to Harrisburg while her small contingent of non-descript security were closely filtered among the not so crowded railcar.

Dickinson was casually watching the people close to him stare at their small colorful devices. Heads were bowed down as if in prayer while their fingers and thumbs were furiously pounding on the front of it. Ever watchful of the men in her charge, she could see the curiosity on Dickinson's face.

"Those are cellular phones. Some people call them *mobile phones*. Portable and rechargeable telephones. You may have seen them when the others were talking to each other. However, the electronics built within these small devices not only allow the user to talk to someone a very far distance away, they also contain other ways to communicate or even entertain," she said.

"Entertain," Morris interjected as Dickinson's expression matched Morris's.

"Yes, sir. Small games can be played while they spend their time on the train going home or wherever they are going."

Dickinson grunted, "Sounds like a waste of time. They should be doing something productive."

Morris commented, "You said it communicates in other ways. What do you mean?"

"Of course, Senator. That little device can text a message from one to another. For example, you would be used to someone writing a letter then having that letter be carried from city to city or even across the states. The time that would take would be days, weeks, or months, depending on the distance. However, like the telephone to which you have already been introduced, it can also send written messages." Sarah produced hers from her pocket and said, "This is just one possible reason you see people looking at them so intently. They could be pressing the correct part of the screen to produce a small note to be sent to someone else."

Dickinson was again a bit gruff in his reply, "Seems to me they would just use the telephone function and tell the person what they want to know."

Sarah grinned at the response. "Many people feel that way, sir."

At that instance, Sarah's cell phone buzzed loudly. Then other phones followed in suit. She glanced at the screen and silenced her phone. Turning the face of her cell phone toward the Senators, she said, "This is a mass notice for an Amber Alert. It tells many people with only one message of something important. In this case, a child is missing."

Morris began slapping his leg and commented quietly, "Hear! Hear! So, one could not use that delicate looking apparatus to tell many people the same message at the same time, could they? I suspect to do so individually would take too much time! Couldn't be done, I say. That little device does have a bit of value I should think."

"I would add that, if the device is used appropriately, it retains a certain level of value; however, when used to simply occupy time, it is a poor distraction," Dickinson said bluntly.

Morris grinned at Dickinson when he said, "Excuse me, Sarah. Might I actually speak to someone? Shall we say, one of the other Senators?"

Sarah smiled agreeingly and placed a call to Carson.

Carson, still at the Old City Tavern, sat down his beer and answered the call. and heard Sarah's explanation. Although trying hard to hide a smile, he sat with a serious face and said, "Senator Hamilton, you have a call, sir." Hamilton, with a confused look upon his face, took the small cell phone, held it up to his ear cautiously, and said, "Hamilton here." Once he heard Morris' booming and carefree voice, the conversation flowed freely. Hamilton passed the phone to Madison who also marveled at the technology. Morris handed Sarah's phone to Dickinson who eventually found the item to be a fantastic tool. To add to the fun, Sarah and Carson decided to use the video feature and added to the statesmen's amazement.

Once the conversation was over, Sarah and her two companions continued to talk about the benefits and distractions of the cell phone and other topics until they arrived in Harrisburg.

While stepping out of the train, Sarah found Morris's attention focused on a gentleman not too far away. Observing carefully, she knew why he was looking. Both could see the gentleman walking with an ever so slight limp. They could also see the metal ankle joint attached to a walking shoe.

"That gentleman has a prosthetic leg, quite unlike yours. There have been many advancements in the medical world, Senator, including prosthetics. Especially within the last 75 years. So much so that the world has Olympians who have competed while wearing prosthetics."

"Is that so?" Dickinson asked. "Tell us more, my dear Sarah," he continued as Morris listened intently. As they continued on their way, Sarah filled them in with as much detail as she could remember.

The trio was enjoying the sites of the state capitol and the hearings they witnessed until their security interrupted them.

~~~~~~~~~~

The day slowly began turning to dusk... but not without a black car following Dr. Benton's group. The windows were tinted such that even a view into the front windshield barely revealed the hands holding the steering wheel.

"Stay close but do not draw attention," said the voice from the one in the back seat who was sitting comfortably in a three-piece black Armani suit.

"Yes, sir," came the quick reply.

Speaking out loud, he said, "J.A.S.P.E.R., call Dr. Benton."

J.A.S.P.E.R replied, "Of course, sir."

The phone in Dr. Benton's pocket buzzed. Always being cautious of his surroundings, he looked around to see who might be watching. He already knew of three cars with tinted windows nearby but made no physical motions that he was aware of them. He apologetically nodded to both men with him and, while holding the phone in his hand, said, "Please excuse me for just a moment," and he stepped away from the other two. He didn't take his eyes off Roger Sherman. While his right hand held his phone up to his ear and answered the phone, his left hand touched his belt buckle and pressed a button. All security for every statesman were immediately notified to go into defensive protective mode and bring everyone back to the facility immediately.

"Hello, Colonel," Dr. Benton said calmly. "How can I help you?"

"Dr. Benton, how is your assignment coming along?"

"As we first discussed, Colonel, I don't have an assignment. We have an opportunity to effect change, and there is a very good chance we may fail. However, the staff and primates are doing just fine, and things are slowly progressing. And again, thank you for funding this opportunity, sir."

"No one is looking over your shoulder, Dr. Benton. You just do what you do. What is the status of this opportunity, if I may ask?"

Paul Tesla, Roger Sherman and Dr. Benton were led by security and placed in a van. As the van pulled away from the curb and slowly entered traffic, the black car began to follow as Benton answered the question, "If you are asking about the test results, I will have my official reports ready for you by the end of the week. But I will tell you, at this point, you will be quite happy. You know I won't say much more than that over these phones. I don't trust them."

"Yes, I agree. I look forward to the reports, Dr. Benton. Please, be careful."

"Of course. I need to get back now. A few of us just stepped out for fresh air. Good day, Colonel." Dr. Benton hung up the call.

An hour later, everyone within the city was safely back in the facility. Morris and Dickinson arrived a little later. Dr. Benton felt fairly assured he would be contacted again once he stepped out of the facility. There hadn't been any communications, so this wasn't a coincidence. His cell phone was programmed with only one number, and that same number was the only one that could reach his phone. However, he did not like being tracked down with this electronic leash. Benton would spare no expense for the safety of the statesmen within his care, and a phone call, even from his benefactor, gave him a twinge that would probably keep him up all night.

"He called you, didn't he?" asked Dr. Rayne.

"Yes. Yes, he did," answered Benton in a rather bland, monotone expression.

"Just wanting another update?"

"Of course."

"You know my next question."

"I do. And the answer is I do not believe he suspects anything other than what our reports tell him. The transportation of a live animal from one place to another place is currently becoming more viable with each test. Our progress on the 8th sub-floor is proceeding in an orderly fashion."

"It just seems like every time we step out, there are eyes watching us. That's a bit creepy, don't you think?"

"They do watch us, and yes, I am of the same mindset. It is 'creepy', as you say. I wonder if I should 'forget' that phone the next time we go outside."

"No. Don't do that," Dr. Rayne said quickly. "You could risk possible backup security measures we have in place. That phone has a level of safety for us."

"Yes, of course; you're right. Any thoughts on what to do?"

"I do. Take a vacation."

"Excuse me?"

"Take a vacation," Rayne replied confidently and held his hands up in quotation marks while exaggeratingly enunciating his words.

"Okay, you have my attention. Go on."

"Go into town. Take the phone. Call him. Do it after you turn in the reports and discuss whatever he wishes. Answer his questions. Then, near the end of the conversation, tell him you will be taking a vacation. Tell him you'll take the phone but ask him to remember that you're needing a little down time. Simply ask him to give you some space. Remind him you have security with you. Tell him you will have a few friends with you and need a break. Remind him you'll have the phone but don't expect it to ring. Tell him you want a vacation."

"You're inferring that we take our guests on our vacation."

Dr. Rayne just smiled at Benton.

"Where shall we go on vacation, Dr. Rayne?"

"Wherever it is, this gets you out of the facility without that proverbial leash, so to speak. Plus, I don't think we need to go together."

"Go on," Benton redundantly motioned his hands for Rayne to explain.

"First, security, sir. I wouldn't think you would want all five statesmen in a single place for any long length of time should, heaven forbid, something arise that might put any one of them or the team in jeopardy. Secondly, since time is not our friend and, as you say, hearts are beating, we might be able to give more experiences, more insights, to the men if they are taken to various places."

"You'll lose those insights on any person who does not witness the same event."

"We can't control that even today, Carver," Rayne said confidently. "If two people witness a car accident from different sides of the street, you get two different stories. If you look at only a part of a picture, you can't see the whole concept from the painter. And I'll close with this; neither you nor I can force the hand of the man who chooses to sign the document as it stands.

It's the different experiences we have in our own lives that have shaped us to make the decisions we have already made. If we put these men in the same place, give them the same experience, then we're no different than Pavlov. They will all find the cheese the way *we* want them to, and I am quite sure that was not our intention. Let's show them what America has become. Show them the good, the bad, the stupid, the genius, and they will come to their own conclusions. These men are very intelligent - ever so much more so than us, I have come to believe."

"Dr. Rayne," Benton said quietly. "I do so admire your perspective and focus. I believe I have a phone call to make about a vacation. Any other bits of wisdom?"

Benton looked very inquisitively at Dr. Rayne. Rayne replied with a smirk, "What? You're telling him the truth. You do need a vacation. But, to be clear, you should tell him. So yes, here's some wisdom for you: I suggest you tell him you will not be working on any 'monkey' business."

PART 2 What If They Knew

Chapter 23

     Dr. Benson's conference call with the Colonel was as easy as Dr. Rayne thought it would be. Benson gave all the proper reasoning and the Colonel agreed a vacation was in order. Of course, the Colonel had some stipulations, but his primary desire was to contact him when Benson and his staff were all safely back in the facility and ready to work again. All the employees dealing with the animal teleportation were elated for the surprise time off. They were given 30 days paid time-off. Each of them knew the work being performed was classified and they would be held accountable. They also knew a polygraph was waiting for them upon their return. Dr.

Benson pulled no punches when it came to the security of his work. He also knew in the big scheme of things, no single person, other than himself and the travelers, could piece together what they have accomplished to this point.

By considering the amount of time off given to the staff from the floor above, Dr. Benson decided to ask each statesman what exactly he might like to learn about next. Dr. Rayne added any other major city was not unlike Philadelphia so, traveling far away from the facility was not necessary but would not be ruled out. Those travel plans were now imminent. That being understood, the statemen gather together to discuss their options.

Madison opened the dialogue, "With consideration to all thoughts that will be put forth, I would encourage us to sit for a day in a congressional session and listen to proceedings. Albeit not being able to object, vote or otherwise engage in the discussions, I think we might be interested in how legislature has moved forward."

"I agree with you, sir." Said Hamilton. "I would like to see this modern-day legislation and try to comprehend what would lend these delegates to make the decisions they have made. I wonder, even now, before I have seen them in action, if they even consider what the Constitution says before they decide to orate in front of other statesmen. Have they passed a test on the contents of the Constitution before being sworn into office? Do they waste their time and cause themselves to be a fool? It may be said that even a fool does not know history is laughing at him. Have they made a mockery of the system by forgetting its purpose? To that end, was I the fool, for having penned by the name of Publius, defending and encouraging this Constitution? Have I, have we, failed to present our case?" Hamilton's face was full of worry and guilt upon making such a claim.

Dr. Carver Benson quickly interjected a response in the fashion of the senate and loudly enough that all other conversations were halted, and Benson was the only person speaking, "To the Honorable Alexander Hamilton, hailing from the great state of New York, I humbly submit to you and your fellow statemen, the following: that we, the people of these United States, live and breathe in the greatest nation that has ever been conceived. Our strength of character, honor and integrity as a nation is unequalled within the realm of all nations. You should be exceptionally proud of the part you have played in making this happen, your Honor. Please, never doubt our gratitude. You are here today, not for us to heave upon your shoulders any guilt for which you claim, but for more of your guidance, wisdom and clarity from the pen you and other patriots so richly wield. In any form of government, any...." Benson paused to search for the right word..." idea, any plan, any snowball, must come from something small, a beginning. As the snowball comes to life and grows, it will meet an obstruction. If it continues to roll, the obstruction may be rolled over and left behind, or it may stick to the bottom and eventually roll back around to the front, or even to the side, should the snowball be pushed off its intended path. Gravity plays an essential roll in the creation of such things. Gravity is the inherent force with which the snowball will grow. Kinetic energy helps move that snowball. A snowball is seldom

291

perfectly round. The concepts of our Constitution are just, your Honor. Just like a snowball it is not perfect. And it has, overtime, grown with Amendments. We call you our "Founding Fathers", "nation builders", holders for the flame of Liberty and have set the framework of our country into motion. You started this snowball. We cannot nor will ever lay any blame for aiding in the creation of the greatest nation on earth. We do, however, need your help. We need you, gentlemen, as a child needs a father, to help us return to the path for which you designed. A path, knowing there will be obstacles ahead that can overcome, and our country be better maintained. We need your help to illicit an integrity of the people that can be held to a higher degree. You two gentlemen," he peered into the eyes of Hamilton and Madison, "penned in the name of Publius, for a reason. That reason holds true to today. We, the people of this great nation, need to hear the words of Publius again. We need the aid of our forefathers to be diligent in the guidance you had once started. Clarify the words that are written and write the unspoken so that this nation could omit our mistakes and misunderstandings. This is what we are asking of you. With your help, we, the people, can and will do better."

Hamilton's quick mind gave Dr. Benson an astonishing retort, "Dr. Benson, your 460 words of encouragement are very aptly put and I, for one, will receive them in the highest regard."

Morris sniped, "Is that right? 460 words? You counted them as he spoke? What kind of genius are you Hamilton?"

292

Roger Sherman spoke, "Both of these men simply outshine us all in any level. And I applaud you equally. Now, shall we settle on visiting the senate for a few days? I, for one, would love to see this and then I have a few more ideas lest my own snowball be maneuvered 'off course' or melted, for that matter." With that, a few bits of laughter came from the group.

Within the hour, Dr. Benson found that the senate was in session and made the necessary arraignments. The group divided up into separate vehicles and with all security precautions, headed for the Senate in Washington D.C. The statesmen thought they would be riding in a motorized vehicle again. They enjoyed that quite a bit and Dr. Rayne was hoping they would be equally surprised and enjoy the plane ride. The statesmen were informed along the way they would be listening to actual deliberations within the U.S. Senate. Roger Sherman was the only man to stop and get a bit nervous while standing on the tarmac of the private runway. After a little coaxing from Dr. Rayne, he proceeded to board. A short time later they arrived.

They were led to a VIP section to listen to the arguments, they were given specific instructions not to interrupt the speakers. The topic at hand was yet another in the vast expansion of the welfare system and entitlement programs.

The current senator from California was advocating for more monies for the recipients of the unemployed. After his opening argument concluded, the senator from Texas gained control of the podium and argued to the contrary.

293

"Please tell me why, in the year 2018, the United States had approximately 92 welfare or unemployment systems programs or 'handouts' with only 2 requiring those recipients to physically 'do something' to be eligible to receive such benefits. Ninety of the programs basically require some menial paperwork and a promise that they are eligible. At the same time, our cities are having a tough time finding employees, due to non-qualifying applicants' or simply do not have the money to hire employees to clean up our cities. And by cleaning up our cities I mean pick up and fill up trash bags or scrub off or repaint areas affected by unsightly graffiti. Why can we not combine the eligibility to receive these benefits of these welfare programs with a program to help the very city they live in, the same city that cuts their checks, the same city that is putting food on their table, the same city where the working people who are paying taxes and let's hold these people accountable to the monies they are receiving.

The California Senator's response was limited in thought, but he responded by declaring this action as having massive liability for the state as the recipient would then be counted as a worker and should any person be hurt while performing such actions would be able to hold that city or state accountable for their injury.

The Texas Senator smiled with this response and gave a concise retort, "That would absolutely be the case for those recipients who would wish to gain something for doing nothing. If nothing is what they wish to do, then nothing is what they should expect, Senator. If they wish to expect a check, then they need to understand they are expected to bring their allotted bags of trash with them or at the very least, have their work verified by an existing authority. The service they perform would be voluntary since they are asking for assistance, not employment. If they are unable to perform such work, then a family member, the church, a charitable organization or a friend should be able to help them, not the government. Even the homeless of any city could do the same work by cleaning up right where they live. Have you seen the trash that surrounds them? Surely, this isn't an unsurmountable task, picking up trash where you sleep. I would even be in favor of recipients being enrolled in a G.E.D. program to finish High School or being involved in the education of a trade. Their grades could be the accountability. I remember as a youth, my parents would not give me any allowance. None. No handouts in our family. However, if we got up early on a Saturday morning, raked leaves and bagged them, we earned ten cents a bag and it was a large bag, mind you. I remember in my childhood when $2.50, that's 25 bags of leaves, would buy me a little something but certainly not enough for the things I really wanted, which, in turn, helped me realize how to work to save money. Why, in a society such as ours, can we not encourage people to work and save money? As to your citing a liability issue, Senator, is it not apparent that we, as taxpayers, are already footing the bill for their health care now? I can't see us being any more liable as they currently lay on their backsides and perform absolutely no function for society at all and continue to collect a check and health benefits. There are statistics showing this type of behavior is generation after generation! We must change! We must be able to see some form of work and effort for the monies they are receiving, if not, we will continue to have recipients who are lazy and not contributing, and we will see the current programs fail and do nothing more than deplete our resources. Put people to work. Help them to feel useful. Give them a sense of accomplishment for a day's labor. Build their self-worth. Encourage them to be better. Expect them to be better and they will expect the same of themselves.

Other senators in the room began to clap in approval for the statements by the Texas Senator. The licentious congressmen either frowned or lowered their heads in disagreement while other remained asleep as if the conservative argument was not relevant. Still, others in the room knew there would be so much more work to do on this subject, it appeared by the applause that this could be worked out for most, if not all, of the current assistance programs if only the arrogance of the socialists would reach across the aisle to try for resolution. Turning around a failing system doesn't happen overnight.

During the afternoon break, Dickinson let out a heated reaction when he exclaimed, "Damn these people! Sleeping or nodding off! In our day we had no time to waste for the people of this country. Ben Franklin may have closed his eyes, but I know from his every response that he was listening! Damn the arrogance of any seat in congress who blatantly shows mistrust of his office!"

Chapter 24

The following day, all five statesmen agreed to sit in and listen to the Legislature again. Revamping health care was the topic of conversation.

A Wyoming senator was orating the true purpose of the healthcare system, reminding the senate of several relevant facts. He began with the fact that healthcare started for the men in the U.S. Navy.

The listened in as he said, "... a pre-paid 20 cents for each seaman. You should recall that these monies were distributed for men who were making a military effort to keep our country safe. They worked for it. They earned it! In the early 1900s, a universal health care proposal was set forth; however, the federal government was not in the picture. The proposal was to let the individual state governments be the responsible parties, keeping the federal government at bay. You should also remember that many workers of that time period had a "sickness fund", provided by employers, and that the American Medical Association (AMA) was opposed to the ideas of "socialized medicine" and "compulsory health insurance"! The Great Depression changed everything."

He continued by explaining, "Hospitals began providing their own type of insurance coverage called Blue Cross. Physicians quickly followed suit by creating their own insurance plan, which they called Blue Shield, and collecting premiums. In 1946, the National Mental Health Act was passed. With the IRS's declaration that premiums paid for by employers became a tax-deductible business expense, the unintended combination of these developments emulsified third party insurance companies as primary health care providers."

The Wyoming senator reiterated that, "While the health care system was changing, employees and employers were paying their way. The government was not giving it away! President Lyndon B. Johnson's 1965 plan for Medicare and Medicaid passed under the Social Security Amendments. I'll remind you this was heavily opposed by the AMA! The insertion of this "socialized medicine", administered by the U.S. government, was still a health care insurance in the present day. However, the federal government was now in control, and it has been a failure!"

The senator continued, "The argument for national health care reform remained a constant source of contention within every level of the political system and would for many years. Each and every president had proposed some sort of change to the system to create one where employees or employers had an opportunity to sign up for health coverage. It was a choice. At the very least, it was an option, even if funded in part by payroll taxes and tax deductions. That is, it was an option until the 1993 Clinton health care plan which required mandatory enrollment throughout all income ranges, which included government subsidies to guarantee affordability. And there you have it. No more choice! Government control. And, it didn't stop there." He paused to look at his audience to see if anyone was paying attention. He paused to look at empty chairs for members not attending the assembly. He mentally noted this happened too often. But, for those who were there he moved on.

"The beast grew hungry for more," he said solemnly.

The Wyoming senator abruptly and loudly protested by challenging the constitutionality of "socialized medicine" and reminded the Congress that Thomas Jefferson himself warned against this very thing called *socialism*. The Wyoming senator concluded his time by reminding those present what Thomas Jefferson meant when the words "promote the general welfare" were written: They were meant to build the economy and challenge citizens to be better than the generation before. Jefferson did not intend for the federal government to promote a welfare system by creating perpetuating programs as a handout to the masses and funded by tax monies! If the federal government continued to pay for our individual bad choices and was then allowed to control aspects of personal choice, then socialism would take a foothold. Step after step, those footholds would gather momentum and America would no longer be governed by the constitutionality of a program but by the will of the elected.

The Wyoming senator, not knowing who was sitting in the gallery, began listing ways to fund health care programs. He proposed taking away the government funding and putting those tax dollars toward other programs or giving it back to the people. He also proposed a "health fee" against the consumables that tend to cause the health issues in our country. As an example, he mentioned the tobacco and alcohol industries. He proposed fees that would be paid by companies that produce tobacco and alcohol. Surely, it would raise the price of such items. However, with the amount of consumption of these items, the increased cost would not be prohibitive to those who wanted them. He was not in favor of another failed prohibition and even admitted he enjoyed a glass of wine or a fine bourbon from time to time. At the same time, he admitted that those individuals who could not afford the increased cost would still find ways to acquire alcohol and tobacco, meaning the addictions associated with these industries and their effects that plague our hospitals would continue. Ideally, however, the "health fee" would result in fewer alcohol-related car accidents; fewer liver transplants; lower lung cancer rates; lower numbers of homeless in the streets due to alcoholism; and fewer addictions starting at young ages, which simply become worse over time and much harder to quit as the person gets older.

The Wyoming senator said he was well aware that the alcohol and tobacco industries would lobby against such an idea paying millions upon millions to prevent such a fee. To a point, they thrive upon such dependencies and low-cost products to produce high-volume sales. He continued by stating he understood that the fee would not prevent alcoholism or lung cancer or change the choices that the addicted would make in the future. But the fee would reduce the cost to the taxpayers who were not alcoholics, even though they might drink. The fee might have lowered the volume of sales in both industries; but spending millions of dollars on lobbyists likely would not change their bottom line as much as they expected. If companies such as these helped produce a solution to an issue created in part by their product, the snowball effect would very well change the number of addicts, homeless, and organ transplants, as well as the level of reliance on government programs paid for by taxes levied on every person in the country. The solution would not solely be the responsibility of these companies as the choice of the consumer must always play a part.

He concluded with an example by stating, "For every man or woman in this country has been faced with decisions that, on some level, would break any given number of the Ten Commandments. We are human, and we will never be able to govern the free will of others. Even our Lord knows this. And we should not try to create a society so controlled by the government that we become puppets to the powerful.

Chapter 25

Madison woke up early. He was not a man who tended to lay in bed, however, on this morning, he didn't stir. His eyes slowly focused on the area around him. A modern hotel-room. His own private bathroom with as much running water as he wished. Light switches and ceiling lights seemed rather handy. Wall outlets, telephone and television served no purpose for him. The table with pen and paper, the clock-radio displaying the current time and the bed were quite useful. He also noted that the feather pillow was truly more comfortable than his own. He was certainly is a different world.

He thought of Benton's classroom and the slow, gradual change it had made for nearly every fifty years of education. He appreciated that. There would have been quite a shock for him, and his fellow statesmen, had Benton not thought this process through as thoroughly as he had. Madison laid in bed being appreciative for the normalcy of his own bedroom, in his own home and in his own time as his mind was heavy for what lay ahead.

He wasn't scared or worried for what may happen today. In fact, he was expecting a good day of learning. But, as Madison continued to lay on his side, he began preparing himself for disappointment. His thoughts turned back to his comment he had made about this 'American experiment'. Why did those words come out of his mouth? There was no ongoing 'experiment' when he argued for a strong national government in congressional meetings, digested strategies with Thomas Jefferson or

Patrick Henry or even simple things such as raising his horses. He also believed it was no accident when Dr. Rayne helped him avoid the pitchfork only days ago. His life was no experiment.

He tossed over to other side and starred at his bedroom door. An experiment was like some exercise in a science lab or baking in a kitchen. If you mess up or burn it, one would throw away and start over. Ah! So, maybe this is what Dr. Benton is thinking as well. Start over.

Questions poured through his mind. Why me? Why now? Why not start with Adam and Eve? Why not with Alexander the Great? Well, those places in time just wouldn't do. There might not be a United States if he started with those. No, Dr. Benton was not playing God. Benton even mentioned that his own life is on the line. The whole team of travelers knew this. Madison knew what it was like to wake up, go to war against the enemy, knowing full-well he could die in battle. Many of his men had lost their lives in a cause they believed in. This was just a different kind of war and he was in a position to come to the aid of Americans. Madison fully believed in Benton's hopes and knew deep down ~ Dr. Carver Benton is a true patriot. Madison knew this was about America ~ the United States. It was about these documents ~ these 'instructions' called The Constitution and the Bill of Rights which govern our country.

Benton wants us to rewrite the instructions for this American experiment. Start over. He is still proving to us that what we have put together was a good beginning but just wasn't clear enough for others to follow. The recipe is flawed. Too much room for interpretation. The result is not so desirable. Too many 'cooks in the kitchen', as it were. Too many laws. Too much government.

Madison spoke to himself, "I shall continue to believe in a strong national government. Yet, I have begun to see where limiting the size and scope of the national and allowing states to be more accountable may be a more suitable solution. Let's just see what this time here in the future continues to show me. Let's just see..." His voice trailed off as he continued to think.

A mere 250 years later, the concept of freedom and liberty has been pushed to the outside and ended up in the crust of what America has baked into today. And this crust was drying up, breaking and falling away from the center. Madison was convinced that if America continues down this path, this "American Pie" would bake itself to death. This inevitable explosion was on the horizon. "Is it already too late," he wondered.

Madison sat up from his bed and began getting ready for the day. He dressed and walked to the bathroom. *This indoor toilet was an amazing thing*, he thought. *These things are in homes across the country?* It's just proof that the 'common man' has more common sense than some of the elitist who can't solve problems for the masses.

Madison hated to be negative. It was out of character for him. He finished getting ready for the day and met the rest of the statesmen.

Chapter 26

Still wearing clothes within the current time period, the entire group found themselves at a local coffee house. Not some national chain, where everything on the menu was five bucks and Christian's were told they were not welcome. Besides, the coffee was decidedly better and less costly at locally owned establishments. Sitting in no particular order around several tables, the group had several small conversations going on at the same time.

As the brew was served, Roger Sherman asked a composite question in his own fashion of not so few words as possible, "The knowledge you maintain is rather amazing, but I wish for you to be more specific within the confines of commerce. You will recall that in 1743, in Connecticut and the township of New Milford, my brother and I opened the first mercantile. Do tell us the history concerning labor, the wages thereof and if there are no objections from my esteemed colleagues, I should first think we will be hearing of details which will astound us and take more than a few moments and secondly, I believe we would be in need of requesting a full pot of coffee and not just a single cup." Sherman glanced in the direction of Madison expecting him to object or make a motion to the contrary of nearly anything he said. Madison and Sherman were known rivals within the Congress and seldom were their wishes in league with the other.

Madison, seizing the moment of the expectation, was not disappointing. He slowly stood to match the eyeline of Sherman and replied, "I wish to add in agreement to this request and suggest a bit of bread to be shared during this informative session. We may be here for quite some time?" Madison nodded just a bit toward Sherman and both men sat down feeling satisfied they had both contributed. The other three statesmen grinned and slowly laughed for a moment and Paul Tesla stood from his chair.

Putting his hand out in front of him with a gesture of noting his own fellow workers he began with a grin and bit of mockery, "If there would be no other offers to answer the question from the Honorable Congressman hailing from the great state of Connecticut, I will begin and accept any additions to this lesson to give these gentlemen a clearer picture of what has transpired over time but first, Dr. Rayne, could you please order up the coffee and snacks of some sort and we shall begin."

Charles Carson, sitting by Dr. Rayne, quickly put his hand on Dr. Rayne's shoulder and responded quietly, "I'll get it. I'm closer, and I think Paul is enjoying this a bit much today."

Paul reminded the men at the table on the history of the labor force in America. He recited statistics between whites, blacks, and other races. He defined and separated the groups into white collar and blue collar and set the tone of the conversation. Paul's ability to pull for information and present it was nothing less than amazing. He formed the otherwise boring statistical information into a mesmerizing story. Other patrons in the coffee shop who were able to hear them began turning in their chairs and listening to the speaker.

306

Paul taught on topics regarding labor in several areas, including farming, even with his main focus-group having just covered this. He went into industrial areas such as unions, ship building, factory work, women in the labor force, blacks with and without jobs, migrant workers and why wages have changed over time.

For years farmers have hired migrant workers to perform much of the work done by hand in the fields. While the landowners were usually white families, the work was predominantly completed by non-white workers who would accept a lower wage. Paul stated that this process hasn't changed much. Still today, part of the labor force are immigrants, legal and illegal, who want to find a better lifestyle here in America than they could have in their own country. They are willing to be paid lower wages in cash and avoid taxes. And there are still employers, farming and otherwise, who will find those people, pay in cash, avoid the government required fees, make a profit and still get the work done. It's a game to some. It's a way of life for others.

For many companies, the use of the advancements in technology, or even better working processes, which promote the ability to produce at a lower cost is a common goal. However, the downside is that it is reducing jobs.

At the end of Paul's conversation, when all questions were answered, he invited his group to go on a bus ride. The large coach bus was waiting for them a block away. Once all the travelers and statesmen were seated, Charles Carson acted as a local tour guide and gave the group a history of the area. By noon, they had driven around the White House, Lincoln Memorial, Washington Monument, Vietnam Wall and other famous tourist places. They also spent a time going through parts of the Smithsonian Museums. While much of this wasn't anything to do with the Constitutionality of any particular subject, the history they had learned in the classroom came to life if a different way.

The day was long but not quite over yet. Carson had the bus driver stop at the Amtrak station where the entire group was given a ticket. Seated on the Amtrak with other passengers, they experienced the two-and-a-half-hour ride back to Philadelphia.

Chapter 27

The following day Dr. Rayne was standing in front of the group. He had been up for several hours during night trying to think of a positive way to propose a thought process to the statesmen. A concept that he, along with Dr. Benson, would hope to shape the thoughts of the statesmen in a direction of growth for America. A direction that could lend a person who wishes to be involved in the decisions of the government would gravitate towards. The two had spoken about this several times and decided Dr. Rayne should deliver the message.

The eight men and Sarah Fleming were seated in Independence National Historical Park and just outside the building housing the Liberty Bell. As the group looked south, Chestnut St. and Independence Hall could be seen not more than 100 yards away. To the north, a newer building just across Arch St. stood there with the words National Constitutional Center. The cool morning air gave way to a very pleasant morning with the sun still rising. The dew along the top of the grass was still glistening. "Good morning everyone." He said and similar greetings were spoken, and head nods were exchanged. "Today's discussion is designed to help you think about the future. While you five are standing here today is no less than the culmination of years of work, research, science and the hopes a several people, we cannot stop and at just giving you a history lesson. What would be the purpose of such a thing if we sent you back without telling you of our own thoughts and ideas. Dr. Benson has already stressed that ultimately, the choice is yours on how you use this information and we, all of us here with you today, agree with this decision and you are free to return at any time ~ travelers, please show these gentlemen you are ready to take them home upon their request."

Each traveler reached into their own pocket and produced the small transport device and showed it to the person they transported. In Charles Carson's case, he showed it to two men. Rayne paused for a moment and watched as none of the statesmen flinched. Their attention was riveted to him. "Very well."

"We are also very cognizant that our views may not lend towards your own. You may be quite disturbed…. angry…. or possibly need more information to form a better opinion. Should your emotions rise and arguments form during this time, we welcome the opportunity to answer questions and discuss viewpoints. Let's begin with a story of sorts.

In a movie shown in 2015 called <u>Bridge of Spies,</u> one of the main characters is a Mr. Donovan. He happens to be a solicitor, a lawyer, such as yourselves. He makes a statement that rings true to our conversation today. The character is having a conversation with a federal agent who has the last name of Hoffman. The Hoffman name is of German descent. Mr. Donovan concedes his heritage is Irish from both his mother and father. However, both men were born in America. They both believe in America but are currently at odds with each other. As an aside, gentlemen, I know from factual accounts in history that several of you have had your own disputes due to your beliefs, but you also know that each of you believes strongly in America and wishes only the best for the American people. Think about this as I continue:

Mr. Donovan clearly states that each man is, by heritage, an immigrant of sorts and they have their differences. He states, "but what makes us both Americans? Just one thing. One. The Rule Book. We call it the Constitution. And we agree to the rules and that's what makes us Americans."

Please understand gentlemen, you are creating this rule book. You are framing the way America works, reacts, grows and lives within the boundaries of law.

At the conclave you were attending before you chose to be here ~ delegates were arguing, orating and otherwise engaged in the formation of a document we call the Constitution. Our independence from the monarchy has been claimed and the Articles of Confederation were ratified in 1781. Our Rule Book is my topic of today's discussion.

"The Constitution talks briefly about a 'citizen'. At the time this was written, this term may, to some, have been inherently clear. To others, it was not and thus it was mentioned in the document. However, over time, it has lost its meaning. It has definitely lost its strength in our sovereignty. Today's definition of a citizen is 'a legally recognized subject or national of a state or commonwealth, either native or naturalized'. Now, let's determine a bit of criteria of what it means to maintain citizenship.

From history, even before your own time gentlemen, we have had a difficult time with who is and who is not allowed 'certain inalienable rights' with regard to citizenship. The Constitution, as it is written, before any amendments, does not define a citizen. What if it did?

In my time such as it is, people have bastardized & profited from that meaning. Let me give you an example: ships carrying visitors on vacation who wish to see our country for a short time might, and often do, have pregnant mothers who, through no fault of their own, must deliver that child while they are on U.S. soil, thus, by definition and default, U.S. citizenship is granted to that child. A child which will likely be taken back to the parent's country or origin ~ raised as a child of that country and will have been issued a birth certificate from the U.S. A child that, in all probability, may not ever be taught to speak English or taught American history ~ will not produce any goods or services in this country ~ will not ever pay taxes to the U.S. government and yet, by birth right alone, has the power to cast a vote.

This practice is not so accidental as one might believe. As a matter of fact, in 2018, television news media reported that there are businesses in Russia profiting from flying pregnant women into Florida, a southern peninsula state, with full expectations of delivering babies for the express purpose with which we have just described. This news program reported the cost of flying each pregnant girl, approximately 20-25 years of age, housing them in a resort hotel, paying for their transportation, meals, hospital stay, the birth, doctor's fees and return to Russia was a rough cost of $100,000.00. I must wonder where this money had come from. How would a young lady acquire so much money? Could it be that the Russian government might be financing this? And what would be the reason for this? To gain a U.S. birth certificate, raise the child in Russia, educate that child in Russia and when the time is right, send that child to the U.S. and educate them in our Universities, in areas of foreign policy, or Information Technology and help them gain jobs within our government. Could it be a long-term plan to undermine the U.S.? Maybe. Maybe not. Perhaps, I should add that it has been reported in the mainstream news that similar programs originating in China pays around ten thousand dollars for their women to perform the same function. Part of the oath of citizenship and of those entering military service is 'to defend against enemies, both foreign and domestic.' Our country's security programs and foreign policies have missed the concept of 'defense' in this regard. To protect against enemies both foreign and domestic. Certainly, these women mean no physical harm to our property, but this practice is directly related to the tax burden placed on the citizens thus, we are not being protected, are we? But it is an interesting concept, is it not?"

This, of course, is our tax dollars at work. But that's not all, those women and children who stay may very well receive welfare benefits. Keep this in mind, simply due to the cultural differences, language or other factors, it takes a long time to assimilate into a city where they were placed in 'maternity hotels'. They would tend to stick together for familiarity. Remember, this has been going

313

on for possibly many years! In the year 2012, as much as 36,000 foreign births occurred on U.S. soil.

The question remains ~ why should this be permissible?

If I were to tell you that the world is keenly aware of our practice to give children born here on U.S. soil a de-facto citizenship, that airplanes packed with pregnant women arrive from other countries and land within the United States for the sole purpose of delivering a child and gain that child's U.S. citizenship, how would you feel?   This 'anchor baby' or 'jackpot baby' practice is allowable due to the 1965 Immigration Act supporting, and in fact, grossly abusing,   the   14th Amendment.   Please   don't misunderstand, the 14th Amendment is also a law passed to follow up the 13th Amendment which freed slaves. The 14th Amendment guaranteed their citizenship of the current human in existence in America for that time period and we applaud this in every way. However, it left the door wide open for future illegal aliens to abuse this law. Remember, this is also the law which allows the births of foreign children to have citizenship based on 'jus soli'.

I believe I've read where several persons sitting in the oval office and others have argued against birthright citizenship or 'jus soli' ~ a Latin term meaning the 'right to the soil'.

Well, do they? Do the 'anchor babies' have a right to the soil for the sole purpose of happenstance or purposeful theft of our tax dollars that support them?   The answer is yes. The answer is yes only due to the way our law is written and, for the past several decades, people are taking advantage of our generosity, our way of life and our hope for a better life in America. Is this not the reason that our countrymen have fought for, argued for, bled for & died for? To get away from monarchies or socialists and oppressive governments where the voice of the people can be heard. To have a strong but less government controlling our lives. To be a free country? Of course, it is and yet there must be a level of control that Americans understand. There must be a government.

I am also aware that many of these women abandon their newly born child with the knowledge that our system will take care of them. The abandoned child may be placed in a home, probably overrun with other children in the same situation, with the hope that the child may be adopted and raised by good parents. Why the mother left them will have a hundred or more reasons we may never know.

Roger Sherman's face began to turn red in anger.

"Yes, your honor." Rayne returned his look and continued, "I understand you have fifteen children of your own and you, sir, have every right to feel anger at the thought of someone abandoning a child. Every good parent should feel the way you do, sir. Unfortunately, that is not the case with mentality or circumstances in today's America. In defense of the children, they would be allowed to stay in the custody of the government which gave them citizenship. Furthermore, those children, again, no fault of their own, are now a tax liability paid for by the programs initiated within the government. The child, who by now is a part of the Child Protection Services, or various other entity names depending on the state the child is found within, and probably has significantly improved living conditions than from where he or she has come from ~ yes, that is a highly probable reason that the parents did this from the beginning. Who wouldn't want a better life for their child? Being a part of the over-crowded and under-funded CPS system and an American citizen, these kids may qualify for free health care or a full college tuition, paid for by whom? By the people of the United States.

These are just examples of situations that have come to fruition in our country. So, I ask you gentlemen, in these cases, should a child, clearly from other countries be given U.S. citizenship due to 'jus soli'? Simply based upon being born within the border of the United States. The Fourteenth Amendment guarantees this right in a very blanket statement and therefore, the answer is yes. A guaranteed citizenship.

In the years that President Donald Trump was in the oval office, he made it known he set out to remove the citizenship of those children who were born in the U.S. when that child's parents were not citizens or, more specifically, illegal aliens. I can't contend that an executive order of such nature would stand up in the congress and it would certainly disrupt millions of lives for the individuals involved. While the idea is sound on the principle that our freedoms and liberties should not be exploited with such blatant disregard for those individuals who have worked hard on becoming a citizen within the laws of the country. On this subject, our nation would not be in this situation were it not for the wording of the amendment.

Please understand, the roots of our country, including your own families, have a   European, African, Native American or some other heritage. At our roots, America is full of immigrants. Period. Our country's true immigrants have performed all requirements necessary to be called U.S. citizens. Why should those that jump over or crawl under our borders enjoy the same liberties? Inclusively, many of the illegals do not pull their own weight either financially or morally. Our country is in decay. Overpopulation in many border cities is upon us, especially in concrete cities overpowering each coastline. We have never been more politically and morally separated than we are today.

"Let me pose this question gentlemen, what if...," he paused. "What if there were precautions taken against such line items as these from the beginning?"

Rayne stopped just for moment to see if any statesman had a comment. Each man continued to be captivated at Rayne's oration. Seeing no signs of questions, Rayne was a bit taken back. Certainly, men of this caliber would have questions. They were well known for their arguments, especially between themselves. He decided to pause for a moment and let their thoughts find a voice.

No one raised a hand or their voice.

"If I may continue with thoughts about being a citizen. If all the people of the United States are considered citizens, what would be on a list of causes for them **not** to be considered citizens.   In my youth, we had a grade in school called 'Citizenship'. Which basically meant that the child was behaving in a manner consistent with being a good child ~ to have displayed good citizenship. When the child misbehaved, the parent would know this because the grade for that child would be lowered. In some schools this may have been a pass/fail situation. In other schools, the grade was such as it was in your own time. High marks for good kids and lower marks for kids that needed attention by the parents. Well, as I said, that's in my youth and I'm unaware if schools continue this type of sort of thing anymore. Too many parents think it is the responsibility of the school system to make a child behave and is someone else's fault when they do not.

"I'd take a lash to any child of mine if they misbehaved in school," Sherman said sternly.

"As would I," added Madison and others showed their agreement.

"My child would have chosen lashes from the schoolteacher over what I would do if they wouldn't behave," Sherman added.

Rayne raised his hands in a calming fashion after every statesman had chimed in. "And I would do the same. But some parent, somewhere, got her feelings hurt so she hired some lawyer and forced litigation upon the school system and screwed that up for many parts of the country. There remain a few sensible places in America where parents will allow teachers or school principals to address the child's behavior by 'lashes' as you say, Mr. Sherman."

Madison spoke up very clearly, "Those that do not allow it are the types of decisions that, to coin your current phrases, 'piss me off'. Why should any judicial proceeding remove a basic corrective action from an educational system? Why would an immediate punishment for an unacceptable behavior be taken away? I am not understanding the cognitive processes from which these outcomes are derived. A teaching system is, by its very nature, designed to help our children learn to stay on the straight and narrow. To gain wisdom through education. I simply cannot fathom how you people live in such chaos as I have witnessed thus far."

Rayne responds in kind, "Mr. Madison, you sir, have the same sentiments of many conservatives today. However, as we have shown you, our population has changed exponentially, and there are many more people who do not share those same sentiments." Rayne moved forward with his thoughts, "I would like to move on with my thoughts of the grades of a citizen but this time, not in school. This time it would be in life. In living a day to day life of making a living, paying taxes, raising a family and producing something of value for the common good. When people who step over that line, those that commit crimes against people and property, the justice system does their best to catch them, prosecute them and incarcerate them. This is very chaotic and has worsened over time. The bottom line is that it is ineffective. I wonder how those citizens would react if the United States had a better deterrent to crime. A better enticement to living as a good citizen.

Dickinson quickly asked, "Is the death penalty not enough of a deterrent? What more are you asking?"

"Ah, Senator. I regret to inform you that the judicial system, in several states, has determined that the death penalty has been deemed inhumane. It seems that we can send our young men and women to the front lines of war to die for our country yet those who commit heinous crimes within our own borders are not allowed the cheapest of deaths of a bullet or a noose, even with due process. Thirty-one states have imposed the death penalty and the remaining nineteen either abolished it or overturned it as a sentence. History and, quite possibly, a memory of your own account, will give evidence for the period when the Constitution was being formed, when the states were in upheaval over capital punishment. Some were arguments between the slave owner and the state as happened in Charleston. More arguments were between the Quaker influences who were against it and others who were in favor. During the continued growth of the United States, being hung until dead was common in most cities. Over time, we evolved to the electric chair and chemical injections. Which certainly urged some of the criminals to think twice but most of them really don't think they will be caught and if they are, they are willing to sit in prison getting fed three square meals a day without a care in the world as most death penalties are not carried out for an average of 178 months (16 years). While other execution dates are still scheduled, the inmates just wait while the tax-payers foot the bill of trying to make sure they don't escape, feed them three times a day, give them time for sports or walk around in the sun. When they aren't outside, many of them lay on a bunk and watch the television. Preachers go into the jails and prisons and try to help with some Christian reform and sometimes it works but mostly it does not. Statistically, many of the inmates conform to the Islamic religion. Many of the prisoners have family members who have also been incarcerated that it seems to be a family reunion within the walls of the penitentiary. All the while, taxpayers also pay the bill for court appointed attorneys who file motions and create paperwork in efforts to have the criminal released earlier and for any of number reasons. Many are counting on the fact that the overcrowded population of the prisons will push out those who have been incarcerated longer so they can let in newly convicted criminals. In 2019, the population was reported as 2.3 million in over 1,700 prisons. In 2025, we're sitting at over 3 million. Several prisons are dedicated specifically to illegal alien population due to language barriers. Most of the inmates there do not speak the English language.

The prisons are so overpopulated these days that if someone had a twenty-year sentence, the judicial system give them credit for three or four days just for spending 1 day inside. Which means they may only serve five to eight years for a twenty-year sentence.

Dickinson raised a hand. "Yes, councilor," Rayne said.

"That would mean your taxpayer pays less for that one individual for spending less time incarcerated. This is counter intuitive to your argument, Dr. Rayne."

"Financially speaking, in this example of only one person, or for argument's sake, even 10 people, you are correct. But, first, if there were no negotiations between prosecution and defense whereby the convicted serves less time and secondly, the time spent in prison were a one to one, day for day sentence, isn't is probable that the criminal might not be willing to forego his freedoms for a known, non-negotiable time and thus, remain a better deterrent. In that case, the prison population would be less, and the taxpayers pay less," Rayne replied calmly.

"Then there's the probability that if the criminal decides not to misbehave on the inside of prison, that person may get out of prison earlier than five years for 'good behavior, which would have kept them out in the first place. Now that's just a kick in the teeth for the American citizen who has always maintained good citizenship! The prison system used to be a place no one ever wanted to go. Now, with the prison population numbering in the millions, it's just an inconvenient vacation or a criminal education for those who have gone to prison multiple times. Here's a question for you; why is it that many citizens and the government, itself, agree that Christian programs are allowed in prisons as a preferred working rehabilitation practice but won't allow such programs to be taught in elementary or secondary schools when the child's mental and moral learning is being developed? Rayne paused for a moment.

I must add the obvious, gentlemen, that I am standing on my proverbial 'soap box', to coin a term you quite probably understand but, I do so without hypocrisy, as I have my own family members that have been incarcerated. I am not proud of that fact and I do not speak of them often. I do not send them money, so they can purchase items of comfort. I do not write them letters, so they can feel loved by someone or involve them in family affairs. I reserve those privileges to my family who possess self-control, fights in the military and sits in a foxhole for weeks on end, can't shower for days, carries wounded off the battlefield and carries their honor proudly. For those who work forty, sixty or seventy hours a week to responsibly provide for their families. The others in my family knew how I would react before they were convicted. Another point in this topic is even with this criminal record, this person and every other criminal, still maintain the right to vote except while behind bars. Why is that? Some states give a couple years grace period after the convict is free of their legal obligation and they are released yet, even that is so negligible. Gentlemen, in the year of 2016, the statistics showed that criminals voted on what was once known as the Democratic ticket. We now know it as the Socialist ticket. Additionally, as our country is so polarized, the popular vote has been closer than a margin of 200,000 votes. In today's population that could be as little as a single county. In that same year, a Virginia Governor abused his powers of pardon and tried to give convicted felons their voting privileges back in time for a Presidential election. Virginia laws admonished this act as an illegal action, but should he have succeeded, there remains a possibility that our country could have had a different president from that election. One that would probably have supported more liberal laws that govern the punishment of criminals.

This is not a new subject in conversation these days. Many other countries wrestle with the same concept. Some countries have totally disallowed it. Some will return the ability to vote after the person has paid their debt to society. Please note that I am not using the term 'privilege' or the term 'right', as I believe that voting should be an honorable act allowed by honorable citizens. It should be earned not just given. Many will argue this point, but it will remain true to the ideal that if something can be earned, it can be taken away. Moreover, if a criminal has chosen to take away the life of another human being, then they should be knowledgeable of the consequences. If they are depriving someone of their life, liberty and pursuit of happiness, why should they be able to vote on matters of law that govern their own lives?

And since the prison system is so over-crowded and costing the tax-payers billions of dollars per year ~ what if these criminals had to stay in penitentiaries where the prisoners had little to no privileges at all during their stay. Where the prison cells were no taller than five feet high and four feet wide. Where the television did not exist. Where meals were served twice a day and must be served by a family member or other benefactor. Other countries already employ these types of prisons and those populations are well under the numbers we have in the United States. I am well aware that ideas such as this would not be pleasant. It is prison! It is not supposed to be pleasant! It is prima facia that the current system does not hold any deterrent to those people who continue to sift through the revolving doors of local jails and state penal systems. My question to you gentlemen is this ~ knowing what you have learned, are ideas such as this constitutional? Because it is certainly evident to me that they are justified.

"As I move on with the concepts of citizenship, I would not rule out the probability of deportation and loss of citizenship by the courts, which would include terminating any travel privileges via a U.S. passport. I will refer you to the results of the 14th Amendment, which currently describes how people may willingly denounce citizenship. What if the Constitution would show those persons who have repeated convicted felonies which meet certain criteria and have not received the death penalty, be deported to countries who will accept them? I did the research. There are places such as this. This is not a new idea. Send them off, and as a voluntary denouncement, remove their citizenship. Should the receiving country decide to place them in their own prison system for a time would be left up the authorities of that country. In my opinion, I feel that five years in a foreign prison would be so much more horrible than a prison style education or inconvenient vacation that is given within the U.S. prison system.

On a side note ~ the prison system in the United States is becoming more privatized and quickly being discussed as 'big business' as the government pays those entities to run federal and state facilities to house inmates. As the increase of population continues to rise, so does the rate of crime and criminals in our penal system. Why is it the government's responsibility, i.e. the taxpayers, to take care of these people. To house them, yes, of course it is but, to actually take care of them. While I'm sure some of these people may very well be the sole survivor for their namesake, maybe we should take a page from the playbook of other countries who have much, much lower percentages of incarceration and require their own family to feed the inmate twice a day. There are cities in France and Scotland that mandate and require family members to feed their son, daughter, brother...whomever, at least twice a day and do their laundry twice a week. The caregiver is forced to live or stay close by to perform those functions. Some families will probably have to share the responsibilities, so they can maintain their own employment which might be many miles away. It is likely not convenient, nor should it be, and it certainly should be embarrassing! I have been told by those who are incarcerated that criminals are not taught 'not to commit' a crime but are taught 'not to get caught' committing the crime. Maybe punishment that affects the family as a whole, that those difficulties may very well be a deterrent to crime. These ideas, if taught at a young age and within the walls of their homes, might have changed the statistics we see in America today.

Would this be a burden on the prison system? Little to no cost on food purchase and storage. People outside the system will cry out how terrible they think this is. That's ok. If they feel the need, let them help bring food to the inmates too. Some will say that's a burden to the family. Yes, I'm sure it will be. Gangs tout their willingness to 'take care of their own' on the streets so, why not let them do so 100%? Financially, it would be less of a burden on taxpayers. There would be monies that could be put to use elsewhere.

I also wonder about honoring the laws of other countries when our system finds that a person is not a citizen of the U.S.? Let's say that prospective immigrant has come into the United States and has had ample time to choose the processes of maintaining U.S. citizenship but has failed to do so and finds themselves incarcerated. Let's also say the country from which this person holds citizenship has a law that permits a limb being removed from their body due to the type of crime committed, such as theft. Should we honor the law of that country and remove a finger or does our diverse morality suggest that is too inhumane?" Rayne could see the body language of the those listening. Legs were uncrossed and crossed the other way. Some gently clenched their hands while others crossed their arms and small scowls could be seen on their faces. Rayne continued with a question.

"Why would that individual believe it is better to steal in the United States and not in his own country?" he asked.

He quickly answered his own question by saying, "Could it be that our laws, which have become so numerous, create loopholes and pander to the lowest standards, are undermining the already minimal deterrents in place and make staying in a U.S. prison or jail seem easier or better as opposed to the swift judgement of their own country? Could it be that this person, like so many others, doesn't care where he lives and will steal no matter what? Whatever options arise to elevate the deterrent level to crime ~ there are always those that will oppose the option. In the field of the creating laws, some solicitors will argue against it based solely on party affiliation or the individual who chose to stand up to the system and suggest such harsher options. Paid lobbyists will join the debates. Eventually, arguments within the House of Representatives and the Senate will arise in "the name of the people", "for the good of the people" or against the person occupying the oval office with intentions of defamation. The result of such acts only delays any positive movement for the country towards new, stricter legislations for making those who would commit heinous crimes think twice about their consequences.

In as much as I have gone into a tangent on the subject of the prison system, permit me to change my direction if I may. Our current system is flawed in that, with few exceptions, it only punishes bad behavior. Why is it that the system does not provide opportunities for rewarding good citizenship?

Even in the majority of our educational grade school system across the nation have removed the grading system called 'Citizenship'. Why? Could it be that someone simply got their feelings hurt ~ that a teacher could not control a child and that child's parent believes the educational system is supposed to raise the child with the morals the parent doesn't have? Whatever the reasons, the system has removed this grading process, and it certainly isn't the cause of the decline in morality for America. The learning process starts with children and in the home and church, does it not?

"Well, gentlemen, I do apologize for my standing on a soap box for a moment. Sometimes I just rant ~ and I fear I'm the only one listening." Rayne stepped backwards away from the them and then turned and to walk away.

If any questions were forming from the men left in the chairs, they were left unasked.

Sherman stood and called out to Dr. Rayne, "William!"

Rayne stopped and turned.

The other four were also standing now and facing Rayne. Sherman waived him back over. "My apologies," Rayne said. "I...I was ranting and..." His comment was cut off by Dickinson saying, "Young man, you have a passion for what you believe in. Please, have no shame. Your convictions bring to light points of thought for all of us and even for the others who are within hearing." Dickinson nodded his head to nearly thirty random people who stopped to listen. The people began to clap when Rayne turned towards their direction. He hadn't noticed the people were behind him.

Madison spoke up, "It is our differences that have gathered the sharp minded men who penned our beginnings and bring us together as a nation. It is these same men, who come with different thoughts that we are torn apart but, we cannot move forward without discussing the differences. Not one human is physically, spiritually or economically equal, Dr. Rayne. Not in any country. We can only be equal in the eyes of freedom."

"Dammit man, speak your mind!" Morris interjected loudly. "I maintain no requirement to agree with your sentiments. Nor you for mine. You may have flooded our minds with educational facts, history and an opinion that may be your own but, I would not know your personal thoughts or ideas you possess should you keep them to yourself," Morris said confidently. "Besides, this is such a lovely day to be outside, is it not? To pontificate on the many concepts and ideals of your time in which you do not like about this country, or you do not understand, is something we are very interested to hear. Mind you, thus far I stand in agreement on the topics you have discussed. Times surely have moved into a direction I would not ever have thought possible so I, for one, am willing to lend an ear. Please, Dr. Rayne, dare to continue."

"Very well then," Rayne replied as he noticed the time on his watch. "Let's have a change of topics. Will there be some subject with which you wish to know my opinion?" he asked.

Sherman raised his hand just enough to catch the eye of Dr. Rayne.

"I recognize the Honorable Roger Sherman from the great state of Connecticut," Rayne said as if he stood in the pulpit with a gavel.

The crowd around didn't have a clue. Rayne and the other travelers casually looked around and not a single person recognized the name of Roger Sherman. Even their security people weren't alerted to anybody making any sudden movements.

Sherman stood from his chair and very calmly began, "It is incumbent upon those who have the power of an office to uphold the integrity and purpose of such office. I fear that

330

the information that we have heard, and the education we have gained, presents a glaring eyesore, by which those most recently who have held the office and their supporters cannot see. They cannot see it as they are either too close to it or focused on another goal. Another possibility is they choose not to see it as it would place a corrective lens in front of them and force them to in proper vision. What they don't see is the long-term erosion from the very purpose for which this government was created. Erosion, by its very nature, is hard to see. Small pieces falling away from the base. Watered down legislation allowing for litigation cracks to be formed in the foundation. A deterioration that have caused those cracks to separate the intention of the law and change the very definition of it. The cracks caused by this erosion appear, to me, sir, to have slowly separated the balance of powers within this governing body. Dr. Rayne, I believe you are expressing the stress from the Constitutional erosion and, in my estimations, could spew forth with more examples, statistics and otherwise overwhelming information. If you were to continue to stand on your 'soap box' as it were, what other piece of information would you convey when specifically dealing with such erosion?"

Rayne stood there knowing exactly what he would say but, all the while, knowing that he was listening to this man ~ a man who had never waisted a word ~ he stood there in amazement. The Honorable Roger Sherman has been soaking in every moment they had spent with him and he regurgitated without reservation or judgement.

While smiling inside himself, he calmly began his reply, "Were I to add to the words of the Honorable Roger Sherman, I would continue his analogy of the long-term deterioration away from intent of our Constitution in terms of the infringement on the executive branch. I believe that our founding fathers, as a whole or by agreement, believed that the House of Representatives would be the best group to logically 'check' the growth of government by controlling taxes over spending instead of giving that power specifically to the executive. However, in doing so, they also push for cooperation or control from the oval office when 'omnibus budget bills' are to be signed without the pleasure of line-item veto.

"Some presidents along the way effectively used their veto power and restrain the spending authorized by Congress. Then Congress did what Congress does and in 1974, it passed the *Congressional Budget and Impoundment and Control Act* whereby effectively removing the intended checks and balances of Congressional Spending. This legally shifted the balance of powers away from the executive.

"Let me say this in a different way. Taxpayers will always wish for less taxes. Congress will always want to spend more and since the spending limit for Congress has been unlocked, Congress will always **borrow** more monies, so they don't increase taxes.

"Gentlemen, you have already been shown that the debt of the United States is in the trillions of dollars and our borrowing limit has outrun its course. No one is lending the United States any more money. As a country, we're moments away from being bankrupt. As a country, our lenders will call in their debts and demand we pay them what we owe. And countries, such as China will call our debt due, and our collateral will be land, oil, minerals, water and anything Congress had allowed in the contracts. So, in my estimations, the United States will be divided among the countries that truly own the land beneath your feet. And that time is soon to be."

"If you wish," Rayne continued, "the internet is full of graphs that support what I'm telling you. And, if the internet can confirm this, then I am not the only person with this opinion. Let me finish out my thoughts with not just spewing forth the issues that support the deterioration of the intent of our governmental system and present possible solutions.

"What if the Constitution protected and defended the powers appointed to the office of the Presidency? It's at this point that you would ask me how. I would reply by more explicitly defining presidential veto powers, including 'Line-Item Veto" from the very beginning. I would define term limits to Senators and House of Representatives. I might add limiting the length of Congressional sessions. I would take away the entitlement sentiments of health care and require the politicians to accept the same health care as their constituents.

"But, the cracks in our foundation; this political erosion, travels in several directions, just like trickling water. The interpreters of the law of the land, known as the Supreme Court, is noted by Patrick Henry as 'the most powerful branch of the government.' He said, "Power is the great evil with which we are contending. We have divided power between three branches of government and erected check and balances to prevent abuse of power. However, *where is the check on the power of the judiciary*? If we fail to check the power of the judiciary, I predict that we will eventually live under judicial tyranny."

"Arguments have been made to justify such infringements by declaring the Constitution is outdated. They also add the contingency that the process of adding amendments is too difficult. Some have displayed the sentiment that the Constitution is a 'living document' and its standards should be changed without adding amendments. However, our country's first Chief justice of the Supreme Court, John Marshall, made this statement to those who would follow him, "The judicial power does *not* include the right to change the Constitution."

"Again, let's ask ourselves some real questions. What if the Constitution clearly stated that future interpretations of the Constitution should not change the intent of the Constitution? Would that mean it would render our country with a limited central government? Perhaps.

"What if the Constitution clearly defined that willful acts to subvert the intent of the Constitution is an act of treason? Or at least make such willful acts be grounds for impeachment. How bold would those in office be if the Constitution was as clear as this? The internet sites President Obama as noting the idea of (the) "Constitution is a living document; no strict constructionism". Conversely, Walter Williams is noted with the sentiment that "Saying the Constitution is a living document is the same as saying we don't have a Constitution."

"Mr. Sherman, your analysis of our country's political erosion is absolutely correct. So finally, one of the main characteristics when speaking of erosion is this; if the erosion is caused by water, it will always take the path of least resistance. Therefore, the Constitution should be resolute from the beginning."

The crowd around had been slowly growing. Applause could be heard when Dr. Rayne concluded his thoughts. There were those that screamed out in disagreement, however, the crowd dissipated as quickly as they had arrived.

Dr. Rayne ended his longer than planned oration with the plans for the following day. "As it turns out gentlemen, congress has a special session tomorrow. I've set up a visitation for all of us that choose to participate. After that, we will be visiting some of the private office areas and possibly meet one or two of them," he said.

Morris spewed forth, "I can't say as I would like to meet any of them. I can't say that they will be able to hold a conversation to the level I would think pertinent. From the concepts of what we have learned thus far, they will not be concerned with the Constitutionality of the ideas or bills that are presented. One side will undoubtedly strip down the other simply because it came from the other side! Do they not concern themselves with trying to make this country great? Half of them delve into tolerance and socialism until when ~ when they aren't tolerant of your opinion!"

"Well, well, well," responded Madison. "Don't look now but I believe our extensive education has struck a chord with the Honorable Gouverneur Morris." The crowd around them gave a quiet laughter as they began to dissipate from Independence Historical Park.

Sarah Fleming found herself standing near Morris and began to make small talk as Hamilton made his way toward Dr. Rayne.

"I look forward to tomorrow Dr. Rayne. Truly. So, I would like to say 'Thank You' up front. I believe this will be most beneficial." Dr. Rayne simply shook his hand firmly and nodded. Dr. Rayne has said enough today.

Chapter 28

The following day consisted of travel to the Capitol Building of the United States. A short train ride later, the group found themselves standing at the East entrance to the historic landmark.

Dr. Benton looked at the expressions on the faces of Hamilton and Dickinson before he commented, "The building has stood the test of time gentlemen. I do not need to recount the beginnings of this building with you, as you two were instrumental in its inception. The physical additions, such as the dome, took several decades for the transformation you observe in front of you. On a personal note; I thank you for holding church services here. That is something I deeply revere. Shall we?" he asked as he properly held his hand out in front to allow his guests to step ahead of him.

The entire group was about to walk up the stairs when Morris noticed the number of stairs. While never one to back down from a challenge, he stopped for a moment to contemplate the potential pain he would be having for the remainder of the day. Sarah, never one to be too far from him, noticed his contemplation and directed his steps around to the handicap entrance and used a public elevator. Dr. Benton nodded to Sarah and understood they would meet on the main floor momentarily. Dr. Benton made a mental note.

As time approached the noon hour, Dr. Benton, Roger Sherman, Alexander Hamilton and John Dickinson followed by their security, were walking down a hallway filled with offices. The remainder of the group had taken another route. As they turned the corner to head to another direction, Dr. Benson starred into the eyes of the Benefactor.

"Good morning, Colonel," Benton said without any surprise in his voice.

Colonel Alan Powers calmly replied, "Well hello Dr. Benton. I didn't realize your vacation included tours or meetings in our nation's capital. I hope you are finding your time off as restful."

"I should think that both of us will do different things to ease our minds and redirect our thoughts away from the daily grind. Today just happens to be a way for me to just that."

"Of course. And who might you be sharing time with today?" asked the Colonel.

Dickinson, who happened to be standing the closest, reached out his hand and eloquently responded, "Tis an honor to make your acquaintance Colonel, my name is John Dickinson."

"A pleasure to meet you, sir. I love your accent. I've traveled extensively, and I cannot seem to place it. Where did you grow up, sir?"

"Not far from here, sir. Philadelphia and Delaware mostly. However, I am also well-traveled," Dickinson replied.

The Colonel politely moved closer to the next person and stuck out his hand. "I am Colonel Powers, sir."

Hamilton did not shake the Colonel's hand. Instead he said, "My name is Mr. Hamilton, and this is the Honorable Roger Sherman," he said as he gently waived his hand towards his colleague. "Wonderful to meet you, gentlemen. Is this the first time to the Capital building?"

Hamilton responded aptly, "I have been to this area long ago, but it wasn't quite utilized in its current state. It's an education to see how it has turned out, sir."

"I see. While I should love to stay and show you around, I believe Dr. Benton is quite capable. I am currently on my way to a meeting just down the corridor. I do hope to see you again soon. Dr. Benson, may I have a word?"

"Of course," came Benson's reply. The two stepped aside and Paul Tesla quickly stepped up and took up the tour guide responsibilities and the group slowly continued down the hall.

"Carver, I didn't know you would be touring the Capital today while on vacation. You should have mentioned it, and I would have made sure you and your group had a private tour guide," the Colonel said.

"Colonel Powers, you are much too busy a man for me to bother you with my vacation plans. Besides, I pretty much know my way around. You know that."

"Yes, I do. By the way, where are you staying? I know you traveled all the way here and would not stay just for a day."

339

"I have a reservation at the Hay-Adams Hotel," Benton replied.

"Of course. I know it well. I should like to stop in later, with your permission, and discuss a few small items. I do apologize, I know it is your vacation time... it shouldn't take too long."

"Very well, Colonel. I believe I should be ready to receive guests around ten PM," he said.

The two shook hands and went their separate ways. Benton caught up with the rest of the group and they all took in part of the special session.

~~~~~~~~~

The knock on the door came precisely at ten PM. Benton set down his glass of 2015 French Bordeaux. He had the bottle brought up from the hotel's famous Lafayette Restaurant earlier. He casually opened the door, stepped aside and allowed Colonel Alan Powers to enter.

The Colonel's demeanor was calm and pleasant. He walked over to the chair where the second glass of wine would be on his left. He knew Benton was righthanded and surmised that since there was less wine in that glass, the other had been poured for him. His observations were rarely wrong, and they were proved successful in this instance as well. Benton had shut the door and had taken his seat.

"Carver," the Colonel said calmly. "We've been great partners for many years now on this project. I picked you because you are damn smart and honest. Yet, I feel I may have someone working for me that isn't honest with me. I've funded this project without too much oversight, and I have never micro-managed. Regardless of the outcome of this meeting, that will not change. Are we understood?" he asked.

"Yes sir. Clearly," Benton replied.

"Seriously, Carver. The door is closed. Just call me Alan. It rarely happens and it is my name. I believe we're closer than those formalities when it remains just the two of us."

"Okay, Alan. I do understand what you are saying. It appears as though you feel deceived by me in some way. Please, ask me your questions."

The Colonel continued, "Truly, I was surprised to see you this morning. I was, however, more surprised by your guests. I mentioned earlier and, you already know this, I've been in many places in the world. I can usually pick out accents from several different countries. But those gentlemen clearly were not from Delaware or Philadelphia. Those places are so close and no one I know speaks with that sort of high level aristocratic and...and..." he stopped for a moment. "Listen, they sounded like they came from early America as crazy as that sounds!"

"Oh, I see," Benton said without raising an eyebrow.

"And their names! Dickinson, Hamilton and that other guy, Sherman. Not sure about him. And the more I thought about it...actually, I haven't stopped thinking about it! Carver, I don't usually lose my composure, but I had a thought that simply consumed my entire afternoon. So, I did nothing else after my meeting except think about our encounter. Here's what I recall, first I saw you. Then I saw several members of your team. Adding to that were the three gentlemen I met and then there were three more larger fellows, whom I will guess as security. Am I wrong?"

"You are correct, Alan. You met three men with those names, and saw the correct number of individuals," Benton said softly.

The Colonel sat quiet for a moment. He had sat in the oval office and spoke to the President on official business that affected the country. He had sat in meetings where someone's life was in the balance. But here, in this moment, his face began to flush as if this was the biggest meeting of his life and he was trying to find his voice. He composed himself, reached into the breast pocket of his suit jacket and pulled out a piece of paper. He handed the piece of paper to Carver Benton.

"Tell me truly, Carver. Is this the man I met today?"

Benton didn't need to unfold the paper that was handed to him. The paper was folded twice as if ready to hand it to the concierge for hailing him a taxi. The white color with the green background clearly revealed it was U.S. currency as a ten-dollar bill.

"Yes," came the distinct answer.

The Colonel's reaction was softly spoken but very pronounced. "Oh my God!"

Chapter 29

The Colonel picked up his glass of wine and gently sat back in the chair and thought about what he had just heard. He did not get angry or seem to be unsettled. At that point, he was just ready for another glass of wine.

When he finally looked at Benton, he raised his eyebrows and gave Benton the look asking for an explanation.

"When you first asked me to join you on this project, I wasn't expecting to reach the goal you had set out for us to reach. Even as advanced as technology is today in 2025, I just didn't believe it. However, your gracious funding allowed me to pull together some of the finest minds in science. Narrowing it down to just a select few and keeping each of them concentrating on a single aspect of the bigger picture, we have achieved the goal you set out, sir. We can properly and continuously transport primates from one point to another successfully. This was your goal, Alan," Benton said, and he paused for a moment. He took a sip of his wine and looked the Colonel in the eye.

"Somewhere along the way, it became a steppingstone to a new goal. I have not lied to you, really. I only gave you the information I needed you to have to continue with the project. I've no idea if it will succeed or not, sir, but it has already done so much that I can barely contain my own excitement some days. Today, you met three very historical men. John Dickinson, Alexander Hamilton and Roger Sherman. All are men who helped influence and finalize the documents that govern our country. You met only three of the founding forefathers that are in our presence today."

"Wait! There are more?" the Colonel exclaimed!

"Yes, two more to be exact. Gouverneur Morris and one of your own hero's, I believe, Alan. James Madison, the 4th President of the United States. My wish, Alan, if you will permit me to try to complete it, is to change America from the beginning. I don't want to play God, I don't want credit, I don't want money and I certainly don't need the headache associated with any of those. I am simply hoping for a better America and to do that, we may as well start with the documents that have governed our country for 250 years. They work! Well, for the most part. But, the men and women in the federal government who have been misinterpreting the intension of laws and then making loopholes to the detriment of the citizens of these United States and moving us away from a God loving country to a place where 'anything goes so it won't hurt someone's little feelings' ~ that crap has got to stop," Benton said.

"Go on."

"Once we helped to develop J.A.S.P.E.R. into what it is today, some of the pieces came together faster but, in the end, my own code made time travel work, Alan."

"Amazing, Carter. Just amazing. Doesn't this have some sort of cosmic repercussions and all that. How do we send them back?" came the questions from the Colonel.

"Me, my team of four, J.A.S.P.E.R and you are now the only people who live in 2025 who know this has happened. The team has traveled back once or twice and not done anything to significantly change the world, Alan, but, of course, now that our new friends have seen the future ~ well, I hope that those documents that have been ignored for some time now get re-written with some clarity. Roger Sherman is known as 'The Great Compromiser' and has signed all four of our countries governing declarations, Gouverneur Morris helped write the preamble, Alexander Hamilton helped found the banking system, John Dickinson has as much, if not more, influence on other congressmen than Thomas Jefferson and James Madison will outlive the others by the time he finishes his time in the oval. I believe they will do everything they can do to help prevent the way this country has turned out," Benton paused for a moment.

"If you knew your child was about to do something stupid, Alan, wouldn't you do something to steer them in a different way?"

The Colonel looked solemnly at Carver Benton saying, "Carver. You are a man of the bible too, so let me remind you of this. Judas tried to force Christ's hands and ended up betraying Him."

"This I know, my friend. I know. If you're saying I'm trying to force a change...then you may be right. And if I'm wrong and the world is worse than it is today, we probably won't know it. There's no guarantee that I will be here discussing this with you. No guarantee that I will be picked by you for this project. Nor any guarantee that either of us will have been born.   It may very well be totally different.   So, I see no point in going down a rabbit hole that I have already been in and out of a million times.   I, and I will add, the entire team, have pledged our lives in the belief of this endeavor.

The opposite may also be true, Alan. If this works, we may not know that either. We probably won't be living in a utopia, I think. But America is a great place at heart and if we can make her even greater...then we have succeeded.

I guess what I need to know from you now is if I still have a job? Is my team still employed? The teleportation of humans is absolutely possible and is working.   You can produce the tele-pads when you're ready and make billions. However, in as much as you funded this, and I certainly owe you everything, I will pass on how to turn these into time travel devices again. I won't do it. You can send me to my grave or throw me in the bottom of a prison, but I am the only one who knows. And, before you try to guess that J.A.S.P.E.R can figure it out, it cannot. The code will act as an irreparable virus and J.A.S.P.E.R. will be no more. There you go, Alan. That is as truthful and arrogant as I hope to ever sound to you, my friend, but truth it is."

The Colonel sat in amazement as Benton poured both of them the rest of the wine from the bottle.   "Carver," the Colonel said calmly.

"Yeah?" came the soft and nearly defeated reply.

"I think you're an even greater thinker than the world has ever known," he said in an easy manner. "And, by any standards, you are the best scientist. I couldn't be any prouder of anyone I have ever known, including my grandfather. So, that says a lot, my friend. So, I only have one more question, if I may?" he asked.

"You pretty much know everything, Alan. I don't think there's anything I've left out."

"But there is," the Colonel said confidently. "May I meet the other two, please?"

Chapter 30

The following morning the Colonel was introduced to the remaining two statesmen. Benton updated the entire team that their benefactor, Colonel Alan Powers, was fully on board with the project and to hold back no information if he asks any questions. The statesmen and the Colonel, along with Dr. Rayne and Dr. Benton had a wonderful breakfast meeting that lasted several hours. The travelers were in the room but pretty much stuck to themselves. The security guards were in the regular dining area for breakfast and sat there until they were needed.

At one point when the group stopped for a bathroom break, the Colonel walked over to the traveler's table and spoke, "Hello everyone. I just had to come over to you and commend each of you for a job well done."

A respectful "Thank you" could be heard from each of them. He continued, "Your extensive knowledge, and yes, even your personal opinions, have given our fore-fathers much to think about. You have opened their eyes to what lies ahead for our country. I'm quite sure that even the collegiate history professors would not have done a better job. Besides, most professors now-a-days teach way too far to the political left anyway. I don't have statistics on this, it's just a feeling that most of them are either old Democrats or younger Socialists, but that's only my opinion." The Colonel thanked them again and went back to his table. The travelers laughed and used their water glasses to toast their efforts.

"Dr. Benton, might I have a word?" the Colonel asked. Benton got up from the table and the two took a walk down the street to Lafayette Square. They shared general chit-chat along the way. Benton knew Colonel Powers would tell him his thoughts in his own time. However, it was much sooner than Benton had anticipated and knew the time was immediate when the Colonel's demeanor changed just a bit.

"Here's the thing, Carver. I'm so amazed at what you have done, I could hardly sleep last night. My brain was firing on all synapse's available to me. I could feel the adrenaline pulsing through my veins. I've never felt so alive. Even now, I feel it. So, make no mistake, I'm fully involved with this project, but I have my doubts."

"I'm listening," Benton said.

"From everything I have gathered in the last twenty-four hours, you plan to be successful. And, I too, hope that you are. But I'd like to let you in on a plan that I have been working on for some time now. An idea that I started even before I found out about the time travel and meeting these phenomenal men. A plan whose goal is, in many ways, very similar to yours." The Colonel caught the attention of Dr. Benton and the two talked for hours.

When the two men had covered the many aspects of the Colonel's plan, Benton said, "I believe I like your plan, Colonel. You're right, you know. Your idea is, in any reasonable concept, very similar to mine. Let's see where it will lead and with this current project, hope it isn't needed."

The Colonel's schedule was always full. He may have been a past Senator, which was also revealed to everyone, and he still maintained relationships with current Congressmen and other potential important figures, yet, every once in a while, he cancelled those top-level meetings when he had a chance to visit great historical sites across the U.S. with the fore-fathers. He loved to hear what they had to say. As promised, he didn't get in the way of Dr. Benton's project.

Over the next couple of months, the travelers and the statesmen took cars, trucks, planes, subways and trains to many places of interest, all while studying the cultures and views of the people of the United States. News events were cussed, discussed, and cussed again as most mainstream media was negative in nature. The statesmen had the opportunity to observe the laziness and selfishness of the country. They wrestled with individual political opinions and unfounded reforms.

They were confused when Americans who wanted to have the fruits of the steel industry, but conservationists refused to allow the steel industry to keep production within our borders. Sherman, being conservative by nature, was skeptical of those decisions effectively hampering the growth of a nation by causing the steel industry to buy product from other countries, whereby increasing the costs of construction for bridges, buildings and other structures.

Over the course of the few short months they were here, arguments flared up from each of the statesmen. The travelers gave them every opportunity to help them form their own opinion. Every side of an argument was thoroughly picked apart, regurgitated and rehashed.

Eventually, frustration sat among them and they could tell they had seen all they wanted to see.

When the project first started, Benton was never sure just how long the statesmen should, or would, stay in 2025 but now he could tell the time for them to return was close at hand.

The statesmen were getting restless to get back to their families or their work. They remembered they were still in the process of building a nation. They were also a bit anxious to use their new education and attempt their task of steering the remaining men who signed the Constitution into believing there should be changes. Changes to keep America from turning out the way it has would be no easy task. The statesmen had no clue how Benton calculated the time spent away but were confident that he would get them back safe and sound and at the right time.

The statesmen woke early. They dressed in their own period clothing and met in the hallway. They walked together down the corridors to the familiar doorway and calmly walked into the classroom for the final time.

Dr. Rayne, Sarah Fleming, Paul Tesla and Charles Carson all stood politely behind Dr. Benton. Each of them had said their farewells to the nation builder's. Dr. Benton had decided that there was no reason to send the team back in time. They had already proven that time travel works. The calculations were completed. On the tele-pads of the 9th sub floor, room 3, pads A and B, five of the nation's founding forefathers were patiently waiting to return home.

They gazed around the room at their surroundings. Gone were the fancy overhead lights and light switches. The large television screen was replaced by the blackboard and chalk. Each man sat in the same desk he had on the very first day. Sarah Fleming stood in the front of the class while the other travelers sat quietly in the back of the room. Dr. Benton stood beside Sarah.

"Good morning, gentlemen," he said. "In a few moments we will walk down the hallway to the tele-port room and humbly send you back to where you belong. Let me clarify, you will arrive in your time about four minutes after you left and in the same place. However, you now have more knowledge than you ever thought possible. This is something dreams are made of. It could also be something to cause nightmares I should think," he said with a slight laugh. Several heads in the room nodded and small gestures in agreement could be seen.

"I have no final words of wisdom prepared for this occasion. I believe we have clarified our intentions. Clarity, gentlemen. Now that you know, now that you have seen, felt, discussed, tasted and learned a bit about

353

this 'American experiment' and, as it could be said, 'walked a mile in our shoes'," he glanced at Sherman as Sherman showed a slight grin.

"What is it that you wish to change?" The question may have been rhetorical, but Dr. Benton just left it hanging in the air to see what may happen.

The room did not sit silent for long.

Morris spoke proudly, "As I believe every man has done, so shall I believe every man will do and that is to levy his knowledge in the direction of his passion, sir. It is, Dr. Benton, exactly what you have done and here we are. I will be ever grateful for the science and medical advancements that have come about, but, in the scheme of law, that is not my passion. I feel obliged to speak of the value of the citizen and their responsibility to the country. Your 35th President, Kennedy is his name I'm sure, said, and I paraphrase, 'to ask what a citizen should do for his country.' It is prima facia that too much of the current population does not do anything *for* this country. Many remain as visitors who wish to be treated as citizens, but their allegiance is not to the United States. Even some who are born here act this way. Within this group of 'illegal aliens', there are those who do not contribute, produce or learn how to be productive! Those are the parasites and feed off those who provide for them! The Continental Congress should discuss ways to encourage citizens, for if a person can decide not to be engaged, then the laws of the country should have the right to eject such persons and not call them CITIZEN! Gentlemen, stupidity and evil will happen, and while some will say that forgiveness should be granted to the poor reptiles, but know that at some point, large scale consequences will occur. That, my friends, is biblical. Yet our country is not surviving as the tax burden and debt are far too much. The consequences of this country's non-action and 'tolerance' choices are killing us. Economic failure is real, and quite sadly, my friends, you are living in it and much of this country is wretched. Change must prevail or destruction will reign." The aristocratic Gouverneur Morris stood proudly and waited for any argument.

None came.

Hamilton unintentionally breathed a heavy sigh as though the weight of the world was upon him. All eyes turned to him and they could see his head handing down when he spoke.

"The honorable Senator Morris is absolutely correct. This country is wretched in many ways. No doubt politically. Again, with proper reference to Mr. Morris' statement, my passion leans to the financial market. Tell me, gentlemen, how does one set up a successful taxation process when you know the one you have previously set up is failing? Yes, the burden of knowledge we now bear obligates us to move towards change, for if we *do* nothing, then we *decided* to do nothing, and it is my own belief that cannot be the course of action taken. A national debt is very understandable to the degree that it remains within the scope of keeping this country safe from those who would wish otherwise. But a national debt, due to mismanagement from the elected within and the failed political machinery to properly sustain itself, compounded by interest, then certainly you must realize you don't really own your country do you. Gentlemen, the owner will someday want what it rightfully theirs," he said.

"Therefore," he continued. "I shall try to place financial instruments in place that will not constrict but be consistent and fair to maintain financial security. What that means exactly I do not know at this moment. Perhaps an open discussion will enlighten me, and a new course will prevail? I will look to the men here in this room who have shared this experience with me for they have the understanding that I do. It is the lot of man to be tricked by false hope and inaction for when we ignore history and fail to learn from it, we shall surely ruin the future."

Gouverneur Morris chimed in, "I like that statement, your Honor. I may steal that and make it my own someday."

"By all means," Hamilton responded.

Dickinson chimed in, "I should like to remind us all, gentlemen, that we are in the midst of the Second Continental Congress. It tis the second as the first failed. Arguments are already in progress. Independence *is* upon us. With the knowledge we now possess, the decisions of this second conclave will only last for a time. If one allows this as settled in his mind, if any man can be content with knowing that his efforts are only temporary in the forming of a nation, then he is not the man to stay in the conclaves which form that nation. There must be change. A sinking ship must shore up the holes left in her or all is lost."

"Well said," Sherman added. "I have learned from our time here, gentlemen. I have learned when good men come together for a cause, share a goal and focus on that goal, they may still not receive the expected outcome. They may come close but no one man can control the choices and activities of another. Particularly when each person has a right to his own decisions in life. Dr. Benton and I are in full agreement on this. What he has done is given us more information than we previously had known. And we obviously accepted his invitation. It is now incumbent upon us to return. We must reflect upon our choices and, when lead, correct mistakes and shore up the holes in our ships," he said looking at Dickinson. "We must pray for wisdom and the right words in our efforts to guiding this country into the future."

The only remaining voice in the room stood quietly. No pressure was on him and none was felt by him except for one item.

Madison looked over at Dr. Rayne and very calmly stepped over to him and stuck out his right hand. "Dr. Rayne, before we take our leave and return to our home, I would be remiss if I did not tell how thankful I am that you saved my life on the day we met. I did not seek out the history books to see if that pitchfork may have killed me. Nor do I wish to know now," he commented sternly. "I do know that I am alive and well. Whether I orate or write my opinions of what I have learned in this time here with you remains to be seen. That I have the chance to do so is...is, well, quite precious to me. It is truly an honor to have met all of you and I thank you for your hospitality," he concluded.

Dr. Rayne stood shaking the hand of James Madison. It was a very surreal moment for William Rayne. To live a hope and burn the memory into his brain. "It is my honor, Senator. An honor indeed," he replied.

Moments later, Dr. Rayne, Sarah Fleming, Paul Tesla and Charles Carson all stood politely behind Dr. Benton. Each of them had said their farewells to the nation builder's. Dr. Benton had decided that there was no reason to send the travelers back in time. They had already proven that it works.

The calculations for transport were double checked. On the tele-pads stood the five statesmen. Each of them was given a gift to take back with them. Their promise to Dr. Benton was not to tell anyone back home of the gift.

James Madison was given a black ink pen. He knew he would keep this at his house where his personal notes were written. The box it came in was personally made by Dr. Rayne. Highly polished wood with small gold hinges. On the top was an engraving which read, "Revelation 1:19". The two of them had talked of this passage the previous week during a glass of whiskey near the end of the day. Dr. Rayne read the passage: "Write the things which thou hast seen, and the things which are, and the things which shall be hereafter." (KJV). Madison remembered very well that Rayne showed him that these are 'red letter' words. Words spoken by Jesus Christ to John, the author of The Book of Revelations. Madison knew he would miss his new friend and that this gift had more meaning than Dr. Rayne knew how to express.

Gouverneur Morris was wearing a new prosthetic leg effectively replacing his old wooden one. It looked exactly like the old one but would never wear out or need repair. It was also much lighter and more comfortable to wear. No one would be the wiser. Morris, ever the lady's man when the time would allow, also kept a small handkerchief that Sarah had given him. Her initials are monogrammed on one of the corners. He had no misconceptions that she would return to the past with him and she certainly believed he would find another female to try and seduce. However, he would never forget that this was the only lady who had ever mentally challenged him, and he would absolutely miss this attraction about her.

Roger Sherman had first thought of what he would want to take back with him if given the opportunity. A bible perhaps? However, the bible he found had copyright page removed but the remainder of the book wasn't changed. Sherman had found that the words of the new Bible were simply not the same as the one he was used to. He wanted to study it on his own time to see if the meaning had been lost over time. He remembered how Webster's Dictionary had changed some definitions to fit the liberal agenda and be more politically correct. He could only guess that publishers would attempt the same with the Holy book. However, the decision ultimately was not his. Instead, he was presented with the new leather shoes specifically made for him. He had already broken them in over the past few weeks and knew that the steps he, and the others, were about to make would be most significant. No one has ever made a change in anything without first taking a step towards that change. Be it figuratively, or an actual foot fall, Sherman was proud to keep the new shoes.

John Dickinson was against taking any artifact back in time before it was created. He thought it might cause problems. However, several weeks ago, in the course of their education, especially in medical technology, Dickinson sat in a chair believing he was experiencing the new ways of testing vision. Carson had noticed him squinting several times while making his notes. As the 'Penman of the Revolution', Carson could only imagine how much Dickinson would write and how his eyes might be affected. Carson kept those results and had a pair of no-line bifocal glasses made in the style of the late 1700's. The glasses worked perfectly, and no one would be able to tell, except for him. When Dickinson eventually accepted the glasses, their conversation was very much to the point. Carson expressed his utmost admiration to a man who, while being very patriotic about the cause of liberty for the country and not a man in favor of championing the plight of an individual, and whom he held in the highest regard as Congressman, a Statesman and a man, stood his ground for the value of others as a whole.

Charles Carson could not think of an appropriate gift for Hamilton and enlisted Dr. Rayne's help. Specifically, since the two of them got along so well. Rayne spent many hours on this but could not think of an appropriate gift for Alexander Hamilton. The man was phenomenal in so many ways that no trinket or token seemed to be the right thing in Rayne's eyes. Hamilton was simply so intelligent and busy that Rayne felt that most things may seem trivial to him. He couldn't give him something to sit on a mantel and collect dust. Surely, something like that would eventually be seen by someone. "But, what to do?" Rayne thought to himself. He couldn't give him the same ten-dollar bill that the Colonel handed to him. Suddenly, that thought made Rayne chuckle at himself, since he didn't even realize he had kept it that night.

Rayne eventually reflected on the life of Hamilton and his struggle with fitting in with the men around him. Men whose names brought prestige and commanded presence far above his own such as Madison and Dickinson, who spent the last months with him in this endeavor. Men who were his political adversaries such as Thomas Jefferson. Men who were, in some ways, his personal mentor such as George Washington. Hamilton's religion, such as it was, held major similarities to his political life, but he was unaware as it continued into his later years.

Rayne knew the history of this man and his demise in 1804. All of this knowledge prompted Rayne make a small item that Hamilton could carry with him wherever he went. It would not cause alarm if found nor would Hamilton need to make any excuses. It would remind him daily of his purpose in life.

Rayne reached over and handed Hamilton a piece of leather. On one side, the leather was smooth and tanned. On the other, it was as rough as a piece of leather could be. The swatch of leather was in the shape of a cross. On the tanned side, the horizontal words were branded "Lord of Lords". On the vertical of the cross were the words "King of Kings".

Rayne explained, "Alexander, we stand here in a bit of an awkward situation. Any man may believe he is an island unto himself and many men do not share their inner most thoughts or beliefs. In this case, history has recorded much of your life. That is, your actions and your beliefs but, if I may say this, despite the historical information, it has been my privilege to relate to you on a more personal level. What I have learned about you is that your religious beliefs are deeper than the stories that are told about you. I also believe you still hold doubts in terms of Christianity. I am fully aware that you believe in the morality of religion to maintain a solid and honest form of government to guide the ways of an individual." Rayne stopped for a moment to gauge Hamilton's reaction.

Hamilton's eyes began to water ever so slightly before he replied, "You see me for who I am."

Rayne gently continued, "I am honored, but I can only see the man you allow me to see. The Lord Almighty sees you for who you are, my friend." Hamilton nodded while staring at the leather cross. Rayne moved on, "Keep this in your pocket, your Honor. When you find yourself in question, about anything at all, be it personal or within the scope of political decisions, rub on this rough side. Remind yourself to pray about your decisions. Years down the road, the rough side will become smoother than the tanned side and you will find that you have been a praying man all along. That you have put your trust in the Lord of Lords. This is my parting gift to you, Alexander."

Hamilton looked up and into the eyes of Dr. Rayne. They reached out and gave each other a very sturdy handshake and Hamilton placed his free hand on Rayne's shoulder and said, "Amen, sir. Amen."

Dr. Benton and his team stepped back from the tele-pads. Dr. Rayne stood calmly with his hand on the button waiting for Dr. Benton to speak. "Make it so," he said calmly. Rayne pressed the button and the statesmen slowly disappeared.

~~~~~~~~~

No sooner were the statesmen gone from the room when Dr. Rayne turned toward Dr. Benton. Rayne's face was stern and determined looking. Gone were the tender wrinkles he had shown moments ago when speaking with Hamilton. His eyes foreshadowed a seriousness that Benton nearly took for anger.

"No," Benton said calmly while looking directly back at Rayne.

"You have not one iota of an excuse not to!" exclaimed Rayne.

The other travelers were in a loss and showed their confusion by whispering to each other if they knew what the subject of this conversation but none of them knew until Benton made the next statement.

"My excuses are my own, and not one iota of them do I owe to you, Dr. Rayne. I do not care to be a fly on the wall. What good can come of it? Why would anyone of us travel back. We belong in this time and they belong in theirs," Benton said.

Rayne looked at the others quietly standing there a bit shocked that Rayne yelled at the boss. Rayne directed his comments at the group in general. "On several occasions, our esteemed leader and I have discussed the option of one of us, just one, follow the statesmen and travel back with the only purpose of watching their progress. Seeing all of our work come to fruition! No one has ever done what we have done! And no one will ever know but us! However, with all of the knowledge we possess here and now, I cannot think of any other person to go back to watch all of this happen but Dr. Benton. His leadership, his knowledge and guidance would best be rewarded by letting his own eyes witness the making of history. A history that he will have helped shaped. A history that has not yet been written due to this project. And he refuses to go!" he said loudly.

Rayne looked at Benton again and said angrily, "This is beyond me, Carver! I just don't understand you sometimes!"

Sarah Fleming and Charles Carson stood there without saying a word, but Paul Tesla could not help himself and opened his mouth.

"I'm quite sure that this is not my place to speak but..."

"You're right, Paul, please don't," Benton said calmly.

"Yes! Speak!" Rayne said confidently. "Paul, please say what's on your mind. We started this all in the same mindset and we will complete this project without reservations of actions or unspoken thoughts."

Tesla looked over at Benton and then around the room before he started talking.

"I..., that is, we, started this project, as Dr. Rayne just said, all of us in the same mindset. And our confidence in this project continued to grow bit by bit. Honestly, I'm sure I'm not the only one who thought this would fail. Time travel. 'Who'd a thunk?' as they say. And then J.A.S.P.E.R. came online due to your modifications Dr. Benton. And with very careful preparations, your love and care for our test subjects were successful from one tele-pad to another. I kept thinking, "Wow! This guy is amazing!" And you have proven yourself time and time again. Tweaking this and modifying that...things which only you thought about. You think so far outside the realm of a common man. If I didn't know any better, I'd say you hold more information in your brain than J.A.S.P.E.R. can find on the internet."

Dr. Rayne raised an eyebrow and wondered where he was going with this statement. Tesla continued, "We...that is, everyone in this room except you, have traveled back in time. We've seen Philadelphia as it truly was two hundred-fifty years ago. The country air is sweet and clean, Carver. The smells of a concrete city are nowhere to be found. There is no paper littering the street. No skyscraper blocking your view. No cars honking and no traffic lights or people on cell phones. Life is so very different compared to what we know today. You, Carver, you can do this, and you should do this! Go experience it.

Is it not you who told all of us that you will finish this project to the very end? Is it not you who have asked us to be a part of this entire history changing event? Is it not?"

Paul stepped over to Dr. Benton and placed his hand on Benton's shoulder and said, "Finish this, Carver. See it through, my friend."

Rayne looked at the other travelers. "Anyone else?"

Sarah's voice was heard next. "You started this project with your heart, Dr. Benton. You *have* done all you can do and now it is time follow your heart one last time. I say go."

Charles Carson rounded out the group by saying, "I once heard a man quote a comic book..." Carson's words hung in the air.

Benton looked at Carson and gently nodded his head up and down. He knew what he meant.

Benton responded gently, "With great power comes great responsibility."

Carson replied, "I will not tug on your heart strings, my friend. The others have done a pretty good job with that already. Have they not?" Charles didn't wait for an answer as Benton wasn't going to give one. That was rhetorical and Benton knew it.

"I will, however, speak to your logic. You have set something in motion that no other person in the history of the science has ever done. I am so honored to have played even the smallest part in what we all have accomplished. This has been and remains a team effort. You didn't do this on your own. However, we followed you during this entire adventure. But the adventure cannot be complete without this final piece of the puzzle. Go, Carver. Be a traveler and be that fly on the wall. Watch with your own eyes and live the dream you started many years ago. You should be the one to own the very last time travel, my friend. Go and come back to us. I believe this is the part about 'great responsibility'. Finish this project. But, be a watcher only." Charles Carson bowed his head and said, "*God, grant my friend, Dr. Carver Benton, the serenity to accept the things he cannot change, the courage to change the things he can, and the wisdom to know the difference. Amen.*"

Benton looked at everyone in the room and said, "Everyone wait here for just a moment, please." Benton left the room but returned minutes later wearing clothing matching the era he was about to visit.

He walked over to the tele-pad controls and checked the settings. He picked up a return teleport button and placed it in his pocket.

Rayne was slightly smiling while standing at the controls and waited for Benton to give the go ahead.

"I'll be right back," Benton said, and he nodded at Rayne.

Chapter 31

The five statesmen found themselves in familiar places. Gone were the fancy lights over their heads and under their feet. No clear glass computer consoles with multi-colored lights, no televisions, radios and no J.A.S.P.E.R. listening to their conversations. They were home and only moments after they left. Not a sole knew they had been gone. The air was cleaner. Their memory was sharp. They knew exactly where they were, and keenly, when they were. They five had met in seclusion before they left 2025 and decided to go to a particular place and meet twenty-four hours later after arriving home. The place was a short horse-ride north from Philadelphia on top of a hill. The grassy hill had few trees on it and the view was spectacular. They agreed they were to meet at a familiar place and each man needed time to get there. The meeting was a bit surreal as the statesmen arrived. Each knowing where the other had been just mere hours ago. They were not standing on the spot where Dr. Benton's underground facility will have been ~ or could be...they were sure they would never know that outcome. They were about to make changes to the country's foundational documents and the future they had just seen was not yet written as far as they were concerned.

Hamilton spoke first, "If that was a dream, gentlemen, I must say that it would not have been the five of us I would have chosen to share in the same dream but I am very satisfied that it turned out this way."

Morris quipped, "If that were a dream, I would be standing here with four women." The other four looked at Morris as he continued, "And, I would have my real leg back." Morris reached down and tapped his new prosthetic limb. "Not a dream," he commented clearly.

Dickinson gently reached up to his breast pocket and felt the pen in his pocket. "We have work to do, gentlemen. I understand we may not see eye to eye on each element for the steps we take but we do have a common goal. I believe it would be prudent for us to maintain a certain level of communication only between the five of us. This will be a task of great undertaking and I fear we will need the strength of the men standing next to us at this very moment to continue down the road in our attempt to repair the wretchedness which occurs in the future and make this country great," he said.

Roger Sherman was looking at the ground, or so it seemed. His eyes were fixed up on his shoes when he spoke. "Where our eyes see, our feet will surely follow," he said gently. "Men...whether ill intentions or good intentions, they will make decisions. For if they don't, then others will make decisions for them. As we are the five that decided to participate in the dream, we all shared, I pray we make wise decisions, gentlemen. Wise decisions with good intentions. May this be the wind that fills our sails. To bring this country together is the still the foremost issue at hand. We now stand in the year of our own time. We know what the future holds. The Honorable Mr. Dickinson is right. We must maintain our common goal and stay in communication. And pray, gentlemen. Pray to be humble in our work."

Madison added, "I am thankful for our dream. When I think about the all of it all, I am grateful to have a larger picture of what our actions and words will do. The weight of such actions is no less heavy if we had the same heart prior to this dream. Do not write any of this down but send business invitations via messenger. We must meet in private and away from anyone from time to time. Are we agreed?"

The men all nodded in the affirmative and then continued with several individual conversations but soon left to return to their duties.

~~~~~~~~~~

The following day the delegates of the Second Continental Congress met to continue their quest on creating a governing document. A new constitution. The country was still very much divided. The five statesmen were very articulate in their respective roles. Despite the time spent in the future, Madison and Sherman remained at odds much of the time. Sherman's arguments were never fully eloquent in the arena he stood in. Largely self-taught about matters of law, his experiences as a county judge, assemblyman, justice of the peace, several political offices and a business owner propelled him into the position he now held. His speech was atrocious according to most however, his common sense prevailed higher than most and he was admired and revered by nearly everyone. John Adams calls Sherman "one of the most sensible men in the world." Not surprisingly, Sherman's orations were largely disputed by James Madison. However, the two of them met in the afternoon on one important topic.

Sherman started by asking, "My friend, shall we work together and create a clause that will allow the government to pass laws *requiring* men and women to act lawfully?"

Madison countered, "I believe we are in agreement, Councilor. Yet, we must come together with the proper wording to present our case. We cannot infringe upon the rights and freedoms for which we are currently seeking from the Monarchy from which we are separating. We shall continue to ask questions. How do we present such an argument to the courts without divulging the knowledge of the future we hold? We are speaking of a law that knows no time or economic status. A law of such nature would not apply to those who would peacefully assemble to protest the actions of the government or other entity. However, when those peaceful assemblies' breakout into physical confrontations, would this be a self-defense or the actions of maliciousness? And we have learned that we know, that we know, that we know....I'm not stuttering, sir...but we do know that the future holds self-centered liberals who will change our words or purposefully misinterpret our meaning for their own goal and not that of the good of the country."

"This is our charge, my friend. We must find a way," came the intense reply.

The two continued to talk about this and a few other items coming up in the conclave. Sherman was showing signs of difficulty with other state senators dealing with other problems they considered more pressing. South Carolina's representatives had very blatantly told the conclave they would not agree to anything that removes slavery from the whole of the constitution and they would not be persuaded otherwise. The Honorable John Rutledge, who, in his mid-40's and above the average age of all the members of this conclave, was a formidable congressman. As a prominent slave owner, his skills as a lawyer, judge, representative and past Governor of South Carolina, earned him every respect from his fellow conclave members. This respect would eventually earn him a nomination from George Washington as a Supreme Court Justice. Even still, he was not the only opponent to face the five statesmen who had a glimpse of the future.

Sherman and Madison decided to call a meeting of the five statesmen. Several conversations must take place to decide how the five could possibly influence the votes of any of the other delegates. Decisions that would, if written in the Constitution or the Bill of Rights, would change the future of the United States.

Chapter 32

Several weeks later the five met in a town not far away from the conclave.   One of Madison's personal friends allowed them to use a room of their house. However, Dickinson requested they meet outside in the sunshine. He wasn't feeling well and felt the sunshine would do him good.   He also felt that the house would echo any arguments that may occur and being outside may quell such disagreements. He wasn't wrong on either account.

A table with a pitcher of cold water was placed in the shade of a tree nearby.   Several chairs were also handy. Once Morris made his way into the meadow and everyone greeted each other in the proper manner, Madison opened the group meeting with a statement.

"I am finding our task to be more insurmountable than I expected.   Our common goal to bring a nation together and, separate from the monarchy which opposes us to do so, is paramount.   Failure must not come into this equation. We may know the future of what will be if we only execute what we know what has transpired, however, I'm finding much opposition in every direction to do more. I have had many conversations on several topics which I feel have truly driven other delegates away from the table of negotiation. So much so that bringing them back to the table may have more of a risk than leaving matters alone. What say you?"

Hamilton responded by raising his hand and no one objected.   He began, "I too have found in the quiet meetings I entertain with other delegates when speaking towards national debt and spending, that is, during time of war or peace, interests rates and the financial machinery that will ultimately lead to the financial crisis of 2025, which we bear witness amongst ourselves, is truly incomprehensible to the men of this age. Admittedly, I cannot confirm that I would understand the amount of debt allowed and created by this country's future elected government should I not have stood where you stood, and heard what you heard, in the year of 2025. Simply stated, it is unbelievable to the men of our time that such stupidity could come from the leaders of this country."

Morris commented in agreement as he was present during some of those same meetings with Hamilton. However, he was very confident in that the banking system which they were both engaged in creating was moving along. His arrogance could not be contained, and he decided to maintain a level of confidence and not agree to any failure of completing at least part of his task.

He started out by saying, "In the matters concerning the existence of our country, I shall give no quarter to the man who puts himself above the whole of the nation. The erratic and contrary democratic chaos, no matter what year one may stand in, must be held at bay in the national theatre when matters of legislation are at hand. We have learned that the Socialists believe the people of our country should live on equal footing, however, we do not nor will we ever. Not financially, economically, in status or in poverty. We are created equal, but we do not live equally. We are all people, and we are all different. And the people who create wealth are, in many cases, the same who provide employment and should not be punished by the government through divisive over taxation or any other instrument. Our country will be destroyed from within, gentlemen, unless we provide the proper footing for that which we are building. Admittedly, this task is much more precarious than changing the landscape of the wilderness."

Morris stopped for a moment obviously recalling a memory he was about to share.

He continued by saying, "I remember over a decade ago, speaking to my close associate, Thomas Paine, of whom you are all acquainted, when the wilderness lands nearby have been changed into a township whereby merchants were able to conduct abundant business. I felt transmigrated by the scene in front of me. My own thoughts, covering the abundant amount of trading that occurred simply by changing the landscape, were transforming. Our adventure in the future, gentlemen, has left me in the same realm of thought. It is quite the task to ask men, who have no understanding of such changes in the economies of our future, of the lives lost in horrendous wars, of the changes in technology or medicine, to comprehend the importance of the words required to prevent such future wonders or atrocities from occurring. Even our esteemed colleague, John Jay, whom we all hold in high respect and maintains a strong vision for a new national government, remains at arms distance in our vision. While the building of a nation is at hand, the men who joined with us to complete this task, are having difficulties going beyond their own vision, just as we have done. Gentlemen, these men have no concept of what it means to fly ~ and yet, we have done so."

Hamilton made a hand gesture and Morris acquiesced to his speaking. "The Honorable Senator from New York remains true to our goal in his own fashion and, we all comprehend, on levels of experience and the intellectual of which our other colleagues are not able.   I, too, remember from our 'adventure' as the Senator calls it, that there exists a very real chance that our nation is in great peril against enemies, not only in the domestic, but from countries outside our borders. Of course, my concern is in the financial realm. Just as Senator Morris pointed out we will be destroyed from within.

How is it that we, five men, working with other honorable men and against time, can ratify a new Constitution and prevent the demise of a country that may only survive 250 years? My heart is one hundred percent into this plan, my friends. My mind tells me we must pursue all ends to the best of our abilities. Many wonderful things will come from our decisions but, make no mistake, as the Senator," Hamilton gestured to Morris, "has pointed out, great wars and destruction will also occur. We are not equal except in the eyes of freedom."

Dickinson had been listening to all the comments and found an opportunity to expound upon the experiences of the other four. After taking a drink of water and clearing his throat he began, "Agreed, and if I may, as we are the ones who shared the 'adventure', I will speak in the familiar. Alexander, Gouveneur, James and Roger, I thank you for meeting me outside today. My health isn't what it should be these days and, while staying in the conclave most hours of the day as you do, it is the sunlight which gives me strength to carry on. In these hours of debate, we must strive in the affirmative for the new constitution to take place. We must free ourselves from the Monarchy for any of this future to occur. As Alexander agreed, we are only free in the eyes of freedom and we must secure that freedom at all costs. These thirteen colony states are in a most fragile condition at this very moment. We must live in the present and continue our path. I pray we are able to keep the distant future in mind as we do so."

In the shade of that sunlight, nearly one hundred yards away stood a lonely figure. His hands were dirtier than what he was accustomed to and his beard was scruffy and unkept. He had been following each of the men with the help of Dr. Rayne's tracking device. A biodegradable chip was placed in Morris's prosthetic leg. At the time the leg was made, Rayne was only hoping that if anyone did travel back, they would at least be able to find Morris. As it turns out, Benton found the entire group on this occasion.

Dr. Benton was far enough away that he couldn't quite make out what was being said. His interpretation of their body language was roughly telling him that their work of changing the documents was slow at best. But even some change could potentially be better than nothing as all. Benton was feeling as though his dream was being slowly taken away from him. However, he truly did not know what they were saying, and he was determined to find out. It was at this moment that he wished he had brought

J.A.S.P.E.R. in its portable form. Naturally, it wouldn't be dependent on the internet for information.   He had developed the portable J.A.S.P.E.R. a couple years ago in case of emergencies such as going to under- developed countries...which is exactly where he was for the time being. "Besides," he thought. "The six-month battery life would have been perfect for this trip." In the end, he was afraid of that if anything happened to himself; if this type of technology would be lost in the past, who knows what ramifications that may cause.

Benton, determined to remain hidden from view, slowly made his way closer to the gathering. While the area was full of trees, it was still a difficult task. He knew a couple of these men were exceptional soldiers. An ambush from a forest line would be something they would be sensitive to and trained in watching for. Benton stopped moving forward when he could hear their voices and slightly understand them.

Benton concentrated and was able to make out some encouraging conversation.   Each statesman spoke of remembering what will happen in the future when they continue to speak to the other participants of the conclave.   Again, he was encouraged for what may happen.

Chapter 33

On September 15th, 1787, two days before history records the signing of the Constitution, the five statesmen met once more. As they had not been discovered meeting in the fields of Dickinson's friend, they had done so again.

Morris's attitude had gotten the best of him of late. The others could tell when he uttered the first words of this meeting. "John Rutledge is a royal pain in my posterior! His quiet demeanor and passive aggressive attitude continue to derail my efforts in saving this country from herself. He refuses to agree to what is needed to prevent this country's future elected from creating the liberal loopholes that will inevitably be the downfall of our economy and liberty's the people of this time have sacrificed!" Morris was agitated enough that he did not sit down.

Madison looked up from his chair and spoke quickly, "Might I remind you that he had his chance to see the future and experience what we have. He chose not to. Even after returning, several of us have had only limited time with him and he refused to listen to any of us. He refused to listen for exactly this reason. He does not want to disrupt the natural development of this country which remains as a sign of his character. He is a great man, Senator Morris. A great man, indeed. And we must not fault him for sticking to his integrity. His forethought in the Constitution is paramount in the very fact that this country will exist as a sovereign nation. We agreed that we mustn't overtly lend our own knowledge about the future to change the decisions of the delegates, by which first establishing a Constitution, therefore the potential changes of such document in the future cannot take place."

"Exactly!" Morris spurted out. "And, I freely admit he is a man worthy of the task set upon him, but if he would give us the liberty of his mind, we may still have the first without the consequences of the second! To have a Constitution written without the negotiations that perpetuate our demise! What could be more insightful and fuller of integrity than this? But he will not listen to reason."

"In this we should rejoice, Senator Morris," Sherman said quickly. Morris quickly turned on his peg leg and waited for the next comment. "We are all aware that this Second Constitutional Conclave has agreed, we must negotiate between all colonies, to meet and keep the opinions of our colleagues undiscussed beyond the confines of Independence Hall. However, Mr. Morris, here, in our private room, the five of us have an understanding of events far more reaching."

Hamilton leaned back in his chair and crossed his legs while listening to the rants of frustration and responses of the others. It was his turn in the pulpit he thought to himself. "Gouveneur," he began. "We must also consider the remaining members of this delegation who, in my estimation, are as frustrated with your own stance in the creation of this nation. They certainly feel as adamant of their constituents' opinions as we do of the knowledge we exclusively maintain. Without publicly disclosing our private adventure, men such as George Mason, and James McHenry, men who remain confidants to you, may not even change their thoughts. You can be rest assured that Patrick Henry will not change his mind regardless of what you say. He will push back based solely on his principles. He is as you are, sir, a man to be reckoned with."

Morris' aristocratic attitude enjoyed the compliment but the better part of himself remained frustrated as he knew Hamilton was right. The participants of this seventeen-week conclave were stern and learned men who held tight to their beliefs. Changing a person's mind, including his own, is not as easy as one would think.

"I admit," Morris said, "that my discussions of not simply rewriting the failing Articles of Confederation and writing a new Constitution have made a few of the other delegates leave the conclave all together. I suppose I too have a passion for what I believe in and tend to be less inclined to give in to the will of others."

Sherman sat quiet watching the exchange between his colleagues. He was remembering some of the wonderful things that he had witnessed during his time with Dr. Benton and his staff. Not everything was so terrible. While they were shown so many negative things, their education also showed them some very wonderful things. Great advancements, brilliant people, inventions, cures for diseases, flying and so much more. He truly loved the flying.

"Mr. Sherman," Madison asked? "A penny for your thoughts?"

Sherman looked up from his blank stare. "My apologies, sir. I was lost in the thoughts of all the bright things that the future holds. And brilliant men, such as Dr. Benton, who are as strong willed as Mr. Morris, Mr. Hamilton, Mr. Dickinson and yourself, of course," he said in a professional manner. "We cannot underestimate Dr. Benton or Colonel Powers as only having a single plan to effect change. Is their dependence on us the only course of action they have planned? I should think not. However, we have two days to complete our task. May we continue to endeavor in our efforts, gentlemen!"

Chapter 34

Two days later on the morning of the 27th, Benton found himself sitting on an outside bench somewhere near Independence Hall. History did not record a time when the final draft of the Constitution had been signed. He only remembered reading of the date. A date on which he had never dreamed of being able to sit outside on a bench and be waiting for the results.

No one else seems to be waiting at the time. The strangers around him went on about their daily lives. During this time that Benton had spent in Philadelphia, he fell in love with the way of life. Things were very different. He noted his appreciation for the things he took for granted. Air conditioning, electricity, the microwave and more. He sat on the bench reading and re-reading the newspaper. He noticed the difference in size and texture of the paper versus the volume sized newspapers of the 1980's, filled mostly with advertisement inserts and then the near non-existent newspapers of 2025, when most news was published electronically and read via cell phone apps or websites owned by the media companies. News that was 'real time' and not something that was printed because it was truly 'yesterday's' news.

He waited. He waited for the men to pour out of the building signifying completion. He didn't know what to expect either. He could recall any account of how the whole of the conclave expressed themselves as they exited the building. No news cameras were waiting with him. No pomp and circumstance.

Eventually, the doors did open and Benton, calmly stood and walked toward the men filing out, listened intently for any sign that his plan had worked. He stood in awe as he watched famous men walking by him. Some had faces of concern while others were simply tired expressions.

A horse drawn carriage pulled up not too far away from him and a lady pressed her face through the window. "Dr. Franklin! What have you given us, sir? A republic or a monarchy?" she asked. Benjamin Franklin answered tersely, "A republic, if you can keep it!"

Benton continued to stand and watch. He saw Madison walking out of the building. His small stature was obvious, but he held his head high and he commanded the respect of many. Madison did not see Benton as he turned and walked down the street in the opposite direction.

Benton wondered if the history records would still record that only thirty-nine men signed the document. That is, thirty-nine delegates, plus the typically non-mentioned Secretary of the Constitution, William Jackson.

Benton did not yet know the constitution was signed in its original form. Not a single word was changed from how he had learned it in his seventh-grade government class. The project failed.

The five statesmen walked away from Independence Hall with the eventuality of a newly ratified country. While so many other delegates of the conclave were excited for the event, there were more than five who's hearts were less than satisfied.

Dedicated men in the cause of liberty and freedom, such as Thomas Jefferson, who, serving as the Minister to France, was not even in Philadelphia. Nor was John Adams, who was out of the country serving as Minister to Great Britain. Many had their excuses of not being able to play a part in this Second Continental Congress, such as John Hancock, Samuel Adams and Patrick Henry. Men who, were they to have their say, might very well have been swayed to change the wording of the Constitution. Other famously dedicated men were clearly frustrated. Not content to sign and purposefully not present on the day of signing were George Mason of Virginia and Elbridge Gerry of Massachusetts. However, it was signed by those who agreed and historically, it remains unchanged.

Dickinson, who's signature was performed by proxy, wasn't present due to illness. Thus, the remaining four who were had decided to meet in a small room of a hotel down the street to share their woes. Just minutes after Morris arrived to meet the other three, they heard the knock on the door.

No one but the four were expected to meet.

On his guard, Madison was closest to the door and cautiously grabbed the round brass knob. His eyes were opened wide as he recognized their guest. Surprised, but always vigil, he quickly checked the hallway for other eyes and found none.

"My heavens, man! You are wonderful sight site to see," Madison exclaimed!

Benton, now clean shaven and easily recognizable, had stepped into the room to complete the joyous greetings from each man. Their expressions of great surprise and happiness would be something Benton would never forget.

Morris' booming voice came next. "My goodness, Dr. Carver Benton! You never cease to amaze. I never expected..." His words trailed off and the large man extended both arms. Benton received the enthusiastic bear hug.

"So," Hamilton said as he stood next in line. "You've become a 'traveler'. It is an honor that you are here with us, my friend. An honor indeed."

The last handshake came from Sherman, and with the gentle grip of an ox he said, "This is a momentous occasion, my friend. How truly good it is to see you." Then Sherman gently placed his left hand over their clasped right hands before he spoke.

Sherman's eyes were steadfast as he looked to Benton. His words stung hard, "We failed, my friend. We failed to prevent the atrocities of the future. We have failed the citizens of the future, the souls that will be lost from war, famine or disease. We failed our grandchildren, great grands and more generations following. Our efforts were not enough, my friend. I wish we could report otherwise." The smiles on all faces quickly faded.

Benton's eyes welled up with tears. This was the most emotional moment Benton could ever remember in his lifetime. Sherman placed a hand on his shoulder as his own eyes filled with tears.

Hamilton's words came next. "We have been yearning for this moment for many years. We have shed blood and tears in our efforts to free this country. We have argued against each other in the cause for freedom so many times I cannot count. We have met with senators from every state, published our thoughts with the help of our patriots and raised our rifles above our heads in the fight for liberty. With every step toward building a nation and to be counted as free men. In this we were only able to initiate a Constitution which you see as unchanged. Believe me, a true failure would have been not to have created The Constitution of The United States. A true failure would to remain under British rule for one minute longer than necessary. This is the dream of liberty. This is the dream of freedom. This has been the dream of many men who have already sacrificed so much in our time. The sacrifice of their own families, children, brothers and sisters. The shedding of blood across many states has already occurred and we know, because of your dreams and knowledge you have granted to us, that more blood will be shed in the name of freedom. This too is our failure. Truly, it is our wish that will have had better news to share with you. Outside of this room, we have stayed the course. But in this room, my friend...in this room, we humbly acknowledge our failure in your quest."

Morris spoke next, "I agree with my colleagues this evening. Our success today is also a failure within your hopes. I fear the evolving socialist's views cannot stop the momentum they have created. The recipients of those who solely rely on funds from any program, governmental or otherwise, will surely revolt against the authorities should the programs be taken away. You should plan for more conflict, Dr. Benton. You will lose these freedoms created today without change in the future. And, we could not help you with the change you desired from us. My heart is laid bare and heavy by our failure."

Sherman made the final comment by saying, "It saddens my soul to feel as though the whole of all our efforts has failed to prevent a land of continuing slavery. However, a failure of preventing the worst of all events in our nation's history ~ not only a first but likely a **Second Civil War**."

The somber sentiments of the room hung thick in the air. A few of the men were seen with tears in their eyes. Others, not unfamiliar with defeat, sat with heavy hearts.

Madison and Benton were both thinking along the same lines. Madison felt sorry for the all the work Benton had done. His brilliant mind, his invention of time travel and moving people from one place to another at the touch of a button. His intentions were good, his plan was sound, however, there would be no Constitution to change if the Second Continental Congress had failed to first come together, united as a sovereign country. For Madison and the other statesmen, this had to be the priority. Of this, there was no mistake.

Benton also believed the same. Without the negotiations between the participating states and a signed Constitution, there would be no United States. No Bill of

Rights would follow and a country, probably, still under the rule of the British. He wondered if that wouldn't be a bad thing? Would he even have the chance to wonder it at all? However, there is a Constitution that was signed. A country in peril of collapse. He could only wonder if the creation of this Constitution, as it stands, will be at the defeat of the future. This American experiment is coming to a close. The next questions are simple. When and how?

Chapter 35

Benton stayed for the rest of the evening and visited with his friend. He explained that he had seen them around town and did his best to keep tabs on the pulse of what was happening without trying to interfere. He believed his interference had already been done by the education they received in the year 2025. He wouldn't take the chance of being written in the history books as someone who might be noteworthy. He was fully invested with the belief that all of the influence on any member of the congress, whether great, small or, unfortunately, none at all, must come from whomever chose to visit the future.

The small contingency continued to talk about the next document to tackle, the Bill of Rights. Madison was particularly interested and promised he would do whatever he could. However, that was yet to be.

The men very politely said their goodbyes and Hamilton, Dickinson and Morris left the room one by one. Madison and Sherman sat back down in their seats.

Sherman spoke first. "It's just the three of us now, Carver." Sherman had dispensed with the formalities. "I want you to know how truly grateful we all are for the gift you have given us. Some could look upon the knowledge of the future as a curse. As you are the last one that shall return to a time when so much political turmoil still exists, you may also think your knowledge is a curse. But, we do not! Our knowledge is, however, an instrument that must be used to change our country for the better. Our political turmoil has changed us, in the here and now. A group of men came together for six days a week and argued nearly everything under the sun. Mr. Madison and I, even with the knowledge you shared with us, rallied against each other more than any other two individuals in that conclave. From all the arguments ~ a nation was born. It was not born out of love for one another, and it twas no easy task. Mind you, arguments, in a smelly room, full of sweaty, angry men fighting for their constituency. Some will say it was very civil. Others will not. Either way, the task was accomplished. You can still do that too, Carver. You still have the power to change the political climate of your time. Truly, you are one of the world's most brilliant minds. The fact that we have breathed the air in the year 2025, and that you are standing in the year 1787, proves that. I believe you will find a way."

Sherman stood and straightened out his shirt and brushed out his jacket sleeves, took a step toward Benton and held out his hand. "Oddly enough, though it has been a few months since we said our last goodbye, I feel as though we have lived a lifetime with you, sir. And," Sherman paused. "I have become fond of your friendship. I shall miss our talks, Carver. And with that, I will take my leave." Sherman stood up from his chair. Sherman's mannerisms were familiar to Benton by now and he knew Sherman had one more thing to say when he took a small step forward, put out his hand, cleared his throat and looked at Benton in the eyes and smiled when he said, "These are the most comfortable pair of shoes I have ever worn. Farewell, my friend."

Benton took hold of Sherman's hand and replied, "Farewell, sir. It has been my honor." Sherman nodded politely, turned and left the room with tears flowing and closed the door behind him.

Madison was still sitting in his chair when Benton turned around. He motioned to the empty chair across from him. Benton sat in the same chair Morris had been in earlier.

"Time," Madison started. "Time is something we can never get back...well, that's what I believed prior to meeting you. If I may, I should like to ask you one question, Carver." Madison looked directly into Benton's eyes and with a firmness in his voice he asked, "Now that you know the outcome of your experiment, are you planning to do it again with other members of this conclave? Perhaps Thomas Jefferson or Benjamin Franklin would produce a favorable result?"

Benton didn't blink an eye and answered without a pause. "No. That was discussed from the very beginning, James. We're not playing at being God. We will accept the result as it stands. To add to that, it appears that this outcome has also not caused any additional negative possibilities. We still have a Constitution as the others mentioned. This experimental project didn't make anything worse for America while attempting to fix future issues. This isn't a failure, Senator, when I think of it from that perspective. So, what will we do now? We will take an idea from a most recent conversation with the Colonel, I believe he has a concept to pursue. We won't travel through time again, but we haven't given up."

"Very good, then. I applaud you on your sentiments. Now then, I will venture that you are not in any hurry to return home? And, at the moment, as time is in your control and you haven't pressed that magic button which is, no doubt, sitting in your left breast pocket of your jacket, I believe we should visit a bit more about this Bill of Rights."

Benton smiled as he saw Madison pick up a bottle of wine and pour two glasses. The two talked into the wee hours of the morning.

PART 3

The Second Civil War

Chapter 36

Benton had returned to find his team settling down in the parlor to talk about their story. In the year 2025, he hadn't been gone but a few minutes. He gave everyone an account of his time spent in the past and concluded by telling them how appreciative he was that they had convinced him to go.

Benton was exhausted. He may be sitting in the year 2025 but, to him, he had literally been awake all night. He excused himself and decided to go find a bed and sleep without setting an alarm clock.

Over the next several months, Dr. Benton and Dr. Rayne and their team continued working. The Colonel had begun to visit the team more often and had spoken to each person individually. They were Benton's team and very loyal to him. He had no intention of changing that

394

dynamic but, he certainly had plans for them in his attempt to resolve the discourse living within America.

In 2026, almost a year to the day Benton had returned, the teleportation project was complete. While it was certainly proven a success with time travel, Benton and his team wanted to be sure there were plenty of tests before it would have been released for public usage. The team had successfully built several tall cylinder walk-in booths, complete with tele-pads built in the bottom. The system contained a voice activated interface for the user to tell the system where they wanted to be transported to and, since the location had a transport booth to receive them, the system worked perfectly. As the travelers were unafraid of the time travel and personally vested in the project, they repeatedly tested the system on themselves. Benton had Dr. Rayne travel around the world with a test booth. He would set it up in remote locations of major cities and program in the coordinates, then name the location. The specific locations in the major cities were predetermined by Colonel Powers so secrecy was maintained. Everything worked as it should.

Satisfied that all possible testing which could have been done was successfully; the Colonel launched his product. Over the next two years, Colonel Powers securely manufactured his teleport product. Several companies, foreign and domestic, tried to reverse engineer it, but due to its security protocols and closed system, in the software and high-end, hardware architecture, none were able. The Colonel was certainly first to market as he hoped he would be. Large corporations were first to purchase tele-pod booths. For some, the traditional 'Go-to-meeting' appointments had a new and literal meaning. The persistent problems with internet meetings failing due to poor connectivity or other issues were a thing of the past for those who had access to a tele-pod booth. The Colonel made billions of dollars. He was already in the top one percent of people of wealth in the United States prior to his first sale. He was now in the top one percent of wealthy people in the *world*.

The Colonel's first plan was to work the system from the inside. Benton was aware that the majority of the Colonel's wealth was inherited. However, it was more than enough for Benton to complete the Colonel's tele-pad project and his own mission. While the Colonel had no knowledge of Benton's mission at the time, the Colonel had a plan of his own to redirect America's path back to the values and intentions of the forefathers. He told Benton that his first plan was already in motion. A plan that had taken years to create.

However, it was time the Colonel gathered up his own trusted colleagues and laid everything out. As one of the Colonel's first money making ventures, he used the inherited franchises as the base of his plan. He spent the following years purchasing as many fast food and hotel franchises to build his empire. He did very well with the profits and wisely invested the proceeds to create even more wealth. He then, with a healthy sign-on bonus, hired the over or under qualified family members of politicians. Whether educated or not, the family of the highly ranked elected officials in each state would run a franchise he owned. Those new employees, the children, brothers, sisters and cousins of the elected officials in state and federal levels of Congress, truly helped the franchises flourish and thus, they enjoyed an easy lifestyle with many amenities and benefits. In some cases, full families were put to work. Everyone pulled their weight, and within months, the facilities were showing great productivity. The salaries paid to the political family members were doubled the prevailing wages for their positions. It did not take long for the employees to become accustomed to large bank accounts, nice cars and nearly every new electronic gadget. The only catch of this plan was to exert pressure on the family, and in turn, the congressman to vote in the direction the Colonel requested. Maybe not as high on the moral code he was raised with by any means, but it was, in his opinion, just as legal as lobbyist, corporate or foreign pressures when it came time to vote. No different than the same democratic billionaire funding multiple socialist campaigns. He knew from experience there were many games, whether they were called 'concessions' or 'negotiations', played at the political level. The Colonel's mindset maintained this plan wasn't any more dishonest than letting locked up, incarcerated felon's, or illegal aliens to vote. Something the Socialist party had lobbied in favor of for many years. He had been in the political system long enough to know that votes could be had if the price was right. It was a long shot, but, not unlike Benton, the Colonel also believed something, nearly anything - even something as drastic as this - had to be done to pull America back to where it should be. He and many other 'average Americans' believed that, though

America was no longer the greatest country in the world, it could be. Colonel Alan Powers, an influential man of means, a past Senator, was willing to sacrifice everything he owned, and pay for as much as was needed, to help achieve this goal. His primary goal was dousing the flames of Socialism burning up our country.

Only time, and an election or two, would tell if this plan would work.

Even with all the positioning he did with politician's families, his efforts never got a chance to be effective enough. The 'free' platform of the Socialist Party in regard to health care, college, medical, welfare and more, were overwhelmed at the voting poles. With the election of 2028, a Socialist government had taken control. By the election of 2032, both the Oval Office and Congress had fallen, and the 'republic' America once was, would be no more.

Even with all the influence and pressure from relatives of his employees voting his way, the liberal votes were sustained by 18% percent. The media confirmed the loss of the oval office and congress were due to the new laws allowing over 10,000,000 current prisoner votes allowed in liberal states. They also include the new laws allowing illegal immigrants who have maintained residence in the liberal states for over 10 years. The media confirmed the two newest voting locations, the District of Columbia and Puerto Rico, whose combined populous are historically very left leaning, contributed the push to socialism. The Socialist candidate promised nearly everything including higher spending amounts for welfare recipients to include a monthly tax-free check for a thousand dollars, no taxes for the lowest of incomes and offset those by raising taxes for higher incomes.

Taxable Income	New Tax Rate
0 - 30,000	0%
30,001 - 80,000	12%
80,001 - 150,000	24%
150,001 - 225,000	35%
225,001 - 400,000	42%
400,001 +	50%

By using an estimated average income of $64,000 on a family of four, they believed people would vote for a candidate who promised lower taxes. Besides, they have always believed the people with higher incomes should pay higher taxes.

The 'stacked deck' the Colonel had implemented was derailed by the "FREE, FREE, FREE' promises touted by the socialist campaigns. The 'Free' label bought many votes of those who want the governmental handouts. Registered socialists' voters were 2 to 1 over federalists. The outcome of this election was psychologically labeled against the socialist's as 'morally disengaged'.

All of the Colonel's positive work that had been done to rebuild America was attacked by the socialists and the remnants of liberals.

The Colonel's plan failed. Sadly, the world witnessed the immediate decay of the country.

Within the first year of holding office, the work of the new socialist president, supported by that party, increased the U.S. debt by over 3 trillion. Economists projected the average debt to increase at the same rate over the next several years. The two major political parties, Socialists and Federalists, threw legal action against each other. Political compromises fell apart as taxes were raised to feed the new social programs that were already financially depleted. The funds for the medical side of social security, Medicaid and Medicare, were drained due to payouts to hospitals for patients of drug overdose, obesity, opioids and more. Additionally, millennials and people under fifty years of age opted out of paying into the program knowing they wouldn't see a dime by the time they would be eligible to receive benefits. Compounding the problem, welfare and free medical programs were extended to the millions of illegal immigrants who were allowed to use the system without paying any taxes into it.

With the acceptance of 'universal free health care' in the United States, the medical profession just billed the government for doctor visits and procedures unless the government found you had the means to pay. And if you pay, the fees were outrageous.

In higher education, the same concept was awakened. With free University education to any willing high school student, the institutions billed the government. Again, unless you had the means to pay, then the fees were incredibly high.

Entrepreneurs and small businesses that used to maintain the countries stability in smaller towns dried up. Capitalism is failing as it is designed to make a profit. Not guarantee the employment of labor. Profit is gained with low costs, not the high wage of an hourly employee. The minimum wage, which was increased to more than $20 per hour by federal decree, caused small businesses to close and unemployment to rise up near 25% and rival the level of the Great Depression. The economic cascading effect of the raised wages destroyed many small towns in every state. In large density populated cities, the increased wage urged manufacturers to purchase A.I. (artificial intelligence) robots to keep their doors open. More jobs were displaced, and more hard-working people reached out to the government. And as robots don't pay taxes, the Socialist began to offset the loss of employment tax, by annually taxing companies for every robot they purchased. In turn, no new manufacturing companies were building in America. They couldn't afford to. However, consumerism was in full swing! The average income American, who typically live from paycheck to paycheck, spent those tax savings. Few literally saved or invested.

The socialist president moved funding away from the country's military to pay for other programs that were now underfunded, leaving the borders, oceans, shipping lanes and overseas bases, less secure than ever before. Young men and women, who, in decades before, were willing to serve their country, no longer had the desire to be a part of "the government". Especially when the same government would pay welfare for not working at all.

Naval ships were shut down as there weren't enough sailors to man the ships safely. Marine and Air Force bases around the world closed for the similar reasons. The apathy of the youth in America had escalated. Still others, older in age, understood the meaning of keeping a job within the government as it was typically harder to be fired from a government job. The country's love of the individual became more important than love of country. The words of President John F. Kennedy on January 20, 1961 fell on deaf ears.

A short two years later, by the end of 2034, America's desperation and the separation between the two parties finally hit the breaking point. She imploded with what was known as **The Second Civil War.**

As much of the American citizens could, they tried their best to make do. Grandchildren, who were now well into their 60's, were in worse living conditions that their grandparents during the Great Depression. An experience America thought would never happen again. The 'haves' versus the 'have nots' turned into the 'can I keep it' verses the 'can I take it'. Some families began to work their jobs in shifts. Some go to work while others stayed at the home to protect their belongings. Those with unregistered guns were glad they kept them but obtaining ammunition proved to be most difficult.

Rioting in streets was much worse after demonstrations have gotten totally out of control. Drug cartels and gangs ruled in many places. The violence was like that of the 1992 Los Angeles riots. Military involvement and late-night curfews were, once again, thrown into motion.

The devaluation of United States currency was worldwide and deemed worthless in several other countries. Ultimately, the U.S. government wasn't able to borrow any more. In America, the people who have already learned the skills of saving, saved as much as they could. Those who have never learned the skill to save and lived paycheck to paycheck finally started saving money. Even still, people who purchased items on impulse continued to suffer. Of those that saved, they took a lesson from the people who had much more than them and made plans to leave.

The United States is as far away from 'united' as she could ever be. Historical enemies of the U.S. laughed and watched the virtual implosion. Some began plotting atrocities to help prevent any recovery as being a world leader. Many allies of the U.S. cried with those who were leaving what was once the greatest country in the world.

The Colonel sat in his office with Dr. Benton and Dr. Rayne. All sat with solemn faces while the Colonel said, "Some days I lay awake at night and struggle with the way America has turned out. I certainly think about it most of the day. I fear I dwell on it too much and live in negativity. Other days I think that the average American doesn't think about it at all. Don't they see the handwriting on the wall? Don't they feel the downward spiral of the government flushing their tax dollars? I...I..." He didn't finish the statement.

Rayne spoke next, "The Byzantine Era, Genghis Khan, the Egyptians, the Romans, the Greeks and, well, you know the histories. They all came to an end. America is very

403

small compared to the empires of the past. Yet, we commanded a presence on the world stage. Countries around the globe used to look up to us as world leaders. I can't help but wonder if this the way the America the Beautiful ceases to be beautiful. We are no longer a shining beacon. Lady Liberty no longer holds the light of America. The light has burned out. Liberty has fled."

Benton looked at the Colonel calmly. "It's time, Alan. Time to start the last plan."

Rayne sat looking confused. "Um, excuse me? What plan?"

The Colonel continued, "Have you ever heard of Britain's Brain Drain?"

"I believe I've heard the term but, go ahead. Tell me," Rayne said.

"Webster Dictionary describes a 'brain drain' as *'the departure of educated or professional people from one country, economic sector, or field for another usually for better pay or living conditions'*. I'm proposing the same concept. The 'why' is already a known factor. The 'how, when and who' are decisions that can be made individually. My plan is to create the 'where'. It's a simple plan to say in conversation but a massive task to put into motion. It is, without a doubt, the last and ultimate solution."

The room was quiet for moment.

Benton's eyes lit up as he answered, "Time to win, William. It's time to win."

Chapter 37

With the Second Civil War continuing in full force and the Colonel's first plan losing to the socialist carrot, he knew it was time for his second plan. Aided by Benton's team, the second plan was about to come into play. He had already sold his franchises after the last election and made a very healthy profit. The Colonel laid out his second plan to Benton and his team.

After hearing the unoriginal but bold plan, each team member, including Benton, remained loyal to the cause and followed all the instructions they were given. This final 'Hail Mary' of a plan for a better country may very well be a win-win situation for those who would choose to be a part of a country where citizenship was earned, and therefore could be taken away, and it truly meant something. Where God wasn't shoved out of the political, school systems, along with discipline. Where people worked hard, and welfare was non-existent via the government. Where consequences for working towards the demise of the country wouldn't be tolerated. Pride for a citizen's country would come from the citizen's willingness to live without the government pandering to the lowest common denominator.

Colonel Alan Powers maintained his wealth in more than a dozen countries and currencies. He laid out a plan for his own team to search the world for about 20,000 - 50,000 square miles of land to purchase. A new 'United America' can begin again. Some states, such as Texas, even with their own sovereign Constitution, tried to succeed, but the federal government prohibited the action. Texas' argument included the changing borders in the Europe when Yugoslavia divided into seven new countries. From the beginning of 1990, over 30 countries have been created from failed USSR or by joining smaller countries into one. The Texas argument was ultimately refused by the socialist government, thus quashing any smaller states from attempting the same idea. The few remaining 'Conservative' states were constantly belittled via the socialist media. The Colonel felt America could not be rebuilt where she is. He was sure he wasn't the only patriot to feel this way. The cancer, known as socialism, had spread. A new country had to be started, just as Dr. Benton predicted.

The United States started out some 250 years ago with 13 colony's negotiating to 'form a perfect union'. The end of this 250-year experiment for democracy has arrived.

Information went out to citizens across America. People yearned for a place to live where citizens wanted to be citizens and could be proud of their country. Where the flag is a banner of pride and citizens looked upon it as a sign of a strong nation.

The Colonels plan would consist of a new Constitution, Bill of Rights and Responsibilities, and a Declaration of Independence to encompass many of the positive ideals which created the United States of America, but also spell out the requirements of being a citizen of the new country. He wanted to clearly fix the loopholes he believed have been abused. The Colonel now believed

Benton's team would be a wonderful option to help draft the documents.

Upon hearing the news, the travelers sat around a meeting table and prepared to work on their assignment. Those who had once believed they had the hardest task of persuading the forefathers into rewriting various parts of the Constitution, now began to believe they were mistaken. Now... they felt the pressure was truly upon them. However, they would not back down. Besides, they didn't have to reinvent the wheel. The original founding documents and amendments only need some clarity, but that was easier said than done.

Paul Tesla thought to himself, *"One must wonder how many congressmen throughout history have thought this same idea of adding to the Constitution for the same reasons as the Colonel. To loosen the federal stronghold of government and give more power to the individual states and hold the citizens accountable. If they did, they obviously failed, or we would already have seen the changes in written form. I pray we succeed in this endeavor. I pray for the people of America."*

As if Charles Carson could read Paul's thoughts he openly said, "We will succeed in our task. We will. We are stepping away from the desolation and opposition of Socialism. We are writing the beginning documents in one accord. Those that are against freedom and liberty, against individual accountability and the honor of citizenship do not have a voice here!"

While Benton's staff began drafting new governing documents, the Colonel's staff sent out the offer to twenty-three different countries around the world with only one question ~ would you sell approximately 50,000 square miles of land and the sovereignty to with it? Both Benton and the Colonel were not surprised to find an eighty percent positive return on their question. Why? It was a fresh bucket of cash to work from and build. New jobs and new economy. New infrastructure and new homes. Some considered it winning a lottery for any country willing to sell land and in need of a stimulus. Billions upon billions! From there, it was only a negotiation. How many billions would it require? Naturally, more questions would follow, but this would be the start. Conversations and negotiations will last for a time. However, this plan, based on the amount of replies, was clearly going to be successful. The 'New America', or whatever it would eventually be called, will happen.

The Colonel's idea wasn't a new concept. The Louisiana Purchase of 1803 came with a $15 million price tag. The U.S. had purchased Alaska in 1872 from Russia for $7.2 million dollars. Many countries purchase property within the U.S. all the time.

Television news stations and talk shows spent a lot of airtime on the Colonel's plan to purchase this much land and build a 'New America'. The requests to be a part of it were, as expected, overwhelming. Billions of dollars were pledged as donations. Sure, many of America's successful were among the donors, but a good portion of the money was from mid-income families too. Even the poor citizens who have survived in the corrupt and decaying inner cities desired to escape and offered what they could.

People who have opened small businesses, created jobs and economic stability wanted to move and take their families and companies and the jobs they created with them. They would rather spend their money willingly to create a better place than have a socialist government eventually force them to pay exorbitant taxes.

The Colonel anticipated that news would spread quickly. He planned on it. In preparation, he made a two-hour television show detailing what the 'New America' would expect of her new citizens. The show would give everyone a fair assessment of what is *expected* of the citizens of the new country. If you don't agree, don't go. It was a free choice. No one was pressured to agreeing to the laws. The opportunity of going would be to live within a new set of rules versus staying and feeding into a socialist country that would soon be taken over by those who called their loans due. The choice was laid out in simple terms. It would be no different than a person deciding to move to any other existing country today. If you don't like what is happening in the United States, you have the option to move out. In a marriage, this is called divorce.

The Colonel lined out the concepts of his plan by starting with a statement. "Living in the new country is an agreement between the citizen and the government. I choose to believe that this would tend to make the lives of the citizens and the running of the government much easier. Walking in agreement could mean knowing the destination and direction of where you are going, knowing the roads to get there and moving along together. Understanding that while you walk in agreement, should there ever come a time when the citizen decides not to be in agreement, that is, not live within laws they have learned, then they have freely made the decision to leave and to allow the remaining citizens in peace. If you decide to live in the new country, you will know the laws the citizens are expected to and choose to uphold. *The concept of legislating a person's heart is impossible.* In the United States, we legislate criminal law and punishments. What if the new government could positively encourage the citizens?" The Colonel's opening statement wasn't extraordinary. It was straight forward and clear and millions of eyes were watching as his TV program aired repeatedly.

The country would begin as a republic and the governing body, with similar checks and balances of the current system, would be established but work in a minimalistic fashion. The leader of the country would have line item veto to prevent any undesired or forced negotiations to the laws. There would be no welfare system except through the charities of churches, families or private organizations. All citizens worked for the betterment of the country. Even after a week had passed of the primetime show being aired, very little of the pledges for donations retracted. In fact, donations were accelerating!

Benton understood that no matter what country one lived in, there would always be those who tried to do wrong. No country with millions of people could, or would, ever be a utopia. That concept is ridiculous. Therefore, a justice system is necessary. As such, he tried to help the people of the new country by setting up a process. Citizens would agree to live within a demerit system which counted down from 500. Once a person runs out of demerits, citizenship is revoked, and they are removed from the country. They would be free to live anywhere else in the world, but not where they decided to throw away the honor of living in the new country.

What if the punishment for minor crimes committed were turned around? Historically, incarceration or some monetary fine is the course of punishment. What if the repercussions were placed on the criminal in a different way? If a person burglarized a home? A burglary is a felony which removes a large number of demerits. All felonies would. Therefore, with a conviction comes with the loss of demerits and incarceration, but what if their own home was taken away? In the current America, jail isn't a deterrent. How many inmates have been incarcerated twice? Or five times, or twenty times? When is enough... enough? Nor are the fines imposing a deterrent. Fines? Most convicted claim they cannot afford the fines and therefore, only a small percentage of the monies are collected! What of the counseling, if any, was sentenced? Has this produced a lesser amount of crime from repeat offenders? What if the afore mentioned burglar has a spouse or children living at home? They would also be displaced, wouldn't they? Yes. What if the would-be burglar would think about that first? And, what if they lost all their remaining demerits due to the crime committed? Then they lose their citizenship and are removed from the country, all with prior knowledge of this being the expected punishment.

What if there weren't any way for lawyers to negotiate a crime to a lesser offence and the law stood as a law and not a suggestion or negotiation? When the definition of a crime is clearly written along with the punishment, and loss of demerits, then the person contemplating the crime will already know what to expect. There would be no need for negotiation by a lawyer at the time of sentencing.

One may claim that the new country is just getting rid of their unwanted citizens. That would be correct! That would be the choice of the person who committed the crime with the knowledge of the penalty. England did this very thing many years ago with the colonization of Australia. This concept isn't new. By not living within the guidelines, those who are expelled from the 'New America' could go back to socialist America where things are more to their liking.

What if you knew of these types of laws *before* you chose to be a citizen here? What if you studied for four years on what the expectations of being a good citizen are in the new country and being allowed to live there? Then there's no way of living your life for which the consequences would be unknown or unfair. For the children in school, the new Bill of Rights and Responsibilities, the new Constitution and governing documents would be taught in all four years of high school. The students would grow up knowing the penalties for crimes and what to expect.

Just like these United States today, people make the choice to break the law already knowing what the consequences could be. However, career criminals obviously do not care about the consequences. If they did, we wouldn't have revolving doors on the local jails or continue to build prisons for those serving life sentences and essentially wasting the taxpayer's dollars. What if being responsible and morally engaged were encouraged?

The new country would also maintain a single place of incarceration for crimes that have not yet resulted in the loss of citizenship. The facility could be a secured patch of land. Those who are incarcerated could be fed by military style premanufactured and packaged M.R.E. (meal ready to eat). What if the shelters in the prison camp were nothing more than canvas tents and cots? They wouldn't have any other amenities than a soldier out in the field. Prison is supposed to be a hardship.

"And what about the military," Sarah asked. "How does the Colonel wish for us to account for the costs of a military?"

Dr. Rayne replied, "I dug into that question too Sarah. Charles and I both had questions on this. His concept is, like several ideas, a consolidation of what other countries have successfully done. We wouldn't need a big military. With that in mind, we eliminate a large portion of costs the government wouldn't have to pay out. However, the security of the country should certainly be addressed. So, let's cover a few points, shall we?"

"For the newest generations of citizens, they would already know what this is like as all kids, male and female, graduating from high school would be required to attend twenty-four months of military duty. Compulsory military service has been in existence in over a dozen countries for decades. This concept isn't new. Obviously, this is a long-term goal but if one would look at the crime rate of other countries who have programs like this in place, such as Sweden, one would know the crime rate is so much lower. In fact, the internet provides statistics showing that Sweden's highest reported crime is harassment and threats while robbery is the lowest. Could it be that the perpetrator already knows the victims have weapons and knows how to use them? It is also known to other countries that this place has a built-in army. A country where all citizens are trained and maintain their own weapons. Israel is another example. So, at the end of their enlistment, they would keep their government issued weapon knowing they could be recalled to duty should the country be in need of such services. Additionally, it would be at the end of their twenty-four-month military time, when they will be offered an agreement that would establish their citizenship and then they are entered into the country's demerit system."

Charles interrupted, "So the young people of the country will learn the country's laws, serve the country and get proper training and enter society before any demerits would be taken away. Doesn't this allow for inexperience and the follies of youth to get in the way of the demerit system?"

"Great question. In some ways, the answer is yes. We must be mindful that countries aren't born overnight. No children have been born in our undefined country as yet. And when they are, they aren't citizens until they learn the laws and decide they want to live in the country. So, we must make allowances along the way. We have to start somewhere.

Paul Tesla slightly raised his hand to catch the eye of Dr. Rayne. "Go ahead, Paul. Ask away," Rayne said.

"You mentioned the ever popular 'T' word," Paul said. "Taxes. Ad-lib on that subject, would you?"

Rayne smiled as he answered, "Taxes? Of course. A five percent tax across the board for every person or business. Keeping a standardized tax rate allowed for businesses to keep people employed and families to thrive. On certain items, such as alcohol or expensive cars, a VAT (Value Added Tax) would be imposed. 'Luxury' items cost more; they always have."

"Five percent! You said five percent," Sarah said adjusting herself to sit on the edge of her seat.

"Sure. The Colonel has requested a simple, across the board rate for all citizens and businesses. The citizens won't be relying on government benefits, payouts, programs and handouts. Low military costs, as we just discussed. And, so much of the infrastructure of the country will be paid up front in the construction of the country. Thousands of less government employees being paid. Hundreds less elected officials collecting a salary. Smaller government. There's a ton of overhead that has

415

already been removed from the government from the very beginning. No tax refunds. Just pay the 5% and budget the rest of your income. The government's responsibility lies with keeping the country, in and of itself, in good working order. Politically and economically. Highways, bridges, waterways, the borders and much more. When I pull back a bit farther, it will be like a very large, gated community. I had not really thought of it like that before but the analogy might fit. However, a sovereign country it will be, and it will operate as such."

"Besides," he went on. "If I'm sitting on the outside and looking into this new concept, I have to say that if the government ever had to raise the tax rate, I would say that it would do so equally for everyone, and by starting at 5%, it is still lower than lowest current rate in the U.S. today."

Charles added, "Plus, the new country is the concept of living up to a higher standard of accountability in citizenship. Those with the means to pay for luxury items would pay the VAT. I know I'm not in the category of having luxury items so keeping a low tax that I can afford is very appealing and I'm getting more excited to live in the 'new America' the more we talk about it."

Rayne continued with more concepts about laws, ideas and the concepts the Colonel and Dr. Benton talked over. Keeping the government in check of itself and working for the people it governs. They discussed how the four branches of the government will maintain checks and balances between themselves so that the citizens are still accountable for themselves and the well-being of the country while still allowing the government to oversee the running of the country. The executive, legislative and judicial may operate in similar fashion of the U.S. while the fourth branch, by whatever name it may be called, would maintain and overall view of the country. A committee of sorts to act like a financial planner to advise the highest office of how the country is performing world-wide and nationwide. A group to step back and look at the country in forms of stability, growth and other categories.

"What about the topic of immigration?" Dr. Rayne asked the group.

Paul responded, "What if the new country, surrounded by its own border, maintains authorized points of entry to the country. Illegal entry to the country will be actionable by deportation out of the new country to an authorized location. The process wouldn't take much time as the Colonel's tele-pad would be available." The group continued to discuss the matter without much rejection to Paul's idea.

"What's an 'authorized location'," asked Sarah.

"I've no idea at the moment but the person wouldn't be around. At this point, as these are only ideas, I'm just thinking this would be a deterrent. If they want to be in the new country, just do it right. If they are escaping something else, then they have certainly ended up somewhere else. I'm not sure this is the best answer, but it did pop in my head." Paul said.

Charles added, "It's a start, what else shall we cover? How about the employees of the government?"

The conversation continued about citizens employed by the small sized government, which includes the elected and appointed people. The elected positions, which may be determined by a lottery draw from a qualified pool, are all on 6-year term limits. The governing body could work more like a board of directors than a traditional parliament. The qualifications for the positions will be tough but fair. The elected are governed by the same laws as the citizens, because in the end, that's all they are. They do not have any life-long career salaries because they can't serve any more than two terms. The elected will choose a health care plan just as their neighbor will. The elected are charged with not perpetuating the growth of the system. Their main goal is to protect the country's integrity, financial stability and economic growth... not to perpetuate the growth of the government.

Dr. Rayne commented, "Listen, the United States has had two and a half centuries of changes. We've endured wars on our own soil and wars in defense of other countries. The United States truly was a superpower! It had millions of people within her borders and maintained international responsibilities costing trillions of dollars, as well as her own national accountability. And with all the changes over time, especially the struggles within herself, which include the most recent change of leaving the citizens at the mercy of a Socialist government, the greatness of what once was 'a nation under God', is no more. I think Benjamin Franklin's intimation was correct. *"If you can keep it,"* he said. And, evidentially, we cannot."

"And to be honest, for me, enough is enough. The United States hasn't been the greatest country in the world for some time. Not in education and literacy, not in science, not in technology or medicine. The United States fails most litmus tests when sitting side by side with other countries, but we do have a few exceptions. We rank high in abortion, drug use, crime and we lead the world in national debt. Doesn't that make you proud? And…" Rayne stopped himself. He wrapped his arms around himself and took a deep breath and sighed.

"I apologize…sometimes I fear Dr. Benson forgot that I can rant when I get passionate on a subject. Seriously, you guys should shut me down when I get like that. Besides, there's nothing in that speech you don't already know."

The others in the group knew all about his rants. No one said a word until Dr. Rayne remarked, "Okay then…where were we?" The group continued working on more aspects of the new Constitution and other documents well into the next morning.

Chapter 38

Fifteen years passed since Benton's time travel project came to a halt in 2025, and the political climate of America showed no improvement. In fact, the deterioration and socialization of the United States was in full swing. Much of the hard work in building America up, creating jobs, employing people to produce a product, raising the economy and securing America's borders by past Presidents of the United States, were severely weakened by the far left in 2028 when they gained the Oval office, Senate and House of Representatives.

Colonel Alan Powers, Dr. Benton and his team were standing near the Reflection Pool of the National Mall. The calm water beautifully framed the picturesque towering view of the Washington Monument. The group was slowly following Dr. Benton as he headed toward the steps of Lincoln Memorial. The normal public crowd had not yet arrived, and the morning air was still and quiet.

Benton began, "I brought you here today for a time of reflection. All of you are historians and experts in your own fields. And, you have given your all in the efforts of what the Colonel, and I feel are categorized as 'righting the wrongs' that this country has faced. I believe President Lincoln did the same. He faced tumultuous political rivalries and the odds were not in his favor. His perseverance is most admirable. He was afforded a huge responsibility, which he fully accepted, when he gave his oath of office. I say these things to you because I think he realized that our country started to falter from the beginning when our country's framers accepted slavery. They wrote, "All men are created equal" and still continued to beat the black man down. The country continued to stomp on those very words by treating the Native Americans as if they were intruders on 'our land'. How arrogant we were. It was their land first. The divisions of our country started before we were even a country. I believe he saw this and made it his mission to change America as best he could, and he succeeded in doing so. Change isn't always easy and, be it positive or negative, it takes time. The processes of change, as all of you are acutely aware, will come with failure before it succeeds. Sometimes, many failures. Presidents of all eras in history have experienced both. Countries have experienced both. It is also apparent that failure and success may run a course like a roller coaster. One rise in success may be followed by the fall of failure. Some may feel the ride down is exhilarating and not wish to endure the slower process of climbing to the top.

"I want to thank you for continuing to work on this project. We have certainly failed to save America along the way however, combined with the Colonel's insights, means and fervor in the same concepts we started with, there is a 'New Country' and as of 2038, she is thriving. She has a strong economy, small government which, I might add, was quickly recognized by the leaders of the world. She has over three million citizens, the lowest crime rate of any country in the world and a waiting list of people who want to live there."

Colonel Powers quickly added, "It is very evident on the world stage that her citizens are very proud to be a part of something that is new and very successful. She is much like a morning such as this. A breath of fresh air."

"I agree," said Benton.

The air was light, and the quietness of the moment was kindly interrupted when Sarah Fleming said, "Dr. Benton, I believe all of us here," she waived her arms politely with her palms up. "All of us, owe both you and the Colonel huge 'Thanks' for allowing us to be a part of this. Our love of country and history have been put to the test. In this we truly grateful! And to add time travel...well, that is a testimony of your zeal, intelligence and fortitude to go the distance to complete a project. It's still the highlight of my life and I could never thank you enough. But what's so much more than that is that the 'New America' is underway. Truly an amazing feat, sir."

Paul Tesla fell into the conversation on que. "To start with an idea and literally have so much support, in such a short time, to start an entire country is absolutely crazy, Doc."

Benson interrupted, "Now that part was all Colonel Powers' concept. Remember, the time travel adventure failed. The Constitution remains the same."

Tesla continued, "That may be so, William, but you allowed us to be a part of it. Sarah is right, we could never thank you and the Colonel, for keeping us around." Tesla using Benton's first name in the conversation was not lost on him. Benton knew they had a real friendship and the compliment had a deeper meaning.

Charles Carson happen to be standing at just the right angle to be a part of the circle of travelers. He stood listening to the nice commentary and compliments. When he cleared his throat, somehow everyone knew he was about to speak. "I'm not sure I'll get through this without my voice cracking so, please, bear with me." He continued to look into the heart of the Lincoln Memorial when he said, "He has always been my hero, sir. He raised a voice for those whose voice no slave owner would hear. He stood in front of men who scoffed at him and, with a certain respect, he defied them for what they stood for. People looked up to him. Not for his height or his towering top hat but because he softly held their respect and boldly demanded their honesty. He spoke the truth. I often wonder if he could use twitter how fast he would have changed the country. In any case, Dr. Benton, please hear me when I say he sits as a monument in the history of the United States as one of the greatest men who has ever held the office of President of the United States. For my entire life, he has been my hero... until I knew you. Until I knew you, sir, because in my eyes, you are more than he could ever be. He sits up there, sir but, I feel if you two were to have a conversation, he would ask you for advice. And you, in your humble way, would give it to the fullest. I am forever grateful for you, Dr. Benton. You are a hero among the heroes of our country, and you are certainly my hero."

"Thank you, Charles. Thank you ever so much. It warms my heart to hear such wonderful things, but you all know that this was a team effort."

"Come now, Dr. Benton, a team will always have a leader," the Colonel said abruptly. "Today is a new day. A new country has been born. Let us be humble in the knowledge that this team has put forth every possible effort. Without a doubt we have found failures along the way however, we have also found successes. Each step, Dr. Benton, each step the team has taken was with a steady hand of the man who led the team. That leader is you. And we thank you very much, sir. So very much."

Looking back into the eyes of the Lincoln Memorial, Colonel Powers asked the question, "Who would ever think this idea would succeed?" He stood there for a brief second and then turned and looked at the rest of the group.

"And yet, it has. One can now ask the citizens of America, who wants to live in the new country?"

Five pair of eyes looked back at him and without skipping a beat, they all looked at Dr. Benton.

One man can make a difference.

The End

~~~~~~~~~~~~~

And A New Beginning

PART 4

Final Thoughts

Now that you have read this fictional work, I wonder if you have MISSED the idea.

It's not about time travel as mentioned in the Foreword of the book. Time travel was just a necessary tool to complete the storyline. But let's cover time travel. The book is not concerned about any time travel paradox's that real scientists or fiction writers may find in this work. As noted by Alex J Coyne in his articles on refliction.com, the Grandfather and Hitler Paradox both place someone in the past to kill a certain person. We aren't here to kill anyone in this storyline. The Predestination Paradox is also not the case here as the travelers are not trying to change their past selves. The Bootstrap Paradox is sending something, including the traveler, back into the past, often

425

to negate the need for its creation. While we do send some trinkets back in the past which are never to be found by anyone, therefore, do not change the course of destiny for those items or their inventors.

Obviously, we have the desire to affect the written words of the Constitution for the following objectives:

a. *To propose changes to the Constitution to better align it with the philosophy of the Founding Father. (e.g. repealing the 14th Amendment and adding an amendment defining citizenship more strictly)*

b. *To guide interpretations of the Constitution and its responsibilities (as it is) to be more consistent with the intent of the Founding Fathers (e.g., originalism/literalism versus 'living document').*

c. *To educate readers about the governing philosophy that underlies the nature of the* **republic** *formed by the Constitution (e.g. decentralized sovereignty, limited central government)*

d. *To defend the Constitution against changes proposed by current-day authoritarians who disagree with the Founders about limited government (e.g. the movements to eliminate the Electoral College and pack the Supreme Court).*

e. *To give readers a look at their own divisiveness or self-destructive decisions which cause a dependency on the government which, in turn, irresponsibly spends the taxpayer's monies.*

The book hopes that people will look at the 'writing on the wall'. People make mistakes. People have always made and will continue to make mistakes, especially when their view is myopic. But, no matter your station, if you do nothing, you have made a choice of accepting the outcome. Someone else will, by default, have made a choice for you. It has been said that CHANGE is doing something WITH someone, not just for someone.

Our founding forefathers made some great choices when they formed our country. Were they perfect? Of course, not. But have you made all perfect choices in your life? I certainly haven't.

We have wonderful medical advancements that have saved lives countless times. We have technologies that are way beyond the dreams of those who lived 250 years ago. Those who made those choices to be inventors or innovators, scientists, doctors, teachers or factory workers are doing wonderful things.

Dr. Benton is a man who thanks God for the failures and progress in his work. He is a praying man. That does not make him any better of a man than a non-praying person, but I think it adds to his character. His desire was to work with the men who started this country in hopes of starting change from the beginning.

We, as a country, a group or an individual, CAN effect change. The history shown earlier in this book is prima-facia of this and we will continue to do so. Dr. Benton's decisions led him to make a machine that would allow time travel! Maybe it really is possible in the future? He decided to try to 'reboot' America. He wasn't the only one to believe a restart was required. Even the floods of the Bible record a restart of what the world is today.

What if our "democracy" is on a path that has already been proven in history?

John Eberhard is attributed to have written about The Tytler Cycle on several websites. Once such site is www.commonsensegovernment.com, where the article suggests the United States in already in stage seven. The article also states, *"We have continually voted ourselves increased benefits, dependent upon the printing presses of the Federal Reserve to sustain our country's ponzi scheme. We have pawned our future and the bill will eventually come due."*

Below is the concept of the Tytler Cycle:

1   From Bondage to Spiritual Faith
2   From Spiritual Faith to Great Courage
3   From Courage to Liberty
4   From Liberty to Abundance
5   From Abundance to Selfishness
6   From Selfishness to Complacency
7   From Complacency to Apathy
8   From Apathy to Dependency
9   From Dependency back into Bondage

Dr. Benton would tend to lean in the direction that America has progressed to the end of Complacency to Apathy stage, living heavily in Apathy to Dependency stage, and creeping into Dependency back into Bondage state. Perhaps we are somewhere between? Where would you place America? What are you willing to do about that?

Alexander Fraser Tytler Woodhouselee (1747-1813) has also been credited with the quote "*A democracy is always temporary in nature; it simply cannot exist as a permanent form of government. A democracy will continue to exist up until the time that voters discover that they can vote themselves generous gifts from the public treasury. From that moment on, the majority always votes for the candidates who promise the most benefits from the public treasury, with the result that every democracy will finally collapse due to loose fiscal policy, which is always followed by a dictatorship.*"

~~~~~~~~~

The many faces of so many countries around the globe have created a rich and colorful world to live in. Each are individual and full of cultures to be visited and appreciated. Each have their own way of surviving with their neighbors. Trading goods and services or ideas and intellectual property. All are successful in their own way. However, each of them will also bear the undesirable. The underbelly that exits permeates nearly every facet of life. No government can legislate the human heart. Every country and culture have devised a way of punishment in their efforts to rid themselves of the unwanted.

429

Ultimately, a criminal will first decide how not to get caught and secondly, if caught, will the punishment be worth their effort. Benton's team has been tasked with devising new, tougher laws that maintain less tolerance than the current system while expecting better quality of the citizens who choose to live in the new country. Their task is very difficult. How will the new country maintain itself as a republic or should it even be a republic? Would it fit into another category?

The separations between Socialists and Federalist are far too palpable and polar, and one must wonder if the elected Senators and Representatives have stopped reaching across the aisle to shake hands in agreement. Have they given up? Is Congress, in the original thought of it by our forefathers, performing as it was designed?

"United we stand, divided we fall." Historic words whose origins are many. Wikipedia shows the origin may come from the Greek author Aesop. It also reports the term as used in the English translation of the Greek Bible in the New Testament of Mark 3:25 (NIV) which reads as red letters, signifying the words of Jesus, "If a house is divided against itself, that house cannot stand." Our nation has never been as divided as it is in our current day. Quite possibly, not unlike any other older generation, I'm afraid for my grandchildren and what type of America they will grow up knowing.

Conservatives, constitutionalists and mid-America that is the right side of the aisle, along with other countries, collectively believe our country is being torn apart from the inside by the Socialist movement, which is the far-left side. Supported by a newly elected government, Socialism spreads throughout the country on liberal media. Our forefathers left a suppressive monarchy for many of the same reasons the characters of this book have set forth. They left their homes to create a new country.

"Socialism is the leading man-made cause of death and misery in human existence," as said by David Harsanyi in 2018 on reason.com. Harsanyi is the Senior Editor of *The Federalist*. What if it is too late to stop the cancer of socialism, or collectivism? Why? Because the contagion is already here.

What if by 2031 the value of the U.S. dollar has fallen yet again? Isn't this inevitable at some point? What if it is no longer accepted as a 'world-wide currency'. The National debt has raised well beyond our capability to pay the interest alone. The potential of 39 trillion dollars of debt continues to rise, and any payment made is upwards of 48% interest.   Like the fall of Argentina, America cannot borrow its way out of debt any longer, so the Socialist must continue their course to over tax and bankrupt the successful.   The Socialist candidate for President in the 2020 election publicly professes taking money from the wealthy to fund the government.   What he is literally doing is stomping on the Constitution and the American dream.   He is literally discriminating against people who have learned to keep their money in the bank. Those who save and invest wisely will be punished for not buying on impulse or lowering their standards.   Based upon Wikipedia's description of the ACLU (American Civil Liberties Union), which states "*The American Civil Liberties*

Union (**ACLU**) is a nonprofit organization whose stated mission is "to defend and preserve the individual rights and liberties guaranteed to every person in this country by the Constitution and laws of the United States." Did you see that? 'Individual rights and liberties'! I believe I have the right to keep my money in the bank! One has to wonder if the ACLU will stand up to the socialist government in defense of the successful?

What if the wealthy all left the United States? Who will the Socialists go after when the successful no longer live in America?

~~~~~~~~~~

The population of our country is increasing at an alarming rate. Online graphs show the percentage of growth is at its highest in the country's history. What if the Socialists stopped the completion of the southern wall between the United States and Mexico and allowing illegal aliens to pour through the cracks and into our country by the tens of thousands daily. Is one of the first stops of illegal aliens standing in a long line and getting on the welfare list? U.S. border towns were overrun with the habits of the illegal aliens pouring into their community. Is their intention to become American? What if the illegal aliens refused to conform to the 'American' way of life, but only expecting to accept the free health care. That is not change for the American citizen. That is theft.

The influx of population in America.... illegal or not...derives predominately from unhappiness. The same reason our forefathers left their homes abroad and created a new country. Maybe their reasons are due to their own failed countries and governments? Maybe they moved for the hope of better employment? Maybe not. It is very probably the general consensus of their mentality was not that they wanted to get a PHD or start a business and live the American dream but escaping the failure of where they were. Perhaps they had no plan at all? Maybe they left due to government oppression? Maybe they left for the idea of the 'land of plenty'? However, if they did nothing to help themselves in their original country, then they arrived here bringing with them their own cultural laziness. And our own government perpetuates their laziness by providing them with fists of tax-payers money.

"When in Rome, do as the Romans do" is a coined phrase during 1777 from Interesting Letters by Pope Clement XIV according to internet sources. Basically, meaning to follow the standard behavior of the inhabitants one visits. But that's just it, we are not gaining visitors to the U.S. "Citizens" are not visitors to our country. Visitors are visitors. Illegal aliens are not visitors. They have arrived here with the intent to stay against our will, the will of the citizens, and being given what is not theirs. If a person's intent was to become a U.S. Citizen, one can only believe they would knock on the front door and request it, not simply jump the border. Of course, the bureaucracy will get in the way and it may take time, but it would be the honorable way to do about it. And millions of immigrants have done just this over many years.

Socialism. Is this the direction the United States wishes to go? I would say our forefathers never intended our country to lead in that direction. We were not created to be a socialist country! The United States was not intended to be an economically homogenized society. Socialism, at the center of its intentions, destroys the republic we were meant to be.

In his August 2019 newsletter, Dr. James Dobson's first paragraph implied a warning to our nation against socialism and those who wish to "fundamentally change" America. Dr. Dobson is a Christian author and psychologist.

~~~~~~~~~~

Envision Monte Carlo, a district of Monaco...on a larger scale...with every class of worker. No slums, no vagrants, freedoms upheld by the citizens, no heavy taxation...and this country remains a Monarchy. I don't believe the 'New Country' would ever open its doors as a Monarchy but the ruler of Monaco has done such a tremendous job of turning it around. It wasn't always like this. It has certainly had a fair share of problems but, with time and guidance and a single-minded focused vision for the future, the problems were addressed, and the country is all the better for it.

Monaco is culturally diverse and maintains an economy inclusive of the wealthy to those who live paycheck to paycheck and all in between. Proof that it can be done!

Isn't it interesting that diversity and inclusiveness are two of the descriptions that some use to describe the United States as the greatest country of the world? Yet, can it be said that those same two words are also the very reasons why our country is being economically and politically torn apart?

~~~~~~~~~~

'Representation without Taxation'...the government was created to have people who represent the citizens of these United States. Including individuals in the population that DON'T pay taxes. Why are the non-tax paying inhabitants allowed to vote? Even after all the arguments for and against who has a right to vote have taken place, what if the voting requirement were to read:

1. IF you are a citizen and
2. A citizen *"In Good Standing"* THEN you have the right to vote.

Why can't citizenship be taken away? In today's America, why shouldn't it be earned? The authorities can take away one's license to drive when one commits enough faults, and in other cases of law, can even revoke a person's passport. What if...

435

...you've lost your citizenship, you can't vote.

...you're not paying taxes, you can't vote.

...you're convicted of a felony, you can't vote, even after release from prison.

~~~~~~~~~~

Does America have more 'money'? Of course not. The government doesn't want to print more money because that leads to inflation. However, the U.S. government is still creating more debt. It does so by not paying off our current debt properly and handing out funds that it just doesn't have in the bank. The benevolence of the United States is admiral but what if it was also detrimental to maintaining the economic integrity of America?

How much money, time and resources have been used to force our country to accept diversity and inclusion? When does the majority say no to negative tolerance? Did parents stop teaching their children good behavior? As a parent or a country, one needs to have a level of tolerance and then hold the line. However, America appears to have pushed that line further and further away from the standards that we were set so many years ago. Things have certainly changed and, in many ways, not for the better. It has been said that parents want to 'build a better life' for their children. At what expense? Do the children of America know the differences between what they _need_ versus what they _want_? What if _they_ knew?

What if our children had long term education of what it means to be an American? What if our country turned back to "a nation under God"? What if the educational system taught our children about the Constitution, Declaration of Independence and other governing documents for more than just a semester here and there? Would the children not 'ask not what your country can do for you but what you can do for your country'? What if parents were more involved in teaching children the difference between needs and wants? What if our children were proud of being a citizen of the United States?

With the changes our country has endured, has it ceased to be the country our forefathers intended?

What if they knew?

The Declaration of Independence

IN CONGRESS, JULY 4, 1776 The unanimous Declaration of the thirteen United States of America

When in the Course of human events, it becomes necessary for one people to dissolve the political bands which have connected them with another, and to assume among the powers of the earth, the separate and equal station to which the Laws of Nature and of Nature's God entitle them, a decent respect to the opinions of mankind requires that they should declare the causes which impel them to the separation.

We hold these truths to be self-evident, that all men are created equal, that they are endowed by their Creator with certain unalienable Rights, that among these are Life, Liberty and the pursuit of Happiness. — That to secure these rights, Governments are instituted among Men, deriving their just powers from the consent of the governed,—That whenever any Form of Government becomes destructive of these ends, it is the Right of the People to alter or to abolish it, and to institute new Government, laying its foundation on such principles and organizing its powers in such form, as to them shall seem most likely to effect their Safety and Happiness. Prudence, indeed, will dictate that Governments long established should not be changed for light and transient causes; and accordingly all experience hath shewn, that mankind are more disposed to suffer, while evils are sufferable, than to right themselves by abolishing the forms to which they are accustomed. But when a long train of abuses and usurpations, pursuing invariably the same Object evinces a design to reduce them under absolute Despotism, it is their right, it is their duty, to throw off such Government, and to provide new Guards for their future security.—Such has been the patient sufferance of these Colonies; and such is now the necessity which constrains them to alter their former Systems of Government. The history of the present King of Great Britain is a history of repeated injuries and usurpations, all having in direct object the establishment of an absolute Tyranny over these States. To prove this, let Facts be submitted to a candid world.

He has refused his Assent to Laws, the most wholesome and necessary for the public good.

He has forbidden his Governors to pass Laws of immediate and pressing importance, unless suspended in their operation till his Assent should be obtained; and when so suspended, he has utterly neglected to attend to them.

He has refused to pass other Laws for the accommodation of large districts of people, unless those people would relinquish the right of Representation in the Legislature, a right inestimable to them and formidable to tyrants only.

He has called together legislative bodies at places unusual, uncomfortable, and distant from the depository of their public Records, for the sole purpose of fatiguing them into compliance with his measures.

He has dissolved Representative Houses repeatedly, for opposing with manly firmness his invasions on the rights of the people.

He has refused for a long time, after such dissolutions, to cause others to be elected; whereby the Legislative powers, incapable of Annihilation, have returned to the People at large for their exercise; the State remaining in the mean time exposed to all the dangers of invasion from without, and convulsions within.

He has endeavoured to prevent the population of these States; for that purpose obstructing the Laws for Naturalization of Foreigners; refusing to pass others to encourage their migrations hither, and raising the conditions of new Appropriations of Lands.

He has obstructed the Administration of Justice, by refusing his Assent to Laws for establishing Judiciary Powers.

He has made Judges dependent on his Will alone, for the tenure of their offices, and the amount and payment of their salaries.

He has erected a multitude of New Offices, and sent hither swarms of Officers to harrass our people, and eat out their substance.

He has kept among us, in times of peace, Standing Armies without the Consent of our legislatures.

He has affected to render the Military independent of and superior to the Civil power.

He has combined with others to subject us to a jurisdiction foreign to our constitution, and unacknowledged by our laws; giving his Assent to their Acts of pretended Legislation:

For Quartering large bodies of armed troops among us:

For protecting them, by a mock Trial, from punishment for any Murders which they should commit on the Inhabitants of these States:

For cutting off our Trade with all parts of the world:

For imposing Taxes on us without our Consent:

For depriving us in many cases, of the benefit of Trial by Jury:

For transporting us beyond Seas to be tried for pretended offences:

For abolishing the free System of English Laws in a neighbouring Province, establishing therein an Arbitrary government, and enlarging its Boundaries so as to render it at once an example and fit instrument for introducing the same absolute rule into these Colonies:

For taking away our Charters, abolishing our most valuable Laws, and altering fundamentally the Forms of our Governments:

For suspending our own Legislatures and declaring themselves invested with power to legislate for us in all cases whatsoever.

He has abdicated Government here, by declaring us out of his Protection and waging War against us.

He has plundered our seas, ravaged our Coasts, burnt our towns, and destroyed the lives of our people.

He is at this time transporting large Armies of foreign Mercenaries to compleat the works of death, desolation, and tyranny, already begun with circumstances of Cruelty & Perfidy scarcely paralleled in the most barbarous ages, and totally unworthy the Head of a civilized nation.

He has constrained our fellow Citizens taken Captive on the high Seas to bear Arms against their Country, to become the executioners of their friends and Brethren, or to fall themselves by their Hands.

He has excited domestic insurrections amongst us and has endeavoured to bring on the inhabitants of our frontiers, the merciless Indian Savages, whose known rule of warfare, is an undistinguished destruction of all ages, sexes and conditions.

In every stage of these Oppressions We have Petitioned for Redress in the most humble terms: Our repeated Petitions have been answered only by repeated injury. A Prince, whose character is thus marked by every act which may define a Tyrant, is unfit to be the ruler of a free people.

Nor have We been wanting in attentions to our British brethren. We have warned them from time to time of attempts by their legislature to extend an unwarrantable jurisdiction over us. We have reminded them of the circumstances of our emigration and settlement here. We have appealed to their native justice and magnanimity, and we have conjured them by the ties of our common kindred to disavow these usurpations, which would inevitably interrupt our connections and correspondence. They too have been deaf to the voice of justice and of consanguinity. We must, therefore, acquiesce in the necessity, which denounces our Separation, and hold them, as we hold the rest of mankind, Enemies in War, in Peace Friends.

We, therefore, the Representatives of the united States of America, in General Congress, Assembled, appealing to the Supreme Judge of the world for the rectitude of our intentions, do, in the Name, and by Authority of the good People of these Colonies, solemnly publish and declare, That these united Colonies are, and of Right ought to be Free and Independent States, that they are Absolved from all Allegiance to the British Crown, and that all political connection between them and the State of Great Britain, is and ought to be totally dissolved; and that as Free and Independent States, they have full Power to levy War, conclude Peace, contract Alliances, establish Commerce, and to do all other Acts and Things which Independent States may of right do.—And for the support of this Declaration, with a firm reliance on the protection of Divine Providence, we mutually pledge to each other our Lives, our Fortunes, and our sacred Honor.

New Hampshire Josiah Bartlett William Whipple Matthew Thornton

Massachusetts John Hancock Samuel Adams John Adams Robert Treat Paine Elbridge Gerry

Rhode Island Stephen Hopkins William Ellery

Connecticut Roger Sherman Samuel Huntington William Williams Oliver Wolcott

New York William Floyd Philip Livingston Francis Lewis Lewis Morris

New Jersey Richard Stockton John Witherspoon Francis Hopkinson John Hart Abraham Clark

Pennsylvania Robert Morris Benjamin Rush Benjamin Franklin John Morton George Clymer James Smith George Taylor James Wilson George Ross

Delaware Caesar Rodney George Read Thomas McKean

Maryland Samuel Chase William Paca Thomas Stone Charles Carroll of Carrollton

Virginia George Wythe Richard Henry Lee Thomas Jefferson Benjamin Harrison Thomas Nelson, Jr. Francis Lightfoot Lee Carter Braxton

North Carolina William Hooper Joseph Hewes John Penn

South Carolina Edward Rutledge Thomas Heyward, Jr. Thomas Lynch, Jr. Arthur Middleton

Georgia Button Gwinnett Lyman Hall George Walton

Articles of Confederation

Transcript of Articles of Confederation (1777)

To all to whom these Presents shall come, we, the undersigned Delegates of the States affixed to our Names send greeting. Whereas the Delegates of the United States of America in Congress assembled did on the fifteenth day of November in the year of our Lord One Thousand Seven Hundred and Seventy seven, and in the Second Year of the Independence of America agree to certain articles of Confederation and perpetual Union between the States of Newhampshire, Massachusetts-bay, Rhodeisland and Providence Plantations, Connecticut, New York, New Jersey, Pennsylvania, Delaware, Maryland, Virginia, North Carolina, South Carolina, and Georgia in the Words following, viz. "Articles of Confederation and perpetual Union between the States of Newhampshire, Massachusetts-bay, Rhodeisland and Providence Plantations, Connecticut, New York, New Jersey, Pennsylvania, Delaware, Maryland, Virginia, North Carolina, South Carolina, and Georgia.

Article I.
The Stile of this confederacy shall be, "The United States of America."

446

Article II.

Each state retains its sovereignty, freedom and independence, and every Power, Jurisdiction and right, which is not by this confederation expressly delegated to the United States, in Congress assembled.

Article III.

The said states hereby severally enter into a firm league of friendship with each other, for their common defence, the security of their Liberties, and their mutual and general welfare, binding themselves to assist each other, against all force offered to, or attacks made upon them, or any of them, on account of religion, sovereignty, trade, or any other pretence whatever.

Article IV.

The better to secure and perpetuate mutual friendship and intercourse among the people of the different states in this union, the free inhabitants of each of these states, paupers, vagabonds and fugitives from Justice excepted, shall be entitled to all privileges and immunities of free citizens in the several states; and the people of each state shall have free ingress and regress to and from any other state, and shall enjoy therein all the privileges of trade and commerce, subject to the same duties, impositions and restrictions as the inhabitants thereof respectively, provided that such restrictions shall not extend so far as to prevent the removal of property imported into any state, to any other State of which the Owner is an inhabitant; provided also that no imposition, duties or restriction shall be laid by any state, on the property of the united states, or either of them.

If any Person guilty of, or charged with, treason, felony, or other high misdemeanor in any state, shall flee from Justice, and be found in any of the united states, he shall upon demand of the Governor or executive power of the state from which he fled, be delivered up, and removed to the state having jurisdiction of his offence.

Full faith and credit shall be given in each of these states to the records, acts and judicial proceedings of the courts and magistrates of every other state.

Article V.

For the more convenient management of the general interests of the united states, delegates shall be annually appointed in such manner as the legislature of each state shall direct, to meet in Congress on the first Monday in November, in every year, with a power reserved to each state to recall its delegates, or any of them, at any time within the year, and to send others in their stead, for the remainder of the Year.

No State shall be represented in Congress by less than two, nor by more than seven Members; and no person shall be capable of being delegate for more than three years, in any term of six years; nor shall any person, being a delegate, be capable of holding any office under the united states, for which he, or another for his benefit receives any salary, fees or emolument of any kind.

Each State shall maintain its own delegates in a meeting of the states, and while they act as members of the committee of the states.

In determining questions in the united states, in Congress assembled, each state shall have one vote.

Freedom of speech and debate in Congress shall not be impeached or questioned in any Court, or place out of Congress, and the members of congress shall be protected in their persons from arrests and imprisonments, during the time of their going to and from, and attendance on congress, except for treason, felony, or breach of the peace.

Article VI.

No State, without the Consent of the united States, in congress assembled, shall send any embassy to, or receive any embassy from, or enter into any conferrence, agreement, alliance, or treaty, with any King prince or state; nor shall any person holding any office of profit or trust under the united states, or any of them, accept of any present, emolument, office, or title of any kind whatever, from any king, prince, or foreign state; nor shall the united states, in congress assembled, or any of them, grant any title of nobility.

No two or more states shall enter into any treaty, confederation, or alliance whatever between them, without the consent of the united states, in congress assembled, specifying accurately the purposes for which the same is to be entered into, and how long it shall continue.

No State shall lay any imposts or duties, which may interfere with any stipulations in treaties, entered into by the united States in congress assembled, with any king, prince, or State, in pursuance of any treaties already proposed by congress, to the courts of France and Spain. No vessels of war shall be kept up in time of peace, by any state, except such number only, as shall be deemed necessary by the united states, in congress assembled, for the defence of such state, or its trade; nor shall any body of forces be kept up, by any state, in time of peace, except such number only as, in the judgment of the united states, in congress assembled, shall be deemed requisite to garrison the forts necessary for the defence of such state; but every state shall always keep up a well regulated and disciplined militia, sufficiently armed and accounted, and shall provide and constantly have ready for use, in public stores, a due number of field pieces and tents, and a proper quantity of arms, ammunition, and camp equipage. No State shall engage in any war without the consent of the united States in congress assembled, unless such State be actually invaded by enemies, or shall have received certain advice of a resolution being formed by some nation of Indians to invade such State, and the danger is so imminent as not to admit of a delay till the united states in congress assembled, can be consulted: nor shall any state grant commissions to any ships or vessels of war, nor letters of marque or reprisal, except it be after a declaration of war by the united states in congress assembled, and then only against the kingdom or State, and the subjects thereof, against which war has been so declared, and under such regulations as shall be established by the united states in congress assembled, unless such state be infested by pirates, in which case vessels of war may be fitted out for that occasion, and kept so long as the danger shall continue, or until the united states in congress assembled shall determine otherwise.

Article VII.

When land forces are raised by any state, for the common defence, all officers of or under the rank of colonel, shall be appointed by the legislature of each state respectively by whom such forces shall be raised, or in such manner as such state shall direct, and all vacancies shall be filled up by the state which first made appointment.

Article VIII. All charges of war, and all other expenses that shall be incurred for the common defence or general welfare, and allowed by the united states in congress assembled, shall be defrayed out of a common treasury, which shall be supplied by the several states, in proportion to the value of all land within each state, granted to or surveyed for any Person, as such land and the buildings and improvements thereon shall be estimated, according to such mode as the united states, in congress assembled, shall, from time to time, direct and appoint. The taxes for paying that proportion shall be laid and levied by the authority and direction of the legislatures of the several states within the time agreed upon by the united states in congress assembled.

Article IX.

The united states, in congress assembled, shall have the sole and exclusive right and power of determining on peace and war, except in the cases mentioned in the sixth article - of sending and receiving ambassadors - entering into treaties and alliances, provided that no treaty of commerce shall be made, whereby the legislative power of the respective states shall be restrained from imposing such imposts and duties on foreigners, as their own people are subjected to, or from prohibiting the exportation or importation of any species of goods or commodities whatsoever - of establishing rules for deciding, in all cases, what captures on land or water shall be legal, and in what manner prizes taken by land or naval forces in the service of the united Sates, shall be divided or appropriated - of granting letters of marque and reprisal in times of peace - appointing courts for the trial of piracies and felonies committed on the high seas; and establishing courts; for receiving and determining finally appeals in all cases of captures; provided that no member of congress shall be appointed a judge of any of the said courts.

The united states, in congress assembled, shall also be the last resort on appeal, in all disputes and differences now subsisting, or that hereafter may arise between two or more states concerning boundary, jurisdiction, or any other cause whatever; which authority shall always be exercised in the manner following. Whenever the legislative or executive authority, or lawful agent of any state in controversy with another, shall present a petition to congress, stating the matter in question, and praying for a hearing, notice thereof shall be given, by order of congress, to the legislative or executive authority of the other state in controversy, and a day assigned for the appearance of the parties by their lawful agents, who shall then be directed to appoint, by joint consent, commissioners or judges to constitute a court for hearing and determining the matter in question: but if they cannot agree, congress shall name three persons out of each of the united states, and from the list of such persons each party shall alternately strike out one, the petitioners beginning, until the number shall be reduced to thirteen; and from that number not less than seven, nor more than nine names, as congress shall direct, shall, in the presence of congress, be drawn out by lot, and the persons whose names shall be so drawn, or any five of them, shall be commissioners or judges, to hear and finally determine the controversy, so always as a major part of the judges, who shall hear the cause, shall agree in the determination: and if either party shall neglect to attend at the day appointed, without showing reasons which congress shall judge sufficient, or being present, shall refuse to strike, the congress shall proceed to nominate three persons out of each State, and the secretary of congress shall strike in behalf of such party absent or refusing; and the judgment and sentence of the court, to be appointed in the manner before prescribed, shall be final and conclusive; and if any of the parties shall refuse to submit to the authority of such court, or to appear or defend their claim or cause, the court shall nevertheless proceed to pronounce sentence, or judgment, which shall in like manner be final and decisive; the judgment or sentence and other proceedings being in either case transmitted to congress, and lodged among the acts of congress, for the security of the parties concerned: provided that every commissioner, before he sits in judgment, shall take an oath to be administered by one of the judges of the supreme or superior court of the

State where the cause shall be tried, "well and truly to hear and determine the matter in question, according to the best of his judgment, without favour, affection, or hope of reward: "provided, also, that no State shall be deprived of territory for the benefit of the united states.

All controversies concerning the private right of soil claimed under different grants of two or more states, whose jurisdictions as they may respect such lands, and the states which passed such grants are adjusted, the said grants or either of them being at the same time claimed to have originated antecedent to such settlement of jurisdiction, shall, on the petition of either party to the congress of the united states, be finally determined, as near as may be, in the same manner as is before prescribed for deciding disputes respecting territorial jurisdiction between different states.

The united states, in congress assembled, shall also have the sole and exclusive right and power of regulating the alloy and value of coin struck by their own authority, or by that of the respective states - fixing the standard of weights and measures throughout the united states - regulating the trade and managing all affairs with the Indians, not members of any of the states; provided that the legislative right of any state, within its own limits, be not infringed or violated - establishing and regulating post-offices from one state to another, throughout all the united states, and exacting such postage on the papers passing through the same, as may be requisite to defray the expenses of the said office - appointing all officers of the land forces in the service of the united States, excepting regimental officers - appointing all the officers of the naval forces, and commissioning all officers whatever in the service of the united states; making rules for the government and regulation of the said land and naval forces, and directing their operations.

The united States, in congress assembled, shall have authority to appoint a committee, to sit in the recess of congress, to be denominated, "A Committee of the States," and to consist of one delegate from each State; and to appoint such other committees and civil officers as may be necessary for managing the general affairs of the united states under their direction - to appoint one of their number to preside; provided that no person be allowed to serve in the office of president more than one year in any term of three years; to ascertain the necessary sums of money to be raised for the service of the united states, and to appropriate and apply the same for defraying the public expenses; to borrow money or emit bills on the credit of the united states, transmitting every half year to the respective states an account of the sums of money so borrowed or emitted, - to build and equip a navy - to agree upon the number of land forces, and to make requisitions from each state for its quota, in proportion to the number of white inhabitants in such state, which requisition shall be binding; and thereupon the legislature of each state shall appoint the regimental officers, raise the men, and clothe, arm, and equip them, in a soldier-like manner, at the expense of the united states; and the officers and men so clothed, armed, and equipped, shall march to the place appointed, and within the time agreed on by the united states, in congress assembled; but if the united states, in congress assembled, shall, on consideration of circumstances, judge proper that any state should not raise men, or should raise a smaller number than its quota, and that any other state should raise a greater number of men than the quota thereof, such extra number shall be raised, officered, clothed, armed, and equipped in the same manner as the quota of such state, unless the legislature of such state shall judge that such extra number cannot be safely spared out of the same, in which case they shall raise, officer, clothe, arm, and equip, as many of such extra number as they judge can be safely spared. And the officers and men so clothed, armed, and equipped, shall march to the place appointed, and within the time agreed on by the united states in congress assembled.

The united states, in congress assembled, shall never engage in a war, nor grant letters of marque and reprisal in time of peace, nor enter into any treaties or alliances, nor coin money, nor regulate the value thereof nor ascertain the sums and expenses necessary for the defence and welfare of the united states, or any of them, nor emit bills, nor borrow money on the credit of the united states, nor appropriate money, nor agree upon the number of vessels of war to be built or purchased, or the number of land or sea forces to be raised, nor appoint a commander in chief of the army or navy, unless nine states assent to the same, nor shall a question on any other point, except for adjourning from day to day, be determined, unless by the votes of a majority of the united states in congress assembled.

The congress of the united states shall have power to adjourn to any time within the year, and to any place within the united states, so that no period of adjournment be for a longer duration than the space of six Months, and shall publish the Journal of their proceedings monthly, except such parts thereof relating to treaties, alliances, or military operations, as in their judgment require secrecy; and the yeas and nays of the delegates of each State, on any question, shall be entered on the Journal, when it is desired by any delegate; and the delegates of a State, or any of them, at his or their request, shall be furnished with a transcript of the said Journal, except such parts as are above excepted, to lay before the legislatures of the several states.

Article X.

The committee of the states, or any nine of them, shall be authorized to execute, in the recess of congress, such of the powers of congress as the united states, in congress assembled, by the consent of nine states, shall, from time to time, think expedient to vest them with; provided that no power be delegated to the said committee, for the exercise of which, by the articles of confederation, the voice of nine states, in the congress of the united states assembled, is requisite.

Article XI.

Canada acceding to this confederation, and joining in the measures of the united states, shall be admitted into, and entitled to all the advantages of this union: but no other colony shall be admitted into the same, unless such admission be agreed to by nine states.

Article XII. All bills of credit emitted, monies borrowed, and debts contracted by or under the authority of congress, before the assembling of the united states, in pursuance of the present confederation, shall be deemed and considered as a charge against the united States, for payment and satisfaction whereof the said united states and the public faith are hereby solemnly pledged.

Article XIII. Every State shall abide by the determinations of the united states, in congress assembled, on all questions which by this confederation are submitted to them. And the Articles of this confederation shall be inviolably observed by every state, and the union shall be perpetual; nor shall any alteration at any time hereafter be made in any of them, unless such alteration be agreed to in a congress of the united states, and be afterwards confirmed by the legislatures of every state.

And Whereas it hath pleased the Great Governor of the World to incline the hearts of the legislatures we respectively represent in congress, to approve of, and to authorize us to ratify the said articles of confederation and perpetual union, Know Ye, that we, the undersigned delegates, by virtue of the power and authority to us given for that purpose, do, by these presents, in the name and in behalf of our respective constituents, fully and entirely ratify and confirm each and every of the said articles of confederation and perpetual union, and all and singular the matters and things therein contained. And we do further solemnly plight and engage the faith of our respective constituents, that they shall abide by the determinations of the united states in congress assembled, on all questions, which by the said confederation are submitted to them. And that the articles thereof shall be inviolably observed by the states we respectively represent, and that the union shall be perpetual. In Witness whereof, we have hereunto set our hands, in Congress. Done at Philadelphia, in the State of Pennsylvania, the ninth Day of July, in the Year of our Lord one Thousand seven Hundred and Seventy eight, and in the third year of the Independence of America.

*With permission from www.ourdocuments.gov

U.S. Constitution

We the People of the United States, in Order to form a more perfect Union, establish Justice, insure domestic Tranquility, provide for the common defence, promote the general Welfare, and secure the Blessings of Liberty to ourselves and our Posterity, do ordain and establish this Constitution for the United States of America.

Article I

Section 1

All legislative Powers herein granted shall be vested in a Congress of the United States, which shall consist of a Senate and House of Representatives.

Section 2

1: The House of Representatives shall be composed of Members chosen every second Year by the People of the several States, and the Electors in each State shall have the Qualifications requisite for Electors of the most numerous Branch of the State Legislature.

2: No Person shall be a Representative who shall not have attained to the Age of twenty five Years, and been seven Years a Citizen of the United States, and who shall not, when elected, be an Inhabitant of that State in which he shall be chosen.

3: Representatives and direct Taxes shall be apportioned among the several States which may be included within this Union, according to their respective Numbers, which shall be determined by adding to the whole Number of free Persons, including those bound to Service for a Term of Years, and excluding Indians not taxed, three fifths of all other Persons. The actual Enumeration shall be made within three Years after the first Meeting of the Congress of the United States, and within every subsequent Term of ten Years, in such Manner as they shall by Law direct. The Number of Representatives shall not exceed one for every thirty Thousand, but each State shall have at Least one Representative; and until such enumeration shall be made, the State of New Hampshire shall be entitled to chuse three, Massachusetts eight, Rhode-Island and Providence Plantations one, Connecticut five, New-York six, New Jersey four, Pennsylvania eight, Delaware one, Maryland six, Virginia ten, North Carolina five, South Carolina five, and Georgia three.

4: When vacancies happen in the Representation from any State, the Executive Authority thereof shall issue Writs of Election to fill such Vacancies.

5: The House of Representatives shall chuse their Speaker and other Officers; and shall have the sole Power of Impeachment.

Section 3
1: The Senate of the United States shall be composed of two Senators from each State, chosen by the Legislature thereof, for six Years; and each Senator shall have one Vote.

2: Immediately after they shall be assembled in Consequence of the first Election, they shall be divided as equally as may be into three Classes. The Seats of the Senators of the first Class shall be vacated at the Expiration of the second Year, of the second Class at the Expiration of the fourth Year, and of the third Class at the Expiration of the sixth Year, so that one third may be chosen every second Year; and if Vacancies happen by Resignation, or otherwise, during the Recess of the Legislature of any State, the Executive thereof may make temporary Appointments until the next Meeting of the Legislature, which shall then fill such Vacancies.

3: No Person shall be a Senator who shall not have attained to the Age of thirty Years, and been nine Years a Citizen of the United States, and who shall not, when elected, be an Inhabitant of that State for which he shall be chosen.

4: The Vice President of the United States shall be President of the Senate, but shall have no Vote, unless they be equally divided.

5: The Senate shall chuse their other Officers, and also a President pro tempore, in the Absence of the Vice President, or when he shall exercise the Office of President of the United States.

6: The Senate shall have the sole Power to try all Impeachments. When sitting for that Purpose, they shall be on Oath or Affirmation. When the President of the United States is tried, the Chief Justice shall preside: And no Person shall be convicted without the Concurrence of two thirds of the Members present.

7: Judgment in Cases of Impeachment shall not extend further than to removal from Office, and disqualification to hold and enjoy any Office of honor, Trust or Profit under the United States: but the Party convicted shall nevertheless be liable and subject to Indictment, Trial, Judgment and Punishment, according to Law.

Section 4
1: The Times, Places and Manner of holding Elections for Senators and Representatives, shall be prescribed in each State by the Legislature thereof; but the Congress may at any time by Law make or alter such Regulations, except as to the Places of chusing Senators.
www.PrintableConstitution.com

2: The Congress shall assemble at least once in every Year, and such Meeting shall be on the first Monday in December, unless they shall by Law appoint a different Day.

Section 5
1: Each House shall be the Judge of the Elections, Returns and Qualifications of its own Members, and a Majority of each shall constitute a Quorum to do Business; but a smaller Number may adjourn from day to day, and may be authorized to compel the Attendance of absent Members,

in such Manner, and under such Penalties as each House may provide.

2: Each House may determine the Rules of its Proceedings, punish its Members for disorderly Behaviour, and, with the Concurrence of two thirds, expel a Member.

3: Each House shall keep a Journal of its Proceedings, and from time to time publish the same, excepting such Parts as may in their Judgment require Secrecy; and the Yeas and Nays of the Members of either House on any question shall, at the Desire of one fifth of those Present, be entered on the Journal.

4: Neither House, during the Session of Congress, shall, without the Consent of the other, adjourn for more than three days, nor to any other Place than that in which the two Houses shall be sitting.

Section 6
1: The Senators and Representatives shall receive a Compensation for their Services, to be ascertained by Law, and paid out of the Treasury of the United States. They shall in all Cases, except Treason, Felony and Breach of the Peace, be privileged from Arrest during their Attendance at the Session of their respective Houses, and in going to and returning from the same; and for any Speech or Debate in either House, they shall not be questioned in any other Place.

2: No Senator or Representative shall, during the Time for which he was elected, be appointed to any civil Office under the Authority of the United States, which shall have been created, or the Emoluments whereof shall have been encreased during such time; and no Person holding any Office under the United States, shall be a Member of either House during his Continuance in Office.

Section 7

1: All Bills for raising Revenue shall originate in the House of Representatives; but the Senate may propose or concur with Amendments as on other Bills.

2: Every Bill which shall have passed the House of Representatives and the Senate, shall, before it become a Law, be presented to the President of the United States: If he approve he shall sign it, but if not he shall return it, with his Objections to that House in which it shall have originated, who shall enter the Objections at large on their Journal, and proceed to reconsider it. If after such Reconsideration two thirds of that House shall agree to pass the Bill, it shall be sent, together with the Objections, to the other House, by which it shall likewise be reconsidered, and if approved by two thirds of that House, it shall become a Law. But in all such Cases the Votes of both Houses shall be determined by Yeas and Nays, and the Names of the Persons voting for and against the Bill shall be entered on the Journal of each House respectively. If any Bill shall not be returned by the President within ten Days (Sundays excepted) after it shall have been presented to him, the Same shall be a Law, in like Manner as if he had signed it, unless the Congress by their Adjournment prevent its Return, in which Case it shall not be a Law.

3: Every Order, Resolution, or Vote to which the Concurrence of the Senate and House of Representatives may be necessary (except on a question of Adjournment) shall be presented to the President of the United States; and before the Same shall take Effect, shall be approved by him, or being disapproved by him, shall be repassed by two thirds of the Senate and House of Representatives, according to the Rules and Limitations prescribed in the Case of a Bill.

Section 8

1: The Congress shall have Power To lay and collect Taxes, Duties, Imposts and Excises, to pay the Debts and provide for the common Defence and general Welfare of the United States; but all Duties, Imposts and Excises shall be uniform throughout the United States;

2: To borrow Money on the credit of the United States;

3: To regulate Commerce with foreign Nations, and among the several States, and with the Indian Tribes;

4: To establish an uniform Rule of Naturalization, and uniform Laws on the subject of Bankruptcies throughout the United States;

5: To coin Money, regulate the Value thereof, and of foreign Coin, and fix the Standard of Weights and Measures;

6: To provide for the Punishment of counterfeiting the Securities and current Coin of the United States;

7: To establish Post Offices and post Roads;

8: To promote the Progress of Science and useful Arts, by securing for limited Times to Authors and Inventors the exclusive Right to their respective Writings and Discoveries;

9: To constitute Tribunals inferior to the supreme Court;

10: To define and punish Piracies and Felonies committed on the high Seas, and Offences against the Law of Nations;

11: To declare War, grant Letters of Marque and Reprisal, and make Rules concerning Captures on Land and Water;

12: To raise and support Armies, but no Appropriation of Money to that Use shall be for a longer Term than two Years;

13: To provide and maintain a Navy;

14: To make Rules for the Government and Regulation of the land and naval Forces;

15: To provide for calling forth the Militia to execute the Laws of the Union, suppress Insurrections and repel Invasions;

16: To provide for organizing, arming, and disciplining, the Militia, and for governing such Part of them as may be employed in the Service of the United States, reserving to the States respectively, the Appointment of the Officers, and the Authority of training the Militia according to the discipline prescribed by Congress;

17: To exercise exclusive Legislation in all Cases whatsoever, over such District (not exceeding ten Miles square) as may, by Cession of particular States, and the Acceptance of Congress, become the Seat of the Government of the United States, and to exercise like Authority over all Places purchased by the Consent of the Legislature of the State in which the Same shall be, for the Erection of Forts, Magazines, Arsenals, dock-Yards, and other needful Buildings;—And

18: To make all Laws which shall be necessary and proper for carrying into Execution the foregoing Powers, and all other Powers vested by this Constitution in the Government of the United States, or in any Department or Officer thereof.

Section 9

1: The Migration or Importation of such Persons as any of the States now existing shall think proper to admit, shall not be prohibited by the Congress prior to the Year one thousand eight hundred and eight, but a Tax or duty may be imposed on such Importation, not exceeding ten dollars for each Person.

2: The Privilege of the Writ of Habeas Corpus shall not be suspended, unless when in Cases of Rebellion or Invasion the public Safety may require it.

3: No Bill of Attainder or ex post facto Law shall be passed.

4: No Capitation, or other direct, Tax shall be laid, unless in Proportion to the Census or Enumeration herein before directed to be taken.

5: No Tax or Duty shall be laid on Articles exported from any State.

6: No Preference shall be given by any Regulation of Commerce or Revenue to the Ports of one State over those of another; nor shall Vessels bound to, or from, one State, be obliged to enter, clear, or pay Duties in another.

7: No Money shall be drawn from the Treasury, but in Consequence of Appropriations made by Law; and a regular Statement and Account of the Receipts and Expenditures of all public Money shall be published from time to time.

8: No Title of Nobility shall be granted by the United States: And no Person holding any Office of Profit or Trust under them, shall, without the Consent of the Congress, accept of any present, Emolument, Office, or Title, of any kind whatever, from any King, Prince, or foreign State.

Section 10

1: No State shall enter into any Treaty, Alliance, or Confederation; grant Letters of Marque and Reprisal; coin Money; emit Bills of Credit; make any Thing but gold and silver Coin a Tender in Payment of Debts; pass any Bill of Attainder, ex post facto Law, or Law impairing the Obligation of Contracts, or grant any Title of Nobility.

2: No State shall, without the Consent of the Congress, lay any Imposts or Duties on Imports or Exports, except what may be absolutely necessary for executing its inspection Laws: and the net Produce of all Duties and Imposts, laid by any State on Imports or Exports, shall be for the Use of the Treasury of the United States; and all such Laws shall be subject to the Revision and Control of the Congress.

3: No State shall, without the Consent of Congress, lay any Duty of Tonnage, keep Troops, or Ships of War in time of Peace, enter into any Agreement or Compact with another State, or with a foreign Power, or engage in War, unless actually invaded, or in such imminent Danger as will not admit of delay.

Article II

Section 1

1: The executive Power shall be vested in a President of the United States of America. He shall hold his Office during the Term of four Years, and, together with the Vice

President, chosen for the same Term, be elected, as follows:

2: Each State shall appoint, in such Manner as the Legislature thereof may direct, a Number of Electors, equal to the whole Number of Senators and Representatives to which the State may be entitled in the Congress: but no Senator or Representative, or Person holding an Office of Trust or Profit under the United States, shall be appointed an Elector.

3: The Electors shall meet in their respective States, and vote by Ballot for two Persons, of whom one at least shall not be an Inhabitant of the same State with themselves. And they shall make a List of all the Persons voted for, and of the Number of Votes for each; which List they shall sign and certify, and transmit sealed to the Seat of the Government of the United States, directed to the President of the Senate. The President of the Senate shall, in the Presence of the Senate and House of Representatives, open all the Certificates, and the Votes shall then be counted. The Person having the greatest Number of Votes shall be the President, if such Number be a Majority of the whole Number of Electors appointed; and if there be more than one who have such Majority, and have an equal Number of Votes, then the House of Representatives shall immediately chuse by Ballot one of them for President; and if no Person have a Majority, then from the five highest on the List the said House shall in like Manner chuse the President. But in chusing the President, the Votes shall be taken by States, the Representation from each State having one Vote; a quorum for this Purpose shall consist of a Member or Members from two thirds of the States, and a Majority of all the States shall be necessary to a Choice. In every Case, after the Choice of the President, the Person having the greatest Number of Votes of the Electors shall be the Vice President. But if there should remain two or more who have equal Votes, the Senate shall chuse from them by Ballot the Vice-President.

4: The Congress may determine the Time of chusing the Electors, and the Day on which they shall give their Votes; which Day shall be the same throughout the United States.

5: No Person except a natural born Citizen, or a Citizen of the United States, at the time of the Adoption of this Constitution, shall be eligible to the Office of President; neither shall any Person be eligible to that Office who shall not have attained to the Age of thirty five Years, and been fourteen Years a Resident within the United States.

6: In Case of the Removal of the President from Office, or of his Death, Resignation, or Inability to discharge the Powers and Duties of the said Office, the Same shall devolve on the Vice President, and the Congress may by Law provide for the Case of Removal, Death, Resignation or Inability, both of the President and Vice President, declaring what Officer shall then act as President, and such Officer shall act accordingly, until the Disability be removed, or a President shall be elected.

7: The President shall, at stated Times, receive for his Services, a Compensation, which shall neither be encreased nor diminished during the Period for which he shall have been elected, and he shall not receive within that Period any other Emolument from the United States, or any of them.

8: Before he enter on the Execution of his Office, he shall take the following Oath or Affirmation:—"I do solemnly swear (or affirm) that I will faithfully execute the Office of President of the United States, and will to the best of my Ability, preserve, protect and defend the Constitution of the United States."

Section 2
1: The President shall be Commander in Chief of the Army and Navy of the United States, and of the Militia of the several States, when called into the actual Service of the United States; he may require the Opinion, in writing, of the principal Officer in each of the executive Departments, upon any Subject relating to the Duties of their respective Offices, and he shall have Power to Grant Reprieves and Pardons for Offences against the United States, except in Cases of Impeachment.

2: He shall have Power, by and with the Advice and Consent of the Senate, to make Treaties, provided two thirds of the Senators present concur; and he shall nominate, and by and with the Advice and Consent of the Senate, shall appoint Ambassadors, other public Ministers and Consuls, Judges of the supreme Court, and all other

Officers of the United States, whose Appointments are not herein otherwise provided for, and which shall be established by Law: but the Congress may by Law vest the Appointment of such inferior Officers, as they think proper, in the President alone, in the Courts of Law, or in the Heads of Departments.

3: The President shall have Power to fill up all Vacancies that may happen during the Recess of the Senate, by granting Commissions which shall expire at the End of their next Session.

Section 3
He shall from time to time give to the Congress Information on the State of the Union, and recommend to their Consideration such Measures as he shall judge necessary and expedient; he may, on extraordinary Occasions, convene both Houses, or either of them, and in Case of Disagreement between them, with Respect to the Time of Adjournment, he may adjourn them to such Time as he shall think proper; he shall receive Ambassadors and other public Ministers; he shall take Care that the Laws be faithfully executed, and shall Commission all the Officers of the United States.

Section 4
The President, Vice President and all Civil Officers of the United States, shall be removed from Office on Impeachment for, and Conviction of, Treason, Bribery, or other high Crimes and Misdemeanors.

Article III

Section 1

The judicial Power of the United States, shall be vested in one supreme Court, and in such inferior Courts as the Congress may from time to time ordain and establish. The Judges, both of the supreme and inferior Courts, shall hold their Offices during good Behaviour, and shall, at stated Times, receive for their Services, a Compensation, which shall not be diminished during their Continuance in Office.

Section 2

1: The judicial Power shall extend to all Cases, in Law and Equity, arising under this Constitution, the Laws of the United States, and Treaties made, or which shall be made, under their Authority;—to all Cases affecting Ambassadors, other public Ministers and Consuls;—to all Cases of admiralty and maritime Jurisdiction;—to Controversies to which the United States shall be a Party;—to Controversies between two or more States;—between a State and Citizens of another State;—between Citizens of different States,— between Citizens of the same State claiming Lands under Grants of different States, and between a State, or the Citizens thereof, and foreign States, Citizens or Subjects.

2: In all Cases affecting Ambassadors, other public Ministers and Consuls, and those in which a State shall be Party, the supreme Court shall have original Jurisdiction. In all the other Cases before mentioned, the supreme Court shall have appellate Jurisdiction, both as to Law and Fact, with such Exceptions, and under such Regulations as the Congress shall make.

3: The Trial of all Crimes, except in Cases of Impeachment, shall be by Jury; and such Trial shall be held in the State where the said Crimes shall have been committed; but when not committed within any State, the Trial shall be at such Place or Places as the Congress may by Law have directed.

Section 3
1: Treason against the United States, shall consist only in levying War against them, or in adhering to their Enemies, giving them Aid and Comfort. No Person shall be convicted of Treason unless on the Testimony of two Witnesses to the same overt Act, or on Confession in open Court.

2: The Congress shall have Power to declare the Punishment of Treason, but no Attainder of Treason shall work Corruption of Blood, or Forfeiture except during the Life of the Person attainted.

Article IV

Section 1
Full Faith and Credit shall be given in each State to the public Acts, Records, and judicial Proceedings of every other State. And the Congress may by general Laws prescribe the Manner in which such Acts, Records and Proceedings shall be proved, and the Effect thereof.

Section 2

1: The Citizens of each State shall be entitled to all Privileges and Immunities of Citizens in the several States.

2: A Person charged in any State with Treason, Felony, or other Crime, who shall flee from Justice, and be found in another State, shall on Demand of the executive Authority of the State from which he fled, be delivered up, to be removed to the State having Jurisdiction of the Crime.

3: No Person held to Service or Labour in one State, under the Laws thereof, escaping into another, shall, in Consequence of any Law or Regulation therein, be discharged from such Service or Labour, but shall be delivered up on Claim of the Party to whom such Service or Labour may be due.
www.PrintableConstitution.com

Section 3

1: New States may be admitted by the Congress into this Union; but no new State shall be formed or erected within the Jurisdiction of any other State; nor any State be formed by the Junction of two or more States, or Parts of States, without the Consent of the Legislatures of the States concerned as well as of the Congress.

2: The Congress shall have Power to dispose of and make all needful Rules and Regulations respecting the Territory or other Property belonging to the United States; and nothing in this Constitution shall be so construed as to

Prejudice any Claims of the United States, or of any particular State.

Section 4
The United States shall guarantee to every State in this Union a Republican Form of Government and shall protect each of them against Invasion; and on Application of the Legislature, or of the Executive (when the Legislature cannot be convened) against domestic Violence.

Article V

The Congress, whenever two thirds of both Houses shall deem it necessary, shall propose Amendments to this Constitution, or, on the Application of the Legislatures of two thirds of the several States, shall call a Convention for proposing Amendments, which, in either Case, shall be valid to all Intents and Purposes, as Part of this Constitution, when ratified by the Legislatures of three fourths of the several States, or by Conventions in three fourths thereof, as the one or the other Mode of Ratification may be proposed by the Congress; Provided that no Amendment which may be made prior to the Year One thousand eight hundred and eight shall in any Manner affect the first and fourth Clauses in the Ninth Section of the first Article; and that no State, without its Consent, shall be deprived of its equal Suffrage in the Senate.

Article VI

1: All Debts contracted, and Engagements entered into, before the Adoption of this Constitution, shall be as valid against the United States under this Constitution, as under the Confederation.

2: This Constitution, and the Laws of the United States which shall be made in Pursuance thereof; and all Treaties made, or which shall be made, under the Authority of the United States, shall be the supreme Law of the Land; and the Judges in every State shall be bound thereby, any Thing in the Constitution or Laws of any State to the Contrary notwithstanding.

3: The Senators and Representatives before mentioned, and the Members of the several State Legislatures, and all executive and judicial Officers, both of the United States and of the several States, shall be bound by Oath or Affirmation, to support this Constitution; but no religious Test shall ever be required as a Qualification to any Office or public Trust under the United States.

Article VII

(Article 7 - Ratification) The Ratification of the Conventions of nine States, shall be sufficient for the Establishment of this Constitution between the States so ratifying the Same. done in Convention by the Unanimous Consent of the States present the Seventeenth Day of September in the Year of our Lord one thousand seven hundred and Eighty seven and of the Independence of the United States of

America the Twelfth In witness whereof We have hereunto
subscribed our Names,

G°. Washington
Presidt and deputy
from Virginia

Delaware

Geo: Read

Gunning Bedford

John Dickinson

Richard Bassett

Jaco: Broom

Maryland

James McHenry

Dan of St Thos. Jenifer

Danl. Carroll

Jona: Dayton

Virginia

John Blair

James Madison Jr.

Connecticut

Wm. Saml. Johnson

Roger Sherman

New York

Alexander Hamilton

New Jersey

Wil: Livingston

David Brearly

Wm. Paterson

Pennsylvania

B. Franklin
Thomas Mifflin

North Carolina

Richd. Dobbs Spaight

Thos. FitzSimons

Hu Williamson

South Carolina

Charles Cotesworth Pinckney

Charles Pinckney

Pierce Butler

New Hampshire

John Langdon

Nicholas Gilman

Robt. Morris

Wm. Blount

Geo. Clymer

Jared Ingersoll
James Wilson

Gouv Morris

J. Rutledge

Georgia
William Few
Abr Baldwin

Massachusetts

Nathaniel Gorham

Rufus King

The Bill of Rights

Amendment I

Congress shall make no law respecting an establishment of religion, or prohibiting the free exercise thereof; or abridging the freedom of speech, or of the press; or the right of the people peaceably to assemble, and to petition the Government for a redress of grievances.

Amendment II

A well regulated Militia, being necessary to the security of a free State, the right of the people to keep and bear Arms, shall not be infringed.

Amendment III

No Soldier shall, in time of peace be quartered in any house, without the consent of the Owner, nor in time of war, but in a manner to be prescribed by law.

Amendment IV

The right of the people to be secure in their persons, houses, papers, and effects, against unreasonable searches and seizures, shall not be violated, and no Warrants shall issue, but upon probable cause, supported by Oath or affirmation, and particularly describing the place to be searched, and the persons or things to be seized.

Amendment V

No person shall be held to answer for a capital, or otherwise infamous crime, unless on a presentment or indictment of a Grand Jury, except in cases arising in the land or naval forces, or in the Militia, when in actual service in time of War or public danger; nor shall any person be subject for the same offence to be twice put in jeopardy of life or limb; nor shall be compelled in any criminal case to be a witness against himself, nor be deprived of life, liberty, or property, without due process of law; nor shall private property be taken for public use, without just compensation.

Amendment VI

In all criminal prosecutions, the accused shall enjoy the right to a speedy and public trial, by an impartial jury of the State and district wherein the crime shall have been committed, which district shall have been previously ascertained by law, and to be informed of the nature and cause of the accusation; to be confronted with the witnesses against him; to have compulsory process for obtaining witnesses in his favor, and to have the Assistance of Counsel for his defence.

Amendment VII

In Suits at common law, where the value in controversy shall exceed twenty dollars, the right of trial by jury shall be preserved, and no fact tried by a jury, shall be otherwise re-examined in any Court of the United States, than according to the rules of the common law.

Amendment VIII

Excessive bail shall not be required, nor excessive fines imposed, nor cruel and unusual punishments inflicted.

Amendment IX

The enumeration in the Constitution, of certain rights, shall not be construed to deny or disparage others retained by the people.

Amendment X

The powers not delegated to the United States by the Constitution, nor prohibited by it to the States, are reserved to the States respectively, or to the people.

Amendments to the U.S. Constitution

Amendment I

Congress shall make no law respecting an establishment of religion or prohibiting the free exercise thereof; or abridging the freedom of speech, or of the press; or the right of the people peaceably to assemble, and to petition the Government for a redress of grievances.

Amendment II

A well regulated Militia, being necessary to the security of a free State, the right of the people to keep and bear Arms, shall not be infringed.
 Amendment III No Soldier shall, in time of peace be quartered in any house, without the consent of the Owner, nor in time of war, but in a manner to be prescribed by law.

Amendment IV

The right of the people to be secure in their persons, houses, papers, and effects, against unreasonable searches and seizures, shall not be violated, and no Warrants shall issue, but upon probable cause, supported by Oath or affirmation, and particularly describing the place to be searched, and the persons or things to be seized.

Amendment V

No person shall be held to answer for a capital, or otherwise infamous crime, unless on a presentment or indictment of a Grand Jury, except in cases arising in the land or naval forces, or in the Militia, when in actual service in time of War or public danger; nor shall any person be subject for the same offence to be twice put in jeopardy of life or limb; nor shall be compelled in any criminal case to be a witness against himself, nor be deprived of life, liberty, or property, without due process of law; nor shall private property be taken for public use, without just compensation.

Amendment VI

In all criminal prosecutions, the accused shall enjoy the right to a speedy and public trial, by an impartial jury of the State and district wherein the crime shall have been committed, which district shall have been previously ascertained by law, and to be informed of the nature and cause of the accusation; to be confronted with the witnesses against him; to have compulsory process for obtaining witnesses in his favor, and to have the Assistance of Counsel for his defence.

Amendment VII

In Suits at common law, where the value in controversy shall exceed twenty dollars, the right of trial by jury shall be preserved, and no fact tried by a jury, shall be otherwise re-examined in any Court of the United States, than according to the rules of the common law.

Amendment VIII

Excessive bail shall not be required, nor excessive fines imposed, nor cruel and unusual punishments inflicted.

Amendment IX

The enumeration in the Constitution, of certain rights, shall not be construed to deny or disparage others retained by the people.

Amendment X

The powers not delegated to the United States by the Constitution, nor prohibited by it to the States, are reserved to the States respectively, or to the people.

Amendment XI

The Judicial power of the United States shall not be construed to extend to any suit in law or equity, commenced or prosecuted against one of the United States by Citizens of another State, or by Citizens or Subjects of any Foreign State.

Amendment XII

The Electors shall meet in their respective states and vote by ballot for President and Vice-President, one of whom, at least, shall not be an inhabitant of the same state with themselves; they shall name in their ballots the person voted for as President, and in distinct ballots the person voted for as Vice-President, and they shall make distinct lists of all persons voted for as President, and of all persons voted for as Vice-President, and of the number of votes for each, which lists they shall sign and certify, and transmit sealed to the seat of the government of the United States, directed to the President of the Senate;— the President of the Senate shall, in the presence of the

Senate and House of Representatives, open all the certificates and the votes shall then be counted;—The person having the greatest number of votes for President, shall be the President, if such number be a majority of the whole number of Electors appointed; and if no person have such majority, then from the persons having the highest numbers not exceeding three on the list of those voted for as President, the House of Representatives shall choose immediately, by ballot, the President. But in choosing the President, the votes shall be taken by states, the representation from each state having one vote; a quorum for this purpose shall consist of a member or members from twothirds of the states, and a majority of all the states shall be necessary to a choice. And if the House of Representatives shall not choose a President whenever the right of choice shall devolve upon them, before the fourth day of March next following, then the Vice-President shall act as President, as in the case of the death or other constitutional disability of the President— The person having the greatest number of votes as Vice-President, shall be the Vice-President, if such number be a majority of the whole number of Electors appointed, and if no person have a majority, then from the two highest numbers on the list, the Senate shall choose the Vice-President; a quorum for the purpose shall consist of two-thirds of the whole number of Senators, and a majority of the whole number shall be necessary to a choice. But no person constitutionally ineligible to the office of President shall be eligible to that of Vice-President of the United States.

Amendment XIII

Section 1.

Neither slavery nor involuntary servitude, except as a punishment for crime whereof the party shall have been duly convicted, shall exist within the United States, or any place subject to their jurisdiction.

Section 2.

Congress shall have power to enforce this article by appropriate legislation.

Amendment XIV

Section 1.

All persons born or naturalized in the United States, and subject to the jurisdiction thereof, are citizens of the United States and of the State wherein they reside. No State shall make or enforce any law which shall abridge the privileges or immunities of citizens of the United States; nor shall any State deprive any person of life, liberty, or property, without due process of law; nor deny to any person within its jurisdiction the equal protection of the laws.

Section 2.

Representatives shall be apportioned among the several States according to their respective numbers, counting the whole number of persons in each State, excluding Indians not taxed. But when the right to vote at any election for the choice of electors for President and Vice-President of the United States, Representatives in Congress, the

Executive and Judicial officers of a State, or the members of the Legislature thereof, is denied to any of the male inhabitants of such State, being twenty-one years of age, and citizens of the United States, or in any way abridged, except for participation in rebellion, or other crime, the basis of representation therein shall be reduced in the proportion which the number of such male citizens shall bear to the whole number of male citizens twenty-one years of age in such State.

Section 3.
No person shall be a Senator or Representative in Congress, or elector of President and Vice-President, or hold any office, civil or military, under the United States, or under any State, who, having previously taken an oath, as a member of Congress, or as an officer of the United States, or as a member of any State legislature, or as an executive or judicial officer of any State, to support the Constitution of the United States, shall have engaged in insurrection or rebellion against the same, or given aid or comfort to the enemies thereof. But Congress may by a vote of two-thirds of each House, remove such disability.

Section 4.
The validity of the public debt of the United States, authorized by law, including debts incurred for payment of pensions and bounties for services in suppressing insurrection or rebellion, shall not be questioned. But neither the United States nor any State shall assume or pay any debt or obligation incurred in aid of insurrection or rebellion against the United States, or any claim for the

loss or emancipation of any slave; but all such debts, obligations and claims shall be held illegal and void.
Section 5.
The Congress shall have power to enforce, by appropriate legislation, the provisions of this article.

Amendment XV

Section 1.
The right of citizens of the United States to vote shall not be denied or abridged by the United States or by any State on account of race, color, or previous condition of servitude.

Section 2.
The Congress shall have the power to enforce this article by appropriate legislation.

Amendment XVI

The Congress shall have power to lay and collect taxes on incomes, from whatever source derived, without apportionment among the several States, and without regard to any census or enumeration.

Amendment XVII

The Senate of the United States shall be composed of two Senators from each State, elected by the people thereof, for six years; and each Senator shall have one vote. The electors in each State shall have the qualifications requisite for electors of the most numerous branches of the State legislatures.

When vacancies happen in the representation of any State in the Senate, the executive authority of such State shall issue writs of election to fill such vacancies: Provided, That the legislature of any State may empower the executive thereof to make temporary appointments until the people fill the vacancies by election as the legislature may direct. This amendment shall not be so construed as to affect the election or term of any Senator chosen before it becomes valid as part of the Constitution.

Amendment XVIII

Section 1.

After one year from the ratification of this article the manufacture, sale, or transportation of intoxicating liquors within, the importation thereof into, or the exportation thereof from the United States and all territory subject to the jurisdiction thereof for beverage purposes is hereby prohibited.

Section 2.

The Congress and the several States shall have concurrent power to enforce this article by appropriate legislation.

Section 3.

This article shall be inoperative unless it shall have been ratified as an amendment to the Constitution by the legislatures of the several States, as provided in the Constitution, within seven years from the date of the submission hereof to the States by the Congress.

Amendment XIX

The right of citizens of the United States to vote shall not be denied or abridged by the United States or by any State on account of sex. Congress shall have power to enforce this article by appropriate legislation.

Amendment XX

Section 1.

The terms of the President and Vice President shall end at noon on the 20th day of January, and the terms of Senators and Representatives at noon on the 3d day of January, of the years in which such terms would have ended if this article had not been ratified; and the terms of their successors shall then begin.

Section 2.

The Congress shall assemble at least once in every year, and such meeting shall begin at noon on the 3d day of January, unless they shall by law appoint a different day.

Section 3.

If, at the time fixed for the beginning of the term of the President, the President elect shall have died, the Vice President elect shall become President. If a President shall not have been chosen before the time fixed for the beginning of his term, or if the President elect shall have failed to qualify, then the Vice President elect shall act as President until a President shall have qualified; and the Congress may by law provide for the case wherein neither a President elect nor a Vice President elect shall have qualified, declaring who shall then act as President, or the manner in which one who is to act shall be selected, and such person shall act accordingly until a President or Vice President shall have qualified.

Section 4.
The Congress may by law provide for the case of the death of any of the persons from whom the House of Representatives may choose a President whenever the right of choice shall have devolved upon them, and for the case of the death of any of the persons from whom the Senate may choose a Vice President whenever the right of choice shall have devolved upon them.

Section 5.
Sections 1 and 2 shall take effect on the 15th day of October following the ratification of this article.

Section 6.
This article shall be inoperative unless it shall have been ratified as an amendment to the Constitution by the legislatures of three-fourths of the several States within seven years from the date of its submission.

Amendment XXI

Section 1.
The eighteenth article of amendment to the Constitution of the United States is hereby repealed.

Section 2.

The transportation or importation into any State, Territory, or Possession of the United States for delivery or use therein of intoxicating liquors, in violation of the laws thereof, is hereby prohibited.

Section 3.
This article shall be inoperative unless it shall have been ratified as an amendment to the Constitution by conventions in the several States, as provided in the Constitution, within seven years from the date of the submission hereof to the States by the Congress.

Amendment XXII

Section 1.
No person shall be elected to the office of the President more than twice, and no person who has held the office of President, or acted as President, for more than two years of a term to which some other person was elected President shall be elected to the office of the President more than once. But this Article shall not apply to any person holding the office of President when this Article was proposed by Congress, and shall not prevent any person who may be holding the office of President, or acting as President, during the term within which this Article becomes operative from holding the office of President or acting as President during the remainder of such term. Section 2. This article shall be inoperative unless it shall have been ratified as an amendment to the Constitution by the legislatures of three-fourths of the several States within seven years from the date of its submission to the States by the Congress.

Amendment XXIII

Section 1.

The District constituting the seat of Government of the United States shall appoint in such manner as the Congress may direct: A number of electors of President and Vice President equal to the whole number of Senators and Representatives in Congress to which the District would be entitled if it were a State, but in no event more than the least populous State; they shall be in addition to those appointed by the States, but they shall be considered, for the purposes of the election of President and Vice President, to be electors appointed by a State; and they shall meet in the District and perform such duties as provided by the twelfth article of amendment. Section 2. The Congress shall have power to enforce this article by appropriate legislation.

Amendment XXIV

Section 1.

The right of citizens of the United States to vote in any primary or other election for President or Vice President, for electors for President or Vice President, or for Senator or Representative in Congress, shall not be denied or abridged by the United States or any State by reason of failure to pay poll tax or other tax.

Section 2.

The Congress shall have power to enforce this article by appropriate legislation.

Amendment XXV

Section 1.

In case of the removal of the President from office or of his death or resignation, the Vice President shall become President.

Section 2.

Whenever there is a vacancy in the office of the Vice President, the President shall nominate a Vice President who shall take office upon confirmation by a majority vote of both Houses of Congress.

Section 3.

Whenever the President transmits to the President pro tempore of the Senate and the Speaker of the House of Representatives his written declaration that he is unable to discharge the powers and duties of his office, and until he transmits to them a written declaration to the contrary, such powers and duties shall be discharged by the Vice President as Acting President.

Section 4.

Whenever the Vice President and a majority of either the principal officers of the executive departments or of such other body as Congress may by law provide, transmit to the President pro tempore of the Senate and the Speaker of the House of Representatives their written declaration that the President is unable to discharge the powers and duties of his office, the Vice President shall immediately assume the powers and duties of the office as Acting President. Thereafter, when the President transmits to the

President pro tempore of the Senate and the Speaker of the House of Representatives his written declaration that no inability exists, he shall resume the powers and duties of his office unless the Vice President and a majority of either the principal officers of the executive department or of such other body as Congress may by law provide, transmit within four days to the President pro tempore of the Senate and the Speaker of the House of Representatives their written declaration that the President is unable to discharge the powers and duties of his office. Thereupon Congress shall decide the issue, assembling within fortyeight hours for that purpose if not in session. If the Congress, within twenty-one days after receipt of the latter written declaration, or, if Congress is not in session, within twenty-one days after Congress is required to assemble, determines by two-thirds vote of both Houses that the President is unable to discharge the powers and duties of his office, the Vice President shall continue to discharge the same as Acting President; otherwise, the President shall resume the powers and duties of his office.

Amendment XXVI

Section 1.
The right of citizens of the United States, who are eighteen years of age or older, to vote shall not be denied or abridged by the United States or by any State on account of age.

Section 2.

The Congress shall have power to enforce this article by appropriate legislation.

Amendment XXVII

No law, varying the compensation for the services of the Senators and Representatives, shall take effect, until an election of Representatives shall have intervened.

The Gettysburg Address

Four score and seven years ago our fathers brought forth on this continent, a new nation, conceived in Liberty, and dedicated to the proposition that all men are created equal. Now we are engaged in a great civil war, testing whether that nation, or any nation so conceived and so dedicated, can long endure. We are met on a great battle-field of that war. We have come to dedicate a portion of that field, as a final resting place for those who here gave their lives that that nation might live. It is altogether fitting and proper that we should do this.

But, in a larger sense, we can not dedicate -- we can not consecrate -- we can not hallow -- this ground. The brave men, living and dead, who struggled here, have consecrated it, far above our poor power to add or detract. The world will little note, nor long remember what we say here, but it can never forget what they did here. It is for us the living, rather, to be dedicated here to the unfinished work which they who fought here have thus far so nobly advanced. It is rather for us to be here dedicated to the great task remaining before us -- that from these honored dead we take increased devotion to that cause for which they gave the last full measure of devotion -- that we here highly resolve that these dead shall not have died in vain -- that this nation, under God, shall have a new birth of freedom -- and that government of the people, by the people, for the people, shall not perish from the earth.

Abraham Lincoln
November 19, 1863

Appendix

The Federalist Papers by Hamilton, Madison and Jay

http://americasbesthistory.com/abhtimeline1800.html

https://www.historyandheadlines.com/10-great-american-achievements/

https://www.brainyquote.com/quotes/quotes/a/alexanderh121863.html

https://en.wikipedia.org/wiki/Social_Security_Act

https://en.wikipedia.org/wiki/Voting_rights_in_the_United_States

https://en.wikipedia.org/wiki/United_States_nationality_law

https://deathpenaltyinfo.org/states-and-without-death-penalty

www.cairco.org/issues/anchor-babies

http://www.breitbart.com/big-government/2015/08/20/u-s-almost-alone-in-granting-birthright-citizenship/

http://onlinemaps.blogspot.com/2012/11/united-states-western-expansion.html

fasttrackteaching.com

https://commons.wikimedia.org/wiki/File:U.S._Territorial_
Acquisitions.png

https://qz.com/784503/what-would-happen-if-felons-
could-vote/

https://www.loc.gov/collections/james-madison-
papers/about-this-collection/

http://findingaids.loc.gov/db/search/xq/searchMfer02.xq?
_id=loc.mss.eadmss.ms009141&_faSection=overview&_fa
Subsection=did&_dmdid=teachingamericanhistory.org/libr
ary/document/speech-on-amendments-to-the-
constitution/

http://oll.libertyfund.org/titles/morris-the-diary-and-
letters-of-gouverneur-morris-vol-1

teachingamericanhistory.org/library/document/speech-
on-amendments-to-the-constitution/

https://www.rapidnet.com/~jbeard/bdm/Psychology/mas
hist.htm

http://www.americassurvivalguide.com/john-
dickinson.php

http://political-economy.com/thomas-jefferson-on-taxes/

https://www.cliffsnotes.com/literature/f/the-federalist/summary-and-analysis/section-v-powers-of-taxation-federalists-no-3036-hamilton

https://www.thoughtco.com/members-in-the-house-of-representatives-3368242

http://history.house.gov/Historical-Highlights/1901-1950/The-Permanent-Apportionment-Act-of-1929/

https://www.history.com/topics/american-revolution/gouverneur-morris

https://en.wikipedia.org/wiki/Liberty_Bell

www.pbs.org/opd/historydetectives/technique/gun-timeline/

https://www.seniorliving.org/history/1800-1990-changes-urbanrural-us-population/

https://en.wikipedia.org/wiki/Battle_of_Sugar_Point

https://www.thoughtco.com/invention-of-radio-1992382

behindthescenes.nyhistory.org/castle-garden-where-immigrants-first-came-to-america/

https://www.libertyellisfoundation.org/ellis-island-history#Laws

https://kids.laws.com/16th-amendment

http://fas-history.rutgers.edu/clemens/constitutional1/sherman.html

https://www.senate.gov/history/1787(to present)

https://constitutioncenter.org/interactive-constitution/white-pages/the-constitutional-convention-of-1787-a-revolution-in-government

https://ia800203.us.archive.org/16/items/writingsofjohndi00dickrich/writingsofjohndi00dickrich_djvu.txt

www.american-historama.org/1913-1928-ww1-prohibition-era/impact-ww1-on-america.htm

https://www.history.com/this-day-in-history/the-indian-citizenship-act

https://www.cnn.com/2012/09/21/opinion/spalding-welfare-state-dependency/index.html

https://www.forbes.com/sites/realspin/2014/03/13/5-ways-the-government-keeps-native-americans-in-poverty/#5ba6f0242c27

https://www.thebalance.com/effects-of-the-great-depression-4049299

https://www.ssa.gov/history/briefhistory3.html

www.bbc.co.uk/history/ww2peopleswar/timeline/factfiles
/nonflash/a6652262.shtml

https://www.cnn.com/2013/08/06/world/asia/btn-
atomic-bombs/index.html

https://www.enotes.com/homework-help/topic/thomas-
jefferson

https://www.cbsnews.com/news/chinas-social-credit-
system-keeps-a-critical-eye-on-everyday-behavior-even-
jaywalking-2018-04-24/

https://www.bjs.gov/content/pub/pdf/crcusdc06.pdf

Fact Monster. © 2000–2017 Sandbox Networks, Inc.,
publishing as Fact Monster.
8 May. 2018 <https://www.factmonster.com/cool-
stuff/entertainment/entertainment-timeline/>.

http://oll.libertyfund.org/titles/morris-the-diary-and-
letters-of-gouverneur-morris-vol-1

https://science.howstuffworks.com/innovation/inventions
/who-invented-the-computer.htm

https://www.fool.com/retirement/2017/02/13/is-social-
security-going-broke.aspx

https://www.history.com/news/5-things-you-didnt-know-about-alexander-hamilton

https://www.christianitytoday.com/ct/2016/february-web-only/god-loved-alexander-hamilton.html

https://www.huffingtonpost.com/matt-j-rossano/hamiltons-religion_b_803677.html

https://en.wikipedia.org/wiki/Economic_Recovery_Tax_Act_of_1981

https://immigration.procon.org/view.resource.php?resourceID=000844

https://cis.org/Report/US-Immigrant-Population-Hit-Record-437-Million-2016

https://www.fairus.org/issue/illegal-immigration/how-many-illegal-immigrants-are-in-us

http://www.bingoforpatriots.com/american-history/13-colonies/colonial-charters-and-early-documents/

https://www.history.com/news/the-birth-of-illegal-immigration

https://www.archives.gov/legislative/features/bor

https://en.wikipedia.org/wiki/Manumission

http://www.azquotes.com/author/10421-
Gouverneur_Morris

http://www.theimaginativeconservative.org/2013/05/poli
tical-thought-gouverneur-morris.html:
Swiggett, Extraordinary Mr. Morris, 225; Morris to Sarah
Gouverneur Morris, April 17, 1778, Sparks,
Life of Morris, I, 158: Morris to Mrs. Lena Rutherford,
January 4, 1804, Morris Papers, Library of Congress; For
references to Christianity, see, for example, Morris to
Washington, May 21, 1778, Sparks, Life of Morris, I, 167;
Morris to John Parish, January 14, 1803, and October 25,
1804, ibid., III, 176-77, 212, 214;
Morris to William Hill Wells, March 3. 1814, ibid., III, 305.

https://www.fairus.org/issue/population-
environment/united-states-already-overpopulated

https://www.loc.gov/rr/program/bib/ourdocs/billofrights.
html

https://en.wikipedia.org/wiki/List_of_amendments_to_th
e_United_States_Constitution

https://www.loc.gov/rr/program/bib/ourdocs/billofrights.
html

https://townhall.com/tipsheet/mattvespa/2015/06/06/ho
w-many-federal-laws-are-there-again-n2009184

http://www.theimaginativeconservative.org/2015/10/the-politics-of-john-dickinson.html

https://www.billofrightsinstitute.org/founding-documents/bill-of-rights/

https://allthingsliberty.com/2017/09/roger-sherman-man-signed-four-founding-documents/

http://www.ushistory.org/tour/first-bank.htm

http://biography.yourdictionary.com/james-madison

To Secure the Blessing of Liberty, SElected Writing of Gouverneur Morris, Edited by J. Jackson Barlow Pub: by Liberty Fund, Inc.

https://en.wikisource.org/wiki/A_History_of_Banking_in_t he_United_States/Chapter_2
https://en.wikipedia.org/wiki/Slave_Trade_Act_1807

https://en.wikipedia.org/wiki/Technology

https://www.battlefields.org/learn/articles/civil-war-facts

http://www.pbs.org/opb/historydetectives/feature/causes -of-the-civil-war/

https://en.wikipedia.org/wiki/Cotton_gin

https://www.eliwhitney.org/7/museum/eli-whitney/cotton-gin

https://www.outsidethebeltway.com/madisons-defintions-of-republic/

https://www.outsidethebeltway.com/a-return-to-the-a-republic-not-a-democracy/

https://www.brainyquote.com/quotes/alexander_hamilton_121863

https://www.jstor.org/stable/2123554?seq=1#page_scan_tab_contents. Baack and Ray, "Special Interests," p.607.

https://bradfordtaxinstitute.com/Free_Resources/Federal-Income-Tax-Rates.aspx

https://en.wikipedia.org/wiki/Taxation_in_the_United_States#Types_of_taxpayers

Hickman, Kennedy. "World War II: The Manhattan Project." ThoughtCo, Jun. 14, 2018, thoughtco.com/world-war-ii-the-manhattan-project-2360698.

https://www.washingtonpost.com/news/volokh-conspiracy/wp/2017/10/18/john-dickinson-during-the-continental-and-confederation-periods

http://www.jesusuncensored.com/roger_sherman.html

https://wallbuilders.com/founding-fathers-jesus-christianity-bible/

https://tenthamendmentcenter.com/2018/07/18/james-madison-refutes-expansive-reading-of-the-general-welfare-clause/

https://www.nytimes.com/1988/07/20/us/farm-population-lowest-since-1850-s.html (A version of this article appears in print on July 20, 1988, on Page A00012 of the National edition with the headline: Farm Population Lowest Since 1850's.)

https://en.wikipedia.org/wiki/History_of_health_care_reform_in_the_United_States

https://www.theatlantic.com/ideas/archive/2018/10/birthright-citizenship-constitution/574381/

https://www.foundationsrecoverynetwork.com/addiction-choice/

https://en.wikipedia.org/wiki/Separation_of_church_and_state_in_the_United_States

https://en.wikipedia.org/wiki/Separation_of_church_and_state_in_the_United_States#The_First_Amendment

https://www.youtube.com/embed/6PzT8vEvYPg

www.refugeeresettlementwatch.wordpress.com

https://www.amputee-coalition.org/resources/prosthetic-feet/

https://www.huffingtonpost.com/matt-j-rossano/hamiltons-religion_b_803677.html

Gouverneur Morris ~ An Independent Life by William Howard Adams. Pub: 2003 by Yale University

https://msuweb.montclair.edu/~furrg/spl/morristopenn.html

Roger Sherman and the Creation of the American Republic by Mark David Hall Pub: 2013 Oxford

https://www.google.com/amp/s/www.biography.com/.amp/people/roger-sherman-9482029

https://teachingamericanhistory.org/resources/convention/delegates/#

https://famguardian.org/subjects/politics/thomasjefferson/jeff0200.htm

https://www.scmp.com/magazines/post-magazine/long-reads/article/2161706/chinese-birth-tourism-pregnant-women-californias

https://www.prisonpolicy.org/reports/pie2019.html

https://en.wikipedia.org/wiki/United_States_Capitol

https://www.youtube.com/watch?v=hKRxZSOqAYw

https://refiction.com/articles/the-rules-of-time-travel-for-fiction-writers/

http://actionamerica.org/fun/tytler.shtml

Barack Obama. (n.d.). AZQuotes.com. Retrieved June 19, 2019, from AZQuotes.com Web site: https://www.azquotes.com/quote/1367261

Walter E. Williams. (n.d.). AZQuotes.com. Retrieved June 19, 2019, from AZQuotes.com Web site: https://www.azquotes.com/quote/1405181

https://davidostewart.com/2012/05/25/five-myths-of-the-constitutional-convention/

https://www.history.com/news/7-things-you-may-not-know-about-the-constitutional-convention

http://worldpopulationreview.com/countries/sweden-population/

https://teleport.org/community/t/is-washington-d-c-conservative-or-liberal/1141/3

https://en.wikipedia.org/wiki/1989_Tiananmen_Square_protests

https://www.investopedia.com/financial-edge/1012/3-of-the-most-lucrative-land-deals-in-history.aspx

https://en.wikipedia.org/wiki/Moral_disengagement

https://www.merriam-webster.com/dictionary/brain%20drain

https://www.dhs.gov/sites/default/files/publications/18_1214_PLCY_pops-est-report.pdf

https://www.tolerance.org/classroom-resources/texts/what-is-a-sanctuary-city-anyway

https://www.bbc.com/news/world-us-canada-44319094

http://www.thefiscaltimes.com/Articles/2013/07/03/9-Changes-to-the-Constitution-How-Would-You-Change-It; Tom Miller of the American Enterprise Institute said the Constitution needs "a better glossary to define and restrain the many open-ended words and phrases in the Constitution's actual text that provide wide latitude for judicial reinterpretation and expansion far beyond their original meaning."

Author Larry Sabato, A More Perfect Constitution, "A Bill of Responsibilities"

https://en.wikipedia.org/wiki/United_we_stand,_divided_we_fall

513

https://books.google.com/books/about/Elements_of_Tec
hnology.html

https://www.insidermonkey.com/blog/11-countries-with-
highest-prison-population-406658/?singlepage=1

https://moneyinc.com/20-countries-currently-debt/

https://www.politico.com/story/2018/11/02/2018-
elections-outside-money-democrats-democrat-alliance-
soros-steyer-956032

https://en.wikipedia.org/wiki/Incarceration_in_the_Unite
d_States

https://reason.com/2018/07/27/sorry-if-youre-offended-
but-socialism-le/

https://top5ofanything.com/list/eafb416e/Countries-with-
the-Highest-Total-Number-of-Abortions

https://www.payscale.com/career-
news/2008/12/unemployment-during-the-great-
depression-are-we-getting-close

http://commonsensegovernment.com/the-tytler-cycle-
revisited/

https://www.printableconstitution.com/

http://www.ourdocuments.gov/doc.php?doc=3&page=transcript

https://www.ourdocuments.gov/print_friendly.php?flash=true&page=transcript&doc=3&title=Transcript+of+Articles+of+Confederation+(1777)

https://treepony.com/phrase-origins-when-in-rome-do-as-the-romans-do/

https://www.thoughtco.com/why-not-just-print-more-money-1146304

https://en.wikipedia.org/wiki/James_Dobson

https://drjamesdobson.org/news/commentaries/archives/2019-newsletters/august-newsletter-2019

https://loc.gov/

https://en.wikipedia.org/wiki/American_Civil_Liberties_Union

https://en.wikipedia.org/wiki/Alexander_Fraser_Tytler,_Lord_Woodhouselee

http://worldpopulationreview.com/countries/newest-countries/

https://quotes.thefamouspeople.com/james-madison-1742.php

https://www.carpentershall.org/walking-tour

Acknowledgments

Thank You to the following:

For the many conversations with my family and friends which spawned some of these ideas and concepts.

David A., Steve S., Charles Y., Robin R., Mallory M., Will B., Ariya A., Jason A., Matt M.

To all who aided in editing and research:
D.D. Duhan
Samuel J. Ayers Ed.D. Director of Graduate Education, Distinguished Practitioner in Residence, Lubbock Christian University - School of Education
Ashley Brewer- Assistant Professor of English, B.A. in English Education
Chris Thomason- Bachelor of Arts.
Judith Smith- Certified Tour Guide of Philadelphia, Department of Defense (*ret.*), Dickinson College 1981
Dale Duhan – Ph.D. Professor of Marketing

516